Praise for Rosanna Ley

'A beautifully crafted slice of escapist fiction'
Heat

'A great page-turner'
Lucinda Riley

'I loved the sultry sensuous feeling . . . a fascinating
story with engaging themes'
Dinah Jefferies

'Impeccably researched and deftly written'
Kathryn Hughes

'Romantic, escapist and mouth-watering . . .
everything you could wish for in a summer read'
Veronica Henry

'The perfect holiday read'
Rachel Hore

'The heat, passion and Latin rhythms come to life in
this compelling tale'
Hello

'A perfect holiday read, to be devoured in one sitting'
The Lady

'Vividly written with a compelling storyline, this is
top escapism'
Closer

'A gorgeous, mouth-watering dream of a holiday read!'
Red Online

'Beautiful, evocative writing'
Sun

Also by Rosanna Ley

The Villa
Bay of Secrets
Return to Mandalay
The Saffron Trail
Last Dance in Havana

ROSANNA LEY

The Little Theatre by the Sea

Quercus

First published in Great Britain in 2017
This paperback edition published in 2017 by

Quercus Editions Ltd
Carmelite House
50 Victoria Embankment
London EC4Y 0DZ

An Hachette UK company

A CIP catalogue record for this book is available
from the British Library

PB ISBN 9781784292102
EBOOK ISBN 9781784292096

10 9 8 7 6 5 4

Typeset by Jouve (UK), Milton Keynes

Printed and bound in Great Britain by Clays Ltd, St Ives plc

For my darling mother, Daphne Squires, with my love

CHAPTER I

The phone call from Sardinia came at the perfect time for Faye. Serendipity, she thought. She'd never been to the island but it sounded like her idea of paradise.

For months she'd been working flat out – head spinning, eyes aching – often until the early hours. Faye looked around her cramped bedroom. Her things were bursting out of the tiny wardrobe and once she'd squeezed herself into the room there was little else she could do but throw herself on to the bed. Which was about all she felt capable of doing these days. Mature students were supposed to have more drive, but perhaps they were more prone to exhaustion, too. So here she was at thirty-three, a qualified interior designer at last, with one big question on her mind – what next?

Was Charlotte's phone call the answer? Faye pulled her week-end bag down from the top of the wardrobe. She was heading back to West Dorset to see her parents. And then . . . she couldn't hold back the grin. Why not? She'd be leaving grey old London, a wet spring and stress levels teetering on the unmanageable. At least for a while.

She threw in a spare pair of jeans and added her washbag, a tee shirt and a jade green cardigan she loved even though it was missing its crucial centre button. Sometimes Faye wondered if *she* was missing her crucial centre button. She had given up a lot to do a degree at the (mature, she reminded herself) age of thirty.

She'd left a well-paid job as a PA in North London. She had also — at least temporarily — lost the good opinion of her mother. Unlike Faye's father, who had pulled her into a hug and told her that he understood . . . *You go for it, love, otherwise you'll regret it for the rest of your life* . . . Molly Forrester was not a risk-taker and did not approve of the quality in her daughter. In her mother's view, Faye should be thinking more about settling down and less about a dramatic career change that could very well end in tears. More practically, Faye had swapped a decent, but costly, flat share in Stoke Newington for this less-than-salubrious room in Hackney, and as a penniless student she could no longer eat out or party as often as she'd like. She manoeuvred her way past the chest of drawers and eyed herself briefly in the long mirror in the corner. Which was perhaps a good thing – she'd looked seriously hungover for days.

Faye chucked a few more odds and ends in the bag and zipped it shut. But it had been worth it. She had always had a strong interest in design. She liked to think that she was creative. All the jobs she'd ever had had left her feeling unfulfilled. And so she'd done some research and applied for this degree course. It fascinated her – how the design of a space could affect an environment, how it could create meaning and evoke feelings. The problem-solving aspect also appealed – how to find better solutions, make things work more efficiently, how to improve a space for the people who used it – and just as importantly, make it look good too.

Faye gathered up the last of her things. She had paid a price, though. Not only had she had to adjust to living on a student grant and in this tiny room . . . not only was she too tired, too broke and too exhausted to go out . . . she had also, much to her mother's horror, lost Justin.

Her gaze drifted to the photograph of them both in Lisbon, still sitting in its silver frame next to the bed, a silent rebuke. Justin. Faye still hadn't quite got her head around it. He had left only six months ago and that was how it felt – as if her long-time boyfriend had simply been mislaid. He hadn't, though. At the time, Faye had pushed the memory of their break-up away because she'd needed to focus on her work. She couldn't give in to any emotional turmoil; all this meant too much to her for that. But now she was having to face the truth: Justin wasn't coming back. She was alone.

So when Charlotte rang from Sardinia . . .

'Faye,' Charlotte said as soon as she picked up. 'I saw the picture on Facebook of you at your degree show. Wow. Congratulations, my love. You did it!'

'Yes,' Faye breathed out. 'Thanks.' It was hard to believe that she could now go to bed before midnight after manic weeks completing her portfolio, her design drawings, the pieces for her exhibition. She was still on a strangely spaced-out adrenalin-filled high. It was like the end of a road with an unpredictable abyss looming in front of her. Scary. Three years it had taken and so much of it had been way outside her comfort zone. Learning to use the various computer programmes, coming up with concepts and ideas that then had to be linked to the material. Faye shuddered at the memory. But Charlotte was right. She had done it – and it felt like it had taken everything.

'I took it all down yesterday,' she told Charlotte. The designs and the posters, the displays of tiles and fabrics. *Sustainability Within Architecture*. The subject of her dissertation, she never wanted to hear that phrase again; she had explored it and analysed it to death. 'It's hard to believe it's all come to an end.'

'Ah, but this is just the beginning,' said Charlotte. She'd always been the optimistic one, even back in sixth form where they'd both studied photography and textiles. They became close friends before going their separate ways after their A-levels. In Faye's case that had been to London to work as a PA, in Charlotte's – rather more exotically – it was travelling around Italy. She ended up marrying an Italian man who ran a hotel in Sardinia.

'I hope you're right.' Faye noticed the thin trail of anxiety in her own voice. She went through to the communal kitchen to grab the bottle of celebratory Prosecco that she hoped was still in the fridge. It was.

'Of course I'm right. With your talent, my love, you'll be swatting them away at the door.'

Faye smiled. As if. She took a glass down from the cupboard. No doubt Charlotte too did her fair share of swatting – and not just because she was a stunning redhead with a figure to turn the head of every Sardinian man on the island. She worked freelance, designing and producing high-end knitwear (she had always been keener on textiles and fabrication than Faye). She and Fabio had no children – yet – but Faye knew that if Charlotte wanted, she could simply relax as the wife of a successful businessman. Instead she had chosen to preserve her own creative identity and Faye respected her for that. As a result, Charlotte understood Faye's decision better than most.

She took a first sip of the chilled bubbles. Heaven. 'You should have seen some of the work at the show,' Faye replied. 'There are a lot of talented people out there.' And just how many design jobs were available anyway?

'I don't doubt it,' said Charlotte. 'But you're the crème de la crème. Any job offers yet? Or interviews?'

'Not yet.' Faye took another sip of her wine. 'I might have to look for something temporary to keep me going,' she admitted. Crème de la crème, indeed.

'But you must be exhausted,' Charlotte said. 'What you need first is a holiday.'

'I wish.' Faye let out a hollow laugh. She put down her glass and drew the wooden blind to shut out the night-lights of London. In Sardinia, presumably, Charlotte would be able to see the stars. Faye let out a small sigh. There had been some interest in her work at the exhibition. One director in particular had approached her and invited her to send over her portfolio. But he had said himself that the project they were working on was in its early stages and they didn't know yet how many people they would need. It was promising, but it would probably be weeks before she heard back. And in the meantime she had to live.

'So why don't you?'

Faye looked around the tiny kitchen. 'I can't afford it.' Her parents had helped her out over the past three years but she was reluctant to ask them for more. She was thirty-three years old. Independent. Or at least, she was supposed to be.

'Can you at least lay your hands on the airfare to Sardinia?' Charlotte's voice grew more serious. 'If not, it's my treat.'

'Oh, I couldn't . . .' But even as she said it, an image from many years ago flickered through her senses. Rippling blue water, white-sand coves, green-cloaked mountains. It was the image of Italy.

'Don't be silly.' Charlotte's voice was crisp. 'And it's not just a holiday, either. Listen, my love. I have a proposition to put to you.'

CHAPTER 2

Back in Dorset, Faye felt herself begin to relax. Everything was so reassuringly familiar. Her mother was baking scones in the kitchen; she had planned a Dorset cream tea following a morning rummage in the antiques market in town. Her father, rangy and fair-haired, in his mid-fifties now and still in good shape, was sitting with his feet up in the conservatory reading the paper; outside, beyond Faye's parents' cottage garden, sheep grazed impossibly green Dorset grass in fields separated by drystone walls that had stood there for centuries. Were her parents even aware of what a rural idyll they lived in? Faye smiled to herself and contemplated the place she had always called home. Her mother had grown up in West Dorset; her father had commuted to and from the city of Exeter most of his life. Faye had moved to London, but she still wasn't sure that she belonged.

'Timeless, isn't it?' she said.

Her father grinned back at her in his usual way. But there was a look in his light blue eyes that stirred some long-forgotten memory for Faye. It hovered there, tantalising; she tried to grasp it, and then it was gone. 'Dad?' She put a hand on his arm as if to anchor him – or her.

He shook some thought away; she saw it. 'Never changes,' he agreed, patting her hand.

'Which is probably why it's so peaceful.' But even if interior design jobs could be found here in West Dorset, Faye wasn't sure she'd come back. London had been a culture shock but she'd quickly become accustomed to the pace and the people; the buzz. It was only now that she was thinking maybe sometimes it was good to slow down.

Faye got up and went to find her mother who was in the kitchen. 'Anything I can do?'

Her mother indicated the bowl on the worktop. 'Help yourself, darling.'

Faye grabbed an apron hanging on a hook behind the door and pulled it on. She washed her hands, dried them and began to rub butter into the flour, feeling the fat slide between the pads of her fingers and thumbs, gradually combining as blissfully as always. She shook the bowl to bring the buttery lumps to the surface. She loved cooking, though she didn't do much of it in London. There never seemed enough time; it was easier to buy salads or microwave dinners for one.

She gave desultory answers to her mother's usual questions. *Yes, I'm fine. Yes, of course I'm eating properly. Yes, I miss Justin.* Her mother would want a lot more detail than that, but Faye wasn't going to volunteer it. Only . . .

Faye glanced up, surprised. For probably the first time ever, her mother wasn't following through. 'Mum?' Her mother's brown eyes were vague, her fingers drifting through a sea of sultanas she was drying in a sieve, in readiness for the scones.

She blinked, shook back a strand of her dark hair, still thick, still glossy, cut in a crisp, no-nonsense bob. 'Sorry, darling. What did you say?'

Faye frowned. She thought of her father in the conservatory, the easy grin slipping from his face. 'Is everything alright?'

'Of course. What do you mean? Why shouldn't it be?'

'Well . . . oh, nothing.' Faye shouldn't complain. It wasn't as if she wanted to answer any Justin questions. Justin had left her because he said he'd had enough. He didn't say what he'd had enough of, so Faye could only assume it was her. Their life together. And she supposed that it was her fault. What boyfriend would put up with a girl who stayed up studying half the night? What boyfriend would be willing to support a crazy decision like Faye's, to study for an interior architecture degree when she already had a reasonable job organising a perfectly nice man's working life as a well-paid personal assistant? Even if it meant that she could work in an industry she loved, doing something more creative and fulfilling? Clearly not Justin, was the answer to that one. Faye wasn't bitter. She liked Justin a lot. She still missed him. She had thought that she loved him and when he left she had braced herself for the emotional fall-out.

But something rather odd had happened in these past weeks. By postponing the pain, by throwing herself into her work, by letting some time go by . . . She had got over the worst of it and was left with simply a sense of disappointment. She'd certainly had a good time with Justin. He was attractive, charming, even funny. But he wasn't enough. She knew that now. She wanted the other, more elusive, kind of boyfriend – the kind who would support her, all the way. If he existed, that was. Apparently there was someone for everyone in this life, but Faye was beginning to wonder.

She brushed the last of the floury crumbs from her hands and set the bowl to one side. She was conscious of a trickle of unease. Everything here was familiar, yes. But things *weren't* the same. Her father wasn't quite his usual self. And her mother had just broken the pattern of a lifetime by not demanding a full explanation of her break-up with Justin. It was totally out of character. Something was going on. Faye took a deep breath. *Come on, now.* She was imagining things. She'd been working too hard, not getting enough sleep. If there was anything wrong, they would tell her. If there was anything wrong, she'd know.

Before tea, Faye and her father went for a walk along the cliff. It was Faye's suggestion. Cliff walking – whatever the weather – was a vital element of a weekend back in Dorset. She wanted to get up high, look out over the vastness of the water, see the sun glinting on the stacked golden cliffs and pebbles of Chesil Beach as they swept in a perfect curve towards the distant hazy point of Portland. She wanted to feel the sea breeze harsh against her skin, combing roughly through her hair. She wanted to clear out the cobwebs of the past few months in hiding.

They parked in the Bay and walked side by side up the steep and raggedy cliff path without speaking – they needed all their breath for the climb. At the top, they paused to look back towards the mismatched roofs of the houses in the Bay and the harbour, its grey concrete jetty pointing out to sea. The water below was olive-glossy, the grass underfoot still sparse and muddy from rain.

'So what's new, Dad?' Faye asked. She realised guiltily that this was a question she probably didn't ask often enough. It wasn't that she wasn't interested; more that nothing seemed to change in her parents' lives. Whereas in London . . . She blinked away the past months of work and Justin – at least for a while. Sometimes, it was as if her other life didn't exist while she was here. Time out. Now that was something she definitely needed.

Her father thrust his hands in his pockets. 'As a matter of fact, something has happened,' he said.

Faye stopped walking. She knew it. 'Yes?' But from her father's expression it didn't look like something bad.

'I've been offered early retirement.' He stared out to sea as if there might be some answers there, his blue eyes crinkling as he squinted into the afternoon sun.

'Ah.' That explained a lot. Faye's father had worked in banking all his life. She knew he'd worked his way up the ladder pretty quickly in the old days. She supposed he'd enjoyed his job as much as anyone – he certainly seemed to get on with the team he worked with. When she'd been growing up he'd often seemed tired, but that was life, wasn't it, for a lot of people? You worked hard, you saved for holidays and you got tired, so you needed them. Faye had been on that treadmill too until she'd taken stock one day and jumped off.

'And?' she probed as they carried on walking. The thrift and buttercups were out on the cliff slopes; a purple and yellow blanket on the green. Early retirement was a good thing surely? Her parents weren't short of money and this would give her father a pension and a chance to do other things. 'You're going to take it, aren't you?' Presuming he had a choice, that was.

'Yes, love, I am.' He threw her a glance she couldn't quite read and increased his pace, striding along the cliff path in his muddy green wellingtons, heading towards Freshwater Beach and the caravan park.

Faye frowned. Something wasn't quite right. She matched his pace, caught him up and linked her arm through his. 'And what will you do with all that free time, Dad?' She laughed. 'Buy an allotment? Do crossword puzzles in bed?'

His smile was a bit like his earlier one – unconvincing. Didn't he want to leave work then? She'd assumed he would. Was he being pushed out? Was that it? 'Only teasing,' she whispered. 'You don't mind, do you? Early retirement, I mean?'

'No, love.' He looked across to the fields on the other side of the cliffs, sloping down to the valley and then up again to the ridge. On the other side were the Nature Reserve and the village of Bothenhampton. 'Course I don't. I'm delighted.'

'Truly?'

'Truly.' He squeezed her arm.

Which should be reassuring. But why, she wondered, didn't he look it?

Later, over tea in the garden, Faye's mother moved back into familiar territory. For Faye, it was almost a relief.

'What about jobs, darling?' she asked, as she spread a thin layer of cream on her scone. 'Anything in the offing?'

Faye shrugged. Her mother was the practical one, the one who worried about paying the rent and what food everyone was eating. Faye took a bite of her scone. Delicious. It was moist and crumbled in her mouth, cream oozing around her mother's raspberry jam. 'I've contacted a few companies and sent them my portfolio,' she said. 'We'll see.'

To be honest, just the idea of actually working in the design world seemed a million miles away from her studying, her degree, where she was now. Could she do it? Could she put it into practice? Was she good enough? Faye had no idea. Her university had a decent reputation within the industry but as she'd already told Charlotte, there were an awful lot of talented people out there. And most of them were younger, fresher and possibly hungrier than Faye. Maturity, she reminded herself, might not be quite the plus point that her personal tutor had imagined it to be.

'Something will come up, love,' her father said with confidence. He looked across at Faye's mother and Faye watched them exchange a glance.

Only she wasn't exactly sure what sort of a glance. 'Actually,' she said, 'something has.'

'Oh?' She had their full attention now.

'Remember Charlotte?'

They did.

Faye swirled a bit of cream from her plate on to her finger and licked it off. 'She's invited me to house-sit for her in Sardinia.' Sardinia: warm, sunny and blessed with more than its share of fabulous beaches. Not to even mention the food, the architecture and the men.

Her mother pulled one of her faces. 'House-sit?' she echoed. 'That's hardly a design job though, is it, darling?'

Which was pretty much what Faye had thought at first. A week or two in Sardinia, she could justify – she had worked hard, she could do with a break, she could still apply for jobs and answer emails while she was away. But any longer than that seemed indulgent.

'Still, Faye could do with a decent holiday,' her father chipped in, bless him. 'After all that work.' He turned to her. 'Plenty of time for finding a job when you've recharged your batteries, love.'

'Mmm.' Her mother looked doubtful as she wiped her mouth with her napkin. Faye knew that before her parents met, her mother had worked in an up-market department store. She stopped working when she had Faye and didn't go back for sixteen years, when she had joined the sales team of a local craft shop. But eventually she'd left that position, too, and now she hadn't worked for years. She kept the house clean and neat as a pin, she cooked dinner, she boiled and baked for the country market – jams, scones, cakes, quiches – and she looked after Faye's father. He didn't seem to have any complaints about that. No, her mother had never been a career woman. Faye wouldn't change that. She had felt cherished as a child; she had been made to feel special. But now she wondered – had her mother ever longed for something different?

Charlotte had explained that her hotelier husband Fabio would be travelling around the chain of hotels owned by his company in northern Italy. 'To work out why their profit performances are low,' she had elaborated. 'To come up with a super-Fabio plan to get them back on track. You know the sort of thing.'

Faye knew. She had met Fabio when he and Charlotte had got married at the old church in Bothenhampton. He was good-looking and supremely confident. Super-Fabio indeed. Faye could see how Charlotte had fallen so utterly in love during two weeks in Sardinia. Charlotte – and the British boys she knew – hadn't stood a chance.

'So where do I come in?' asked Faye. 'Don't tell me Fabio needs a PA to keep him organised, because I won't believe you.'

Charlotte laughed. 'You're right, he doesn't. But I'm going with him.'

'For moral support?'

'You're joking. He doesn't need that, either. No, to give me a chance to see some of Italy. We hardly ever get away. That hotel is Fabio's baby.'

'Oh, I see.' Now things were becoming clearer. Faye wondered if Charlotte wanted a different kind of baby for herself and Fabio. 'A sort of holiday, do you mean?'

'Holiday? That's even funnier. Fabio's a complete workaholic and you know me, I can work wherever I lay my hat. And my knitting needles, naturally.'

'Naturally.' Faye chuckled. 'But why do you need me?'

'To house-sit. To feed Fabio's precious tropical fish.'

'Ah, yes, the fish.' Charlotte had told her about the aquarium which apparently now took up half the width of their living room.

'And to be on hand in case of burglary,' Charlotte added.

'Nice.'

'You know what I mean. Fabio's paranoid.'

So he wasn't perfect, thought Faye.

'And before you ask, there's no reason why we should be burgled. We've never been burgled and there's practically no crime here in Deriu.' Her voice changed. 'Apart from when Giorgia Volti disappeared – but that was years ago, and before my time. But like I said—'

'Fabio's paranoid.'

'Exactly.'

'And is there anything else I have to do?' Faye asked.

'Simply enjoy yourself for a few weeks or so in Sardinia.' Charlotte's voice was persuasive now. 'After all that studying into the small hours, Faye, you need it.'

But Faye knew her rather well. 'And?' she said . . .

'And Charlotte has two friends who own a theatre,' Faye told her parents now.

'A theatre?' Her father shot her a quizzical look.

'A theatre,' she confirmed. Theatre was everywhere when you came to think about it. The whole of life was a drama.

Her mother's brow wrinkled. 'What are the names of these friends?'

'Alessandro and Marisa Rinaldi,' Faye told her.

'Rinaldi . . .' Her mother had been looking at her very intently. But now she looked away, into the garden, her eyes unfocused, as if she were lost in thought.

'We met Bruno Rinaldi,' Faye's father said. 'He stayed with us when Charlotte and Fabio got married.'

'Of course, yes.' Faye remembered him – dignified, well mannered and rather charming.

'He mentioned having two grown-up children, didn't he, Molly?'

Faye's mother seemed to bring herself back into the room with some difficulty. 'Yes,' she said. 'He did.'

'He wasn't much older than us,' Faye's father said. 'What's happened to him? He's still around, isn't he?'

Faye wondered if she was imagining the tension in the room. 'No,' she said. 'Charlotte told me he died some months ago.'

Her mother let out a gasp.

'We didn't know him well,' her father said. 'But I'm sorry.'

'What is it that Charlotte's asking you to do?' There was an odd expression on her mother's face.

'Take a look at the theatre – initially. After that . . .'

'And will you go?'

'It needs renovating,' Charlotte had told her, barely able to keep the excitement out of her voice. 'It's been left to rot for years. It needs restoration and a total redesign.'

Faye tried to think how much she knew about theatre design. Very little. 'I don't—'

'And you –' Charlotte cut her off – 'could very well be just the woman for the job.'

'Yes,' Faye told her mother. 'I certainly will.' Turn down a holiday in Sardinia and the chance to see one of her closest friends – not to mention a rather intriguing project in the offing? Truth was, she couldn't wait.

CHAPTER 3

Faye had managed to book a last-minute budget flight to Olbia. It was a stunning place to fly into. As they approached the coastline of Sardinia, Faye peered out of the plane's porthole window, taking in the sight of little islands, rocky bays, boats moored in an almost circular harbour and turquoise water that looked more like the Caribbean than the Med. In the distance, behind the busy port, the mountains were cloaked in green trees and scrub, a few wisps of cloud gathered around their summits.

Faye felt a jump of anticipation. She'd had a few wobbles this week thinking about the project that she'd already half-committed to by coming here. Charlotte hadn't gone into too many details. 'We can discuss it properly when you arrive,' she'd said in answer to Faye's questions. During her time in Sardinia, Faye reflected now, Charlotte had adopted a certain Italian breeziness that seemed a characteristic of the Mediterranean temperament. At any rate, she had seemed determined to get Faye to Sardinia at all costs.

Faye wasn't sure why. She had no practical experience in the workplace and redesigning an entire theatre – even a little theatre – sounded more than a tad ambitious for someone who'd only just finished her degree. 'Nonsense,' Charlotte had declared, when Faye said as much to her. 'You can at least give them some ideas.'

'Okay,' she'd agreed. She was getting a free holiday, after all. 'I'll try my best.'

Charlotte met her at the airport, where they hugged, told each other how good the other one was looking and got into the car to head for Deriu. Charlotte drove west into the interior through forests of cork oaks, the trees bent and shadowy with lavender-grey lichen, many of them stripped to the waist of their rugged bark. There was a sense of stillness in the landscape here that drew Faye, but much of the effect was lost; during the journey, Charlotte chatted non-stop – about her work, about Fabio's work, about their forthcoming Italian trip. And when those subjects were exhausted she moved on to questions – about Faye's degree (*I don't know how you did it*), about her break-up with Justin (*definitely not the right man for my girl*) and then reminiscing about the good old days at college.

Faye wasn't complaining. She was enjoying simply sitting back in the passenger seat feeling the warmth of the late spring sun through the car windows and soaking up the scenery. They passed through the woodland of cork trees and olive groves, the maquis of shrubby vegetation randomly identified by Charlotte – in the middle of unconnected sentences – as myrtle, blackthorn and arbutus. 'Even in the winter the island looks green,' she threw in. 'Beautiful, isn't it?'

'It is, yes.' Faye could see that her friend was proud of the island that she had made her home. Charlotte was thriving here. She ran a small, successful business and she seemed happy. It was true that she was looking better than ever, dressed this after-noon in an elegant loose silk shirt in dove grey over close-fitting black trousers that flattered her petite frame, her auburn hair cut pixie-short these days in an immaculate style that accentuated the shape of her scalp, her high cheekbones and slanted green eyes.

'So what did people do in Sardinia before tourism?' Faye asked her.

'Agriculture, shepherding, mining, cork.' Charlotte rattled them off. 'Lots of crafts – especially basket-making and rugs. And then there's coral – wait till you see the coral, Faye.'

It wasn't until they crossed a bridge over a wide river lined with bamboo and date palms that she stopped talking. Faye realised this was relevant. She waited.

'This is it,' Charlotte said.

'Deriu?'

She nodded.

Her friend had described it, but words hadn't done the little town justice. The jumble of buildings lay mainly between the far riverbank and the hill beyond; both the town and the river were backed by mountains which stood, tranquil, seemingly untouched for centuries. Faye could see what looked like a castle on the top of the hill, the other old buildings sheltered beneath. The cluttered houses were painted various shades of pastel, the river snaking from the cradle of the lush mountain valleys in the east through to the sea beyond. A line of ribs, inflatables and other small boats were moored along one side of the tree-lined river.

'That's the *centro storico*, the old mediaeval town.' Charlotte pointed towards the castle on the hill. The lower reaches of the old town were in shadow. 'It was originally founded by the Phoenicians – because of the fertility of the soil and the river, I should think. The sea and the marina are over there.' She gestured ahead. 'And we live on the riverbank.' She laughed. 'Like Ratty and Mole from *Wind in the Willows*.'

'It's glorious.' And this was to be Faye's home for the next month or two. How fabulous was that?

Charlotte smiled, drove on and pulled up outside a converted riverside building.

Faye looked up. It was big, more like a factory, though it had clearly been made into several houses.

'These places were tanneries in the eighteenth and nineteenth centuries,' Charlotte said. 'Reminders of the days when Deriu exported fine leather all over Europe.'

'Not anymore though?' Faye asked. A few of the buildings had been converted into large and elegant houses while others still seemed derelict.

'Sadly, no. That was back in Deriu's glory days under Spanish rule,' Charlotte told her. 'The old tannery next door's been made into a museum if you're interested in the history.'

'Oh, I am.' Faye shot her a warm smile. 'I can't wait to explore. And see the theatre, of course,' she added.

Charlotte blinked. For a moment she seemed to lose a trace of her self-possession. 'Thanks for coming, Faye.' There was something in her expression as she turned towards her that made Faye wary.

'What is it?' Faye kept her voice low though they were still in the car and there was no one anywhere near to hear her. It struck her that Charlotte had been talking so much to stop herself from saying something else, something she didn't want to think about, perhaps. 'Are you okay? Is it Fabio?'

Charlotte shook her head. 'No, it's not Fabio. We're fine. I'm fine.'

Thank goodness. 'What then?' Faye sighed. 'Is it the theatre?'

Charlotte bit her lip. 'There are some things I didn't tell you about the theatre, my love,' she admitted.

Faye should have known. It had all sounded far too good to be true — a dream job in a dream location. Why should she be so lucky? 'Go on.'

'It's the townspeople.' Charlotte glared out of the car window at an unfortunate couple who were simply strolling along the banks of the river. 'They don't like change.'

'Who does?' Faye shrugged.

'Yes, that's true. But some of them can be rather confrontational. Rather vocal.'

'Vocal?' Faye felt a growing sense of unease.

'And they've started this campaign.'

'What sort of campaign?' Faye had visions of a march along the riverside under the palm trees. Of placards, banners, hate mail even. Her sense of foreboding increased still further.

'Oh, just a petition,' said Charlotte. 'It's nothing, really. Small town politics.'

But important enough to upset Charlotte. 'A petition asking for what exactly?' she pressed.

'For the little theatre to be restored to its former glory,' Charlotte said. 'For everything to be made exactly as it was before. People in this town are very . . .' she raised an eyebrow, '*traditional* in their beliefs. You'll see.'

Faye wasn't sure she wanted to. If Charlotte had mentioned the words confrontational, campaign and petition to her before, she probably wouldn't have come. She was here to relax, not get involved in a war with the townspeople of Deriu. She had done some research about theatre architecture before she came — she didn't want to appear a complete novice and it was obvious to her that the architecture of a theatre was integral to its use within the community. However, she had intended to wait until she saw the actual building before she delved too deep.

'But your friends own the theatre, don't they?' she asked. 'Surely it's their decision how to redesign it?'

'Exactly.' Charlotte nodded. 'But . . .' She hesitated. 'Let's just say there's been a bit of a dispute.'

'A dispute?' Faye mentally added this to the list of words that wouldn't have persuaded her to come here. 'About what?'

'About the ownership.'

Faye stared at her. 'So your friends might not own it at all?'

'It's complicated, Faye.' Charlotte put a slim hand on her arm. 'This isn't England. Some things — like property deeds, for example — aren't as black and white here in Sardinia. They're more a murky grey.' She opened the car door. 'Come on. Let's go inside. I can't wait to show you the house. We had it converted five years ago.' She smiled back at her. 'If only you'd been a bit quicker getting that degree of yours, you could have come over to do it for us.'

'But . . .' Murky grey? There must be deeds, surely? And if Charlotte's friends didn't actually own the theatre, then how could they employ her to work on its design? 'You should have told me,' she said crossly, following Charlotte out of the car. 'About the theatre, I mean.' Charlotte had dragged her here on false pretences, luring her with promises of sun in Sardinia and an exciting project to work on to boot, and here she was being dumped in the middle of a war zone.

'Faye.' Charlotte put down the suitcase she'd got out of the back of the car and pulled her into a hug. She held her by the shoulders and looked her straight in the eye. 'I'm sorry, my love,' she said. 'But if I'd told you everything, you might not have come.'

'Exactly,' muttered Faye, though it was hard to be angry with Charlotte when she was looking so contrite.

'But here you are, in the most beautiful part of the island,' Charlotte said, 'and all I'm asking is that you go and see the theatre and talk to the Rinaldis. If you don't want to get involved in the project, then don't. You can stay in our house as long as you want, feed the fish for Fabio, and then go home when you're ready. You'll still have the promised holiday. Okay?'

Faye could hardly argue when it was put like that. 'Okay,' she agreed.

'Great!' Charlotte swung away and picked up the suitcase. 'We can always find someone else to feed the fish if you want to leave early, though I hope you won't,' she said. 'And as for the theatre . . .' She led the way up the steps to the front door. 'Marisa and Alessandro will explain everything.'

Faye had mixed feelings about this. What other important nuggets of information might Charlotte have left out? She thought of her mother's reaction to the name Rinaldi – it had been odd, to say the least. In fact, both her parents had been acting out of character; it was unsettling. Faye wanted to know what – if anything – was going on. 'Why didn't Bruno Rinaldi's wife come to your wedding?' she asked Charlotte.

'She died before we got married,' Charlotte told her. 'She was an actress. I never knew her, but it was a huge tragedy in the village. Marisa says that everyone in Deriu loved her.'

'I see.'

'Then Bruno died a few months ago,' Charlotte explained. 'It's hit them both hard. Marisa, especially.'

Which added even more complexity to the project, Faye found herself thinking. Not to mention emotional turmoil. 'When are we going to see the Rinaldis?' she asked. Hopefully there'd be a bit of a chance to relax and take in her surroundings first. She wanted to explore Deriu Marina and the tannery museum by the river, not to mention that intriguing *centro storico*.

'Very soon,' sang out Charlotte as she slotted her key in the lock and opened the door. 'As a matter of fact, I've invited them to dinner tonight.'

CHAPTER 4

Less than two hours later, Faye was sitting on the sleek, cream leather couch in Charlotte and Fabio's open plan sitting room, doors open wide on to the terrace overlooking the river, a glass of chilled Prosecco in hand. They were waiting for the Rinaldis to arrive.

'They're both lovely,' Charlotte had assured her. 'Marisa in particular has become such a dear friend of mine, so I know you two will get on.'

Faye hoped so. Although the better they got on, the harder it might be to say 'no' to her theatre project.

Charlotte had proudly shown her around their home, which they'd bought and had restored a few years ago. Faye scrutinised it carefully with her new designer's eye. Like the old tannery it had been in a previous life, the house was arranged on two levels, the lower one comprising an open plan kitchen along with the dining and sitting area. The kitchen combined minimalism with warmth. A glossy black granite worktop flanked a black-and-white range cooker, and a massive top-of-the-range fridge conveniently dispensed soda water and ice at the touch of a button. The kitchen gadgets – and there were quite a few – were all tucked away in softly gliding cupboards, and the washing machine and dishwasher were in a utility room behind. The kitchen floor had been constructed from a natural porous limestone that felt surprisingly warm and comfortable under-foot, and a matt black slate lined the area behind the cooker. It was immaculate – and tidy. Faye smiled to herself. It was the kitchen of a successful professional couple with no children.

'Do you like it?' Charlotte spun around. 'Do you think you could be comfortable here?'

Was she serious? 'Oh, I could probably manage.' Faye ran her fingertips over the gleaming granite. Though she might be reluctant to do any cooking. This kitchen seemed far too pristine for anything so everyday.

In the sitting-room area, a contemporary, free-standing black and steel wood-burning stove was surrounded by classy leather furniture that echoed the building's beginnings. It was a clever touch, Faye thought. The sweet scent of leather mingled with the flowers artfully arranged in a vase on the wood and glass coffee table. The floor in here was a wooden parquet with unusual tinges of red and green – olive and cherry wood, Charlotte told her. One of the walls was wood-panelled and the others were painted a clean white. Deeply piled rugs of richly patterned burgundy and moss green added vibrancy and texture to the room. Hanging from the ceiling was a classic art nouveau chandelier and on the far wall was the *pièce de résistance* – Fabio's tropical aquarium. Faye gazed in. The floor of the aquarium had been laid with grey pebbles and white gravel; aquatic plants and purple coral created hiding places for the yellow, orange and iridescent blue fish swimming languidly around their home. Faye liked the fluidity; the movement of the fish in the water was restful. She could see why Fabio was so proud of it.

'What do you think?' Charlotte took Faye's hands and cocked her head to one side. 'Is our home to your taste?'

'It's really stylish. You've done it beautifully.' And Faye meant it.

Decor was subjective, but Charlotte had a good eye and had clearly brought her skills to the project. She had retained the sense of space and height in the old tannery, which had a high, beamed ceiling, but also injected some necessary warmth into the living space to make it a home. Faye cast another look around. 'Did you and Fabio agree on everything or did you have carte blanche?'

'We argued. We fought. And then – of course – I let her have her own way.' Fabio had come in without them hearing. 'Faye.' He stretched out his arms. 'It is wonderful to see you.'

'And you, Fabio.' Faye noticed immediately how well her friend's husband spoke English these days. 'How are you?'

'Very well.' Fabio strode over, grabbed her shoulders and kissed her enthusiastically on both cheeks. '*Bella*,' he murmured, leaning back to take in the sight of her. 'You are looking beautiful.'

'Thank you.' Faye smiled at the extravagant compliment. Italian men were such charmers – who wouldn't want to believe them? And she wanted to say the same to Fabio. He was certainly looking very dapper. Clean-shaven with his hair trimmed close to the scalp, his dark eyes twinkled. He was dressed in a well-cut and stylish navy suit with a pale lilac shirt, Italian leather brogues on his feet.

'*Ciao*, my love.' Fabio greeted his wife with an affectionate embrace.

Charlotte smiled up at him. 'I'm just going to show Faye her room and then I'll be back down,' she promised. She turned to Faye. 'Dinner is a joint effort tonight,' she explained. 'I'm in charge of seafood but Fabio's pasta is to die for.'

Faye could hardly wait. She'd eaten nothing since the dry cheese and pickle sandwiches on the plane and she'd been up since 6 a.m. She followed Charlotte up the wooden staircase. It led to two bedrooms, each with its own lavish bathroom. Her bedroom was painted white throughout and had wooden beams and a vaulted ceiling with a cherry wood parquet floor. The bed was big and made up with plump white pillows and crisp, luxurious bed linen. On the bedside table was a glossy magazine: *Ciao!* – presumably the Italian equivalent of *Hello* magazine. Faye looked out of the window. There was a wonderful view of the river below, the old town of Deriu and the mountains, the scrub glinting golden-yellow in the early evening light.

It was a paradise, thought Faye. Even if she only stayed here a week, she was going to enjoy every minute.

The front door was wide open and a light knock followed by the sound of footsteps announced the arrival of the Rinaldis. There was much excited chatter in a fast and furious Italian, which Faye struggled to follow. And then she was being introduced to a small dark-haired woman of about her own age with huge velvet-brown eyes and a wide smile. 'This is Marisa,' said Charlotte. 'And this is Faye Forrester.'

Marisa clasped Faye's hand warmly. 'I am so happy to meet you,' she said in perfect English. 'Thank you for coming. You are a godsend.'

'Your English is excellent.' Faye was surprised. She'd assumed she'd have to brush up on her Italian for this job. Though Sardinian was a different language, of course – many words were similar to Italian, but there was more of a Spanish influence, as Charlotte had already told her.

'Thank you.' Marisa smiled wistfully. 'Our mother taught us. It was very important to her.'

'I met your father,' Faye said softly. 'He came to Charlotte and Fabio's wedding.'

Marisa's face lit up. 'Of course,' she said. 'I thought your name was familiar. He stayed with your parents, yes?'

'Yes.'

'They were very kind to him. He told us. Are they well?'

'Yes, they are. Thank you. But I am very sorry for your loss.'

Marisa bowed her head, but not before Faye saw her dark eyes fill with unshed tears. 'I wish I too had visited England for Charlotte and Fabio's wedding.' She reached out and squeezed Charlotte's hand. 'But I did not know you, and we were not close with Fabio back then.' She leaned forwards conspiratorially. 'My brother, he was, I think, a little jealous that our father was so fond of Fabio.'

'Ah, I see.' Faye had been uncertain about meeting these two after what Charlotte had told her this afternoon, but she was drawn immediately to this attractive girl with the heart-shaped face and big smile. As far as ownership of the theatre and potential disputes were concerned, Faye thought, she might not be the godsend Marisa hoped for, but she would definitely be giving them the benefit of the doubt.

'Marisa is a primary school teacher here in Deriu,' said Charlotte.

'More wine, I think,' Fabio announced, heading to the kitchen.

Charlotte grasped the arm of the man who had his back to them as he talked to Fabio. 'And this,' she said, 'is Alessandro.'

He turned around to face Faye. '*Buona sera, Signorina.*' His voice was deep, though not unfriendly. Faye was surprised by the dark blue eyes that confronted her.

She blinked. '*Buona sera,*' she repeated back to him.

'So you are the designer.' He too spoke in English. His gaze raked over her.

Faye was slightly taken aback by his direct approach. She straightened her shoulders. He had none of the easy warmth of his sister but he certainly looked dramatic enough to own a theatre. His black hair curled around the collar of his white linen shirt, and his eyes were nothing short of compelling. He was slim-hipped and tall for a Sardinian man, she guessed, topping her by around two inches. Apart from the blue eyes, he reminded Faye of his father. 'I've only just qualified.' She gave him an equally direct look back. If he could get straight to the point, so could she. 'I don't know yet if I can even be of any help to you and your sister.'

He nodded, as if he'd already worked this out for himself. An attractive man, Faye had to admit, but unlike his sister and his father, definitely lacking in people skills.

Fabio reappeared with a bottle of wine and Charlotte ushered them out towards the terrace where she had laid the table. 'Plenty of time to discuss all that later,' she said. 'Let's eat.'

It was still light and Faye was warm enough in her sleeveless maxi dress although she had brought a wrap downstairs just in case. The sun was dipping down in the west behind the house and the lights were coming on by the river, sending yellow beams on to the softly rippling water. The cutlery and crystal glasses Charlotte had set on the crisp white tablecloth gleamed. They sat down. Faye was between Marisa and Fabio, with Alessandro sitting opposite.

Charlotte brought the first course – a delicious chickpea and wild fennel soup – to the table and the conversation flowed pleasantly enough, touching on local issues (but not on any disputes, Faye noted). The soup was light and left an aniseed taste on the tongue. She helped Charlotte clear the bowls.

'So what do you think?' Charlotte whispered as they stacked them into the dishwasher. 'Aren't they lovely?'

'Marisa seems very sweet,' Faye agreed cautiously.

Charlotte laughed. 'Alessandro will grow on you,' she said. 'He can be a bit prickly, but he's a good man. You'll see.'

The next course was Fabio's infamous pasta. 'La Pasta Sarda,' he told her, which turned out to be *fregola* – small, round and a little like couscous – which positively melted in the mouth. Fabio served this with mussels, prawns, squid and clams in a rich and garlicky tomato sauce, with what Charlotte told her was *pane carasau,* a crisp Sardinian bread, on the side. Over this course, they talked about Charlotte and Fabio's upcoming Italian trip.

'What are you hoping to find?' Alessandro asked Fabio. He scooped up some pasta and one of the tiny succulent *vongole*, clams.

Fabio shrugged. 'Who can know? I must see how each hotel operates. How they market themselves, how they manage their staff and their accounting. Everything.'

'And then?' asked Faye. She looked up from peeling one of her prawns. This was the kind of food she loved – messy but delicious.

Fabio picked up his glass and took a sip of wine. 'And then I deal with it,' he said. 'My company, they want to . . .' He hesitated. 'How do you say? Make things more the same?'

'Standardise?' It was a shame, thought Faye. She popped the prawn into her mouth. Independence was a concept fast disappearing in world commerce, it seemed. The hotels were part of a chain, yes, and she could see that profit was the driving force, but she didn't like it. She preferred to stay in independent hotels, eat in independent restaurants and shop in eclectic, one-off boutiques rather than department stores. It might take more

31

time and the quality wasn't always consistent, but surely it made life that bit more interesting. She scooped up some more *fregola* and tomato sauce and decided not to make her views known at this point in time. She had only just arrived, after all.

Rather to her surprise, Alessandro took up a similar position. 'So that every hotel is the same as the next?' he growled. 'I hope you will not introduce a fast-food outlet too?'

Fabio laughed. 'I agree with you, my friend,' he said. 'But do not fear. There will be no fast food. The accounting method may be the same but our hotels have a reputation for being exclusive.' He eyed Faye over the rim of his glass. 'And different.'

She smiled. 'I'm grateful to you all for speaking in English for my benefit,' she said.

'It is good for the practice,' Fabio replied. 'Charlotte and I speak it together sometimes. And I need it for work, of course.'

'Exactly,' Alessandro put in. 'We cannot expect tourists to speak Italian, let alone Sardinian.' And although he smiled as he said this, Faye couldn't help but feel that it was a dig.

'You're right,' she said. 'The British are very lazy about learning languages.'

'Not only the British.' Fabio began to collect the plates. Charlotte got up too and Faye realised that there was going to be another course. She hoped that her stomach could take it.

Alessandro raised an eyebrow. 'The Italians too perhaps,' he said. 'How many of you speak our language when you come to live over here?'

'Practically none,' Fabio agreed, apparently not worried in the least by what was obviously a bone of contention for original Sardinian islanders like the Rinaldis. He turned to Faye. 'Apart from within their close family circle, most Sards speak

Italian as much as their traditional dialect,' he said. 'It is easier that way.'

'For you especially, my friend,' Alessandro chipped in.

'Dialects can be different in just a few miles,' Marisa added. She was a born peacemaker, Faye could tell.

Fabio rolled his eyes. 'And so their colloquialisms can be a complete mystery.'

Faye laughed. 'When did you first come over here, Fabio?' she asked.

'In my early twenties, when I started working in the hotel industry.' He clapped Alessandro on the back. 'That was when I first met Marisa and Alessandro's father Bruno. He owned the hotel I still work in.' Fabio shook his head sadly. 'He took me under his wing.'

Faye recalled what Marisa had told her about Alessandro's jealousy. Clearly, he had got over it. The two men were obviously good enough friends for a bit of banter not to affect their relationship.

Fabio took the plates out to the kitchen and returned a minute later with another bottle of wine. They were drinking a *Gallura*, a straw yellow Sardinian white that was almost too easy to drink, Faye thought ruefully.

'Your island is very beautiful but also very small, my friend.' Fabio laughed as he began to refill their glasses. 'Whereas Italy . . . What can I say? Her language is the most historic and the most revered in the whole world.' He puffed out his chest and they all laughed.

'Though, to be fair on tourists, you speak Italian, Faye.' Charlotte came back to the table with a tray of silver foil parcels. She unwrapped one and a gush of lemon-fragranced steam whooshed out. 'Or you used to.' She looked around the table. 'Fresh sea bream,' she said. '*Orata*.' She began to serve the fish.

'With baked *melanzane*.' Fabio brought another bowl to the table.

Goodness, thought Faye.

'We both did A level Italian at college,' Charlotte told the others. 'And Faye and I spent a summer in Italy.'

'You did?' Alessandro seemed surprised and Faye was glad to prick the bubble of one of his preconceptions, at least. He was, she decided, rather tricky.

Even so, they were all looking at her as if they expected her to suddenly switch to fluent Italian. She felt herself blush. 'It was just a few weeks,' she protested. 'I don't speak it fluently. Certainly not anymore.' But what a summer. She exchanged a glance with Charlotte. They had both stayed in Naples, with different families, but they had been able to spend a lot of time together.

'Ah, Naples,' Charlotte sighed dreamily, ignoring her husband who had responded with something rather rude in Italian. She sat back at the table and there was a pause while they all sampled the fish. It was good. Faye was glad that Deriu was by the sea; this was her kind of food. Although she didn't think she'd eaten so much in one sitting in her entire life.

Faye had adored Naples, although she knew that Fabio, coming from Milan as he did, took the view of many northern Italians that anywhere south of Rome was full of peasants and to be visited at your own risk. Naples had been hot and busy that summer when she and Charlotte were seventeen; the scents of Italy were stamped into every side street, seeping from every brick and stone; operatic arias drifting from open windows, the sweet, pungent smell of roasted peppers, tomato and garlic exiting every doorway. The life was on the streets. And Naples was about as real as it got. Faye had loved the noise and the bustle, the pizza and the ice cream, the glorious views of the Bay of Naples from her bedroom in the house up on the hill.

They had both enjoyed short, uncomplicated romances with Neapolitan men: Faye with the son of the family with whom she was staying, Charlotte with his best friend. Those boys had flattered them, looked after them, shown them the sights of Pompeii and Herculaneum, the Catacombs, the Royal Palace and the Castel Nuovo. They wooed the girls in the back streets of Naples and even took them to Capri on a friend's small boat.

They had left the Amalfi coast at the beginning of September, vowing to return, and Charlotte had done just that at the first opportunity, travelling by train to Genoa and then going by ferry to Sardinia. She met Fabio and made her life here. Faye, on the other hand, apart from a few days in Rome with a girlfriend eight years ago and a weekend in Venice with Justin, had never been back.

But she would make up for it now. 'Why did your parents feel it was so important for you to learn English?' Faye directed the question at both Marisa and Alessandro. 'Charlotte tells me your mother was an actress?' She was impressed by the Rinaldis' fluency, and it furthered her determination to brush up on her Italian this trip and use it whenever she got the chance. She was not going to be one of the lazy tourists so derided by Alessandro.

'Yes, she was.' Marisa spoke quietly. 'And she often performed in English language plays.'

'I see.' So she had experienced the benefit of being bilingual and wanted her children to have it, too.

'But it was not only the English language that she thought

important.' Marisa spoke quickly, and Faye imagined that she could detect a hint of resentment behind her words.

'Oh?'

'It was our entire education,' Alessandro said smoothly. He lifted his glass as if to make a toast. 'And naturally, we thank her for it. Marisa, at least, has used her education skills wisely in becoming a teacher herself.'

Faye glanced across at Marisa but she had her head down, focusing on the neat forkful of fish she was about to eat. 'Was your mother born in Sardinia too?' Faye asked. And what about Alessandro, she was thinking. Had he also used his education wisely? What did he do for a living?

'Ah, no,' Alessandro replied to her question. 'She was Italian like Fabio here, from northern Italy.'

So these two were half-Italian, half-Sardinian. Faye guessed that many islanders had gone to mainland Italy where there were more opportunities. But Sardinia was beautiful enough to have drawn plenty in return. What did it feel like to have grown up here, she wondered, to have lived here forever?

'Our mother also lived in your country for some years,' Alessandro told Faye. He had finished his bream and *melanzane* and now he placed his knife and fork together and wiped his lips with the crisp white napkin beside his plate.

'Really?' Faye was surprised.

'She joined a company of actors, travelling the UK.'

'On tour,' supplied Charlotte.

'Yes. And then she came to Sardinia, to the little theatre at Deriu, restored and ready for her to perform in.'

Ah yes, thought Faye. The theatre. She mustn't forget the theatre, the main reason for her being here.

At last they were all finished. Charlotte got to her feet to clear the plates and Faye rose again to give her hand. 'Is that where she met your father?' she asked Marisa and Alessandro when she returned. 'At the theatre here in Deriu?'

'Yes, it is.' Marisa's expression grew more animated. 'His parents owned *il Piccolo Teatro*. It was love at first sight, you know. They were a golden couple. Sofia and Bruno Rinaldi.'

Faye did not miss the quick glance sent Marisa's way by Charlotte as she brought in the dessert. '*Seadas*,' she announced.

'Traditional Sardinian fritters with honey and pecorino,' supplied Fabio.

'Wow.' Faye eyed the fritters warily.

'It was our mother's destiny to join the new company,' Marisa said. 'And of course, to fall in love.'

There was another silence around the table as everyone took in the sight of the impressive dessert. Charlotte had certainly pulled out all the stops. Faye wondered when anyone was going to tell her about the petition, the ownership dispute, the confrontational townspeople. At the moment the story was simply of a charming romance.

'You must miss them both very much,' she said. Sofia in particular must have been quite young when she died. Faye wondered how it had happened. She'd ask Charlotte later; she didn't want to dwell on such a sensitive subject here at the dinner table.

Once again, Alessandro's eyes were on her. He reached out for his sister's hand and squeezed it. 'We do,' he said.

Faye tasted her dessert. The fritter had an intense flavour – both sweet from the drizzled honey, but also salty from the pecorino, with a hint of lemon.

'It is *corbezzolo* honey from the strawberry tree,' Fabio told her.

'Bittersweet,' added Alessandro, casting what seemed like a knowing look around the table.

Bittersweet indeed, thought Faye. 'So the theatre must have an interesting history,' she said, determined to keep the conversation on track.

'Oh, yes.' Marisa nodded. 'It is part of the identity of our town.' She glanced at Alessandro but didn't elaborate any further.

Fabio sat back and looked around the table. 'Coffee, anyone?' he asked.

They all said that coffee would be perfect and Charlotte suggested that they take it in the sitting room. They drifted inside, Faye casting a final reluctant glance towards the still and moonlit night, the gleaming darkness of the river, the crescent moon and the stars in the satiny sky.

'I'd love to see it as soon as possible – the theatre, I mean,' Faye said. And she wanted to know its story. She sat down on the couch next to Marisa. Although they were very different, she felt that this girl could be a friend and ally. Not that Faye needed a friend and ally for a week's holiday in Sardinia. But still . . .

Alessandro came and stood beside his sister. 'There is no time . . .' He looked at his watch.

'Oh, I didn't mean—' *Now*, she was going to say. She wanted to see the theatre tomorrow when she got a chance to explore the *centro storico*.

'—like the present,' he finished.

'Sorry?' Faye blinked at him.

'Why not?' He strode back to the open door and looked out at the terrace they had just come from. 'A theatre is made for the night-time, *non evero* – is this not so? It is at night-time that a theatre will come alive.'

'Well . . .' Faye could think of a few reasons why not. One, it would be rude to leave Fabio and Charlotte's dinner party so abruptly. Two, it was late; she'd got up early to travel here from the UK and she was ready for her bed. She'd eaten so much at dinner she wanted to sleep it off, not start walking the streets. She waited for one of the others to voice an objection but they didn't.

'It is a good idea, I think,' Marisa said at last.

Faye glanced at Charlotte, who shrugged. 'It's up to you,' she said. 'If you're not too tired . . .'

Faye was tired, but maybe a walk might do her good after all this sitting, eating and drinking. She was longing to see the theatre – more than that, she was intrigued. And the soft night air was irresistible. 'How far is it?'

'Not far.' Alessandro leaned over and picked up her wrap from where she'd left it hanging over a chair. He handed it to her. Faye couldn't work out if the expression in his eyes was a plea or a challenge.

Whatever it was, Faye rose to it. 'Okay,' she said. She turned to Marisa. 'Let's go.'

CHAPTER 5

Ade stared out into the night-time garden. He couldn't see much; it was too cloudy, and there were no lights on out the back — just fields and sheep and hills. He should go up. He'd made up his mind, so now he should go and tell her; it was only fair. He turned around and made his way upstairs.

It was Sunday — a day usually dedicated to the garden, he thought, not without a slight trace of bitterness. It was the sameness that got him, the regularity; it made him want to chuck his gardening trowel in a ditch and take off somewhere. This morning he had suggested as much to Molly.

'Such as?' she asked mildly.

'A day out in the New Forest?' he said. 'Lunch on the beach at Weymouth?'

Molly had that sad look on her face. 'I promised I'd call in and see Mum,' she said. 'And then I thought I'd bring her back to have dinner with us. If I'd known . . .'

'Never mind.' Ade knew that he sounded irritable. He rubbed the back of his neck. He was irritable. And he knew that he should give Molly some notice — if he gave her some notice, she might even come. But wasn't that the point about spontaneity? It had to be, well, spontaneous.

So he had gone for a long walk on his own, starting off from home, heading up through the Nature Reserve and then down to the Bay. Ever since Ade had told Molly about his early retirement, the atmosphere had been strained between them. Though maybe it had been tense before that too and he just hadn't noticed.

Ade stomped through the wood, waiting for the exercise, the fresh spring air, the musty woodland smells to clear his head the way they always did. The atmosphere hadn't always been strained between them, of course. He had loved her once. Ade stopped for a moment as he realised the magnitude of this thought; the past tense of it. He continued to walk on, more slowly now. Did he love her still? Did it matter that when he went for a hike he always went alone, or with Faye? Did it matter that every evening they sank into separate armchairs to watch TV or read the paper or a book? Exchanging the odd word, yes. But alone, he thought. That was the truth. Living separate lives.

Ade paused by the Nature Reserve gate as he always did. It was a steep hill and he had to pace himself. June, he decided, was his favourite month. Around him, trees, bushes, plants, wild flowers were growing in earnest; they meant it now. Days were long, sweet and mild; even people looked brighter and more hopeful. Ade was hopeful too. He walked on. It wasn't as if he was lonely. He played golf with colleagues, tennis at the club in town. Friends – couples – came round for dinner or drinks from time to time; there was the occasional trip to the theatre or cinema, the usual sort of stuff. Middle-class stuff. His lip curled. And he had no one to blame but himself. He had allowed his life to slip out of his control; he had become what he had once vowed never to be. How had that happened? And more to the point, was it too late to change?

The path emerged on top of the ridge. Ade loved the

ridge: the short sparse grass, the distant hills and fields with grazing sheep; the view from here down to the Bay. He climbed up to the worn wooden bench to sit down and take in his surroundings for a moment. The sun was glimmering through a faint mist, sending a sheen of light, like liquid honey, on to the surface of the ocean. Ade was happiest walking the Dorset cliffs, the combination of vast sky, endless ocean, and high ground always made him feel good. Maybe over the years the sense of infinity he found here had made him feel that he wasn't trapped, that he hadn't made the wrong choice all those years ago, for the right – or even the wrong – reasons. Maybe, Ade admitted to himself, it made him feel free.

But that was an illusion. He took the path down to the Bay now, first along the ridge and then down to the road. This led to the disused railway track that passed through the Bay, where a café had been set up in the old station. He liked that. Lots of people complained that there was no longer a railway station here or in Bridport, but Ade rather liked the sense of isolation it lent this part of West Dorset. The café at the station was a nostalgic nod to the past. The past . . . Ade sighed. He couldn't blame Molly for any of it.

He thought back to the first time he'd seen her in the Electric Palace. Pretty Molly Thomas with her neat, dark, shining hair, pink lipstick, dark doe-brown eyes catching him short and pulling him in. Ade was living in Exeter – he was in Bridport for the weekend for a mate's wedding. He was already working in banking. It was a five-year plan. He could still hear his father's voice – *get a good education, a career. You can travel the world later. Get yourself going first* . . .

Ade smiled and nodded to a couple sitting outside the café with coffee and a bun. There were people inside, too, and the car park was half full already. The Bay had always been quiet until they filmed a TV series here a few years ago. Since then everything had changed. People came to stare as if transfixed by the golden cliffs, to identify the local newsagent's that had featured in the series and the restaurant that had been used as the police station. Ade still loved the place, though; the quirky mix of old and new, the tang of fish coming from the boats in the working harbour, the fresh air tainted with salt, the screech of seagulls in the wind. Even the blowsy kiosks by the harbour had a place in it all. It was real life here; it was never meant to be manicured.

He had fallen for West Dorset and Molly Thomas that weekend and pretty soon Ade was back here most weekends that followed. His dad was wrong though – Ade couldn't travel the world later. Because later, he would still be working in banking and if he left – even for a year – he'd go down a few rungs of the ladder and all that work would have been in vain. He wouldn't have let that stop him, mind. But when Ade met Molly, everything changed. She fell in love with the man his father had wanted him to be and he fell in love with what he imagined she could be. It hadn't seemed so complicated at the time – but that was because of the chemistry.

He walked alongside the harbour, past the moored boats and the eager-faced kids with their fishing nets looking for crabs, the kiosks selling fish and chips and candy floss, the white fishermen's cottages. He walked along the ginger-pebbled beach – there was a high mound of pebbles acting as a sea defence and the Bay needed it; in winter the harbour had been known to flood and West Cliff could be cut off for days.

Ade struck out up the pathway of West Cliff. This slope was more gradual and he walked slowly, taking time to admire the beaches below, their sand exposed because the tide was out, and the view of the Bay and the treacly cliffs stretching out towards Burton and beyond. The problem was that good chemistry didn't last forever. There was a time, early on, when Ade realised that he and Molly were not on the same trajectory in life. They had that spark and similar backgrounds – which took them a long way – but Molly wanted what her sister had: the stability of a hardworking husband, the joys of a young family, the sure knowledge that support from a relative was never far away. He couldn't blame her, losing her father the way she did when she was just seventeen. But Ade wanted something else.

He'd told Nina that. Never anyone else. He'd told Nina because she understood. He'd told Nina because she recognised the other Ade – the one he was meant to be and had always intended to be. Ade passed the alleyways that led to the Cliff Walks. He'd always fancied living here – having this view every day, at all hours, but the blustery Bay wasn't Molly's thing. Too many motorbikes, she said. Too many tourists in summer and too much wind and rain in winter. Too extreme in every sense of the word. Too much drama.

'What kind of something else?' Nina had asked him.

'Something risky,' he said without really thinking. 'Something unsafe.'

'You want to test yourself?'

'Maybe.' Ade thought about this. 'I want to see things,' he said. 'I want some different experiences.'

'Something to tell your grandchildren?' She was laughing at him now.

'I want to know I've lived,' he said. 'That's all.'

Molly would have maintained that he was living here in West Dorset. But the world was a big place. And Ade wanted to see a lot more of it before he was through. Ultimately though, as Ade had found, Fate had a way of grabbing the reins and taking you an entirely different way.

At the top of the cliff, Ade paused again and looked around. He could never tire of gazing at the sea. It had a different mood every day, every hour sometimes. He blinked. Was that what was the matter with him now? Was he bored?

Back then . . . just as he was thinking he really should do something about his relationship with Molly, after two years of travelling between Bridport and Exeter and creating the kind of steady pathway that in Molly's eyes could only lead to one thing . . . Just as he thought he couldn't stand one more month at the bank, one more week, one more day. Just as he thought, *now's the time, today, tonight* and almost just as he opened his mouth to tell her . . . Molly gave him the news.

Ade walked on through the green meadow at the top of the cliff. He would walk on to Eype, he decided. There was a farm café across the Down. He would stop there and have a bite to eat before heading back.

She had grabbed the lapels of his jacket. 'I'm pregnant,' she'd said, brown eyes dancing. 'Say you're pleased?' There was the smallest of pauses, a heartbeat. 'You are pleased – aren't you, Ade?'

He had stared at her, confused. She had stolen his moment. His mind computed the differences between them in a flash, what they both wanted and what he had been going to say to her that night. The chemistry didn't matter and neither did their backgrounds; it was their future that mattered. Ade gave in to panic. 'How did that happen?' His mouth was dry. He kept staring at her as if she might suddenly say – *only joking, Ade, relax, only joking*. And what then? Would he tell her he was leaving? Could he tell her that? He wasn't sure that he could.

'Silly.' She giggled, still not realising. 'I think we all know how it happened.'

We all? 'How many people have you told?' He licked his dry lips.

'Only my mum.' She blushed. 'I was sick. She took one look at me and she guessed.' But Molly was hesitating now. 'Ade?' She grabbed his hand. 'You are pleased?'

He took her in his arms. It wasn't her fault that he was a restless bastard. 'Course I'm pleased.' He stroked her hair. 'Daft thing. I'm bloody delighted.'

One of the things Ade liked about this area was that every beach was different. The Bay had its working harbour and high cliffs, while here there were great swathes of green down and a steeply shelving pebble beach with Golden Cap squatting in the distance to the west. Looking back, he couldn't say that any of it had been hard. Marrying Molly, living in West Dorset and commuting to Exeter every day for work, becoming a father to the baby girl he soon adored more than he could have dreamt possible. Faye. It shamed him how he had woken up sweating in those early days, imagining conversations where he persuaded Molly to have an abortion, to take this prospective responsibility — their child, for God's sake — and flush it down the toilet. Thankfully for all of them he had never voiced these thoughts out loud — especially after what happened later. But they had been in his head and that was bad enough.

He was young. He'd felt trapped. He had been bloody trapped. But Molly was a good wife and it hadn't been so very difficult to throw himself back into work, into his golf and his tennis. Best of all had been watching Faye grow into an adorable toddler, a little blonde charm-machine with his eyes, his hair, his build and Molly's wide, beaming smile.

Ade climbed up the steps from the beach and headed for the Down and the farm café. There was nothing to get home for. Molly and her mother would be sitting peeling vegetables and making conversation; in all these years he'd never become fully part of their little circle. His own parents were dead and gone and he was an only child. And Faye . . . well, Faye was in Sardinia now. At least she'd found herself an adventure. He smiled.

So when it came, that bolt from the blue when Faye was seven years old and everything in his garden was calm and rosy . . . it turned his world around. *She* turned his world around. *Nina*. But . . . He could see the café now. It was quiet; not many people came this far off the beaten track at this time of year. It was a 'but' that seemed to deny a thousand possibilities and more.

Things were different now, he reminded himself. He had been given another chance. Now, he could grasp his freedom. There was no Nina. He felt a momentary rush of nostalgia, because he had always kept a small piece of her in his heart. But it wasn't too late for Ade. And it wasn't too late for him and Molly either, despite everything.

For better, for worse . . . Back at home, Ade went into the bedroom where Molly was pulling on her nightdress. Without make-up her face looked more vulnerable. But he had made his decision. He had considered the consequences and he wasn't about to let anything change his pathway this time.

'Molly,' he said.

'Mmm?' She glanced up. She looked worried and he hated that, wished he could take a fingertip and smooth that frown away.

'I've been thinking,' he said, 'about this early retirement thing.'

Molly raised a perfectly plucked eyebrow. 'Oh?' She waited. She watched him.

'This is our chance.' He grabbed her hands. 'Our time, Molly.'

'To do what?' But she was smiling, thank God she was smiling.

'To travel, Molly. To see the world. To get away and do something new, something different.'

Her brow creased. 'Something different,' she echoed.

'We can afford it,' he said. 'What's to stop us?'

She hesitated.

Ade sighed. 'We need to do something. You and I need to do something. Before . . .' Before it's too late, he was going to say. Separate lives could soon become separate worlds. He and Molly . . . all that joined them now was Faye, and she was busy building her own life.

He stopped. Molly was regarding him seriously. 'Molly?'

'But, Ade, I don't want to do anything different,' she said. 'There's Mum and Kath and the kids. I couldn't leave them. I love my life here.'

Ade stared at her. She loved her life here. 'But, I . . .' His voice tailed off.

'I'm sorry, Ade,' said Molly. 'But the truth is, I don't want to go anywhere.'

CHAPTER 6

Faye crossed the bridge, Alessandro by her side. How on earth had she managed to get herself in this position? She had only agreed because she'd assumed all three of them would be going.

But Marisa had turned around at the last minute. 'Alessandro will take you,' she said. 'I will wait here. I must talk to Charlotte before she leaves tomorrow.'

Faye stared at her in dismay. 'But . . .'

'Alessandro lives in the old town,' Marisa explained. 'I live in an apartment near here – just down the river.' She pointed. 'And I have heels.' She stretched out her shapely legs. Her black strappy sandals were very lightweight and very high.

'Do not worry,' Alessandro interjected. 'I will not leave you to return alone.'

Once again, Faye had the sensation of not being in control of events. She fixed Alessandro with a look of determination. 'I'm not worried,' she said. 'But perhaps it's best if I see the theatre with you both. Tomorrow?'

'Of course.' Marisa put a hand on her arm. 'We will do that too. But please will you go now with my brother? It is quite safe and it is not far.'

Faye wondered who or what she was referring to as safe. Alessandro perhaps? But she knew when she was beaten. 'Alright,' she said, trying to hide her reluctance. She didn't want to seem rude.

'*Andiamo*,' said Alessandro. His navy blue eyes gleamed. 'Let's go.'

So they left Fabio clearing up after the dinner party and Marisa having a heart-to-heart with Charlotte – no doubt with her heels off by now, curled up comfortably on the leather couch – while Faye was walking into the *centro storico* of an unknown town late at night with a Sardinian man who had already proved himself more than a little unfriendly.

The silence hung between them as they left the bridge and took a side street that led uphill. It was less lit up here than it had been down by the river and although some of the windows of the tall, narrow houses were still illuminated, others were dark and seemed vaguely forbidding with their peeling paintwork and high, inscrutable balconies. Faye repressed a shiver and pulled her wrap closer around her shoulders. Alessandro Rinaldi wasn't the easiest man to be with. The tension was almost tangible. 'Tell me about the history of the theatre,' she suggested. That would be a good start.

'It was built in the 1820s,' he said. He continued to stride up the hill as if it were nothing. The occasional wrought-iron lamp lit their way with a dull orange glow, but it was still hard for Faye to keep her footing on the unfamiliar and uneven cobbles. He waited for her to catch up. 'But even before that, there was a group of amateur players. They used the annex of the school to rehearse in and they put on performances for the townspeople for almost thirty years – especially at carnival time.'

'That must have been quite something.' Through her research, Faye was aware that theatre had long been integral to the Italian culture, and that there were still some old amphi-theatres in Sardinia. 'So what happened? Did the schoolchildren chuck them out?'

To her relief he gave a low chuckle and offered her his arm. She took it. Rather some unwanted contact than a sprained ankle. But he wasn't so bad. He felt warm and solid and sud-denly they seemed more in step. The houses were no longer forbidding. Most of the balconies were crammed with window boxes and the peeling paintwork had a charm of its own. The fragrances of jasmine and basil hung honeyed in the air and every so often she caught snatches of an Italian pop song or aria drifting down from a high window. The old town was lived in.

'Educational needs changed,' he said. 'Perhaps there were more children, I do not know. At any rate, the king had to ask the Gov-ernor of Deriu to stop the amateur theatre using the annex.'

'That's a shame. Which king was it?' Faye enquired.

'Victor Emanuel I of Savoy,' supplied Alessandro. 'Our island has always been a target for pirates and marauders. We have been ruled by plenty of others.' He straightened his shoulders. 'But we Sardinians are independent. My father's ancestors may have suffered isolation and hardship, but we like to feel that we remain un-captured. We are a proud race.'

Faye glanced across. She could see that in him. The pride and the independence – and possibly a bit of pirate too, she thought. Who would dare to try and capture him? She smiled to herself in the darkness. 'So what happened to the amateur players?' she asked.

'In return for losing their premises, the king promised to help support the building of a new civic theatre. If the company could raise part of the necessary money, he said, they could own the theatre as a . . .' He hesitated. 'How do you say?'

'A consortium?' Faye was beginning to suspect the reasons behind the dispute of ownership Charlotte had told her about. Meanwhile, they had emerged from the street into a small square.

'Exactly. A consortium of local families. Deriu was a rich place at this time. There were many associations and societies, a civic library, and successful industries such as mining and leather. In fact, Deriu was one of the first places in Sardinia to have street lighting and an aqueduct.'

Faye remembered what Charlotte had told her about the tanneries. 'So what happened?'

He glanced across at her. 'The port was destroyed by a storm in 1880. My great-grandfather drowned at sea that day.'

'Oh.' Faye sensed the emotion behind his words. 'I'm so sorry.'

'The town suffered an epidemic of cholera,' he continued softly. 'The mines were closed. We returned to what you might call our "pastoral roots".'

'Until tourism,' she said.

'Until tourism,' he agreed.

'And you?' she asked him. 'What do you do for a living, Alessandro? Are you an actor too, perhaps?' It was possible – though he might also have taken over his father's business interests.

He laughed. '*Non*. Me, I am more like my grandfather. I took to the sea.'

'As a fisherman?'

'As a boat-builder.' He stopped walking. 'We have arrived. This is *Piazza del Teatro*, Theatre Square.'

Faye let go of his arm and looked around her. A couple of old street lamps lit up the small square, which was lined with historic buildings and date palms, completely deserted as if lost in time. In the centre stood a small fountain dribbling water – a shallow and cracked basin balanced on a narrow column of stone set in the middle of a stone bowl – and a wooden bench under a small, bushy tree. Faye peered at the buildings. One looked like a church and another . . .

'And this is our little theatre.' Alessandro gestured towards it. For the first time, she detected real warmth in his voice. 'Our *Piccolo Teatro*.'

Faye moved closer towards the eroded steps that led up to the building. It was hard to see clearly in the dark, but the facade of the theatre was certainly in desperate need of restoration. Situated as it was on the hill and raised up on the steps, she guessed that it had been at the mercy of the wind and rain for a long time without any defences. The paint was flaking and there seemed to be some sort of vegetation growing out of the roof; the place looked sorry for itself, indeed. She moved closer still. But despite its state of disrepair, it was beautiful. At the front, a rose window presided over a large wooden door surrounded by crumbling stone pilasters. Faye could see the evidence of its former glory in the elegance of the decorative plasterwork, even in the dim light from the orange lamp glowing at the bottom of the steps.

'Once, there was always a billboard outside advertising the plays,' Alessandro said sadly. '*Da Non Pedere* – not to be missed.' He shook his head as he led the way up the steps. 'But no more.'

'How long ago was that?' Faye asked him. They climbed the dozen steps and at the top, she ran her finger along a crack in the stonework of the wall; it was jagged and deep, as if the little theatre had suffered a severe body blow. Before she came to Deriu, Faye had assumed that the theatre would have fallen into disrepair in the 1930s and 1940s. So many buildings had. Much of the world had suffered from the Depression, and many buildings had been left to fall derelict, or been bombed and never repaired. But Alessandro remembered the theatre as being fully operational in his lifetime. He remembered the billboards, and both Rinaldis had talked about seeing their mother on stage. She sneaked a look at him. Alessandro couldn't be any more than late thirties. So the theatre had been left to rot for only twenty years at the most.

'It was closed down nineteen years ago,' he said.

Faye nodded. But what had happened nineteen years ago? 'When your mother died?' she asked softly.

Alessandro stiffened and for a moment she thought he wouldn't answer at all. 'Yes.' He frowned. 'My father could not bear the thought of the theatre existing without her. He could no longer bear to see the place, let alone run it. It reminded him only of the old days, the good days. And so he closed it down. That is natural, *non*?'

'Of course.' She wondered why he was so defensive.

'*Andiamo*,' he said. 'Let us go in.'

Alessandro lifted a stone urn that stood outside the entrance and groped under it. He produced a large key. Faye raised an eyebrow. They obviously weren't worried about people sneaking into the theatre and ransacking it. Or perhaps there was nothing left to take? She ran her fingertips along the pilaster to her right; its surface was powdery, it seemed to be disintegrating under her touch. Was this a listed building? Did such a thing even exist in Sardinia? She shook her head. It was daunting. Quite frankly, with a project like this, she wouldn't know where to start.

Alessandro inserted the key in the lock, gave the door a firm push and, reluctantly, it creaked open to reveal a dark foyer. He led the way in, flung open another door, flicked a switch and then stepped aside. '*Il Piccolo Teatro*,' he announced.

Faye drew a sharp intake of breath. The theatre was in a traditional horseshoe shape with three loggias or open galleries and a box providing a small private seating area on either side of the auditorium. The curtains – velvety and dark lilac – still hung across the stage where the eye was immediately drawn to an elegantly designed stucco ceiling. The faded colours must have been vivid once, the stucco crisp and new. The seats in the auditorium were faded red and dusty, the grey and white marble floor chipped and worn. The ravages of time and damp had left the theatre looking tired and unloved. But there was an atmosphere in the place – a kind of electricity – that stopped Faye in her tracks, that held her suspended as if she were waiting for the musicians to start playing in the empty orchestra pit, for the actors to stride forth on to the stage, for the curtain to rise.

Alessandro seemed pleased by her reaction. 'There are three hundred seats.' He brushed his hand along the back of the nearest one and Faye saw the dust motes dance in the air.

'Quite a lot for a town this size,' she observed. The *centro storico* of Deriu didn't seem to cover a large area, despite the big castle on the summit of the hill.

Alessandro shook his dark head. 'Not so many for a town that once had royal approval,' he said. 'People came from all over Sardinia and beyond to see performances in this theatre.'

'What sort of productions were they?' asked Faye.

'Straight plays, opera, comedy.' He shrugged. 'This theatre, it has always been popular and successful. We think that is why . . .' His voice trailed.

She waited. 'Why what?' Why other people wanted a slice of it?

Again he shrugged. 'It is of no matter.'

Faye watched his expression as he stared towards the stage. Was he remembering his mother treading those boards? 'It must be very emotional for you,' she said carefully. 'Coming here . . .'

'It is.' His voice was low.

Faye gently touched his arm. 'So why now?' she asked. 'Why do you and Marisa want to restore the theatre now?' She had to ask these questions. She needed to know.

'My father – he died three months ago.'

'I know. I'm so sorry.' Faye bit her lip. And yet this little theatre seemed so bound up in family tragedy; why was it so important to restore it?

He shook his head as if to brush the emotions away. 'Our family was rich once,' he said. 'We owned land, buildings.'

And a share in the original civic theatre, she presumed.

'Much of it was lost but my father sold the hotel he owned to the company Fabio now works for. He left money.' Alessandro looked around the dilapidated auditorium. 'My sister and I wish to use some of it to restore the theatre in memory of our parents,' he said. 'It is where they met. If the theatre lives on, their memory will live on, too.'

Faye nodded. 'I understand.' She had to admit that it was a lovely idea. Bruno Rinaldi might not have wanted to be reminded of his wife's days of fame and glory in the theatre, but he hadn't tried to sell the place, had he? He too must have been clinging to the memories. And besides, it didn't seem fair that the town was deprived of its theatre because one man was grieving for his late wife.

Alessandro led the way towards the stage and the orchestra pit. 'Almost twenty years . . .' He spoke as if Faye wasn't there. 'It is a long time for the place to be empty, for the stage to be bare.' He let his words hang. 'I remember my mother best as Lady Macbeth, you know, in the play by your William Shakespeare. Her voice was so strong, her presence so powerful . . .' He held out his hands in front of him as if they were covered in blood; Faye remembered that scene.

Lady Macbeth. Faye looked up at the dusty lilac curtain. And with his words she was transported back to her first real visit to a theatre, not a pantomime or a musical, but a performance of *Macbeth*, which she was studying at school at the time. She remembered climbing the staircase up to the top balcony, the smell and feel of the short-haired red brocade on the seats at the Theatre Royal in Brighton, where they were staying with some of her father's relatives. She remembered the buzz of voices, the hush as the lights dimmed, the feeling of anticipation, and the excitement as the curtain rose on another world; a world that – for the next few hours at least – became the real world, the only world that mattered.

'Thank you for showing me your theatre,' Faye whispered. Perhaps she had been mistaken about this man. He was direct, yes, but there was nothing wrong with that. He had suffered a great loss and he was dealing with it as best he could. She thought of her own healthy parents, and how fortunate she was to still have them both. They too had something special – something she could only hope to emulate one day, and now with her father's early retirement, their lives could be even better.

Outside the theatre, a shadowy figure was loitering by the fountain. Faye thought she could smell a faint scent of orange blossom in the night air.

Alessandro squinted into the darkness. 'Pasquale?' he called in Italian. 'Is that you?' He bent towards Faye. 'He is always hanging around,' he muttered. 'Practically lives in the place.'

'*Si*.' The figure took a few steps towards them and now Faye could make out his features in the lamplight. He was probably in his seventies, of medium height and upright in stature, sporting a dramatic shock of white hair. As he drew closer, she saw that his face was lined and weathered, his eyes sharp and bright as a bird's.

'And who is this?' He too spoke in Italian. His smile was broad and welcoming.

'Faye Forrester.' She held out her hand.

'Pasquale de Montis at your service, *Signorina*.' He gripped her hand firmly and bent his head so that for a moment she thought he might kiss it.

'*Buona sera, Signor*,' she said.

'English, *si*?'

She nodded. '*Si*.' So much for brushing up on her Italian.

'You look it,' he said. 'Tall, fair, slender.' He scrutinised her from head to foot. 'You are interested in our theatre?'

'It's a lovely old building.' Faye glanced at Alessandro. She wasn't sure whether her presence was supposed to be public knowledge. Alessandro still hadn't mentioned any ownership dispute. She'd seen the theatre but she pretty much remained in the dark.

'It is, yes.' Pasquale rubbed his hands together with satisfaction. 'And it holds a great many memories for me, as Alessandro here will tell you.'

'You were an actor?' Faye was intrigued. She wouldn't be surprised. There was something about his gestures, slightly larger than life, and the way he held himself poised; even the projection of his voice.

'Ah, yes, it is so.' Pasquale looked down modestly. 'I cannot deny it, *Signorina*.'

Faye laughed. She was conscious of a slight tug on her arm. She glanced at Alessandro who had his eyebrows raised.

'We must be going.' He glanced pointedly at his watch and at that moment the church bell let out a low clang. '*Ciao*, Pasquale.'

Pasquale raised his head to gaze intently at Faye. 'We will meet again, *Signorina*,' he said.

Faye smiled. He was an interesting character. 'I hope so.'

Alessandro took her arm once more and set his usual brisk pace across the cobbles.

'You don't like him?' she asked when they were out of earshot.

He gave one of his little shrugs. 'I have no feelings either way.'

Faye wasn't convinced. Alessandro was a man who seemed to have very definite feelings either way – about everything.

'He played opposite my mother in the old days,' he went on. 'They were friends, I suppose. He was *nervoso* – of a nervous temperament, you know? She was always kind to him.'

Kind to him. An unusual way to describe a relationship between colleagues, thought Faye. And yet there was something about Pasquale that drew her sympathy. Perhaps he too had suffered when the theatre was closed down. Perhaps he'd had a hard life. Or perhaps, as an actor, he was good at making people feel what he wanted them to feel.

'Was he good?' she asked.

'Good?'

'At acting.' Their steps seemed to echo on the cobbles. Faye noticed that in the short time they'd been in the little theatre, most of the remaining lights in the houses had gone out. The people of Deriu, it seemed, had now all gone to bed.

'He would say so.' Alessandro laughed without humour.

'More importantly, he likes to think that he . . .' His voice faded. He looked cross about something. The reflective mood he'd been in while they were inside the theatre had completely dissolved.

'Owns the theatre?' Faye guessed. She felt him tense by her side. 'Charlotte told me there was some sort of dispute.'

Alessandro slowed his pace. He looked around the dark, narrow street but did not look at Faye. '*Niente*,' he said. 'It is nothing. I am surprised Charlotte even bothered to mention it.'

'Nothing?' It hadn't sounded like nothing.

'Nothing we cannot take care of.'

Faye sighed. They had reached the bridge. She was conscious that she'd drunk several glasses of wine over the course of the evening and that this was probably a conversation best saved for a more sober frame of mind. But she liked Marisa – and even Alessandro, though Charlotte had been right and he was prickly. Seeing the theatre had affected her deeply; it had seemed to reach out to her. She wanted to help.

'Alessandro,' she said. 'You do see that I can't get involved with any renovations or designs until ownership of the theatre is fully resolved, don't you?' She didn't add that in her opinion she'd been brought here under false pretences. Not that she'd made any promises. But she did feel that her holiday in Sardinia had come with a clause attached – to help Marisa and Alessandro with the restoration of their theatre.

His eyes positively glittered in the darkness. 'It is resolved.'

'As far as you are concerned, perhaps.'

'As far as anyone is concerned.' They paused at the bridge. There were still some lights on in the houses by the river – including Charlotte and Fabio's, which Faye could see from their vantage point. The water was sleek and still.

'But—'

'Will you trust me on that?'

Faye wasn't sure what to say. Could she trust him? After all, they'd only just met and she didn't know the full facts of the situation. Why should she?

'Perhaps you should trust me,' she said, 'with the truth.'

'The truth?' He let out a bark of laughter and turned away from her towards the river. 'We have the paperwork,' he said. 'Our family has owned the theatre outright since the early 1900s. Is it our fault the townspeople now see a chance to make some money out of the place and suddenly want to be involved with it?'

'Is that what's happened?' Faye wasn't convinced. Surely it must be more than that? People couldn't suddenly claim owner-ship to something legally owned by someone else.

'And in any case . . .' His voice softened and to her surprise he took hold of her hand that had been resting on the parapet. 'Marisa – and I – we are only asking for some ideas from you.' His tone suggested that it was his sister who had wanted her here, not the man by her side.

'Of course.' Nevertheless . . . It was one of those moments – an early June night in Sardinia, the warm air balmy and comforting as down on the skin, a crescent moon escaping for a moment from a hazy shroud of cloud cover, the stars stamping the night sky with silver, a handsome man dark-haired and blue-eyed . . . a moment so perfect it could almost be a cliché.

'Thanks for walking me back, Alessandro,' Faye said softly. 'I can make my own way from here.'

He drew away slightly. 'The night – it is still so young,' he said.

'Perhaps.' Faye felt the night had seen more than enough

61

drama already. 'But I'm tired. Shall we meet again at the theatre tomorrow – with Marisa?'

He let go of her hand. 'As you wish,' he said. 'Marisa and I will both be working tomorrow but we can meet you there in the evening, at eight?'

'That's fine.' It would give Faye all day to explore in peace. She knew where they kept the key to the little theatre now. Tomorrow she would go back and take another look at the place – on her own, sober and with her notebook in hand. And she would talk to people – Alessandro and Marisa were hiding something from her, she was sure, and she was determined to find out what it was. The next time she met up with Alessandro Rinaldi, she would be prepared.

CHAPTER 7

Molly had known it would happen – it was just a question of when. Life and marriage could trundle along without disruption for years, but if there was a fault line, it could crack at any time.

She pulled her mind back to her creative writing class; though she did wonder why she was doing it. Did she really want to access her writer within; did she even have one? There were other questions she could ask herself, too: like why had she enrolled in Spanish conversation? It was hardly a requirement for the kind of holidays in Spain she'd ever taken. And although Pilates undeniably kept her fit and toned with a strong core, frankly, she'd never enjoyed it. She could also ask herself why she allowed a book club to dictate her reading habits and why it was necessary to knit and bitch when she could just as easily simply knit in the way she had always done.

Molly knew why. She was filling her life with other things and other people so that she didn't have to think too much, so that she wouldn't notice the empty spaces. It didn't work, though, not entirely. Covering holes at surface level didn't mean they were no longer there. But Molly didn't dare contemplate the alternative: to uncover and embrace them.

The writing class was taking place in Molly's old school, which was a little surreal – she kept seeing a vision of Miss Lethercott in her black batwing gown ranting about grammar as she brushed chalk-dust from her hands. It was a motley group ranging from Ron (he had written several novels – all self-published – and seemed intent on reading excerpts from every one aloud to the group at the slightest opportunity) to Molly, who was here mainly because the pottery class had been full and who had so far hardly written a thing.

Tonight, they were doing a writing exercise about the colour red. Jo, their tutor, explained that the exercise was designed to develop their creativity, to show how colour could be linked to character, to emotion, to landscape. They would, Jo had suggested, be surprised at what might emerge.

Molly spent a while being unsurprised that nothing had emerged, until a picture arose in her mind. She found herself writing about a red dress, describing it on the page down to the last button, zip and detail. Molly had been wearing the dress the first time she met Ade, in the Electric Palace. Molly was nineteen going on twenty and desperate for something, for life, to happen. She remembered that feeling so well, even now.

Ade had happened. He was casual, he was spontaneous, and he didn't appear to have any hang-ups. *Red*, she wrote. Ade seemed to offer up so many opportunities for Molly to change her life. Red for passion, for a bright flame. Red for autumn leaves, for November, for their first kiss. Ade had happened and he'd never known about the gap he filled. She hadn't told him because she didn't want to frighten him away. And when you don't tell someone something right at the start, it turns out that it's surprisingly hard to tell them later.

Bright flames didn't last forever, of course. Molly knew that. She looked around at the group. They were all writing furiously. Jo smiled back, an encouraging smile. Bright flames were replaced by something less exuberant and less warm. Molly frowned. Beige perhaps? But beige wasn't right. Her love for Ade had never been beige. More green. There had been life and growth — she thought of conception, of pregnancy, of the newborn — and often a sense of summertime. But how could you stop someone from leaving? Summer didn't last any longer than autumn. She had thought once that ropes could bind them, but ropes could also stop someone from feeling free. And then . . .

Red didn't have to be about passion. It could also be about death. Molly screwed up her eyes. That was too hard. She'd seen death first-hand on two occasions. She wouldn't be writing about that.

Instead, she began to doodle. Perhaps an art class would be more productive? Every season ended, that was the thing. Long days grew shorter; there was a chill in the wind and a darker tint on the leaves of the trees; even the sun began to set in a different position in the sky. People grew restless — especially Ade, she thought — and things that seemed solid and real seemed to disintegrate in front of her very eyes.

When it happened, when Faye was only seven years old, when Molly looked up at Ade as he walked in the door that evening and saw that he wasn't looking back at her, not really, Molly had been filled with a sense of inevitability. It was so strong, that feeling, that she could conjure it even now. Something had happened. Someone had happened. And all the empty spaces leapt up to remind her they were still around. Why should he love her? Why should he stay with her forever? Why should anyone? He didn't know her secret, he didn't know what thoughts plagued her in the middle of the night, because Molly had never told him; she had never told a soul.

The next day Ade had phoned to say he'd be late home from work. It was the second time that week. Molly told him that was fine, then she put down the phone and burst into tears. Her mother had been with her at the time. 'What is it?' she had asked. 'What's wrong?'

'It's Ade.' And Molly had told her what she knew.

'Are you sure?' her mother pressed.

Yes, Molly was sure. She didn't need to see a hotel bill in a pocket or lipstick on his collar. There were so many other signs. She couldn't not see – even if she tried very hard.

'It happens.' Her mother remained composed although her lips tightened and Molly knew that she shouldn't have told her, that she'd be against him now. 'Talk to him. Tell him it has to stop. There's Faye to think of.'

Her mother went home and Molly dried her eyes and put Faye to bed same as always and set to, making a beef casserole. But she never challenged Ade; she never let him know. She didn't want to make him choose; she wasn't brave enough. She had done one brave thing in her life, and it seemed she had used up her quota. She forced herself to stay silent and she buttoned it all up inside. One loss and now the threat of another.

Red sky, she wrote now. *Red for danger. Red for stop. Red for blood*. She had also cried when it was confirmed that she was pregnant again a few days later – she had suspected as much but not told anyone this time – and cried again two months on when she lost it. She had cried a lot that autumn. She couldn't believe how many tears; how great the sense of loss. And yet in the end, Ade had made a choice.

Molly drove home after the class. She wasn't sure that she would go again. She had signed up on a whim, but it seemed that creative writing could be surprising after all, and not in a good way. She wasn't sure that she wanted all these memories, thoughts and losses to swim to her surface; it was safer not to think sometimes.

She wondered how Faye was getting on in Sardinia. That had brought back some memories too, but of course it was a long time ago now. It was very sad to hear about Bruno. But there was no reason why . . . She flicked the indicator and took the turning up to the village. It was a Dorset hollow, carved out, she supposed, by centuries of wear and tear: the tread of horses' hooves, cattle and villagers walking to town, the furrows made by cartwheels and rain, and now the weight of modern traffic. The trees and ferns grew high on either side, lining the lane, and a flagstone path led past the church.

When Molly had offered to put up one or two of the wedding guests for Charlotte and her family, she hadn't dreamt they would be allocated someone like Bruno. Molly drove past the houses on the raised pavement. Bruno. It was astounding how you could look at a person and recognise their losses. Molly had pretended not to, of course, but the poor man was wearing his grief like a human billboard, and it seemed that he recognised her losses, too. It was funny, she thought, how easy it was to tell everything to a stranger.

The lane was narrow and Molly had to wait for a car coming the other way. At the end of the road she took the turning towards the old chapel and home. Ade would be there and he would want to talk – again. But she couldn't explain to Ade how she felt, why she couldn't leave her mother, any of it, really.

Sometimes, Molly wondered if it would be easier if he did leave – if he just walked away. It would be a burden lifted at least. No more worrying about when it might happen. But . . . She realised she was gripping the steering wheel so tightly that her knuckles were blue-white. There had already been two great losses in Molly's life. Could she really cope with a third?

CHAPTER 8

Pasquale de Montis paced the dusty floorboards of the stage in *il Piccolo Teatro*. He came here often. The truth was, he loved this place. More than that, it was so close to his heart that it was part of him. He had begun here with his beloved Papa when his father had worked as a caretaker, looking after the theatre almost as if it were another child, and he had ended up here on this very stage at the climax of his career. He had seen *Piccolo Teatro* in its heyday – been part of that heyday, he liked to think – and he had seen the theatre grow sad, forlorn and neglected. Others had stopped visiting the place, thinking there was nothing to see, but Pasquale had never felt that way. He continued to come here, to tread these dusty boards. It was his thinking place, his refuge, the home of his heart; a place where he could get away from everyone and be safe, alone with his most private thoughts.

For a moment, Pasquale stopped his pacing, faced the drawn lilac curtain that separated him from the auditorium. He remembered those precious moments when the performance was about to begin – moments when the house lights dimmed and the audience grew quiet. The palpable anticipation in the air. And he knew that they were waiting for him . . . not just him, of course, he was not so vain as to think that, but . . . that feeling was what made it so special, what made an actor want to be an actor, in his mind. It certainly wasn't the money.

Pasquale looked up to the ceiling, to the faded decorative stucco. An actor in Sardinia would never be a rich man. In a permanent company there could be regional or even national funding; a man could get his yearly *stipendio*, but it was not a lot unless one got lucky and made the big time. Still worse, there might be payment for performances only and not rehearsal time. It was hard. But it was worth it. If Pasquale was already on stage, he would glance across at whichever cast member might be with him and the *attori* would exchange a look, then look away, look inward, get into character in that moment. If he were backstage, he would do the same. And then.

Pasquale cleared his throat and flung one arm out in front of him as if he had an audience once again. King Lear perhaps: '*Who is it that can tell me who I am?*' He spoke aloud, quite pleased with the sound and the desperate emotion the words conveyed. The acoustics here were as good as ever and he liked to think he could still project, that his voice still owned a certain clarity and timbre. And it was a good question. All men were the sum of their parts: their childhood, the acts of their adulthood, their joys, their fears. Ah. Pasquale allowed himself a small inward smile. Lear was one of his favourites. He had played King Lear in England during his two years touring with the repertory company there; a satisfying time for many reasons, not least because that was where so many of the English plays belonged. Here it would be different. *Chi è che mi può dire chi sono?* Fine, so far as it went, but great Shakespearean prose did not translate well to Italian or Sardinian. In Sardinia, half the cast barely knew the origins of the plays, the meanings . . . His eyes glazed as he remembered. Not so Sofia. But then Sofia had always understood how he felt and agreed with him too. Like him, she was a purist. Like him, she had respect for form.

Pasquale thrust aside the dusky curtain so that dust motes flew into the air. *La prova generale,* the dress rehearsal might be expected to go badly; there was no audience to speak of. He looked out into the dim auditorium. Of course there was no one there. 'I am a man more sinned against than sinning,' he muttered. Lear again. Tragedies had always been his forte. Not for him the comedies of life or the stage. He felt things. Pasquale struck himself on the breast. He felt things *here*.

He did not delude himself that without an audience he was doing any more than speaking his part out loud. He was not a crazy man. But it was *per divertimento* – it gave him pleasure. And sometimes he could lose himself in it. He could pretend that things were as they once were, that none of the bad events had happened, that he was still an actor on stage, that people still watched him and listened to him and wanted what he loved to give. Ah. He was not deluded though; Pasquale knew the truth.

He returned to the other side of the curtain – the private side. '*Merda, merda, merda,*' he whispered; this was the 'good luck ritual' preceding a performance, the spoken words that would build to a crescendo as everyone stood in a circle, before finally breaking out and slapping one another for good measure. He shook his head. He did not need it now, of course; those days were gone. Nevertheless . . .

Pasquale's career had been varied. He had never intended to travel as much as he had – throughout mainland Italy, England, all around Sardinia – for his heart had always belonged to Deriu. But under the circumstances he had been unable to resist. It was not simply the fact that belonging to a touring company was so different, so much more professional than he was accustomed to— He cocked his head, imagining that he heard voices. But, no. There were no voices, not anymore. Here in Sardinia, theatres often closed between June and September because no one wanted to spend time indoors.

One never knew what obstacles might occur before production – perhaps the set designer, the *scenografo*, might suddenly announce he had not enough money for the requirements of the production, or an actor might declare that he was no longer able to perform. There was always an unpredictability about the thing. Here in Sardinia, workshop auditions for the cast of a production took place only four weeks before the first performance – and they included a mix of drama students and amateurs as well as more experienced actors like Pasquale.

Pasquale recalled the director in Sassari who had departed from the conventional traditional interpretation of *A Midsummer Night's Dream* in favour of something he described as 'post-apocalyptic' theatre. Naturally, it wasn't entirely to Pasquale's taste. But he could comprehend the vision. He was a creative; he could understand the creative mind.

He had only travelled abroad for a few years. And then he had returned here, to his hometown, to this theatre, to his mother and all the people who knew him; returned home basking in a certain success, it had to be said, although he didn't wish to be arrogant about the matter.

Pasquale drew a line on the floor in the dust with the toe of his shoe. The dust was a travesty, a symbol of decline. What had happened to this theatre was a tragedy. By God . . . He sank to the floor, on to his knees. No sooner had he returned here to Deriu than things had started to go wrong. He buried his head in his hands – just for a moment, no one would see. It had been, he realised in hindsight, the very slow beginning of the end.

But he must stay strong. Pasquale got to his feet and dusted down his trousers. He jumped. Was that a noise from somewhere backstage? He shook his head. Old ghosts. They were nothing to be frightened of. He had gone beyond that now. He had no one to fear.

He turned around, frowned. The important thing was to keep control. The past was past. He was old now – though at seventy-seven years, he was still fit and that was a blessing when he thought of his poor Papa. Pasquale was old, but he was not finished. And there had been rumours recently about *Piccolo Teatro* that had made his actor's hackles rise. It was said that the Rinaldis intended to do up the theatre, to restore it to its former glory. Pasquale had felt a frisson of the old excitement mixed with terror race through him when he had heard those words. Did that mean he would lose his refuge from the world outside? Did they think that they could so easily recreate something so special? Memories, he thought. They still had the power to affect a man. They alone would never be taken away from him.

Nevertheless, it had been a surprise yesterday evening to see Alessandro Rinaldi emerging from the theatre with a stranger. A woman, an *attractive* woman, it had to be said. Although he had never married, Pasquale liked to think he was a good judge. Was she involved with Alessandro Rinaldi, perhaps? Romantically involved? He didn't think so – though there might have been something . . . But if she were . . . Pasquale shook his head once again. That was not his business. The Rinaldis were not his business. Not anymore.

More to the point, if they were romantically involved, why take a woman to a disused theatre? It wasn't even as if the little theatre meant much to Alessandro Rinaldi. What did he know of its past? He hadn't been much more than a child in its glory days. He hadn't had his name plastered on the billboards outside; he had never had his name in lights – and neither had his father, come to that. But if Alessandro and the woman were not romantically involved, then why had he taken her there? Given the rumours, this was a more worrying scenario. In that area, certainly, Alessandro Rinaldi could not be trusted. Would he ignore the wishes of the townspeople, just like his father before him? After all, nothing was settled.

Pasquale flicked his gaze back and forth around the stage. He peered into the wings and finally, satisfied that all was as it should be, he returned to the front of house. Everything seemed the same. What should he do? Nothing, yet, he decided. A decision would be made in good time and then he would see. For now the theatre was safe. For now he could come here and remember and dream . . .

Pasquale walked slowly up to the foyer and turned around for one last look, before letting himself out of the old oak door. He locked it carefully behind him, turning the ancient key, lifted the urn to one side and replaced the key under the warm stone. He did not usually visit the theatre in the evening – the last thing he wanted was to have his reverie interrupted by one of the Rinaldis. But during the daytime he was safe. Alessandro was building his boats and Marisa was teaching in the school. No one else was interested. No one took any notice of him, not anymore. Pasquale sighed. Such was life. *Who is it that can tell me who I am?* He'd had his moments, though. No one could take those away.

'*Bon giorno, Signor.*'

The voice took him by surprise. He jumped guiltily and glanced around.

She was standing at the foot of the steps looking up. 'You have been visiting the theatre?' Her voice was soft, her eyes kind. Pasquale had the feeling that she might understand. He relaxed.

'I do no harm, *Signorina*,' he said. Though he shouldn't have to explain himself to her, some stranger. He didn't want her to report back to Alessandro Rinaldi though, didn't dare risk that he might change the hiding place of the key.

'Of course you don't.' She put her head to one side, as if waiting for him to say more.

'I enjoy the remembering,' he said. He walked down the steps.

She nodded. 'Your days on the stage,' she said. 'It must have been a wonderful time.'

He glanced at her quickly but she did not seem to be making fun of him. 'It was.' He regarded her more closely. 'And you?'

'Me?'

'You have returned to *Piazza del Teatro, Signorina*,' he said, stating the obvious.

She spread her hands. 'It's a lovely square.'

Very well. Pasquale looked around at the piazza he had grown up in, the square lined with date palms that he knew so well. Tired cobbles, a cracked and dribbling fountain, a myrtle tree. It was nothing so special – not to a tourist, anyhow. So she could play the game of being elusive, of hiding her true intent. But Pasquale would not give up so easily. He inflated his chest. He was Pasquale de Montis. He was his father's son. 'You are staying in Deriu?' he enquired politely.

'Yes. At Fabio and Charlotte Odini's. Do you know them?'

'Everyone in Deriu knows everyone else,' he told her gravely. 'Which means we cannot do anything without someone hearing about it.' He did not want to be unkind, but he hoped this might make her think.

She laughed. It was a nice laugh and he felt proud that he had caused it. Perhaps old Pasquale de Montis had not lost his touch after all.

'So there are no secrets in Deriu?' she asked. 'Is that it?'

On the contrary, thought Pasquale. They all had their secrets. Old Enrico Volti had his reasons for being a suspicious old bastard, but if he thought something was going on with the theatre, then something probably was. 'It does not truly belong to them,' Volti had said. 'And it is time for the townspeople to reclaim it.' Brave words. But Pasquale knew more than most about the value and persuasion of words. 'Who knows?' he said. 'I think everyone, he has his secrets, *non*?' He scrutinised her carefully. Did she? 'So what do you think of our little theatre?' He was curious. Perhaps she was just walking by. But perhaps not.

He sensed her hesitation. 'It's a beautiful building.'

'It was.' Pasquale looked up at the facade. To him, the stonework seemed to crumble a little more every day. He empathised.

'And perhaps it will be again?'

Pasquale frowned. Was she trying to tell him something? Or was he reading too much into it? 'Perhaps,' he said. He took a deep breath. 'This is the reason you have come to Deriu, *Signorina*?' he asked. 'To see our theatre?'

He saw that she was surprised and did not quite know how to respond.

'Not really,' she said at last. 'Charlotte is an old friend of mine from college.'

'Ah.'

'But you're right, I am interested in the theatre. Which was why Alessandro brought me to see it last night.'

He nodded. 'I see.' She was a nice girl, but not very good at pretence. Nevertheless, he would bide his time. Everything would be revealed to he who waited. 'So you have come to see it again?' he asked. 'Alone?' He raised an eyebrow. Now that, he was not happy about. He felt protective about the place, he could not help it.

Again, she hesitated. She pushed back her long fair hair with the fingers of one hand. She was a natural-looking girl, he thought. A classic English beauty. A bit wishy-washy for his taste perhaps – he had always gone for dark and sultry. This one was cool, and certainly no actress. 'I was just looking around,' she said. She pointed up the hill. 'I've walked up to the castle.'

He nodded politely. 'It has excellent views,' he said. 'It is a natural vantage point left over from the days when we had to worry if there was a foreigner approaching the town.' He noted her surprise. But it was best to be forewarned, he thought. Others, such as Enrico Volti, might be a lot less kind and a lot more direct with the poor girl.

'And I've visited one of the museums.' She fanned herself with the map of the town she was holding. It was getting rather warm; Pasquale had noticed as much. 'It's probably time to go home for lunch now.'

'A good plan, I think.' Pasquale smiled. 'And I will do the same.'

'You live close by?' The young woman seemed to want to talk some more. She paused at the bottom of the steps.

'I grew up over there.' He indicated the house directly opposite the theatre, facing them on the other side of the square. It did not look much, but it was a solid place. They had running water and electricity and it was comfortable enough.

She looked across. 'Oh, I see. Facing the theatre. How lovely.'

He nodded. He liked that she appreciated that – the proximity. 'My father was the caretaker of *il Piccolo Teatro* when I was a young boy,' he said. A caretaker, that was, in the proper sense of the word. It was not a job, more a vocation. 'My father was a practical man; clever with his hands. He used to help making the scenery too. He could make almost anything.'

She nodded encouragingly.

'I used to follow him around looking for chores.' He had been too young to do anything useful, he supposed. But he had enjoyed just being there, trailing after his father's heels. And he did not think his father minded him being around. Pasquale's memory – long ago though it had been – was of a father who liked the fact that his son was so attached to him and the theatre that was his life. And Papa would have been proud, Pasquale thought, to have seen his son acting on that stage – if he had ever had the chance.

'You loved it even then?'

'Ah, *si*.' It had not lasted long enough, that time. Pasquale had so few memories to draw on of his Papa, before they lost him. And once he was gone . . . 'Even the smell of a theatre is special,' he said. 'The scent of greasepaint.' He smiled. 'And of anticipation.'

'Yes.' Her expression changed. 'It's such an amazing colour . . .'

He gave her an enquiring look.

'I suppose it's the colour of make-believe.'

The colour of make-believe . . . Pasquale blinked at her in surprise.

He heard his mother almost before she spoke. The door being flung open, followed by the harshness of her tone.

'Pasquale!' she shouted. 'Where are you?'

'Over here, Mama.' He lifted his hand to wave, though he wanted to ask this young woman what exactly she had meant by the colour of make-believe.

'What are you doing, eh?' She glared at him, at both of them.

'Nothing, Mama.'

'Come away from that place right now, for the love of God. Come and eat.'

'I am on my way.' Pasquale glanced at the young woman. He didn't like her to hear how his mother spoke to him, but guessed she wouldn't understand what had been said. His mother could speak Italian, but she rarely bothered. My own language is good enough, she would say. If someone wants to speak to me, they can use that or not bother to speak at all. 'My mother,' he said. 'She still has not forgiven me for not giving her grandchildren.'

The young woman laughed once again. She held out a slim white hand. 'Goodbye, Pasquale. It was nice to see you again.'

He took her hand and raised it to his lips without touching. '*Arriverderci, Signorina*,' he said. 'Until we meet again.'

He walked briskly across the square and into his house without looking back. He shut the door and turned into the front room that looked out on to *Piazza del Teatro*. From there he watched her from the other side of the shutters, curious as to what she would do.

The young woman looked around her, hesitated, then ran lightly up the steps to the theatre. He watched as she bent to move the stone urn, picked up the key, looked round again. She put the key in the lock and slipped inside the theatre.

78

Pasquale clenched his fist. He wanted to race back there, to protect the building as his father had once protected it, but he could not. She had as much right to be there as he did – perhaps. And the truth was that he had liked her. No doubt she was harmless. But who was she?

Pasquale went into the kitchen for his lunch. He did not know, not yet, but he would make it his business to find out.

CHAPTER 9

When Faye arrived once again at *Piazza del Teatro* just after eight that evening, to the low clang of the church bell, the Rinaldis were already there. Marisa stood at the bottom of the steps while Alessandro waited at the top, looking as if he couldn't help but take the superior stance. But that, Faye told herself, was not her problem. She must remember what Charlotte said when she left this morning – *Faye, you can walk away any time*.

'*Ciao*.' Faye greeted Marisa with a kiss on both cheeks. Once again, she thought she could smell the fragrance of orange blossom, but there was no orange tree here, just the tree by the old fountain which had green, shiny leaves and small white flowers like stars.

'Did Charlotte leave okay?' Marisa looked sad. 'I will miss her.'

'Yes, she did.' Faye would miss her, too. She felt more than a little stranded here now that Charlotte and Fabio had gone. Dropped in it. But there were compensations, the house by the river was elegant and luxurious and the little town of Deriu was charming.

After they left, Faye had spent the rest of the day exploring the mediaeval *centro storico* that she had so far only seen at night-time. It was made up of steep and narrow cobbled streets lined by tall, skinny houses painted every shade from vibrant turquoise to deep ochre. Brightly coloured washing hung on balconies; vines, bougainvillea and blue jasmine clambered over old terracing and clung to crumbling stone. The streets led to small piazzas housing eccentric-looking churches with massive wooden doorways and decorative rose windows, fruit and vegetable markets, jewellery and cork stalls, and quirky bars and cafés.

Faye had walked along the stone ramparts of the castle on the top of the hill and looked down through the grove of olive trees and prickly pears to see the river winding from the valley in the east between the lush green mountains towards the sea. Below her were the terraces and cluttered rooftops of Deriu – old and new – and she could see the boats of the marina beyond. She had ducked into the tiny castle chapel nestled among the walnut trees and marvelled at the mediaeval frescoes, still bright and vibrant all these centuries on.

Then there had been that rather strange encounter with Pasquale de Montis here in the square. He had seemed a bit suspicious of Faye, but she liked him. He was theatrical, as one would expect, but Sardinians and Italians were more dramatic, more physical than the British anyway. He was an interesting character and it was obvious he had the little theatre's best interests at heart, which had to be a good thing.

Finally, she had returned to Charlotte and Fabio's apartment to eat, after which she found herself caught up in *la passeggiata* that she remembered from her time in Naples – the traditional walk taken by many of the villagers around the town streets with the purpose of observing, chatting, taking exercise and exchanging opinions and news, at a time of day when the sun was no longer too hot and before they returned to their own houses for the rest of the evening.

'*Ciao*, Alessandro.' Faye went up the steps to greet him, conscious of the warmth of his dark olive skin as she dropped a light kiss on both cheeks. She tried to pinpoint the scent of him . . . wood and oil with a cool streak of lemon, she decided.

'Did you have a good day?' For a moment the dark blue eyes met hers. Faye wondered if he'd guessed she'd been back here. Maybe she hadn't left the key in quite the right position? She decided to play dumb. 'Very nice, thank you.' She told them what she'd done and what she'd seen, leaving out her encounter with Pasquale and her second visit to the little theatre. 'I like your town. It's delightful.'

Alessandro raised an eyebrow. 'I am sure our town is very happy about that,' he said. 'And now – to the theatre.' He swung open the wooden door. 'After you.'

Faye entered the foyer and the other two trooped in behind her. *Il Piccolo Teatro* was beginning to feel like an old friend. The dim lighting, the lumpy, red brocade seats, the crumbling stucco and shadowy lilac curtain all seemed very familiar now. This afternoon, she had almost tiptoed around, taking a closer look at the open galleries and the private boxes, examining the materials of the place and the designs painted on the ceiling and walls. She had only stayed for fifteen minutes or so, but it was long enough to get the feel.

She turned to face them. 'Perhaps you should start off by telling me,' she suggested, 'what you have in mind for the theatre? Do you see it as retaining its exact sense of history? Or do you see it in a more contemporary light? Fulfilling some different purpose for the town, perhaps?'

Alessandro's brow darkened. 'Its purpose is to be a theatre,' he said. 'We want it to be restored to its former glory. We want plays and opera to be performed here exactly as they used to be.' He looked at her as if she were crazy to suggest anything else.

Faye nodded. 'I see.' She could certainly see his intransigence. And she could understand his point of view. It was important for the historical identity of the theatre to be preserved – even if it wasn't a listed building, it would be criminal to destroy the character that made it so special. But this was not the 1800s. Was there still as much of a call for a theatre of this type in a town like Deriu? She turned to Marisa, who hadn't yet said a word. 'Marisa, do you agree with Alessandro?'

Marisa walked along the back row of seats, trailing her hand across them. 'I do, yes, up to a point,' she said at last.

'If there are enough funds available, you'll need specialist help as far as restoration is concerned,' Faye told them. It certainly wouldn't be a simple job. She spread her hands. 'I'm a newly qualified interior designer. While I'd love to help you with some ideas for redesign, I'm not an expert on traditional Sardinian theatres. If you want the theatre to be simply restored to its former look and purpose, you don't need someone like me. You need a restoration expert, a good team of builders and skilled craftsmen.' She didn't want to turn down the job – not yet anyway – but this was an unusual situation, and she wanted everything to be clear from the outset.

'Exactly!' Alessandro thumped the back of the seat nearest to him and a flurry of dust particles spun into the air. 'Did I not say that, Marisa?'

'Yes, yes.' His sister dismissed this with a gesture of her hands. 'But I wanted an objective opinion. I wanted some new ideas. You never listen to me, Alessandro. We have to ask ourselves this, will the theatre survive if it is simply restored – again?'

Alessandro straightened his shoulders. 'We will make sure it survives,' he said.

'And in the future? We will not be here to look after it forever.'

He was silent, gazing out towards the stage as if it might tell him something.

'No doubt our ancestors said the same thing when they took over the theatre and invested in it.' Marisa turned to Faye. 'It was in the early 1900s. They had the money, and of course the local government wanted the theatre to survive. Everyone wanted the theatre to survive.'

'But no one else was willing to pay for it,' Alessandro put in.

'As you say.' Marisa turned away from him. 'But the point I am making is that no one wanted *il Piccolo Teatro* to fall once again into disrepair. And yet it did.'

'No one except our father,' Alessandro said darkly.

Marisa shrugged. 'He had his reasons.'

'How do *you* think the theatre can survive?' Faye asked her. She would at least try to be objective, but she doubted Alessandro would listen to her either. Marisa, at least, seemed to have more grasp of the reality of the situation than her brother. His view was more romantic – and that was not the only romantic thing about him, she found herself thinking as she glanced across at his dark features. She hadn't forgotten that moment on the bridge last night, the look in his eyes, the way he'd taken her hand and suggested that the night was still young. Faye shivered. She was having a 'what if' moment. On reflection, she reckoned it had been a lucky escape.

'I think perhaps we should do something to make the theatre more . . .' Marisa hesitated, sent a silent appeal with her eyes to Faye.

'Useful?' suggested Faye. Now here she could be of some help.

Even when Sam Wanaker had the Globe Theatre famously reconstructed, he had included an education and exhibition centre. The important thing, surely, was to attract people to the theatre.

'*Useful?*' Alessandro bellowed. 'It is a theatre. It does not have to be *useful*.'

He made it sound like the worst thing imaginable. And yet utility — along with beauty and durability — was meant to be a core principle of architecture, or so Faye had been taught. 'What do *you* want the theatre to be?' she asked him. 'What do you want it to achieve?'

'The theatre is a place to celebrate the arts and literature and performance,' he said. 'I should have thought that was obvious.'

'Alessandro.' Marisa went to him and put a gentle hand on his arm. 'Calm down. Faye is asking the questions she has to ask — it is her job. As for me, I want the same thing as you do. We are on the same side. We are just talking.'

'Talking. Eugh.' He brushed her away and strode right up to the stage. 'Talking only causes more problems.'

Faye could see that Marisa needed more help. 'If you were to decide on some sort of redesign,' she began, 'then we would have to talk, because there are so many alternatives to consider, depending on how you intend to use the space.'

'Alternatives?' he growled.

'Even if its sole use continues to be that of a theatre . . .' Faye took a deep breath. But she had done her research and it was part of her remit to give an opinion. 'Potentially, the layout could be completely changed.'

They both looked blank.

'A theatre doesn't have to have a stage here —' she pointed — 'and hidden wings.'

'What?'

'There are theatres built in the round. And in Japan, they often have a platform connecting the back of the auditorium to the stage.' She gestured down the centre aisle, trying not to feel like an air steward pointing to floor lighting.

'What for?' But even as he spoke, Alessandro half-turned away from them as if he'd heard enough already.

'For the actors to come on stage in a different kind of way.' She tried to remember exactly what she'd read about it. 'They can pause as they come on, they can talk to the audience, even explain their roles in the upcoming performance.'

'Really?' Marisa frowned.

It did sound a bit odd, Faye had to admit, especially if you had only experienced traditional theatre. 'It's a kind of halfway house between fiction and reality, if you like, where . . .' Her voice trailed as Alessandro spun around. But it was Marisa he addressed.

'Can you not remember Mama?' he demanded. 'Can you not still see her on this stage, wearing that long blue velvet dress with the necklace that glittered at her throat?'

Faye watched him, spellbound. Once again it struck her that he could be an actor himself – he had the presence and the voice for it, as well as the looks. He turned his attention to Faye. 'Halfway house between fiction and reality?' he muttered. He shook his head. 'Spare me.'

'It's a transitional concept.' Faye stood her ground, though she was aware that she'd probably already gone too far. He had a point – it had sounded a tad pretentious. 'And it was just an example.'

Marisa looked close to tears. 'Yes, Alessandro.' She spoke in a small voice. 'Of course I remember Mama. But that is the past. We must look to the future now. It is our responsibility to protect the theatre through the centuries to come.'

Faye looked from one to the other of them. They were alike in appearance – both dark with aquiline features – and although their eyes were different, they had the same high cheekbones and curly black hair. But in character, Faye guessed that Alessandro was the tempestuous one. Nostalgic, sentimental. He was looking for a memory of his beloved mother. Whereas Marisa . . .

'I'm simply making you aware of other possibilities,' Faye said. She had found the idea interesting, but maybe it had been inappropriate to mention it here – she had probably done more harm than good. She had the feeling that once again she was way outside her comfort zone. 'I'm not necessarily recommending it to you,' she added weakly.

'We are grateful for that, at least,' said Alessandro.

Faye ignored him. Sarcasm, as everyone knew, was the lowest form of wit. 'A theatre is also about the people,' she said gently to Marisa. 'Architecture works with the space and helps create the style and the meaning of a building. Part of a designer's job is to make the people who use it feel good about the space they're in.'

Alessandro let out what sounded to Faye like a Sardinian curse. He did not look impressed.

Faye sighed. She was clearly wasting her time. 'Why did you ask me here?' she asked them.

'A good question.' Alessandro sat down on the edge of the stage. 'We made a mistake. We must apologise.'

Marisa took a step towards Faye. 'Please do not think us ungrateful,' she said. 'Alessandro, he has his ideas . . .'

Alessandro let out a contemptuous snort.

'But when I realised the strength of feeling in the village . . .' Her voice wavered.

'Strength of feeling?' At last, Faye thought, they were getting somewhere. Surely they could tell her now?

'I wanted to get some new ideas,' Marisa said. 'Some different ideas.' She looked defiantly towards her brother. 'Before we approached an architect or made any definite decisions. As I said before – I don't want to live in the past. Our parents are dead and gone. I want to move on.'

'Of course.' Faye bowed her head. But wherever Marisa wanted to move on to, she clearly felt she had to settle the responsibility she felt for the theatre first. Faye understood. And she'd do her best to help her. She was lucky to have both her parents healthy and happy; her maternal grandmother, too. Marisa had Alessandro, but at times she must still feel alone.

Marisa gave a little nod. 'I was upset one night – about the theatre and the problems it was causing in the village.' She bit her lip. 'Charlotte told me about you, and I thought it would be great to have someone young and energetic to come over with all the newest ideas and—'

'And we could not ask anyone from around here,' Alessandro cut in dryly.

'Why not?' Faye had wondered about this herself. London might be more of a hub for the latest design ideas than rural Sardinia, but even so . . .

The door opened and Faye glanced round in surprise. A small group of men and women were standing in the entrance, in the foyer, and on the steps behind. They looked rather forbidding. Their apparent leader, a small, gruff-looking man in his early sixties or so, stepped forward and spoke rapidly to Marisa and Alessandro in a dialect Faye had no hope of understanding. He was flinging his arms around as he spoke, his chest thrust out and his nostrils flaring. His body language said angry.

'What's going on?' Though this delegation, she guessed, answered her question. They couldn't ask anyone from round here because round here everyone heard what was happening and the Rinaldis' legal ownership of the theatre was being brought into question. Faye had the feeling she was about to find out much more about the dispute over the ownership of the Little Theatre of Deriu.

CHAPTER 10

Marisa took her arm. 'Do not worry,' she said. 'It is only Enrico Volti and a group of people from the village. Alessandro will handle it.'

Alessandro looked as furious at the intrusion as the intruders did with him. He strode towards the group, eyes glinting and they all started yelling at each other and gesticulating wildly. No one seemed to be listening to anyone else.

That was what you called an ownership dispute, thought Faye. But where had she heard the name Volti before? She tried to remember. And then she saw a familiar figure with a shock of white hair emerge from the foyer. Pasquale.

He ducked through the crowd and to her surprise, came to stand by her side, a sad expression on his weather-beaten face. 'They are arguing,' he said.

'They certainly are.'

'About who owns the theatre.'

Faye eyed him thoughtfully. She would take a guess that he knew a lot more about what was happening in Deriu than he let on. 'Who does own it?' she asked him. 'The Rinaldis seem pretty sure that they do.'

By now they were all talking at once, Marisa and Alessandro included, and it was hard to make herself heard above the hub-bub. Faye wondered if the little theatre had ever seen a drama like this before. Possibly. The Sardinian race appeared to be very volatile.

Pasquale blinked at her in surprise with his bright bird-like eyes. 'Naturally, the residents of Deriu consider the theatre to be their property, *Signorina*,' he said rather primly. 'It is, after all, a civic building. It was given to certain families who represented the townspeople back in the early 1800s.' He nodded. 'This is what they are saying, what they are claiming.'

'But that was an awfully long time ago,' Faye pointed out. She noticed that the women of the group were as vociferous as the men and there was no sign of the row abating. Alessandro had told her the original history. But Marisa had also said that their family had restored the theatre a hundred years later when it fell into disrepair. 'What about later, when the Rinaldis got the place up and running again?'

'Ah, so you know about that?' Pasquale nodded. 'And yes, he is saying that now.' He indicated Alessandro who was indeed saying something – and rather forcefully. 'He is reminding them of that time and of how no one else in Deriu was interested in the theatre back then and how his family were granted the ownership in return for all the money and work and—'

The leader of the opposition group shouted something back and spat on the floor. Clearly, he wasn't convinced of the argument.

'He says it is old history,' Pasquale told her. 'He says that now it is a matter of corruption.'

'Corruption?'

'Yes. That is what Enrico Volti is accusing their family of.'

Goodness. Faye didn't think that would go down very well with the Rinaldis. It was very different, she reflected, to the way things might be disputed in England. 'What does Alessandro say to that?' she murmured.

Pasquale's bird-like eyes narrowed in concentration. 'He says that giving the theatre to the Rinaldi family was the only way – at the time,' he added darkly, 'for the theatre to survive. He says that the townspeople are ungrateful –' he hesitated – 'bastards. He asks if Enrico is crazy. He says why would the Rinaldis have put so much time, effort and money into the theatre if it did not even belong to them?'

A reasonable question, thought Faye. Marisa had tears in her dark eyes and Alessandro flung his arm around her. He was certainly protective, Faye could say that for him. 'How can it be resolved?' she whispered. And what was she doing here, anyway? From what she had heard so far, only one of the current (possible) owners had any interest in her ideas. The other didn't even want her around.

The angry voices suddenly died down as abruptly as they had started. Everyone began to move towards the stage. 'What's happening now?' asked Faye. They'd already put on quite a performance.

'They have decided to hold a meeting,' said Pasquale.

'Now?'

'Now,' he said. 'Come, *Signorina*.'

Faye wasn't sure that she was even entitled to be here but the drama was too compelling. She followed Pasquale and joined the others on stage. But she couldn't help noticing that a few of the townspeople threw her dark, suspicious looks as she did so. Did they know who she was and why she was here? Did they want her gone? She supposed so – and it wasn't a pleasant feeling.

A couple of the men carried a table through from the back and others brought chairs from somewhere in the wings. No one seemed particularly happy but one of the men slapped the ringleader of the delegation on the back and someone else arranged a chair for Marisa. Bottles of beer appeared from one of the women's baskets as if this had somehow become an amicable and social occasion, but within minutes, they were all arguing and shaking their fists at one another again.

Faye glanced up to see Enrico Volti, the ringleader who'd been doing most of the talking, pointing right at her. She flinched and made herself sit up straighter. She'd been right in her assumption – they didn't want her here. But this wasn't her argument and she hadn't done anything wrong, so she refused to feel intimidated. Volti shot her a dirty look before letting loose a torrent of Sardinian dialect. Faye struggled to understand. She was getting the gist. He was accusing her of interfering in the business of the town, of being a stranger, an unwanted stranger.

'Enrico Volti's family was once one of the richest in Deriu, along with the Rinaldis. Though it is hard to believe, I know.' Pasquale tutted quietly.

'But not anymore?' Faye watched the man warily. He was black-eyed and looked dangerous.

'The family put their money into mining,' Pasquale explained. 'At the beginning of the nineteenth century, this country had dozens of great mines – lead, iron, copper and silver. And that was just the start of it. There was work for anyone who wanted it.' He sighed. 'But over the years, the profit margins, they decreased. Even in my lifetime. They had taken everything from the ground, you know?'

Faye nodded. 'So the mines closed?'

Pasquale leaned closer. 'In 1963, *si*. And when the mines closed, the Voltis, they lost much of their fortune.'

Faye had read that there were skeletons of the old mining towns remaining all over Sardinia. Tunnels, railways, houses . . .

'What exactly was Enrico Volti saying about me?' she asked. Pasquale seemed quite happy to retain the role of interpreter that he had adopted. She wondered if he always stayed in the wings. He was the kind of character, she suspected, who was more drawn to centre stage.

Pasquale hesitated. 'He was complaining that the Rinaldis had brought in a foreigner to decide the business of Deriu. He says it is not right, not proper.'

He had a point, thought Faye. 'And what did Alessandro say in his defence?' She spoke lightly, but it mattered, she realised, it really did. She had few enough friends here.

Pasquale glanced at her curiously. 'He said that this is their theatre and that to ask your advice was their joint decision.' He paused, listening. 'He said that you are an expert and being an outsider means you can be objective in your opinions.'

'Oh.' Alessandro's response was a turnaround. But one that Faye was grateful for. She felt ridiculously touched that he'd stuck up for her.

'He also said that nothing has been decided.' Pasquale put his head on one side as he regarded her. 'Is this true, *Signorina*?'

'Yes, it is.'

There was a lull in the conversation at the table and she found herself staring at Alessandro as he thrust his hand roughly through his hair. To her embarrassment, he glanced over and saw her watching him. With an effort, Faye brought her attention back to Pasquale who was still talking.

'That is Volti's wife Carmela sitting beside him.'

Faye looked at her. Unlike some of the other women, she

wasn't saying much, but her dark eyes darted from one speaker to the next.

On the other side of the table, voices were raised once again and Enrico Volti was holding forth, chin held high. A blue vein pulsed in his neck and Faye watched, fascinated. It seemed that no one dared interrupt him.

'After the tragedy, Enrico Volti lost even more,' Pasquale said. 'Some say he lost his reason.'

He was milking the drama like any good actor, Faye couldn't help thinking. But, 'What tragedy?' She should find out some of the history of the village – then she might discover more about what was going on.

Pasquale crossed himself. 'Their daughter Giorgia – she disappeared.'

'Disappeared?' For a moment Faye was hardly aware of the people sitting around her, the buzz of their voices, the slamming of fists or beer bottles on the table. And then she remembered where she had heard the name Volti before: Charlotte had mentioned it when she'd claimed there was next to no crime in Deriu. *Apart from when Giorgia Volti disappeared*, she had said.

'No one knows where or why. The whole village helped look for her. Enrico spent weeks, months, years searching.' Pasquale looked mournful; for a moment Faye swore she saw a tear in his eye. 'His business suffered. He drank. He gambled.' Pasquale's words hung in a dramatic pause. 'Some say he lost his mind.'

'That's very sad.' Suddenly, Faye felt sorry for the man – and the woman – at the end of the table. They had lost everything. 'But what does that have to do with the theatre?'

'Nothing, of course.' Pasquale spoke quickly. 'But he is bitter. He blames the Rinaldis for much that has happened to him, for his misfortune – possibly unfairly. The two families . . . they have always been competitive.'

Faye thought 'competitive' was putting it lightly – they seemed more daggers drawn. It was one of those Italian-type feuds, Faye guessed, dating from mediaeval times when rival families coveted one another's land rather than their theatre.

'The Rinaldis always had special favour in days gone by.' Pasquale was still speaking. 'Deriu was an important royal town once, you know.' He puffed out his chest. 'The Voltis, they were often overlooked. Perhaps they were not so pretty.' He laughed and cast a glance towards Marisa and Alessandro, who were now hunched together talking in undertones. 'Who knows?' Pasquale shrugged. 'And so, Volti, he began the petition.'

'What sort of petition?' It must be the one Charlotte had mentioned. Faye wondered why it had been left to this man to explain to her exactly what was going on in Deriu. She couldn't blame Marisa and Alessandro, though they had been somewhat economical with the truth. But why had Charlotte dragged her over here to this hornets' nest? She decided to have it out with her friend at the earliest opportunity.

'The petition to bring the theatre back to the people,' he said.

Faye was beginning to see. She was also getting the glimmer of an idea. Marisa had said it herself: they must look to the future. They had a responsibility to *il Piccolo Teatro*, yes – but perhaps they had another responsibility, too. A responsibility to the community they lived in. After all, the origins of theatre went back to the rites and religions of the earliest communities when people sang, danced and sacrificed to appease their gods. Theatres and communities were intricately woven together; they always had been.

Enrico Volti was the first man to get to his feet and scrape his chair back on the stage. He looked miserable. He was no longer making eye contact with the rest of the group; he seemed beaten.

'What's been decided?' Faye asked Pasquale.

He folded his hands in front of him. 'Nothing.'

'Nothing?'

He shrugged. 'The Rinaldis have documents of sale,' he said. 'Alessandro is a stubborn man – he will not give an inch.'

Faye could believe that. 'But . . .?' She almost felt that this wasn't a fair conclusion.

'The townspeople do not have the money or the power to get legal advice or to take things further, *Signorina*,' Pasquale said. 'For now, the matter is closed.'

For now. Those two little words said a lot, she thought. She looked up to see Enrico Volti shooting another venomous glance her way. 'Won't that make them even more angry?' she asked Pasquale.

Pasquale cocked his head to one side in that bird-like way he had. 'I think so, yes.' He followed the direction of her gaze. 'What will you do, *Signorina*?'

Faye hadn't thought about it. Her first instinct was to get away from this place, but she was stubborn enough not to be driven out. And was it fair on Marisa and Alessandro? And Charlotte? She had, after all, promised to at least give them some ideas. She turned to Pasquale as they joined the others leaving the table. 'I'm sorry I wasn't totally honest with you earlier today, Pasquale,' she said. He had been kind to her. Without his help, she wouldn't have had a clue as to what was going on tonight. 'The truth is, I didn't know about all this – and I wasn't sure who I was supposed to tell about my reasons for being here.'

'Please do not give it another moment's thought, *Signorina* Faye.' He gave a little half-bow.

'And thank you – for acting as translator.'

He smiled. 'It was nothing,' he said. 'I am happy to be of service.'

Faye eyed him curiously. It was one thing staying in the wings, but . . . 'Whose side are you on, Pasquale?'

'Side?' He licked his lips, looked around him.

'Who do you think should own the theatre?' After all, he loved it perhaps more than anyone. Yet he had appeared to stay on the sidelines; he had not got involved.

'The theatre – it belongs to itself,' he said. And with one last enigmatic glance around the stage, he slipped from her side.

Faye looked for Marisa and Alessandro but they were still talking – or arguing – with one of the men from the village. '*Ignoranti*,' she heard Alessandro mutter. '*Basta!*' Enough!

He might think them ignorant, she thought. He might tell them that he'd heard enough, but it would just lead to more tension and hostility. Both of which she could do without.

Her mobile rang and Faye went outside to take the call. It was her father. 'Hi, Dad. It's good to hear the voice of reason.'

He gave an unconvincing little laugh. 'What's up?'

'I couldn't begin to tell you.' Faye walked down the steps and looked back at *il Piccolo Teatro*. It stood serene in the dusk as if unaware of the myriad of problems within.

'Well, I don't want to add to whatever's bothering you . . .'

Faye was immediately on the alert. 'What do you mean? What's happened?'

'These conversations should be had face to face.' He sighed. 'I know that.'

'Tell me, Dad.' Faye braced herself. What could it be?

Something to do with his early retirement? A health issue? 'Is it Mum?'

'It's both of us, my darling.' His voice cracked.

'Both of you? You're scaring me now.'

'We're okay,' he said, though he didn't sound it. 'And nothing will change. Nothing at all.'

Faye wished she could believe him. But it sounded as if something was about to. She gripped the mobile more tightly. 'Dad?'

'We both love you, you know that.'

'Of course I do. For God's sake. What is it?'

'We're separating,' he said. 'Your mother and I. I can't begin to explain it to you. Not like this. Not now. But . . . we felt we had to tell you. We just hope you'll understand.'

Ade still wasn't sure how it had happened. He would have thought there was a big gulf between wanting to go off travelling and divorce. But apparently there wasn't. He had thought he knew everything about Molly's life and what made her tick. But he didn't. Anyway. It had happened and now he had to deal with it.

He was in shock. He stood at the bar of the Black Horse pub in Exeter with a very decent pint of cider and looked around at his companions. His team. They were a good group of guys and he'd miss them – the camaraderie, the working together to meet deadlines, the problem-solving. He'd even miss the commute to work. Two hours of every working day spent in the car, sometimes more, depending on traffic. It was a lot of his life. It had turned out, though, that those hours in the car were valuable. They provided thinking time, a chance to unwind from work and leave it behind, and an opportunity to listen to music – his music, the music that Molly had always winced at, as loud as he liked. He could even listen to Radio 4 – there was a wealth of fascinating stuff there and it was a lot more fulfilling (he felt rather superior about this) than slumping in front of a soap opera at home. Yes, it was surprising how life-enhancing a commute could be.

Once, many years ago, he'd considered buying a flat in Exeter that he could crash in during the week. He'd also considered guesthouses for a while. But his commute wasn't quite long enough to justify it and he'd always wanted to get back to Dorset. Only now he was wondering, why had he? Wouldn't he trust himself if he didn't go back home? Though the one time he hadn't . . . but that was silly. West Dorset was his home. Molly was his home. Only not anymore.

Ade returned to their table with the drinks. 'Here you go.' He put them down on the table.

'Cheers, Ade.' They helped themselves.

'Where's it going to be, then, mate?' Brian asked, supping his pint. 'Outer Mongolia, Timbuktu or what?'

'Lyme Regis most likely,' Ade joked – though it was hard to joke at a time like this. As far as his team was concerned, Ade and Molly were spending every evening looking at holiday brochures. As if. In fact, he hadn't even gone home this week. He was renting a short-term flat; how short-term, he had no idea. He wasn't sure what he felt yet. Stunned, certainly. Scared, definitely. But was there something else? Something a bit more liberating? He'd like to think so. And this was what he was trying to focus on.

When Molly had told him that she didn't want to leave Dorset, Ade had changed tack. 'A shorter trip then,' he'd said. Marriage was about compromise. Ade knew that more than most. 'Six months? Less? We could go trekking up the Himalayas? Go on safari in Africa?' Though perhaps these were too energetic and far-flung. 'Tour Europe? Spend a few months down under?' He chuckled.

'I don't want to, Ade.'

'Which one?'

'Any of them.'

And Ade had looked at her closed features and felt his anger rise. 'Why not? What the hell's wrong with you?' Yeah, he shouldn't have said it. But it was too late now.

Ade heard himself laughing and joking with his team as if he were observing himself from above. Was this what a near-death experience was like? Dis-association? He wasn't really here with them; he knew that much, and he could imagine their comments afterwards. Most likely, they felt sorry for him. Got out just in time, they'd probably say.

He thought again of Molly. He had overreacted. But she'd taken a sharp pin to his bubble.

'Leaving you behind, Ade,' one of the guys said. They were almost ready for top-ups and he'd barely touched his pint.

Ade laughed uncertainly. Everything was a bit uncertain lately. He wasn't drinking as much as he usually did; he felt the need to keep things clear. And he realised how he'd built it up in his head. This new opportunity. The freedom. The chance to get close to his wife again. The only trouble was, he hadn't shared the fantasy with Molly.

Molly had coloured. She looked as if there was a lot she could say and wanted to say. 'Nothing. But my life's here.' She had walked away from him then, yet another unfinished conversation, and he'd been left frustrated as ever.

After her writing class he'd brought it up again. He wasn't going to let it go; she must know that.

'Is it because of your mother?' he'd asked her, almost the second she walked in the door. What else could it be? Ade was at a loss. But her mother also had Molly's sister Kathryn. She worked full-time but she didn't live far away. Molly's mother wasn't young, but she was healthy. She didn't need a carer.

'It's because of lots of things.'

Because of your lack of adventure, he thought. Because everything has to be sure and known. 'What about me?' he asked. He'd felt injured, unappreciated. All these years commuting to Exeter. All these years working in the bank – when his life could have been so different.

'Oh, you.' Molly managed to impart considerable disdain into these two words. 'Why does it always have to be about you?'

Ade was speechless. He'd worked hard for his family all his life. Why the bloody hell shouldn't he have something now?

He put his hands on her shoulders, tried not to notice how she flinched. 'Think, Molly,' he said. 'Aren't there things you want to do with your life? Places you want to see? We can afford it if that's what's bothering you.'

She shook her head. 'It isn't that.'

'What then?'

She shook her head again.

Ade let his hands fall. It was hopeless. This was hopeless. 'We've got to do something,' he said. He'd said this before. *You and I need to do something*. The words seemed to hang in the air between them. They both knew what they meant.

'All very well for you to say that now,' she whispered.

'But, Molly –' Ade looked at her face. He couldn't believe the wrong turn the conversation was taking. He struggled to get back on track. 'I'm only saying . . .'

Molly turned away so that he couldn't see her expression. But he noticed that her knuckles were white. 'Why don't you go on your own, Ade?' she said.

He blinked at her. That hadn't been the idea at all. But now that she had said it, he found himself thinking about it.

Freedom, he thought. It was what he'd wanted – once. Could it still be possible? Did he even want it to be possible?

'After all . . .' She turned back and there were tears in her eyes that shocked him. 'You've never wanted to be here, not really. All these years.'

He stared at her. All these years? What did she mean? 'Molly?' He frowned. 'What are you talking about?'

She took his hands. 'Did you ever really want to marry me, Ade?'

He couldn't believe it. 'You idiot,' he said gently. 'Of course I did.'

She didn't let go of his hands. 'And if I hadn't been expecting Faye?'

'Oh, Molly.' It was so long ago. 'What's brought this on?' Molly had always been good at avoiding confrontation, at putting her head in the sand. And in a way Ade had appreciated that. He didn't want one of those wives who let rip at the slightest thing, who got upset if their husband forgot to bring them flowers or Valentine's cards, or analysed every imagined slight to death. But he knew. His wanting to leave, that's what had brought this on. He had meant it to be a new start, not some sort of ending. Only. He tried to stay calm. 'Molly. We have a life together, don't we?' It was so unlike her, getting upset like this. She was always so sensible. And yet he thought of what he'd just said – *we've got to do something*.

'Tell me though, Ade. Be honest.'

'Back then,' he sighed. 'I was young. I didn't know what I wanted. But I always wanted you.' This wasn't exactly true, but what was the point of dredging up the past? No, of course he wouldn't have married Molly. He wouldn't have married anyone, not then.

'And now?' she asked. 'Do you want to be with me now?'

'What do you mean?' For God's sake. He tore his hands through his hair. 'Of course I do.' What was she saying? They were married. They had Faye. They were a family. They had a house in West Dorset and a life together. Yes, he had said that something had to change, but only so that things would be better.

'You're the one who wants us to turn our lives upside down,' she said. 'Because you're not satisfied with what we have.'

'It's not like that.' But somewhere inside, Ade knew that she was right. He wasn't satisfied. Sometimes he felt as trapped as he had at twenty-two. His working life at the bank coming to an end was only the catalyst.

He looked at the group sitting around the table in the pub. The jokes had got bluer and the faces redder. It was true. Retirement was a big thing. If he were going to divide his life into segments, this would be the start of a new one. Not of old age, whatever this lot thought – he was only fifty-six for Christ's sake – but maybe his last opportunity to do some of the things he'd wanted to do at eighteen. He wasn't ready to settle down to a life of golf and gardening. He'd go crazy. He wanted an adventure.

'Isn't it?' Molly was still staring at him intently.

He bowed his head. 'It's not you, Molly,' he said.

'Isn't it?' she said again.

'Molly . . .' If only she had brought this up before, if they had discussed these things years ago . . . Then maybe things between them might have taken a different course. And yet Ade knew that these were the sorts of conversations that could bring the scum to the surface, that could end up destroying a quiet and satisfying relationship. *Quiet and satisfying*. Two words he wouldn't wish to be inscribed on his tombstone. 'Why don't you want to come with me?' He pulled her closer, trying a new approach. 'What are you worried about?'

'Nothing.' Her face was passive. 'Why do you want to go, Ade?'

That was easy. 'To have an adventure. To take a few risks. To find some excitement, some life . . .' This sounded more critical than he'd intended. It also sounded vaguely dodgy. Ade thought of Nina. He often did think of Nina, usually with regret. Nina had spun into his life from nowhere and through her he had found the man he'd always hoped to be. He was still there. The explorer, the devil-may-care. Ade hadn't meant to be unfaithful to Molly. But he couldn't regret it. Nina was too important to regret.

'I knew there'd come a time,' Molly said.

Once again, Ade had the sensation that this conversation was slipping away from him. He wasn't sexist but women often did that, he'd found. It was as if they were operating the conversation on two levels and you didn't realise it until you said the wrong thing – and then it was too late; you were damned. Why, he wondered, did women always have to over-complicate everything?

'How did you know there'd come a time?' he asked. 'What do you mean? You and me, we're a team, right? We've always been a team.'

'Teams support each other.' Molly's voice was clipped. 'Teams are honest with each other. They work things out together.'

'When haven't I been honest?' Ade had intended to sound aggrieved; he even felt aggrieved, damn it. But his voice broke. The truth was that he'd often not been honest with Molly. Particularly not about Nina.

'You don't need me to tell you, Ade,' Molly said. 'You've never forgotten her, have you, really?'

For a moment, Ade stopped breathing. 'Who?' It was instinctive, wasn't it, to deny? Never admit to anything, someone had told him once.

'I don't know her name.' She shook her head. 'Whoever it was I lost you to, when . . .'

When we lost our baby, thought Ade. That time. 'I don't know what—' he began, out of habit. What you're talking about, he was going to say. How the hell had she found out? It was years ago.

'You do,' she corrected. 'I'm sorry, Ade, but you do know – very well.'

'Molly—' But Ade realised that he had run out of things to say. They had been distant from one another for so long. The well of platitudes, of affection, whatever it was between them – for now, he had no bloody idea – was empty. She had found him out. She had always known.

Molly was looking at him sadly and he felt a shit, an absolute shit.

'It was a long time ago,' Ade said. 'I'm sorry, Molly.'

She said nothing.

Ade spread his hands. 'But I stayed with you,' he said. It was all he could think of. 'I never left you.'

'You did leave me, Ade. That is exactly when you left me.'

He stared at her. 'What are you saying, Molly?' But he didn't want to hear it. He had wronged her. He had betrayed her. And he had imagined that she was unaware.

'I should have done it,' Molly said. 'I should have done it when I had the chance.'

Done it? Ade felt the ground slipping from under him, ground he had always been very sure of. 'Done what?'

'Taken my chance.' She stood very upright and still. 'Found a new life.'

'When was that, Molly?' He kept his voice low, but his mind was racing. Had there been another man? How could there have been? Wouldn't Ade have known about it?

'I couldn't talk to you,' she said. 'I never could. I could never . . .' Molly hesitated, 'share things with you, Ade.'

Ade tried to stay calm. 'What things?'

But she just gave one of those little shoulder shrugs of hers. 'It's funny,' she said, 'how I could recognise grief in a stranger, and he could recognise it in me.'

The woman was talking in riddles. How had they got from travelling to grief-stricken strangers? Ade didn't have a clue. 'What stranger?' He could hear his own voice, louder now.

'It gives you a shared bond,' she continued, as if she hadn't heard him. 'You confide in one another, you share secrets, they learn the heart of you. It brings you closer together.'

Ade had had enough of this. 'Have you slept with another man, Molly?' he asked her. He realised his fists were clenched. He had no right, but just the thought . . . 'Have you been unfaithful to me?'

She shook her head as if he'd missed the point. 'I've fought for you and I've tried to make you happy, Ade,' Molly told him. 'But it's too late. Our time's up. We should accept it. Our time is up.'

Ade felt as if he'd suffered a body blow without knowing where it had come from. Had there been another man? He had no idea. And if there had – could he even blame her after what he'd put her through? But what did she mean about someone learning the heart of her? *Jesus* . . .

That was what happened, Ade thought now, when you

allowed your life to become too polite, too domestic. That was what happened when you stopped seeing, stopped listening; it was what happened when you started leading separate lives. When had they last made love? Ade couldn't remember. When had they last shared a candlelit dinner and talked, *really* talked? When had they last walked along the beach together? Held each other, looked into each other's eyes? How did that happen? How did a couple forget to do these things? How did they lose each other this way? How the hell did they fall so easily out of love?

CHAPTER 12

The first flight available was the day after tomorrow. Faye had already told Marisa she was leaving, though not the reason why. She didn't want anyone to tell her she was overreacting. She just wanted to find out the full story. She wanted to be there – with them.

'What are you talking about?' Faye had asked her father. A reel of pictures swam through her head. Holidays in Cornwall, picnics on Chesil Beach, day trips to London; the three of them. Sports Days at school when her father took the afternoon off work and afterwards took Faye and her mother for fish and chips in the harbour at the Bay. Walks and talks; games and laughter and . . . her whole life, Faye thought. Her family. Of course there had been bad times, too. There had been low points and illnesses and the occasional full-scale row, but that was when you found out how strong your family really was. Her parents had always been together. They'd always been there for her. They were the one thing she could always be sure of, the one constant she could go to when things got rough, whenever she didn't know where else to turn. And 'one' was the operative word. They were one unit. They were her parents.

'Faye.' Her father's voice was distant as she stomped down the cobbled streets, across the bridge, along the riverside path, oblivious to it all. She wasn't going back into the theatre. She was heading to Charlotte and Fabio's in a daze. 'Faye, love. Are you alright?'

'Of course I'm not alright,' she muttered. 'I don't understand what you're talking about. What's happened? Why are you doing this?' An awful thought occurred to her. 'Is there—?' She thought of her father with another woman. Impossible. Her mother with another man. Equally so. They still held hands, for God's sake! But then suddenly she couldn't remember the last time.

'It's not that,' he said. But his voice was uncertain.

'What is it, then?' She opened the door to Fabio and Charlotte's place, stepped inside, and shut the rest of the world out with relief.

'We want different things,' he said.

'What?' She kicked off her shoes, tried to compute what he was telling her. After all these years? 'What different things?'

He sighed. 'You know I've always wanted to travel.'

'Oh, for heaven's sake, Dad.'

'And your mother doesn't. With this early retirement . . .'

'So that's it.' Suddenly Faye could imagine. 'It's upset you. It's turned your life around. You don't know what you want to do—'

'But Faye, love, I do know what I want to do,' he interrupted her. 'That's the problem.'

'Let me talk to Mum. Is she there?' Faye flopped down on to the leather couch. She felt as if she needed the support. She felt as if everything solid she had built her life on had been pulled from under her.

'No, she's not.'

'Where is she?' Faye frowned.

She heard him hesitate. 'She's at home, I suppose.'

'And you're not?' Faye realised that things had gone even further than she'd imagined. 'You haven't left her? Not already?'

'I'm still working, Faye,' he said. 'It's my last week. I'm in Exeter.'

'But . . .' But he had always commuted to work.

'It was amicable, love,' he said. 'We both agreed—'

But Faye didn't hear what they had both agreed. She didn't want to. 'I'm sorry, Dad. I'll have to talk to you later.' She pressed the red button, cut off the conversation. She was stunned.

Two minutes later, she tried her mother. She didn't pick up – and Faye didn't want to ask herself why. She paced the room, thinking, going over it all.

Half an hour later when Marisa appeared at the door, Faye felt a little more in control. It was some sort of mid-life crisis on her father's part, no doubt. They were doing that thing she'd read about – silver splitting, or whatever it was called, when people realised their time was running out and they wanted . . . something different, he'd said. But, no. They were making a big mistake. There was too much history to let their whole life together go. It was up to her to make them see.

'*Ciao*, Marisa.' Faye didn't invite her in. She didn't want to talk to anyone.

'You did not come back to the theatre,' Marisa said. 'Did we frighten you away?'

Faye shook her head. 'I'm sorry,' she said. 'But there's been a bit of a family crisis.' It certainly felt like one. She wasn't sure exactly what she was going to do, but she certainly couldn't do anything from Sardinia. She had to get back there and talk to them. She had to sort this out.

Marisa's velvet-brown eyes widened. 'You are leaving Deriu?'

Faye remembered Charlotte's words: *Faye, you can walk away any time.*

'I have to,' she said. 'I'm sorry.' She had to go back to the real world where people who had been married for thirty-four years suddenly decided to part. And she must get a job. This wasn't a job, not really. It had been interesting to look at the theatre, make a few sketches, and let herself begin to imagine what could be done with it. But it was self-indulgence, a fantasy. And besides, Marisa and Alessandro needed to decide what they wanted first – if the townspeople of Deriu allowed them to.

'I understand.' Marisa looked crestfallen. 'I thought you would be an ally,' she said ruefully.

Despite herself, Faye smiled. 'Stand up to him,' she said. 'You've got the right idea. I'm sure it will work out in the end.'

The following day, Faye packed her things. She texted Marisa to ask her to feed Fabio's fish and Marisa sent a message back telling her that yes, she would, she had a key and that Faye musn't worry. She didn't try to phone her mother again. As her father had said, this was something that had to be done face to face. And if he was still in Exeter, then he could come back down to Dorset and talk to them.

It was only eleven in the morning and Faye wondered what to do with herself on her last day in Deriu. She'd barely skimmed the place, she thought, and yet she'd imagined she'd be here for weeks, soaking up the sun and the atmosphere, getting a taste of Sardinia and taking a well-earned rest. Rest? So far she'd been flung into the centre of a long-standing town feud and refereed the differences of opinion between Alessandro and Marisa Rinaldi. And now this. She felt as relaxed as a cat on a hot tin roof.

When the doorbell rang she guessed it would be Marisa again.

But Alessandro stood there, looking very laid-back in shorts and a loose tee shirt with dark sunshades that effectively prevented her from reading his expression.

'Oh, hello.' Faye had to admit she had been rather relishing the prospect of spending some more time with him, even though he was possibly the most opinionated man she'd ever met in her life. Unfortunately, he was also one of the most attractive. But perhaps it was for the best. With everything else going on in her life, she really didn't need to be seduced by some Sardinian Lothario. Not that he had tried to seduce her, exactly, but surely she hadn't imagined the look in his eyes . . .

'Faye,' he said. It was, she realised, the first time he had addressed her by name. 'What is going on here?'

Faye looked around. 'Nothing.'

He pushed his shades down his nose a little so that she could see his eyes. 'Marisa tells me you are leaving already? Is this true?'

Faye's fingers tightened on the doorknob. Shouldn't he be pleased? He'd made it clear he didn't want her or her ideas anywhere near his precious theatre. 'Aren't you working today?' she asked him. Those eyes really were a very surprising shade of blue.

'No.' He glanced behind her. 'Are you not going to invite me in?'

'I was just . . .'

'Running away?'

She opened the door a little wider. 'I'm not running,' she said. 'It's a family problem, that's all. I need to get back to sort it out.'

'Ah.' He followed her inside. 'Shall we have coffee? We can talk about this family problem, if you like.'

Faye raised an eyebrow. 'Yes, we can have coffee; I'll put some on. But I don't want to talk about it, if you don't mind. It's personal.' She didn't care how stuffy this sounded. And if she did want to confide in someone, he wouldn't be the first person who sprang to mind.

'We could stop for coffee somewhere on the way to the beach, perhaps.'

'The beach?' Faye wondered if he always talked in riddles.

'Certainly, the beach. I know a place where it is perfect to swim.'

He would.

'But do we have time?' Alessandro looked around the room. 'You are leaving when?'

'Tomorrow morning.'

He clicked his fingers. 'Then yes, we have time. You cannot leave without visiting the beach. You are here in Deriu. Have you even seen our marina?'

She shook her head. Since she'd arrived, everything had happened so fast. As for Alessandro, he did have a way of taking over. Faye wasn't sure how she felt about that, but she could certainly see how Marisa found it hard to make her views known.

'What else will you do?' He walked over to the French windows and flung them open. 'It is a beautiful day.'

He was right; it was. And as he said — what else would she do? Sit around thinking about her parents all day? She had come all the way over here. She should take advantage of what little time she had left.

'OK. Why not?' Faye noted his quick smile of satisfaction. She guessed that he usually got his own way.

Upstairs, she changed quickly into a bikini under her sundress and grabbed a beach towel from a cupboard. She threw a few things into a bag – a thin cardigan in case it got chilly which could double up as a beach pillow, some flip-flops and suncream. She was downstairs again in five minutes.

He swung around, beaming. 'You are ready, good.' He nodded his approval. 'I like a woman who does not . . . what do you say?'

'Dither? Faff about?' Faye grabbed her sunnies and a wide, floppy hat. 'Come on then. What are we waiting for?'

They walked round to the side of the house where he had parked his car, a vintage Alfa Romeo, the colour a faded moss green. Not flash, she thought, but very nice.

'Jump in,' he said. 'First, we will go to the marina.'

Deriu Marina, she saw immediately, was a working port. Pleasure crafts were moored in the bowl of the harbour and other boats glided effortlessly in and out, but there were also fishing trawlers, fishmonger stalls and men and boys fly-fishing from the mouth of the river and the bay. A shack had a sign pronouncing it to be the diving centre, with the *I Quattro Mori*, the Four Moors Sardinian flag, flying high. By the jetty, fishing nets had been stretched out to dry; one man squatted on a threadbare net, carefully mending it by hand. Beside the marina was a little railway track with a café which reminded Faye of the disused railway line and tea station in the Bay back in West Dorset. Trains were still running here though, and white and blue jasmine scrambled over the building.

'The trains were used for mining,' Alessandro told her. 'That is my boatyard over there.' He pointed, regarded her seriously. 'Later, I could show you around, perhaps?'

'Perhaps,' she said. She couldn't decide what to make of him. His family had money – his father had been a well-to-do businessman – and yet Alessandro was a craftsman, a traditional boat-builder. He dressed well, but casually. And he drove an Italian classic car, albeit a well-worn model from the sixties.

There was a beach at the marina, but clearly that wasn't what Alessandro had in mind. 'The beach we are going to is at an old mining village, only a few kilometres away,' he said. 'But first – the coffee.'

He took her to a backstreet café. 'It is the best coffee in Deriu.'

It was certainly better than any Faye had tried yet. Strong and rich, but not bitter.

'Are you feeling better?' Alessandro asked her after she'd taken a few sips.

Strangely, Faye realised that she was. She nodded, surprised at his concern. 'Yes. Thank you.'

Alessandro was watching her intently and she fidgeted under his gaze. 'May I ask,' he began. 'Do you have a family of your own back in England? Children? A husband?'

Faye almost spluttered into her coffee. 'No,' she said. 'No children. No husband.'

'Is it so strange to ask this?' He leaned back in his chair. 'In Sardinia, most women are married with a baby by the time they are twenty-five.'

'Not Marisa,' she pointed out.

'Not Marisa,' he agreed. 'For some years Marisa has been married to her job.'

'And now?' Faye got the impression that perhaps this was no longer the case.

'She visits Rome.' He smiled. 'There is a man there, her boyfriend. She met him when he came to Sardinia on a vacation.'

'Ah.' Faye wondered what was holding Marisa to the island now, apart from her schoolchildren. Perhaps it was the little theatre. Perhaps Marisa couldn't leave until the theatre had been restored in her parents' memory. 'And you?' she asked.

'Me?'

'Do you have children? A wife?' She took another sip of coffee. Alessandro was an unusual man. He hadn't been in the least friendly and yet he seemed determined to whisk her away – first to the theatre and now to the beach. It would be easy to write him off as a bit of a womaniser, but maybe there was more to him than that. Sadly, she wouldn't have the time to find out.

'Do you think if I had a wife she would let me take a beautiful woman for coffee and a trip to the beach?' he asked.

'But would she be able to stop you?' Faye teased, responding, she knew, to the glint of humour in his eyes. So she was flirting. So what?

He laughed. 'Maybe not. But –' he leaned closer again – 'if I were married, I would not want to go to the beach with a beautiful woman. I would be going with my wife, don't you think?'

'I hope you would,' said Faye. But even this jokey conversation made her think about her parents and her father's bombshell. There couldn't be anyone else for either of them – could there?

He was still watching her. 'You are thinking of this problem you have to go back for, *non*?'

'I was, yes.' He was too perceptive. But for goodness' sake, her parents were adults; she was an adult. Lots of people got divorced. Was it really the end of the world? Yes, she thought. It was the end of her world, in a way; at least of the world she knew and loved. If this happened, if they separated, then nothing would be the same again.

'If it is not your children and it is not your husband . . .' His dark brows drew together into a frown. 'Is it your parents? Is one of them ill? Is that it?'

That would almost be better. Faye immediately hated that she'd thought that – even for a millisecond. She shook her head. 'They're separating.' She couldn't believe she'd told him. But there was something about this man that drew her and it had just spilled out.

'Ah.' He moved the salt and pepper canisters on the table carefully to one side. 'And this news – it was a shock?'

'Yes.' She sighed. 'They've always been so happy together.'

He nodded.

'They've never had any big problems.'

He nodded again.

'And apparently there's no one else involved.'

He waited.

'So I can't see – why.'

She was worrying with her fingers at the placemat in front of her.

'Faye.' Gently, he put his hand on top of hers. He didn't take hold of it, he just let his palm rest over her knuckles. 'So you are going back to find out the reasons,' he said.

She felt the warmth seep into the back of her hand and slowly she felt it unclench and relax. 'Yes.'

'You are hurt, upset, confused. You need to find out why they have made this decision.'

'Exactly.' Faye was relieved that he didn't try and talk her out of it, or that he didn't point out the obvious – that maybe her parents were never as happy together as Faye had always believed. 'You don't think I'm wrong to want to talk to them?' she asked him. She had never interfered in their lives before, but she supposed she'd never had to.

'Of course not.' He dismissed this with a wave of his hand. 'They are your family. Family is everything – especially here in Sardinia.' He paused. 'But remember, Faye . . .'

'Yes?'

'Parents sometimes do things that surprise us,' he said softly. He drank the rest of his coffee and pushed the cup to one side. 'Sometimes it is hard to remember that they are people, *non*? Not just our mother and our father. But people with their own lives.'

Faye looked at him more closely. This man was full of surprises. She could see that she had underestimated him. 'Is that what happened to you?' she asked. 'Did one of your parents surprise you?'

'Yes.' At last he withdrew his hand and got to his feet. 'My father surprised me. Before he died, he told me something, something that—' He broke off, as if realising who he was talking to and what he was saying. He took a deep breath. '*Andiamo*,' he said. 'We should not talk of that now. It is nothing. We must remember that this is your last day in Sardinia. And so. Let us go to the beach.'

As they left the café, a girl came sauntering by. She was in her late twenties, Faye guessed, slender and attractive with raven hair, an impressive suntan and plenty of gold bling. Faye saw her look at Alessandro, eyes narrowing, before she stopped short at the sight of Faye.

'Alessandro,' she snapped. She let loose a torrent of dialect. Faye didn't even try to keep up, but it was easy to get the gist. She put one slender hand on his arm and gestured at Faye with the other. Her face was flushed and angry. Not a wife perhaps, but a girlfriend, certainly.

Faye felt a stab of disappointment. She might be leaving Sardinia, but that didn't stop a girl from having her dreams.

Alessandro, however, didn't seem bothered in the least, although he did let out a small sigh. He spoke back to her, still smiling, and then removed her hand firmly from his arm and waved her off. '*Ciao, Jana.*'

Faye hovered uncertainly. The girl was looking daggers and Faye couldn't blame her.

'*Andiamo*, Faye.' Alessandro took her arm. 'Let's go.'

'Who was that?' Faye disentangled herself as they walked back towards the car. She already seemed to be thoroughly hated in the village of Deriu — perhaps it was a good thing she was leaving.

'Her name is Jana.' He didn't elaborate.

'Why was she so angry?'

He laughed. 'Jana is always angry,' he said. 'She is a lovely girl, but . . .' He shrugged.

Faye remained unconvinced. She had looked as if she had every right to be angry. Her hand on Alessandro's arm had been a gesture of possession. And the way he had reacted was a clue. A clue to the personality of this man.

CHAPTER 13

They drove up through the mountains and along a narrow mountain pass, past green gorges and a deep ravine. A lone motorcyclist passed them like an angry mosquito; otherwise, there was little traffic around. Faye tried to distract herself from the sheer drop beneath them by admiring the striking red rock formations and dramatic scenery, taking some comfort in Alessandro's confident driving.

Alessandro looked across at her and smiled. 'We have to go up,' he said, quite reasonably, 'before we can go down.'

At last, to her relief, Alessandro swung off on to a dirt road leading to a small town nestling in the foothills; the mountains sloped down towards the sea as if they were taking a little rest.

'The old mining town,' he said.

Faye looked around. Several lonely rows of uninhabited, half-derelict buildings were a bleak reminder of the town's once prosperous mining history. But beyond them, the sunlight was glancing off the surface of the sea, soft arrows of white cloud breaking up the brilliant blue sky.

'I wanted to show you this old town, this beach.' He parked the car on a patch of grass surrounded by tamarisk trees.

Faye climbed out. It was late morning now and the sun was so hot she was glad of her floppy hat. She looked around her curiously. What was so special about this place? And why did he want to show it to her?

Alessandro led the way through a wooden gate and along a sandy boardwalk flanked with bamboo, over some dunes and dry grassland decorated with the occasional clump of slim, delicate wild lilies, and past the skeletal remains of more buildings, the husk of the mining works. She could see a fort standing on the distant headland.

'This was the old warehouse.' He pointed to a large faceless, roofless, windowless building surrounded by rubble. 'And this was the yard where goods were stored.'

Faye looked from side to side as they walked, aware of the grainy boards under her feet, stretching out over the dunes. Portions of stone wall stood sombre and upright in the sand like gravestones. Ahead of them, the glassy blue ocean shone.

The place was very quiet – not only unlived in, but forgotten too, she thought, though she could see a few people sunbathing on the far side of the bay, some small children playing in the shallow waves. There was a strange monochrome quality to the landscape: at first glance, the sand, earth and stone buildings all seemed to be the exact same shade of light terracotta; everything camouflaged except for the thick vegetation on the far hillside and the sudden blinding blue of the sea. But as they drew closer to the sculpted cliff, Faye realised that the stone was in fact greyish-brown, quite dark in places, and in other areas marbled with white, red and silver. The bay itself was keyhole-shaped, the remains of an old pier jutting out into the ocean.

'The zinc was sent from this cove to the port of Carloforte,' Alessandro said, 'on small boats with lateen sails.' From the expression on his face as he stood there looking out to sea, Faye guessed that he could see them still.

'Where was it taken after that?' And did Alessandro still make boats with lateen sails? Faye was keen to visit his boatyard, but she suspected that they wouldn't have the time. Traditional boats and a classic car, she thought. A theatre that he wanted to restore to its original nineteenth-century splendour. Alessandro was a man with one foot firmly rooted in the past.

'It would have been sent by steamship to northern Italy or France,' he said. 'Zinc was much in demand. Other minerals too.'

But that demand had left behind a legacy, she thought. Of cliffs and mountains with half the heart gouged out of them, of deserted towns where there had once been thriving populations, of lost, roofless buildings now crumbling to the ground. There was no use for a mining village in this day and age. There was no infrastructure – it couldn't become a seaside town for tourists or islanders without the injection of a lot of cash. And the same applied to the little theatre, she found herself thinking. It shouldn't be left to become an anachronism of itself. Whatever Alessandro thought, it had to have some use, some purpose specific to the present, for it to survive. Faye held on to the handrail and stepped down to the beach. But that wasn't her problem now. She had a different problem – and it was waiting for her in West Dorset.

'Where shall we sit?' She prepared to put her towel down on the sand, though she realised it was not actually sand at all; the beach was made up of tiny quartz-like stones and shell so fine that they were more like dust.

'This way.' Alessandro glanced around, before ducking under a high, overhanging ledge.

They were going to sit in a cave? She gave a mental shrug and followed him. But it wasn't a deep cave, she saw at once. On one side was a foothold and as she watched, Alessandro put one foot on this and swung the other up so that he was standing above her. He beckoned her up to join him. Faye swung her bag over her shoulder and did so. She'd ask questions later, she decided. Clearly, he knew where he was going; she'd have to trust him.

Alessandro squeezed through a hole in the cliff – the remnants of a tunnel made during the mining years? – and held out his hand to help her through. It was strong and warm, a practical, boat-builder's hand.

'Where are we going?' They were on a different path now, more like a goat track, quite steep with bits of loose rubble and stones making it harder to negotiate – at least in flip-flops – and hidden from the beach by trees.

'You will see.'

Faye was intrigued. 'What kind of trees are these?' she asked Alessandro. They had dark green, shiny leaves and star-shaped flowers and reminded her of the tree in *Piazza del Teatro*. She even thought she could detect the faint scent of orange blossom drifting in the sea air.

'Myrtle,' he said. 'We use the leaves in cooking.'

'Ah.'

'And the berries to make our traditional liqueur.' He glanced back at her. 'The root and the bark are still used for tanning leather, which is why you'll find several myrtles in Deriu.'

'There's one in *Piazza del Teatro*,' she murmured.

'That is so, yes.' He gave her an appreciative look, as if surprised. She smiled to herself. He was quite the chauvinist – expecting women to take ages getting ready, expecting them not to notice their surroundings, expecting them to do what *he* said. But despite this, she had to admit she was enjoying his company. He'd given her some good advice about her parents, he was interesting to talk to, and this outing had already turned into an adventure.

They scrambled along the path, making their way towards the headland. Ahead, an archway had been cut into the limestone cliff – also man-made, surely? It was low and deep, and Faye didn't see it until they were almost on top of it; the interior of greyish-brown stone was in deep shadow.

He turned. 'This way.'

She followed him through. The path here was flat but she couldn't quite stand upright. All she could see was Alessandro half-crouched ahead. And then he emerged from the tunnel, stepped aside and Faye caught her breath. Wow. In front of her, framed by the stone archway, was the most perfect bay she had ever seen. The rays of the sun illuminated the glittering blue-green sea and white jewelled sand and gilded the limestone rocks beyond. She saw a black cormorant dive under the water and emerge a few moments later, head bobbing in the waves. Faye stepped out from the archway of the cliff. The tiny bay was deserted.

'You cannot see this bay from the ocean; it is well hidden,' Alessandro told her. He strode across the sand and threw down his bag; in seconds he was stripping off his shorts and tee shirt. His body was tanned and toned, but he wasn't a fitness freak, she could see. His arms were strong and muscular – from all that boat-building, no doubt.

'A secret bay.' Faye marvelled as she made her way over to join him. Beyond the white sand was a dried-up riverbed that led into the valley between the maquis-shrouded slopes behind. On either side were the sculptured cliffs. The bay was sheltered and perfectly positioned. From this location, they couldn't see the rest of the ocean, and the rest of the ocean couldn't see them. And Faye could see how: this inlet began from just below the centre of the main keyhole bay, where the cove narrowed and then widened. The shape of the first bay and the nature of its sharp angle were what concealed this beach. 'It's beautiful,' she said. 'So peaceful.'

'Not always. See the sand up there on the plateau?' He pointed. It was over a hundred metres from sea level, she reckoned. 'That's how far the sea can fling the sand in a winter storm, when we have the *mistral*. The shape of the beach, it is always changing.'

That, thought Faye, was what could happen in paradise.

'Coming in?' His hands were on his hips. The challenge was unmistakeable.

'Try and stop me.' Faye slipped her sundress from her shoulders and ran laughing down to the water's edge where foam crept up the beach, drawing back to leave dark arcs on the white shoreline. The first silky touch of the ocean took her by surprise — it was colder than she'd expected — but Alessandro was catching up, so she stepped through the waves. A few quick skips as the tide surged around her shins and she plunged into the water.

'I am impressed,' he said when she surfaced. He dived in, came up right next to her, his curly dark hair plastered to his scalp.

'By what?'

He laughed. 'The speed of the woman.'

Expecting women to be slow, she thought. Faye smiled as she settled into a breaststroke, swimming towards the waves, rising with them, letting them carry her into shore, swimming out again, flipping over on to her back to stare up at the cloudless sky. Drifting. At peace. She was more used to the temperature now; it was invigorating, slightly chilling and tingling on her skin. She saw a dark jellyfish trailing through the water nearby and swam a few strokes away. There was always danger, she reminded herself, as well as change, in paradise.

'It is perfect, *non*?' Alessandro was beside her again.

'Yes.' She smiled as he dived through another wave and re-emerged. It was indeed perfect and Faye was loving every minute. 'Who comes here?' she asked him. 'Who knows about this beach?' In England, she reckoned there was nowhere left that people didn't know about. It seemed different here in Sardinia, with plenty of unpopulated rocky bays to discover and explore.

Droplets of water clung to Alessandro's brown shoulders. 'A few locals. Walkers sometimes. There is a path, much higher.' He pointed up to a ridge. 'But most of the time you can be alone.'

A bolthole, thought Faye. Why did he need a bolthole? She turned again, thought about her parents. How could two people live together for so long, be so much a part of one another's lives, share a daughter and a history, and then simply break up? It didn't seem possible. It seemed wrong. It had to be wrong. She closed her eyes and willed the tide to take it all away – everything her father had told her.

'Do you come here often?' she asked Alessandro. An old chat-up line, but he wouldn't know that.

His eyes gleamed. 'As often as necessary. I have a boat here, look.' He gestured to the shore and Faye saw a small wooden craft with faded red and green paintwork, half-hidden under an overhanging part of the cliff.

'I take her out to other secluded bays,' he said. 'Some places you cannot even reach by land. Sometimes, you can see the monk seal off this coastline, although he is rare.'

'It sounds wonderful.' Faye heard the wistfulness in her own voice. How she would have loved to have spent more time here, to have got to know this coastline, the town of Deriu, the Sardinian people.

She let the tide take her back into shore once again; Alessandro was right behind her. As she emerged from the shallows, she turned to him, suddenly shy. 'Thank you for showing me this place.'

'It was my pleasure.' He got to the bags before she did, reached down for her towel and tossed it to her. Faye wrapped it around her shoulders. She was glad of its warmth; out of the water she felt chilly and more vulnerable.

'But you know, when you have spoken to your parents . . .'

Faye looked away. She didn't want to think about that anymore, not now.

'You can come back here, yes?' He was holding his towel but looking at her, waiting for her response.

'What for?' she asked. She pulled her towel in closer. 'We both know that if the theatre is to be restored to the way it used to be, then you don't need me to tell you how.'

He bowed his head to roughly towel-dry his hair. When he looked up again it was tousled and sticking up all over.

Faye laughed. He looked like a little boy.

'You came here for a holiday,' he said, 'as well as for a job.'

'Well, yes . . .' But as the job hadn't worked out . . .

'We asked you to come here.' Alessandro took a beach sarong from his bag and spread it on the sand. 'Shall we?'

Faye sat and he sat down next to her. 'Marisa asked me,' she reminded him gently. 'Or at least Charlotte did. I never got the impression it was your idea.'

'This is true.' Alessandro gazed out to sea. 'Things have changed, Faye,' he said. 'That is why I came to see you this morning.'

'In what way?' Faye hugged her knees. Perhaps it was the petition and what had been said at the meeting. Perhaps Alessandro had had second thoughts.

'I want to hear your ideas for the theatre.' He held up his hand before she could speak. 'I know you need to go back home. I understand that you need to talk to your parents.' He let his voice hang. 'But after that . . .'

'Yes?' Faye waited.

'After that, I am asking you to come back here,' he said. 'Please.'

'But why?' Faye picked up some of the sand and shell in her palm and let it trickle through her fingers. Why had he changed his mind, she meant. But also — what did he want her to do?

'My family worked hard to repair and recreate our theatre,' he said. 'And now it feels as if the villagers are trying to rob us. Of our theatre, and the memories too.'

Faye could see why he felt that way; the Rinaldis had put so much into it. When he put it like that, it was hardly fair for the rest of the community to try and take it away from them. But . . .

'We need someone objective.' He leaned on one arm and turned to face her. 'I feel you can help us. I feel you understand.'

Faye remembered how he had defended her at the community meeting the night before. 'You mustn't feel guilty,' she said. 'I came over here not knowing if redesigning your theatre was a job I even wanted to take on.'

'But I saw it in your eyes that night,' he said.

Faye was surprised. 'What did you see?'

'You loved it,' he said. 'Never mind about all those things you

130

told us – about theatre in the round and fiction and reality.' He laughed and she had to laugh with him. 'That is not the point. You loved our little theatre. It touched you, did it not?'

She nodded. 'It did, yes. It's charming. But—'

'No more but's.' His eyes glinted. 'I do feel guilty, yes, and so does Marisa. We have talked this over. We want you to come back and work with us – for a while at least. We want to listen to your ideas for the theatre and we want you to help us design a restoration that everyone is happy with.'

'Everyone?' That was a tall order.

He shrugged. 'If you are willing to give us some of your time, we would like to make you a proposition. We will pay for your flight back over here and for the time and work you decide to do for us. Once the initial plans are made, you can stay as long as you like – just as you originally intended.' Alessandro turned back to face the sea. 'What do you say? Deriu is not such a bad place to spend some time, *non*?'

'It's a beautiful place,' she said.

'*Molto simpatico, si*.' He gave a small nod of satisfaction. 'It was not a good start. But we can do better, I think.'

Faye smiled. She thought of her parents and what her father had told her. She thought of Charlotte and Fabio's house and the warm but shadowy town of Deriu that had already shown signs of creeping into her heart. She thought of Pasquale and Marisa and this man who had brought her here to this secret beach. Yes, to seduce her. But not in the way she had expected. She must go back to West Dorset – at least for a day or two. She must speak to her parents and find out the truth. But why let this ruin the rest of her plans? 'Alright, Alessandro,' she said. 'I'll come back.'

'Fantastic.' His eyes shone. He turned to her and lifted her chin so that she was looking straight into his eyes. He was so close, his hand still cool from the water, his hair clinging damply to his neck. 'I am happy to hear that.'

Was this just about the theatre? Faye searched his expression for an answer to her unspoken question. But she couldn't see one. All she could see was the navy of his eyes, the slant of his cheekbones, the shape of his mouth . . .

'Thank you, Faye.' His lips were so close to her cheek that she could feel the brush of warm air as he spoke. He let his hand rest for a moment on her shoulder and she felt an instant streak of desire, a bolt of warmth that wasn't just from the sun above them. She thought of the woman they'd seen outside the café – Jana. Quite clearly, she thought she had some claim on this man. But what was the truth?

He drew away, his gaze still on her mouth. '*Buon viaggio,*' he murmured. 'You will have a good journey and I shall see you when you return to us.'

What do you want from me, she thought again. But she was coming back to Deriu. And then, she would find out.

CHAPTER 14

Pasquale was heading down to the marina on his battered bicycle. He called her the Silver Lady because she had once been elegant and her chrome had shone. He was going to buy some fish.

'Make sure it is fresh,' his mother had said. She hobbled outside to see him on his way, dressed as ever all in black and wrapped up as if it were winter. Her sparse iron-grey hair was hidden under the shawl she wore and her blackcurrant eyes were sunken in the leathery dough of her face. 'Make sure you get it at the right price, too; he will swindle you, given half the chance. Make sure he guts it. And get him to wrap it up properly in newspaper, not a plastic bag. Fish sweats in plastic.'

'Yes, yes, Mama, I know.' Pasquale often shut her voice off in his head. *Per l'amor di Dio* . . . He loved her, but a man could only take so much. She could not help it; she was old. But it was not easy sometimes.

People asked why he'd never married. The other men he played dominoes with in the bar joked and speculated about it quite often. Pasquale joined in, of course. He knew them all so well and they liked to think they knew him too. They might have their suspicions – they'd known him for years after all – but Pasquale was adept at playing his cards, like his dominoes, close to his chest. He chuckled to himself. Sometimes in response, he'd cast a glance in his mother's direction as if to say: *she's answer enough, eh?*

Pasquale wobbled a bit on the bike as he came to some treacherous uneven cobbles. It was mean of him, but just a joke. Everyone knew what a matriarch she had been, and still was; everyone knew how much he cared. People might speculate; many folk had nothing better to do. But Pasquale de Montis could recognise a beautiful woman as clearly as the next man. He always had.

The Silver Lady gathered speed as she was travelling downhill and Pasquale had to wrench the handlebars from side to side to keep her straight and true. He had known many beautiful women and played opposite them too, but there had only ever been one woman for Pasquale. *'Did my heart love till now? Forswear it, sight! For I ne'er saw true beauty till this night.'* Romeo e Giulietta. He would practise that bit later on stage, he decided. It didn't sound quite right in his head as he tumbled down the hill from the old town on his bicycle. And he couldn't start speaking out loud, not here; that would make the villagers speculate all the more.

Marriage . . . Pasquale braked at the end of the road and waited for a passing car. The surface of the river gleamed like a snake's skin on the other side; it wound sinuously from the valley between the mountains, moving forward to the sea. Pasquale turned right towards the bridge and the marina. Marriage was a big commitment for a man. Plus of course he had his mother to look after. It seemed to Pasquale that he had always had his mother to look after. Heigh ho. Even so – he would have if he could have.

'Be careful how you pack it in the basket.' She had still been talking as he rode away. 'Fish is a delicate thing. And don't fall off that bicycle. I do not want our fish to be splattered all over the road.' As if, he thought, she was more worried about her precious fish than she was about her only son.

But what choice had he had? Pasquale reached the bridge, puffing a bit on his journey's last leg, which was uphill. He had stepped into his father's shoes so young – or tried to. Not that he could live up to his father, as his mother was fond of telling him. He could never match his achievements and he would not presume to even try. His father was a hero.

A bit of downhill now as he reached the rise and Pasquale let out his breath in a whoosh as he descended the bridge and freewheeled on to the marina. He could never live up to the reputation of a man like that, but he had done his best. And he hoped that he too had been loved in his way.

Who would have thought a man like his father could have come from such lowly beginnings? The caretaker of the local theatre, who spent his days greasing and oiling machinery to keep it in good working order, fixing lights, keeping the auditorium and foyer clean and tidy, seeing to the toilets, repainting – especially the outside of the windows which often needed doing because they were so close to the sea. Pasquale trailed after him like a dog, holding nails, hammers or paint pots, occasionally trusted to sweep the stage or run errands to the hardware store.

Ahead of him now, Pasquale could see the ocean. It was visible almost everywhere in Deriu. From the top of the castle, of course, as well as from the back of his own house in the upstairs bedroom occupied by his mother (Pasquale preferred to look out at the theatre from the front of the house) and from the dilapidated roof terrace they rarely used. The little theatre also had a sea view – a clear one from the window in the foyer and the dressing rooms at the side. The little theatre stood so high on the steps from *Piazza del Teatro* that it had views as fine as the castle – but like the castle, *il Piccolo Teatro* caught all the corrosiveness of the salt air and the winter winds and storms. It needed a lot of looking after.

Pasquale remembered his father's soft, gentle voice. 'We are here to make sure everything runs smoothly, my boy.' As if it were an honour to serve in the theatre – a sense that had been instilled in Pasquale too. 'You and I, we are the background cogs.'

Pasquale chuckled. *The background cogs*. He had liked that, although he had gone on to be a foreground cog, someone who loved the attention of an audience – or even craved it, as his mother liked to say. But he had stayed in the theatre. Even back when he was a boy, he had known he would do that.

'When all goes smoothly, no one thinks about what we do,' his father had added. 'But we have the satisfaction of knowing. And if anything should go wrong . . .' His face had darkened. 'Then we will be the first ones called to order.'

Which was hardly fair, thought Pasquale, as he swept down to the harbour, his thin legs pedalling madly, the Silver Lady rattling her chain in the wind, past the fishing boats and the cafés to the stall where the best fisherman sold his catch of the day. Two children ran into the road in front of him and Pasquale rang his bell fiercely as he swerved to avoid them. 'Be careful! Look where you are going,' he shouted for good measure. Children today!

He had never wanted children. 'Because you are still a child yourself perhaps,' his mother had told him once. But she had laughed and chucked his chin and her little black eyes had glittered. So maybe she did not mind so much . . .

It was true. Things could always be different. Pasquale braked abruptly as a stray dog bounded from the pavement towards him and the Silver Lady responded, almost sending him over the handlebars. But life was what it was and with his father dying so terribly young and in such tragic circumstances, Pasquale had been forced to devote his time and energies to looking after his mother, even when he was still at school. And later, what time and opportunity did he have for a wife, for children? That, at any rate, was what he let the men in the bar believe.

Pasquale surveyed the fish stall. As ever, the fish looked surprised that they had been caught, eyes wet and wide, scales gleaming. He sniffed. Not even a few hours since they'd been happily swimming in the sea, he'd guess. There was a massive bluefin tuna – they usually made an appearance from the end of May till September – some red snapper, a tub of squid and octopus, a tray of fat sardines, langoustines, mussels and a few scrawny crabs. He took his time and made careful choices.

His mother would come down here herself if she could. She'd denied old age for decades, clumping along the cobbles to fetch bread, meat and vegetables with the best of them, but in her nineties now, she had finally succumbed to being housebound – or as good as. She still cooked, though, and directed Pasquale (who was used to being directed, it had to be said) as he carried out chores and looked after the house. In the evening she still liked to play dominoes, just as her son did, though she had to lean forward and squint to see the number of dots. She never made him feel guilty when he strolled down to the bar to see the old cronies and play there while he drank a beer or two. Perhaps she thought it made him more of a man.

Having made his purchases, Pasquale carefully packed the fish away in his bicycle basket. He glanced across at the beach café. And then he saw them. Well, well . . . He wheeled the Silver Lady out of sight, propped her against the wall and slipped round the side of the building so that he could watch them unobserved – from the wings, as it were.

He looked confident as ever, so sure of himself. Pasquale ground his teeth. Just like his father before him, he didn't even have to try.

Pasquale thought of the nerves he himself used to feel before a performance, dancing into terror in his stomach. Would he forget his lines? Would he trip? Would he still be able to make them feel it? Only as he stepped on to the stage would the adrenalin surge through his body, only as he spoke the first lines would he know – he could do it; he had them. It would be okay.

He was leaning forwards, his elbows on the table, looking into her eyes, feeding her a load of nonsense. Pasquale snorted in disgust. Women fell for it every time; they lapped it up, the old charm offensive, as if they did not have a brain in their head. Making them feel special, making them feel they were the only woman in the whole world worth looking at. Pasquale knew how it worked, though he'd never been able to pull it off himself. He couldn't understand how the women were fooled by it. Perhaps it simply made them feel good. But what did he want with her? Was it just the obvious or was there more?

He said something to her and she laughed – not a polite laugh, but a throw-back-your-head laugh that reminded Pasquale so vividly of Sofia. He gave a little start. Yes, she used to laugh like that. It had been a wonderful feel-good sound.

A waiter appeared with their bill. She picked up her purse; he waved it away. He pulled his wallet from his back pocket and they both got to their feet. They had been on the beach, Pasquale guessed. She was wearing a sundress and her shoulders were freckled and tinged with pink from the sun. Their hair was still damp – one fair, one dark. Pasquale frowned. So why had they met and what did this mean?

He slunk away. He did not want them to spot him, laugh at him, feel sorry for him – any of the things that sometimes occurred. He returned to the Silver Lady, relieved to see that the fish was still in the basket. Otherwise his mother would not be pleased, and she was more than capable of thwacking him over the head if he didn't get out of the way fast enough.

What did it mean? It meant that – as he had guessed – their relationship was not merely professional. Colleagues did not go on outings to the beach unless they were on very friendly terms. Which worried Pasquale. He had seen it all before. She was a nice girl; he wouldn't want her to get hurt. Did this mean that she was staying in Deriu? Did it mean that Alessandro Rinaldi would continue with his plans for the theatre? Pasquale felt a shiver of foreboding as he mounted the Silver Lady. He feared so.

Later, after his meal back at home, Pasquale sat in the front window watching the theatre as he so often did. He saw Alessandro Rinaldi rounding the street corner, on his way back to his own house. Pasquale hesitated, but he was alone.

Pasquale slipped out of the front door. There were some kids hanging around the piazza; he had seen them before. He didn't like the way they loitered on the steps to the theatre. 'What are you doing?' he demanded.

'Nothing,' they said. But they looked shifty.

'Get along with you then,' he said, waving them away.

Swiftly, he cut through the square so that he came upon Alessandro just as he approached his place on Via del Carmine. '*Bone die*,' he said in greeting. '*Tutto bene?* All is well, I hope?'

'Ah, Pasquale.' Alessandro looked like the cat that had got the cream. 'It is going very well. It is a lovely day, is it not?'

Pasquale looked up at the sky. It was pale blue and there was a pleasant light breeze. June was his favourite month on the island – a time when all was fresh and hopeful and summer had not yet burned out its heat. But perhaps Alessandro was not talking about the weather. 'Indeed,' he agreed. 'And can you tell me – what is happening now?'

'Happening?' A shadow crossed Alessandro's brow.

'With the theatre.' Pasquale hopped from one leg to the other. It was important to be in the know, especially where the theatre was concerned. If there was news . . . he would like to be prepared.

'How do you mean, old fellow?'

What else could he mean? 'Are you continuing with the restoration?' He held his breath. *To be or not to be, that is the question.*

'Of course. We all want to see the theatre up and running, *non*?'

Pasquale tried to look non-committal. 'But Enrico and the others—'

'What can they do?' The shadow seemed to flare into anger. 'They cannot fight it. They do not have the means.'

Pasquale nodded. 'Possibly,' he conceded. 'But there are other ways . . .' There were always other ways.

'You do not get something for nothing in this world, Pasquale,' Alessandro told him. 'You know that.'

Pasquale frowned. Something for nothing? What did he mean by that? 'Ah,' he said. 'So there will be much rebuilding, I suppose.' He hated the thought of this, of his theatre suffering under the blows of men and machine, the stage dismantled so that he could no longer slip inside the theatre and dream of the past. All that history crumbling to nothing, all those memories –

'I do not know yet,' Alessandro said. He grinned. 'As little as possible if it were up to me. Are you worried about the noise, *vecchio mio*?'

'The noise? No, no.' Pasquale had not even considered this, though his mother would hate it, he knew.

'Good man.' He slapped him on the back and Pasquale nearly fell over from the force of it. 'We will keep you informed.'

'*Grazie*.' Pasquale acknowledged this with a small nod of his head. 'And the girl?' he asked.

'The girl?'

'You know.' Of course he knew.

'She is leaving Deriu,' Alessandro said. 'But do not worry, old fellow.' And he actually chuckled. 'She will be coming back.'

CHAPTER 15

On Fridays, Molly always had morning coffee with her mother. Ade had no idea about the elderly – he had lost his parents some years ago – but Molly had made it her business to know. She had made a promise.

Her mother's security was connected to routine. It wasn't that she *had* to have morning tea at seven, a bath on Tuesdays and Saturdays and a trip to the supermarket on Thursday mornings. It was that the routine established by these predictabilities made her feel secure. Molly's mother's security had been snatched away from her by the death of her husband. Molly would give anything to have her father back, but that was impossible. The next best thing was to help her mother manage without him. And she had done that for years.

She prepared the coffee in a cafetière she'd bought her mother many Christmases ago, pouring the boiling water on to the grounds and inhaling the fragrance as it infused; it was invariably even better than the taste.

'How's Faye?' her mother called from the lounge where she was sitting on the pale blue sofa with the white rose pattern that had been in the house for as long as Molly could remember. 'Have you heard from her?'

'Oh, yes, she's fine.' Molly felt a small surge of guilt. She placed the lid firmly on the cafetière. It always helped to be doing something. When she'd found out about Nina she'd made a beef casserole big enough to feed an army (as if, she thought, her husband could be lured back through his stomach). When she lost her baby, she'd walked along the beach to Freshwater on the verge of collapse, stamping her very grief into the stones.

Molly waited for the coffee to brew. She had intended to call her daughter this morning, but . . . She didn't want to get Faye upset and she didn't want Faye to get her upset. She had to keep control. Molly sighed. She couldn't afford to let loose, to break down, to fall; it was too much of a risk. But sometimes the responsibility of maintaining everyone else's happiness did get her down. Give Faye some space, she thought. Just a day or two to digest the news. Then she'd talk to her, then she'd deal with it. When she felt strong enough. When she'd worked out exactly what she was going to say.

'How does she like Sardinia?' came the voice from the other room.

'I'm sure she's having a good time.' A picture flashed into Molly's mind, of a man with kind brown eyes and a very sad smile – a man who seemed to understand. She pushed down the plunger of the cafetière, enjoying the rush as the dark coffee filtered through.

She had never meant to say as much as she had to Ade, but having held back for so long, it had simply poured out. At her creative writing class she had been thinking and writing about passion and death. And what had he said? He wanted to 'find some life'. That was it. That was what made her flip. It wasn't just what he had done, how he had behaved, or his assumption that she hadn't even known he was having an affair. She wanted him to know that she had always known; that she was not stupid and could have left if she'd had a mind to. Because of Ade, she had told her story to another man, got close and allowed him to learn the heart of her.

Molly blamed her creative writing class too. That conversation with Ade had happened when she was already half-opened by all the words that had been flowing from her mind, her pen. Red. It was the colour that had started it all off, plain and simple. Go on then, Ade, she had thought. Find some life somewhere else, why don't you?

'And the theatre? Is Faye going to take the job?'

Too many questions. Molly sighed. And she suspected there had been a few she hadn't heard. But at least they took the focus away from her situation. 'I'm not sure.' How on earth was she going to tell her mother about Ade? So much for certainties, for routine.

Of course, she could have said 'yes' to her husband when he first mentioned travelling. She knew what he wanted. She could have gone away with him. She had considered it – for a moment, despite all the tension between them – because she thought the alternative, losing him, might be one loss too many. But then she had looked up at him and read his mind and thought: enough. She was his wife. She'd had it with being second best.

Molly put coffee cups and saucers, the milk jug and cafetière on to a dainty primrose-patterned tray. Everything her mother owned was dainty; Molly had vowed to escape from this tradition in her own house, but to her horror, she found herself buying similar things: a fine porcelain tea set with a pattern of delicate violets, fragile slim-stemmed wine glasses, antique furniture with marquetry and fleur-de-lys, neatly stitched muslin curtains that billowed decorously in the breeze . . . Molly's precious possessions filled her house and smirked at her. It seemed she had inherited the dainty gene.

'How have you been, Mum?' she asked briskly as she took the tray through.

'Very well, thank you, dear.' And she looked it: eyes of cornflower-blue still bright and curious, hair thick and white; all her faculties intact. Ade was right; her mother didn't need a carer.

'Here we are.' She kept her voice breezy. She put down the tray and shot her mother a beaming smile.

'What's wrong, Molly dear?' her mother asked.

Faculties a bit *too* intact, Molly amended. 'Why should anything be wrong?' she countered. Her mother didn't know her darkest secrets, but she still knew her rather well. And she had been there when Molly received that phone call from Ade to say he was working late, again; when she returned from Freshwater beach and wept for two hours, hardly stopping. It should have been Ade's shoulder, but it never was.

'It's obvious,' her mother said. 'You're not really listening to me. You're somewhere else. What's happened?'

Obvious . . . It had been blatantly obvious to Molly, too, when Ade dropped his bombshell, even as she was considering it – that he wanted to get away, that he'd always wanted to get away. And – worse – that he'd never got over her, the woman with no name. She could almost *see* him thinking of her, that look in his eyes. He was so transparent. It made her feel slightly sick. How stupid did he think she was?

Molly plumped up a cushion on the armchair to distract herself. Perhaps she had been stupid, back then, when she had tried to keep him. But she'd had seven-year-old Faye to consider and another little one on the way that she hadn't even told him about. But it was different now. Did she want to go away with a man who was still thinking about another woman? Did she want to spend time with a man who had nothing to say to her, who looked through her sometimes as if she wasn't even there? Did she want to break her promise to her father for a man like that? No, she did not. They had tried and they had failed. She'd had enough. It was more honest this way. And wasn't it about time for honesty?

'Is something wrong at home?' Her mother had poured the coffee. Molly added milk and took her own cup over to the table and chair opposite.

'Oh, Mum,' she said.

There was a pause. Molly felt too many emotions rising to the surface. She didn't think she could bear it. She tried to remember to breathe.

'Molly?' Her mother was leaning forwards, her eyes concerned.

'There's still a few bluebells out in Langdon Woods, you know, Mum.' Molly swallowed. The flowers were already past their first and second flush but it was such a rewarding walk, looking down over Seatown with Golden Cap ahead and the sea gently shimmering below. 'Shall we go and see them after coffee?'

Her mother put her white head to one side. 'That would be lovely, my dear,' she said.

Molly knew that her mother was waiting. She looked out into the garden of her childhood. Neat borders uncluttered with weeds, plants precisely spaced a specific number of inches apart, bushes trimmed, trees pruned, lawn pristine as a bowling green. Her mother employed a gardener now and Ade mowed the lawn most weekends. It seemed impossible to believe that she and Kathryn had spent so much of their childhoods in that garden. Kathryn had played with her dolls, dressing them in different outfits – she had continued this tradition as an adult by running her own boutique in Dorchester – while Molly had preferred her toy farm animals. Pigs, lambs and cows had bounded over the lawn, launched themselves into the forsythia, and performed somersaults through her mother's washing hung out on the line to dry. It wasn't unusual for a pig or a rabbit to emerge from a shirtsleeve when her mother was ironing.

At the back of the garden were raspberry canes and a trellis for runner beans. Molly and her father used to pick them; Kathryn and her mother had prepared them, washing the fruit for jam, running the beans through the slicer ready for dinner. Molly thought of her mother's ancient aluminium jam pan and big wooden spoon stained with juice, of the thick, syrupy, seeded liquid that emitted the stickiest, most pungent scent ever. She could smell it even now if she just closed her eyes.

Her mother must have spoken again but Molly had no idea what she'd said.

'Ade and I have decided to separate,' she said calmly. She sipped her coffee. There. It really wasn't so hard to say out loud – especially to her mother who knew almost everything, at least about that time. Molly didn't quite dare look at her, though.

'Oh, my dear.' Her mother got to her feet and reached out for her.

Molly got up and let her take her in her arms. Her mother's bones felt fragile and she smelt of lavender and face powder. But Molly would not crumple. She would not let her mother worry about what would happen now. 'It's alright,' she murmured into the soft white hair. 'Really, Mum. I'm fine.'

Her mother drew back and looked at her intently. There was a glimmer of wetness in her cornflower-blue eyes – a tear? 'Is there – ?' She hesitated. 'Someone else?'

Who did she suspect? Molly? Or Ade? Yes and no, she thought. Molly tried not to remember the way Ade's light blue eyes had darkened back in those early days, when he was thinking about *her*. Ade's other woman had been a part of their lives for so long. He might not see her anymore, but she was still in his head and maybe even his heart. As long as she still possessed a part of him . . . 'No,' she said. Because that wasn't it.

'Then why?'

Molly sighed. 'People change,' she said. 'A lot of couples split up nowadays. It isn't so terrible. Divorce is common, you know that. No one has to stay with someone –' *who they don't love anymore*. Go on, say it, she thought. Ade hadn't. Ade hadn't said anything about love.

Molly's mother's face clouded. 'People don't take marriage seriously enough,' she said. 'Your father –'

Molly switched off. She didn't want to think about what her father would have said. But it was too late. She felt the panic rise in her chest and she breathed, deep from her belly, as she'd been taught. She counted the beats. She waited.

How she missed him still. From here, she could see the black-and-white photograph on the dresser in its silver-plated frame. Her father as a young man, hair slicked back, dressed to kill in a sharp waistcoat and loose trousers, sleeves rolled up, a beer glass in his hand. It had been taken at her christening. Molly liked to think of herself, just a baby, somewhere in the background of the photograph. She liked to think of her father turning and holding out his arms. *Where's my sweetheart?* Molly suspected he would have done that. He was her world. And she liked to think that she was a big part of his. As a child, she'd adored him. She'd loved him and as she got older, she'd respected him, too.

When Kathryn was born, he had taken her aside. 'It's very special to have a baby sister,' he said.

'I know, Daddy.' Molly was looking forward to holding her, to reading to her, to teaching her everything she knew. Though as it turned out, Kathryn had not wanted to listen and she and Molly hadn't been as close as she had hoped. She loved her, but Kathryn's fierce independence and easy sense of style had never completely belonged in their family; she was a one-off.

'But you'll always be my special sweetheart,' he whispered. And Molly had snuggled into his arms and smelt his unique scent of cloves and pipe tobacco and she had felt as happy as she could ever be.

Twelve years later he was ill and she was saying goodbye to her world far too early, at seventeen.

'Let's go and see the bluebells,' Molly said. She put down her coffee cup and got to her feet. 'A bit of fresh air will do us good.'

'Blow the cobwebs away,' added her mother and they exchanged a small smile.

Molly parked the car in the woods and they walked through the gate to the path. The hill and the tall trees were on one side, the shady ground still blanketed with bluebells. On the other was the view of Seatown and the ocean.

'Oh my goodness, I'd forgotten how lovely it is here,' Molly's mother exclaimed.

Molly took her arm and they began to walk cautiously along the path towards the Cap. They wouldn't go up it – it was far too steep for an elderly lady – but they could still catch the best views. The air was full of damp, early summer and the rich, honeyed scent of the flowers.

'You're being very brave, my dear.' Her mother gripped her arm more tightly.

'Not really.' *Be brave, my sweetheart*, her father had said to her that day. She knew he was dying. They'd brought him back home, but they didn't know how long he would have. *Be brave*. But Molly wasn't brave. Look at her. She was a mess and she'd made a mess of her marriage. *Look after your mother for me*. And something had passed between them. A feeling of love. An understanding.

Molly knew that in some way she was as culpable as Ade. She had never trusted him enough. She had never told him her own secrets. More than that, she had created the distance between them once she knew that he'd been unfaithful; she had worn the armour she needed. It would probably happen again and this time she would be ready. She remembered her determination. *I will not be hurt again*.

'I didn't even know you argued,' her mother said weakly.

'We don't.' It was funny, Molly thought, that rows were considered a bad thing. The right sort of row could let out necessary emotion; the right sort of row could help you understand the other person's point of view and enable the relationship to move on.

'What will you do?' Her mother stopped walking.

'Nothing.' That was easy. 'Ade's got his early retirement package and his pension; he's leaving me the house.'

'That wasn't quite what I meant.'

Molly patted her mother's hand. 'It will be alright.' They turned to survey the bluebell wood, the hazy indigo of the flowers like a mist draped gently over the ground.

Molly's phone pinged and she reached to get it from her bag. 'Oh,' she exclaimed, as she read the text.

'What is it?'

'It's Faye.' Molly replaced the phone in her bag. 'She wants me to pick her up from the airport. She's coming home.'

CHAPTER 16

Her mother had come to Arrivals to meet her. Faye spotted her immediately on the other side of the barrier – she looked small and slightly fragile in her summer jacket and blue skirt with a print of yellow sunflowers.

'Mum!' She waved and saw her mother's answering smile – tentative perhaps, but at least it was there. When she got close enough, they hugged.

'How was your flight, darling?'

'Fine.'

'You should have warned me you were coming.'

Faye scrutinised her mother's face. There was no telltale redness around her eyes, no lines of sadness around her mouth. The dark bob of her hair was neat as ever and her make-up was immaculate. Anyone would think that nothing had happened. 'You should have warned *me*, Mum,' she said.

Her mother flinched and seemed to snatch an extra breath. 'Mum?'

'I'm sorry, darling.' She ducked her head. 'You're right. It's been very sudden. I'm still getting used to the idea myself.'

Faye felt immediately contrite. This was her mother – a woman who found it hard to show her emotions. That didn't mean she wasn't hurting. Faye took her arm. 'Are you alright?'

'Yes, I am.' Her mother patted her hand. She almost sounded convincing. 'Sorry, darling. Let's go and find the car.'

'I know I should have rung you straightaway,' she said, when they were driving away from the airport on the broad sweep of the A38, green fields on both sides. She sounded distracted, not quite with her.

Yes, you should have, thought Faye. She knew the way well enough. The route just clipped the edge of the Mendip Hills. To the west were Wells and Wookey Hole caves, to the east the elegant city of Bath.

'But I didn't trust myself.' Her voice became quieter still.

Faye waited for her to go on.

Her mother threw a quick look across at her. 'I didn't want to get too emotional. Especially with you being away from home.'

'Oh, Mum.' Faye digested this. 'I understand that. But I just wanted to talk to you.'

'Yes, of course.' Another quick look. 'Well, you're here now, darling.' And although she was trying to sound bright, Faye could feel the flatness behind her words.

She took a deep breath. 'So what's this all about?'

'Didn't your father tell you?'

She was being evasive, Faye realised, which was not a good sign. 'Not in detail.' And not that she'd given him much of a chance. 'What's happened between you two?' What could be that big, that momentous to break up a couple who had been together for thirty-four years?

'Nothing, really.'

Nothing? Faye looked across at her mother as she flipped the indicator and prepared to head towards the Mendips. She could almost see the shutters coming down. 'Something must have happened,' she said gently. 'Is it Dad? Has he done something?'

'No one's blaming anyone. No one's suddenly done anything. That isn't what this is about.' Her mother pressed rather sharply on the accelerator, taking the turn a bit too fast.

This sounded rehearsed to Faye. 'Then what is it about?' She gave up looking at her mother and stared out of the window instead. She was beginning to feel like a child again. Faye usually loved this journey – the route took in lots of little villages, farmland, as well as the hills and vales of the Mendips. But it wasn't likely to be giving her any pleasure today. 'And don't give me all that stuff about wanting different things – I've heard that already from Dad.'

Her mother glanced across at her once more then quickly looked back to the road. It was narrower now and more winding. 'It is about our future, though,' she said, as if she'd only just come to this conclusion. 'He's right, in a way. It's about the way we want our lives to be from now on.'

Faye realised that her mother was gripping the steering wheel so hard that her knuckles were white. 'Mum?'

'I'm sorry, my darling, and I know this is terribly hard to hear, but although it seems like a sudden decision to you . . .' She hesitated. 'In fact, it's been coming for years.'

For years. Faye thought about this as they turned right at the Mendip Inn and continued down the hill towards Shepton Mallet. This was something she hadn't considered, and didn't want to either. There was an awful finality to it. 'You haven't been happy together for years?' she asked bleakly. 'Really?'

'It's hard to explain.' Her mother's voice was softer now. 'Especially to you. You're our daughter. I can't discuss all the details of our marriage with you; it wouldn't be fair to your father. It wouldn't be right.'

Faye tried to process this. 'But why now?' She had told

Alessandro that she needed to find out why her parents had decided to separate, but what she had really thought was that she could make them talk to one another and sort it out. She had hoped that their separation had merely been one big misunderstanding. But now she felt helpless, because clearly, that wasn't it at all.

'Because of your father's retirement, I suppose. He wants to do things, to travel. And I don't.'

'But that doesn't mean you have to break up your marriage.' Faye shook her head. It made no sense. It wasn't enough. They passed through the bustling little town of Shepton and soon were surrounded by countryside again. 'Can't you come to some sort of compromise?'

'No,' her mother said. 'I really don't think that we can.'

Faye thought about this. It had been coming for years, her mother had said. They hadn't been happy for years. This was hard to take. Faye felt betrayed. As if everything she had believed in had been nothing more than a pretence, a fairy tale. 'So you looked at each other one evening and said, let's call it a day? Is that it?' She knew she sounded bitter. She *was* bitter.

'Of course not. I told you it was a difficult decision and—' Her mother had a pained expression on her face and Faye could see that this was hard for her. 'Your father's plans brought other things to the surface.'

'What things?' It was hard for her, yes, but Faye needed some answers.

'Just things. It's complicated.'

They had come to Street on the Fosse. Fosse Way, the famous old Roman Road. *Complicated*. Faye waited for her mother to continue.

'You shouldn't have come back early because of us.' Her mother sighed. 'We wanted you to have a proper holiday. We—'

'Mum. How was it complicated?'

'I can't tell you, Faye.' She shook her head and put the fingers of one hand to the bridge of her nose. Faye realised that her mother was pretty much at the end of her tether. 'We've made our decision, and that's all there is to it. I'm afraid you just have to accept it, my darling.'

Faye resisted the urge to bang her head on the dashboard. She thought of Alessandro, of the long and lazy lunch they'd had at the beach bar back in Deriu Marina, of the way he'd looked at her in the secret bay. He had seemed to be promising so much more. But did she want to go there? It could be awkward if she was working for the Rinaldis; everyone knew not to mix business with pleasure. And then there was Jana – clearly, something was still going on between them, and the last thing she wanted to do was butt in on someone else's relationship. But on the other hand . . . She examined her mother's set expression as she drove through the green Somerset countryside. Was this what happened when love went wrong? It was enough to make anyone feel disillusioned.

'Do you still love him?' Faye asked her mother. They were her parents. She had to try everything.

For a moment, her mother didn't answer, and then she frowned. 'There was a song once,' she said. 'What's love got to do with it?'

Faye shook her head. She sat back in her seat. They were almost in Dorset now, almost at the Beaminster Tunnel where a couple had died in their car a few years ago, following a landslip after prolonged and heavy rainfall. Faye shivered. It had taken more than a year to rebuild the tunnel. But what about the families of those poor people? Had they been able to rebuild their lives? 'Where's Dad?' she asked.

'He's coming round tonight. He wants to take you out to dinner.'

'Will you be coming with us?'

'No, darling.'

They were dealing with this separately, Faye realised. And this made her even more afraid.

Faye felt like crying when she saw her father. He'd always been easier to reach somehow, the emotions closer to the surface. But now, he looked confused and older, and he hugged her a bit too tightly. Faye was cross with him. Why had he allowed this to happen?

They went to a traditional old pub down in the Bay where the walls were plastered with pictures of the past – fishermen with wooden boats and grizzled faces, men in the 1930s playing water polo in the harbour, the Bay when it had flooded, the time when snowfall left the gingerbread cliffs with a layer of icing on the top. It was a warm and pleasant evening and there were quite a few people around – it was always busy in season. The Bay itself was a bit like a theatre, Faye found herself thinking. People arrived in their cars, coaches, and on motorbikes, water rushed in from the river to the harbour, then the people left and the water too. Like the emptying of an auditorium . . . Faye shook her head to dispel the image. It was hard, it seemed, to get the Little Theatre of Deriu out of her mind. Even the curved, red upholstered bench seats in this pub reminded her of it.

She sat down while her father went to fetch menus and drinks. Had she loved the little theatre on sight? Alessandro seemed to think so. It hadn't just been the theatre, though, and despite herself, Faye smiled at the recollection. It was the memory of her childhood visit to the Theatre Royal in Brighton, the memory of a time when everything had seemed innocent, uncomplicated and perfect. And it was the passion in Alessandro's voice when he had spoken of his childhood memories and of seeing his mother on stage. Faye understood about memories, even more so now. What could she do to help the Rinaldis? On the plane coming back here she had made some initial sketches and jotted down a handful of ideas, though planning permission would obviously be an issue if the structure of the building was to be altered in any way. She was looking forward to sharing her thoughts with Marisa – and Alessandro, of course – when she returned to Deriu.

But for now, she was determined to get some answers from her father.

'This is so awful,' she blurted when he returned and sat down opposite her. 'What's going on, Dad? I couldn't get anything out of Mum.'

She saw his shoulders droop slightly. He looked weary, she thought. As if retirement had edged him into a different time of life. 'I don't know what to say, love,' he told her. 'I really don't.' He handed her a menu. 'Nothing's "going on", as you put it. Your mother and I have just decided to go our separate ways.'

That again. Faye glanced down at the menu and made her choice. The waitress appeared and they ordered their food.

'I don't know what to say, either, Dad,' she said. 'I can't believe it. I can't understand it.'

He shook his head. 'Maybe it's for the best. Sometimes you stay with someone for the wrong reasons.'

'What sort of reasons?' And how could it be for the best? There was no one else involved. They would both be lonely apart.

'Because you're used to one another? Out of habit?'

Faye was stung. 'This is Mum you're talking about.'

'Yes.' He hung his head. 'Yes, of course. And I didn't mean it like that. Really. I don't know what I'm saying these days. Sorry, love.'

'It's alright, Dad.' She didn't want to upset him. Faye looked around the bar where they were seated. There was an old man with a border collie at his feet sitting in the corner supping a tankard of real ale, a young couple deep in earnest conversation at another table, and one or two locals at the bar. Faye was conscious of a weird sense of role reversal. 'Whose decision was it?' she asked.

He shrugged. 'A bit of both, I suppose.'

'Have you even thought it through?' She searched for the right words. 'Is there anything I can say to change your mind?'

'I don't think so, love, no.' He reached out and took her hand. 'I know you're upset, but we have to make our own minds up. Your mother and I, we have our own lives to live.'

Faye thought of Alessandro and what he'd said about parents not just being parents, but being individuals, too. 'But what will you do? Where will you go?'

'I don't know yet, Faye.' His voice sounded bleak, but there was something else. Some sort of light in his eyes.

This made her want to weep. 'Where does it leave me?' she asked.

'It's not about you, Faye, my love,' he said gently. 'I'm sorry, but it's not.'

'I know that.' She felt the tears pricking at her eyelids now. 'But it still affects me.' And neither of her parents seemed to understand.

'You're right,' he said. 'Of course it does.'

The waitress brought their food and Faye swallowed back the tears. She leaned forward. 'You could do more,' she said. 'You could talk to her again. You could try a bit harder.'

'Faye . . .' Her father shook his head and frowned. He picked up his fork and began to eat.

She prodded the salad next to the fish on her plate. The food looked delicious but she seemed to have lost her appetite.

'People grow apart,' her father said. 'It happens.'

But not to you, thought Faye. They were her parents. *Not to you*. 'Do you still love her, Dad?' she asked him just as she had asked her mother earlier. Because that was what it came down to, surely. 'Do you?'

'Faye.' He put out a hand and covered her hand with his. Once again, she was reminded of Alessandro and the warmth of his skin on the beach back in Sardinia. 'The truth is – I honestly don't know.'

CHAPTER 17

The first person Faye saw when she returned to Deriu was Enrico Volti. One of the Rinaldis had organised a taxi from the airport – Faye had half-expected Alessandro to meet her, but no doubt he was working in his boatyard; she shouldn't, she reminded herself, expect too much.

Enrico Volti couldn't have known she was returning to the town. His expression when he came stomping along the riverbank and saw her standing outside Fabio and Charlotte's house, gazing in reflection at the boats gently rocking on the water, the date palms and tall houses forming a colourful background beyond, was thunderous. Faye flinched, but stood her ground.

He walked right up to her, let loose a torrent of *Sardu*. Faye understood. He wasn't pleased to see her.

She straightened her back and faced it. 'You should talk to the Rinaldis,' she told him in Italian, which he must speak perfectly well – they all did. 'I'm not your enemy. This ownership dispute has nothing to do with me; I don't know anything about it.' She made a gesture of finality with the edge of her palm, sweeping it away. She had been wondering whether or not to head over to the theatre this afternoon and she was still frustrated from her abortive attempt to sort things out at home. Her parents' separation appeared to be a *fait accompli*. She was in no mood for bullies.

He looked surprised at the fact that she spoke Italian and Faye was glad that the fluency she'd developed during her time in Naples hadn't left her. She kept her gaze level and waited for his response. No doubt, like most bullies, he only took such an aggressive stance with someone he perceived to be weaker than him. 'You do not belong here, *Signorina*,' he growled, in Italian this time. 'You should leave right now. Go home.'

'Are you threatening me, *Signor*?' Faye kept her cool. During her time in Italy she had seen how the Mediterranean temperament could flare into anger one minute, dissolve into beaming smiles the next. She didn't think she had any reason to be scared – at least not yet.

His eyes narrowed. 'I am simply telling you, *Signorina*. If you know what is good for you, if you will listen to an old man who knows more than you of what goes on here in Deriu, if you have any sense at all – you will leave.'

'To make things easier for you, *Signor*?' Faye felt sorry for him – she remembered what Pasquale had told her about Enrico's daughter's disappearance – and she had sympathy for his views on the ownership of the theatre. But she would not be dictated to by a diminutive, wild-eyed Sardinian man who didn't even know her or what she hoped to achieve here.

He shrugged. 'It is of no matter to me,' he said.

Was it a front? She softened. 'Even if I were to leave, they'll only get someone else.'

'And I will continue to fight them,' he muttered.

His fists were clenched. Faye raised an eyebrow. 'You should try different tactics, *Signor*,' she said. 'You might find that people are more on your side than you think.'

Enrico's gaze slipped over her shoulder and Faye turned around to see Carmela scurrying along the riverbank path towards them. 'I am sorry, *Signorina*,' she said breathlessly to Faye. 'What has he been saying to you? He has not upset you, I hope?'

'Strangers,' spat Enrico, provoked by his wife's appearance into another outburst. 'They know nothing. Nothing. They come here. They interfere. They take our property—'

'Enrico,' Carmela soothed, plucking at the sleeves of her husband's raggedy jacket. 'No one has taken anything.'

'They know nothing of our customs, our lives, our village ways—'

'I'll listen if you want to tell me,' said Faye. 'I'd like to know more about Deriu and its people.'

'Eugh!' Enrico turned away in disgust. He shook his fist. 'You tell them I will not be giving up,' he said. 'You tell them I have a plan, that I will not make it easy for them. You tell them that the Rinaldis do not own Deriu as they think they do.'

Faye was surprised at his passion. She had already seen that he felt strongly about the theatre and the community, but he seemed to really have it in for the Rinaldis personally. 'You should tell them yourself, *Signor*,' she said. 'I'm not your messenger.'

For a moment there was a stalemate between them. Faye looked at this tobacco-skinned man, who was probably not much older than her father, his dark eyes burning with fury. She saw him getting the measure of her and then his expression changed, as if he were thinking of something – or someone – as if he were remembering . . . But before she could say anything more, he let out a snort of derision or frustration, or both, and stomped away.

Faye let out the breath she was holding. What had Charlotte said? *Simply enjoy yourself for a few weeks . . . It's a paradise . . . Relaxed holiday.* She was having a laugh.

'Please do not think badly of him, *Signorina*.' Carmela did not immediately follow her husband along the riverbank. 'You see, he has never been the same since our daughter Giorgia . . .'

'I'm so sorry, *Signora*,' said Faye. 'I heard about your daughter. Does your husband think——?' *That she was abducted*, she was going to say, which would explain his unfriendly behaviour to any stranger who came to town. But how did you say that to the girl's mother?

'That the Rinaldis are somehow responsible?' Carmela clicked her tongue and drew in a breath.

Hang on a minute. Faye blinked at her. That wasn't what she'd been going to say at all. 'Well, no, I thought . . .'

'Who knows what that man thinks?' Carmela looked towards her husband's diminishing figure as if he were a complete mystery to her.

'But can you tell me –' Faye touched her arm – 'why he's so passionate about the theatre belonging to the community? Is he a theatre lover himself?'

To her surprise, Carmela threw her head back and laughed – a full, throaty laugh. 'Him? No.' She put her hands on her hips; her expression grew serious. 'It is for Giorgia that he fights for the theatre.'

'For Giorgia? How can it be for Giorgia?'

'She loved the theatre.' Carmela's expression grew dreamy. 'She longed to act, to sing, to be on stage. She was always the centre of attention wherever she went, that girl of ours.' Her pale brown eyes filled with tears.

Faye could almost see the girl conjured up by her mother's words, so full of life. How sad it was that her parents didn't even know what had happened to her; it was a terrible thing to be unable to resolve the disappearance of your child. A thought occurred to her. 'Enrico supports the restoration of the theatre then?'

'Oh, yes.' She nodded. 'He does indeed. He is obsessed by it.'

'So why not let the Rinaldis do what they want to do? Why not let them pay for it to be restored?' Faye was confused. If the community could not afford legal fees to support their claim for ownership, then they could hardly afford the cost of repairs and restoration. They might get a grant of course, but that would be years in coming.

Carmela shook her head. 'He does not trust the Rinaldis,' she said. 'He does not trust them to do as they say they will, to look after the theatre. Or even the community, come to that. It is his pride. He does not want them to have anything to do with it.'

'But why not?' What had they done for him to feel like that?

But Carmela was already moving away as if she had said too much. 'I do not know anything, *Signorina*,' she said. 'That is all I can say.'

She followed her husband's footsteps, leaving Faye in even deeper reflection than before. What exactly was going on in Deriu? And whatever it was – did she really want to be a part of it?

An hour later and Faye was still trying to dismiss what Carmela and Enrico Volti had said to her. Strange things could happen when someone was dealing with the trauma of losing a child. They were both probably looking for someone else to blame. Faye had no doubts about Marisa and Alessandro's commitment to the theatre project, although it hadn't even progressed to the ideas stage yet. But she would see it through as promised. She had arranged to meet up with both Rinaldis tomorrow evening, she would share her ideas then and see what they thought. In the meantime, she'd refresh her memory on a few details by visiting the little theatre.

She climbed the crumbling steps and rooted for the key under the urn as before. But as she entered the foyer she heard voices – actually just one voice – coming from the auditorium. Faye stepped slowly inside. The theatre was dark but for a single, weak spotlight focused on the stage. The lilac curtain was raised and a lone man stood in its glow. She smiled. It was Pasquale de Montis and he was quoting lines – from Shakespeare, if she had to guess – in his own language. The dialect was fast but also musical. Faye closed her eyes to listen more clearly. The rhythm was not the same as Shakespearian English, but it had a beauty of its own. As for Pasquale – he was quite clearly lost in another world.

At the end of the monologue she gave a little clap and walked forward.

Pasquale jumped. 'Who is there?' he shouted, squinting into the light.

'Faye Forrester,' she called. 'Hello again, Pasquale.'

'Ah, it is you, *Signorina* Faye.' This seemed to calm him. He walked up to the edge of the stage and sat down. '*Buona sera*. Good evening to you.'

'You were rehearsing,' she said. 'I'm sorry to interrupt you.'

'Alas, no.' He observed her closely when she came within range of the spotlight. 'I was reminiscing. The good old days, you know?'

'I know.' She smiled.

'It is weak of me,' he said, returning her smile. 'Which is why I do it only in secret.' He held a finger to his lips and raised his eyebrows.

'I won't tell anyone,' she promised. He was a sweet man.

Ruled by his mother as much as by his love for the theatre, she guessed; there was an air of romantic nostalgia about him that drew her. And what was wrong with being lost in the world of the past, the world of the theatre he had adored? She sat beside him on the stage.

'So you are back in Deriu.' He nodded as if he had expected as much.

'I am, yes.'

'Because of the theatre?' he asked. 'Or because of Alessandro Rinaldi?'

She shot him a glance. How perceptive he was. She would never have guessed. But then, he behaved like someone on the sidelines of life, when he must so often have been centre stage.

'Because of the theatre,' she replied. For now. 'But tell me something.' She thought of Enrico Volti.

He spread his hands. 'Anything.'

'What would you like to see for the future of your town's theatre, Pasquale? How would you restore it if it were up to you?'

He seemed to consider this, feet dangling, head on one side. 'You are talking to the wrong man, Faye,' he said. 'May I call you Faye?'

'Yes, of course. But why is that? Why are you the wrong man?' She would have thought him the right one — at least the one closest to the theatre itself.

'Because I am deeply ashamed to say that I would not change it at all.'

Faye looked around her. The spotlight was still switched on and, through the cluster of dust motes, it illuminated a couple of broken planks that created a gaping hole in the stage, rotted folds in the lilac curtain, cobwebs matted into the ceiling and

167

some broken masonry left in a crumbling pile by the wings. 'You'd leave it in the state it's in at the moment?' she asked. 'Unused and closed to the general public?' She was surprised. 'Just so that you can come here and be alone on the stage with your memories?' She spoke gently — she didn't want to hurt him — but it was a selfish attitude, nonetheless.

'Not just because of that.' He let out a long sigh. 'I know you must think badly of me. I think badly of myself.' He gave her a mournful look. 'But I could not bear to think of other feet treading these boards, other men playing those parts, other voices speaking my lines.'

Faye saw the pain in his eyes. 'It must be hard,' she said. 'But wouldn't other productions being performed here bring back the memories of those times? Wouldn't it please you for the place to be revived? For you to see it again as it once was or even —' she took a breath — 'for it to be serving your community in other ways?'

'You think me selfish.' Pasquale fixed her with eyes as black as sloes even in the rays of the spotlight. 'But sometimes, the memories — they are too difficult, too heady. After I am dead, perhaps . . .'

'And your father?' Faye went on. 'What would he say about it? He was the caretaker here, wasn't he? How would he feel about the place looking like this? Wouldn't he want the theatre to be saved?'

'Saved?' He put his head to one side, considering. 'When you put it like that, yes, he would.' His expression changed. 'He was so good at saving things himself, you know.'

'I am sure he was,' said Faye. Poor Pasquale. She felt so sorry for him. 'So that is why you are on nobody's side.'

'Side?'

'In all this arguing about who owns the theatre.'

He smiled. 'It does not matter who owns it,' he said. 'The Rinaldis will get what they want.'

'Why do you think that?' Faye was curious.

'Because,' he said, 'they always do.'

CHAPTER 18

Faye was conscious of Alessandro's presence as soon as she entered Marisa's apartment that evening. He was standing on the far side of the large open-plan living room but quickly made his way towards her. 'Faye, how lovely to see you. A drink? Some wine perhaps? We have a local *Vermentino* chilling in the fridge.' His navy blue eyes gleamed. 'I heard that the vineyard owner grows the vines opposite the sea to make more of the reflected light.'

'Which may be why this one is rather strong.' Marisa rolled her eyes. 'Be warned.' She gave Faye a warm hug and seemed pleased to see her. So far, so good, thought Faye.

'Spoilsport.' Alessandro grinned and went to fetch the wine.

Which gave Faye a few moments to compose herself. She wondered if Marisa knew of their outing to the beach. Not that anything had happened exactly – nothing significant, that was – but they had at least established a connection, which Faye was certain didn't just exist in her imagination.

Alessandro set the glasses down on the table and came over. 'Faye.' He kissed her enthusiastically on both cheeks and she briefly inhaled the scent of him: the sweetness of wood and oil with that bitter streak of lemon; the scent of Sardinia, it seemed.

'It's great to see you, both of you.' Faye smiled. 'It's good to be back.' Mentally, she crossed her fingers. She hoped.

Alessandro poured the wine and passed around the glasses. 'To the three of us,' he toasted. 'And to *il Piccolo Teatro*.'

'Us and the theatre,' they echoed.

Faye took a sip of her wine. It was golden yellow and smooth and tasted of nectarines.

'So, Faye, could you start by telling us how the process works?' Marisa led the way over to the large central table where Alessandro had first put the tray of glasses.

Faye followed her. She knew that Marisa lived alone; her taste was reflected in the more feminine look of her apartment than Fabio and Charlotte's bigger place upriver. There was a large, ornate Venetian-style oval mirror on the wall opposite, a pretty glass lampshade on the ceiling above, and colourful cushions and a throw on the L-shaped sofa. The walls were painted a pale shade of chartreuse, and there were Moroccan-style rugs on the wooden floor. It was homely with a mish-mash of styles, the house of a woman whose career was more important than her home. She probably, Faye suspected, didn't have much spare time for considering decor. It was a good space though, with high-beamed ceilings and a lot of character. She'd love to get her hands on it.

Marisa was still talking. 'Do we discuss our ideas first? Do you make some drawings? How do we begin?'

'I need to know a bit more about what you both want,' Faye said. 'What sort of feel we're aiming for. And practical things, too – like the sort of numbers you envisage using the theatre, for example.'

They both nodded, apparently receptive. Good progress so far, thought Faye. 'But first and foremost, we need to agree on the concept,' she continued. 'Maybe we could do that tonight? Throw around some ideas and see how we go.'

'Of course.'

'I'll do some sketches while we talk.' Faye pulled her sketch pad out of her bag. She had already started a rough outline and made several notes. 'Later, I'll create some mood boards when I have more of an idea where we're heading style-wise.'

'Mood boards?' Alessandro raised an eyebrow.

Faye was not to be deflected. 'Mood boards,' she confirmed. 'They're pretty standard procedure, just ideas, really. To get a sense of atmosphere, style and . . .' She faltered.

'Mood?' he supplied.

'Exactly.' Faye looked down at her notes. 'We need to survey the space, of course. I'll measure up, take pictures, look around and check on things we need to address. Then we'll start drawing up the initial plans.'

'It's exciting.' Marisa's dark eyes shone.

Faye smiled. 'We'll also need a structural engineer to check any proposed structural changes to make sure the building will work on a practical level.'

She glanced across at Alessandro to gauge his reaction.

He shrugged. 'It all sounds possible,' he said guardedly.

Faye consulted her notes. One step at a time, she reminded herself. 'How hard is it to get building plans approved here in Sardinia?' she asked.

'Not hard,' Alessandro said. 'But definitely time-consuming.'

'That is the Sardinian way.' Marisa agreed with a smile.

'And is the theatre a listed building?' Faye had been concerned about this.

'No, it is not listed anywhere.' Marisa tapped her fingernails on the tabletop. 'According to *patrimonio culturale,* buildings like *il Piccolo Teatro* should be preserved and protected as artistic sites, but our theatre was derelict for so long that I think it was, how do you say, "off the radar"? Here we are fortunate, *non*?'

'We are.' Listed or protected buildings were always harder to work with. Architects and designers had less freedom, though there were more guidelines to follow, which could be helpful.

'What happens after that?' Marisa asked.

'Once the designer's plans are accepted by the relevant authorities for any architectural changes,' Faye went on – she was not going to assume that she would be the designer in question – 'you must employ a good contractor who understands your intentions and will follow the plans to the letter without cutting any corners. The designer will work on any new furniture and source what you need for the interior plan and decor.' She took a breath. 'Each phase will be signed off with you, the client, to make sure you're happy as work progresses. More or less, that's how it all works.'

'It is a long process.' Alessandro made the point again. He was watching her closely.

'It can be.'

'So you will be around a long time.'

Faye saw Marisa cast a surprised glance at her brother and she flushed. 'Not necessarily,' she said. 'I could be here at the start to help get things moving and make sure the plans reflect what you're looking for. Then you could employ a site manager to be here in situ.'

'You would trust a site manager with your plans?' Alessandro spread his hands. 'You would trust the builders in Sardinia?' Once again, he arched a dark eyebrow.

Faye couldn't tell how serious he was. 'We could liaise,' she said. 'And I could visit the site from time to time. Plus you two will be here to keep an eye on things.'

She could see them thinking about this. If the project had been in the UK, of course she would stay closer to it. But this was Sardinia – and anyway, they might decide after this initial meeting not to take things any further. She smiled. 'But we're getting ahead of ourselves.'

'Concept,' said Marisa.

'Concept,' Faye agreed. She took another sip of the rich white wine.

They spent the next hour and a half talking it through, Alessandro disappearing from time to time to top up their glasses. Marisa and Alessandro both wanted to retain the historical feel of the interior: the cylindrical bezel at the entrance adorned with swags and garlands, the three-level loggia and private boxes and especially the elegantly designed ceiling with its four medallions representing comedy, tragedy, melodrama and romance. They were so faded that they were practically unrecognisable at the moment; all the plasterwork, paintwork and stucco would need considerable restoration. The loggia and boxes were features reminiscent of the time when audiences would survey other theatre attendees as well as the stage, when theatre was a place for socialising and being observed as much as viewing a performance; they did not provide a direct focus for the spectator. They were integral to the theatre's history. The character of the little theatre was its best feature, and Faye agreed that they must retain it.

'But how can we bring it into the present day if we keep it exactly as it was?' Marisa asked.

'One thing we should consider is the seating,' Faye said. 'The stage, the ceiling and the entrance certainly provide the charm.

But the seats exist for the performances. What if the present seating was removed?' She loved the faded red brocade seating of the theatre, but it was lumpy and uncomfortable to sit on and far too restrictive for modern-day purposes. Besides, the cost of restoring it would take a large chunk out of their budget.

'So everyone has to stand?' Marisa frowned.

'No, no.' Faye drew a quick sketch with her pencil. 'You can get seating now that's removable and easily stored. There are various options — it depends on the flooring, but they're all quick to assemble and space-efficient, not to mention comfortable and stylish. I can show you some examples online.'

'Ah,' said Alessandro. 'Now you have it, now you don't.'

'Exactly. Portable seating has revolutionised the multi-functional venue industry. It means we can create a much more flexible space.'

'Multi-functional venue?' A shadow passed over Alessandro's brow. 'Flexible space?'

Faye slowed down. She recalled his reaction last time such possibilities had been mentioned. 'So the theatre can be used for other purposes. It can host casual events and more formal productions. It can become more complex, even ambiguous. It can adapt.'

'By multi-tasking?' Alessandro grinned.

'Exactly.' Faye was relieved that he was at least willing to consider it. In her view it was the only way to ensure the theatre's long-term survival. 'Having movable seating is useful for theatre productions as well,' she added. 'The director can be more innovative with staging. The audience isn't so —' she hesitated, again aware of their previous conversation on this subject — 'fixed'.

'What kind of events are we talking about?' asked Marisa.

Faye knew she still had to tread carefully. 'You tell me. What could your community here in Deriu do with a theatre space? Concerts? Exhibitions, perhaps?' Alessandro couldn't object to that, surely? 'If the seating was removed, the auditorium space would make a fabulous gallery for local artists to exhibit in.'

'*Si, si.*' Marisa clapped her hands. 'It would be perfect. The atmosphere of the theatre could add a whole new dimension to an exhibition.'

Faye nodded, pleased that she was getting the idea. 'And it also shows off the theatre,' she added. 'It brings people to the space. It adds a contemporary feel to the old theatre; a sense of vitality and optimism.'

'And maybe the auditorium could also be used for big meetings?' Marisa said. 'Conferences? Civic events?'

'Why not?' They must cater for a range of people with different practical requirements, also for visitors from other cultures who had diverse expectations and wanted a range of experiences. That was the future, as Faye saw it.

Marisa clicked her fingers. 'Farmers' markets,' she said. 'Local food stalls.'

'I am not so sure about that.' Alessandro was not looking so cheerful now. 'Do we want a food market in our theatre? It could be a bit messy, *non*?' He still thought of it almost as a sacred space, Faye realised.

'Wedding receptions!' There was no stopping Marisa now. 'Parties.' Her eyes sparkled. 'Big parties.'

'Whoa now.' Alessandro put both hands firmly on the table. 'It is a theatre, remember?' He caught Faye's eye. 'Primarily always a theatre, yes?'

'Yes,' she said. 'Primarily.' She exchanged a quick conspiratorial glance with Marisa. Sometimes new ideas had to come more slowly.

'Our theatre is not a party venue,' he said fiercely.

Marisa's dark eyes flared. 'But can you not imagine, Alessandro, how wonderful it would be? The whole village dancing in the auditorium?'

Alessandro shuddered. 'No. I cannot.'

'The point being . . .' Faye intervened. One thing at a time, she thought. Alessandro's objections could not be wiped away in one meeting, nor even in a day or month. It was important for him to still have his memories and his dreams. 'That it's a beautiful, atmospheric and usable space,' she finished. 'And that it can be used by the community for whatever you please – to promote the arts through inspiration and discovery.' She let that sink in. 'You two own the theatre –' and if Pasquale was to be believed, they would continue to do so, despite Enrico's efforts to the contrary – 'so you and Marisa get to decide what happens in it. As much or as little as you choose.'

Alessandro nodded slowly. 'It makes sense,' he said, 'if the theatre is being made use of . . .'

'Then it stays part of the community,' Marisa completed. 'And it survives. It serves our town of Deriu. And the townspeople will work hard to keep it going.'

Faye could see Alessandro mulling this over. It was hard for him, she could tell. She thought of Enrico Volti and Pasquale de Montis. All of them had their memories and their reasons for loving the little theatre. All of them had a vision for its future – even if their visions didn't completely coincide. But if only they could work together instead of against one another . . . Alessandro had such clear recollections of his mother performing on that stage; it meant so much to him, and Faye loved that. It was asking a lot for him to imagine something that must seem so different. Although she too loved the little theatre, Marisa didn't seem to have the same sense of nostalgia. But maybe Alessandro had been closer to his mother, or maybe Marisa was too young to remember so clearly. Marisa, Faye thought, was more of a pragmatist; Alessandro a dreamer.

'And what else could we do?' Marisa asked eagerly. 'How else could we change things?'

Alessandro shot his sister a disapproving look. 'Change is not always the answer,' he said.

'Buildings can develop according to need,' Faye said. 'They can breathe and live and evolve; they can grow new additions upward and outward through different interior design.' She looked from one to the other of them, trying to get her point across. This was what had attracted her to interior design in the first place, this sense of possibility and interaction. 'Buildings respond to the rhythms of the people using them. And the exterior changes too, of course.'

'Yes,' Alessandro said. 'It weathers and cracks.'

'Yes, it does.' Faye noticed that he was looking sceptical, but she'd had an idea. 'But even if the theatre becomes more contemporary, you can still hold on to the past.'

'How so?' He frowned.

'Well, for example, you could make the foyer into a sort of museum of memories.' Faye could see it in her mind's eye.

'A museum?' He leaned forwards, more interested now.

'With snapshots of the past.' Faye had seen this done in various venues in the UK. It would be a good way of holding on to the theatre's history, of keeping the historical connection alive. 'You know the sort of thing: pictures of how the building used to look back in its heyday, before it was restored, then during the restoration. Snapshots of old performances, the actors who performed here, and people like your father and mother and grandparents who owned the theatre and helped keep it alive. Ticket stubs, old programmes,' she went on. 'Anything of interest to visitors of the theatre.'

'What a great idea,' enthused Marisa.

'It could look fantastic,' Alessandro agreed.

Fantastic. A big word. Faye was encouraged. She grinned at him and, almost to her surprise, he grinned back. 'People would come to the theatre because it's such a beautiful building,' she went on. 'Or it will be, once we're finished. Then they'd see the display, get a sense of the history, have the whole story.'

'It would inspire them to visit an exhibition or a play.' Once again Marisa took up where Faye left off. 'Or a musical event, perhaps.' She nudged her brother. 'What do you think, Alessandro?' She turned to Faye. 'The auditorium has amazing acoustics.'

'It all sounds good,' said Alessandro. He was looking approving now. 'I like the idea of the photographs of the past. And the foyer is quite big. Photos on the walls, do you think?'

'Or in display cases.' Faye wondered about suggesting a small café; she had seen this work very well. But perhaps she would save that one for later.

'And a few old programmes, did you say?' Marisa glanced at her brother again. 'Alessandro has a whole pile over at his place. Photographs, too. Masses of them. He is such a hoarder.'

As she had thought – one foot rooted in the past. Faye smiled at Alessandro, who gave her a modest smile in return. 'It is true,' he said. 'They are my souvenirs.'

'You could even have some Deriu tourist information leaflets available from the box office if you wanted to,' said Faye. 'Why not? You could make the little theatre the hub of the community.'

'The hub of the community,' Alessandro repeated. Faye could tell that he liked that.

'A tasteful hub,' she teased. They exchanged a look and Faye felt a small shiver run through her. This time, she had enjoyed the process of bouncing ideas from one to another. She really felt that they were getting somewhere.

'I can't wait to get started.' Marisa looked excited as a child. 'Perhaps I could organise an art competition for the children. A new sign for the theatre? We could show the best ones in the foyer on opening night.'

Opening night . . . Faye smiled. Marisa was really looking ahead. 'It would benefit the entire community,' she said. 'And it would bring more visitors to Deriu.' She hesitated. 'If you want them, that is.' She guessed that tourists were not universally appreciated by those who lived on the island. But arguably, they were needed.

Alessandro gave a non-committal shrug. 'It is our future,' he said. 'We have lost most of our past industry.'

Faye thought once again of that deserted mining village. So much had been taken from this landscape and yet it was still stunningly beautiful, rugged and unspoilt.

'You are right.' Alessandro picked up his glass and took a slow sip of the wine. 'Tourism will increase. Our island has a lot to offer, do you not think?' He addressed this to Faye. And although his question was casual, it seemed loaded with meaning.

'Oh yes,' she said. 'Fabulous food, a great sense of history, glorious beaches . . .'

Marisa looked from one to the other of them. 'Speaking of

food,' she said, 'time for a snack, I think.' She got to her feet and moved to the kitchen area.

Alessandro watched her go. Then he turned his attention back to Faye, leaning closer so that she could feel the warmth of his proximity, so that she was aware of the scent of his skin. 'And how are things with you, Faye?' he asked. 'Did you find out what you needed to know back home?'

'Not really.' Faye fingered the stem of her wineglass. Not at all, actually. She was still struggling with it, still feeling unsettled. She hesitated. She hardly knew this man, but he seemed to invite her confidences. 'I feel as if my parents don't match my memories of them any longer,' she said. 'As if they've become different people somehow. Or maybe they always were.' Would he understand?

Alessandro sat back in his seat, let out a sigh and glanced towards the kitchen area to check that Marisa was out of earshot. For the moment, she was. 'And now you wonder,' he said thoughtfully, 'all these years. Were they just pretending?'

'Yes.' That was it exactly. She wondered how he knew.

They were silent for a moment, digesting this, and then Marisa reappeared with a tray of food. 'Here we are,' she said.

'Wow.' It was a feast.

'We have pecorino Sardo and some salami; this is *bastone di cardinal*.' She pointed.

'Cardinal's stick?' Faye tried a literal translation.

'*Si*. It's a sweet salami made with dried and candied fruits and nuts.' She moved on. 'The twisty biscuits are *acciuleddi*.' She offered the plate to Faye.

Faye took a bite. 'They taste a bit like deep-fried sweet pasta.' She recalled the *frappe* she had eaten at a *festa* in Naples. 'They're delicious.'

'We drizzle them with honey.' Marisa looked justifiably proud of her simple snacks. 'And this is *ficareddi* – a kind of figgy macaroon.'

Faye had never heard of this one, either. She had a taste.

'They're made with ground almonds,' Marisa told her. 'With *liquore di mirto.*'

'Ah.' Now this Faye had heard of, though she had not yet tried it. The infamous Sardinian *digestivo* made from purple myrtle berries. Now that she'd identified the shrub from the beach she'd visited with Alessandro and the little tree in *Piazza del Teatro*, she'd seen the myrtle tree almost everywhere she went on the island. The white flowers were fully open now and the aromatic scent of the myrtle – like aniseed mixed with orange blossom – seemed to hang in the very air.

They ate and drank and chatted of other things before Marisa cleared away the food and they returned to the subject of the theatre.

'How would you change the theatre structurally?' Alessandro asked Faye. 'If it were up to you?'

'We should ask a good builder to take a look at the place before we decide anything,' Faye said. 'And the structural engineer. But I was thinking it might be possible to build an extension at the back, if funds allow.' There was currently a small patch of wasteland at the back of the building that she assumed was part of the original plot. It seemed a shame not to utilise it, but the work wouldn't be cheap and it depended on how far the Rinaldis wanted to go.

'What would we use it for?' Alessandro asked.

Faye considered. 'Workshops, maybe? Writing workshops? Art workshops? A small and intimate studio space for people to come and learn a craft?'

'Great idea,' Marisa said. 'It is so cramped at the back there – especially in the dressing rooms. Maybe we could enlarge those a bit while we're doing it. And there is a room at the end used for costumes which is just wasted space.' For a moment her voice faltered.

'Marisa?' Faye wondered if she was having second thoughts.

But she shook her head and regained her composure. 'The place – it gets to me sometimes,' she said.

'The theatre?'

'The theatre, Deriu . . .' She grew quiet. 'The memories,' she whispered.

Alessandro grasped her hand. 'Do not worry, little one,' he said. 'We will do it – you and I. It will come together – you will see.'

Marisa nodded.

But Faye wondered. Did Marisa want to leave Sardinia? And if so, was the restoration of the theatre keeping her here, or the job she loved? What about her boyfriend in Rome? Or was there more to it? She sensed something deeper, some darker sadness hidden in Marisa's eyes.

She brought her attention back to their discussion and looked down at her sketch pad. 'I think we need a centrepiece. Something special which represents our concept somehow.' She had been thinking about this; it was why she had wanted to return to the theatre yesterday afternoon.

'Do you have something in mind?' Alessandro had let go of his sister's hand but his expression remained serious.

'There's a beautiful rose window in the foyer,' Faye said. 'I think we could make much more of it.'

'For example?'

'Have you noticed how it frames the sea?' She turned to face him. His eyes were the blue of the sea, as a matter of fact. Not when it was calm, but when a storm was approaching.

'I have, yes.' A small smile twitched at his lips. Another connection, she thought. She actually felt it.

'At the moment it lacks impact,' Faye said. 'There are too many glazing bars and some of the glass is obscured. We might consider one clear plate-glass oval window to maximise the sea view.'

'Perfect,' said Alessandro.

'After all,' said Faye, 'this is your little theatre by the sea.'

'I like that.' Alessandro's eyes gleamed. 'Our little theatre by the sea.' He let his gaze drift beyond her to some point unknown. 'And perhaps we can think of another way to make the rose window more of a focal point? Maybe something decorative around the frame?'

Faye watched him considering the problem and she smiled to herself. This was a turning point. He had made a positive contribution. It meant that he was now fully on board.

She leaned back in her seat with satisfaction. She felt that they had gone as far as they could tonight. They needed to consolidate and reflect before they moved on to the next stage. 'So to sum up, our concept is to bring the theatre into the twenty-first century and make it a vibrant hub of the community – the arts centre of the town – combining the new with the old through strong connections to its theatrical history.' She looked from one to the other of them. 'Are we agreed?' They nodded their assent.

Alessandro got to his feet, long and lazy, and went to fetch the wine.

'We were right to ask you to come back,' he said when he returned. He looked into her eyes, just for a moment.

Faye found herself wondering what was behind them. If eyes were the windows of the soul, then what could she learn about Alessandro Rinaldi?

He refilled their glasses with a flourish. 'To our concept for *il Piccolo Teatro*,' he said.

'Our concept.'

CHAPTER 19

'She is back then? Eugh.'

Pasquale glanced up from his dominoes. He had been waiting for this, of course. It was one of the reasons he had come to the Caffe Rosa tonight. To see which way the wind might be blowing. The speaker – Enrico Volti – clearly did not require an answer to his question. And Pasquale did not need to ask whom he was talking about. They had their share of tourists in Deriu, but the *Signorina* Faye – she was not a tourist, and they all knew it.

'You saw her?' Pasquale selected his tile and played it. There were four of them in the game tonight so they were playing the block version and the boneyard – the home for the spare tiles – was empty.

Tomasso and Jiseppu shifted uneasily in their seats. Jiseppu took a swig of beer. Neither said a word. They were Enrico's henchmen – they would always wait for his lead.

Enrico swore softly. '*Si*. I saw her.'

Tomasso took a draw of his cigarette, coughed noisily and made his play. Jiseppu frowned and followed suit. They exchanged a look. Pasquale ignored them. Enrico was the one to listen to, the one to beat. He might have lost the light of his life, he might have lost his money, but the old bastard still knew how to win at dominoes.

'Where?' Pasquale asked.

'Up by the river.' Enrico fingered his tiles, picked up one, and tapped it on the table with a light clackety-clack. 'Looked very much at home. Answered back to me, she did.'

She would, thought Pasquale. A man would never be able to tell that one what to prepare for his dinner. But he didn't blame her. It wasn't her fault that she had been dumped here in Deriu by that friend of hers who was also an outsider, without the least idea of what and who she was taking on. Like a lamb to the slaughter. He clicked his tongue.

'Who is she, anyway?' growled Jiseppu. 'Where is she from?' He lifted a hand to indicate to Rosa that he required more beer. Rosa ignored him. She wiped the top of the bar clean and began washing the glasses used by a group of people who were just leaving. She'd bring the beer over in her own good time.

Pasquale watched as Enrico placed his tile end-to-end with the eight that was already there. The other side was a blank, damn it. They'd been shuffled and the tiles stood on edge so there was no way he could see, but it was as if he knew what Pasquale had in his corner. The other end of the chain was no use to him; he'd be forced to use his last blank. 'She is from England,' he told them, pleased to convey the information, happy to be the man who knew. 'She is an "interior designer".' He gave these last words a special emphasis, placed his tile on the table end-to-end with Enrico's and didn't meet the other man's eye.

'Interior designer – pah!' Enrico swore again.

Tomasso and Jiseppu both laughed so much that Jiseppu nearly rocked himself off his rickety wooden chair. Tomasso spluttered as he took another swig of beer. Pasquale held back. His mother didn't like it when he came home reeking of alcohol and she always let her views be known at the highest vocal pitch possible. Besides, he liked to stay in control. He enjoyed the comradeship of these men in the bar, he liked playing dominoes, and he relished a chat about village affairs. But at heart he had always been a bit of a loner.

People didn't realise that because they only saw what was right in front of their faces. People were – mostly – unaware of complexity. Just because a man liked to be on stage, performing in a theatrical production – just because he savoured being the centre of attention at certain times – didn't mean that he didn't also enjoy being in the wings at other times; watching, waiting, listening. Pasquale watched as the others played their hands.

'What does she want then?' Tomasso asked. He grimaced, displaying nicotine-stained teeth. 'What does she want with our theatre?' He spoke freely – they all spoke freely – because they were the only ones in the bar now that the last group of people had gone. The younger villagers went to Bar Portici to watch the sport, the football; Rosa's was the old way of life.

Pasquale repressed a sigh. 'She is employed by the Rinaldis,' he said.

Enrico swore again. Pasquale wondered how much he'd had. Time was when Enrico Volti hadn't bothered much with the bar, the dominoes or the beer. But the man had lost his love of life when he lost his daughter, that was for sure. Pasquale crossed himself at the thought and Enrico shot him an enquiring look.

'Hey – Rosa!' Jiseppu shouted again. 'Do you not have beer to sell, eh? What are you waiting for, my love? I am here. My glass is empty. I am still waiting for you as I have waited all my life. What does a man have to do to get a drink?'

'He has to be patient,' Rosa yelled back. Nevertheless she

poured the beer and brought it over, her flat shoes flapping on the old flagstones. Jiseppu reached out a hand to pat her generous bottom but she saw it coming and slapped it away. He shrugged.

'So what will happen?' he asked, returning to the subject, and Pasquale was pleased to note that he addressed the question to Pasquale as much as to Enrico. That was how things were when you listened to what was going on around you as Pasquale did. You learned things. This gave a man power – the power of knowledge, and the power to change things sometimes.

Pasquale shrugged. 'They will go ahead with the restoration, my friend.' He glanced at Enrico who was staring in front of him as if in a daze. 'Unless someone stops them,' he added. Though why should they want to stop them? The Rinaldis were putting their hands in their pockets. Did they not want the old theatre to be restored? They did not, after all, have Pasquale's agenda to consider. Did it really matter so much who owned it? But it did, of course it did. There was pride at stake, there was dignity. There was the past and there was the future.

Jiseppu and Tomasso shifted their dominoes and drank more beer. Tomasso was still smoking and the fug of cigarette smoke hung heavy in the small bar although the doors were open to the night air.

'Can we stop them?' Jiseppu asked Enrico.

Enrico played his tile. It was a double blank. Pasquale sighed. He knocked on the battered wooden table to signify that he was unable to play.

'We could try.' Enrico grinned mirthlessly at Pasquale, his black eyes glinting. 'We could have another meeting. Discuss our next move. Eh, Tomasso?'

Tomasso nodded, grunted, played his next piece.

What was the point, Pasquale wondered, of all these meetings? As they all knew, the people of Deriu were powerless. Without money, how could they fight the Rinaldis?

'They will get what they want.' It was as if Jiseppu had read his mind.

'They have always owned the village.' Tomasso agreed with a glum expression. He lit another misshapen cigarette from the butt of the old one and inhaled sharply.

Enrico hit the table with his fist and they all jumped, the dominoes shuddering too. 'They will not always own it,' he muttered. 'Not while I have breath in my body.'

'But what can we do?' Tomasso asked. 'How can we stop them?'

The play went on. Pasquale drummed his fingers on the table-top. The conversation was like the chain of dominoes on the table. It went on, it doubled back, it repeated itself; there was only so far it could ever go. Pasquale had been party to this discussion so many times over the past weeks. But as Enrico had said before – without money, what could they do? Pasquale had more reason to hate the Rinaldis than anyone – except perhaps Enrico – but even he could not think of a way to stop them getting what they wanted.

'We could scare the girl away.' Jiseppu raised his scraggy eyebrows.

Pasquale flinched. He did not like that idea. 'They will only get someone else.'

'Can we do nothing?' Jiseppu too knocked on the table. 'Pass.' Just the two of them had a chance of winning the game now. 'We must do something.'

'Ask Pasquale here what we can do. He knows about the theatre.' Enrico gestured towards him and Pasquale felt a rare flush of pride. His mother might think him a fool, not fit to be called the son of his father, but Enrico Volti knew that he was worth more. Enrico Volti knew that he had more to give.

The other two looked his way. Pasquale shrugged modestly.

'He talks to the Rinaldis.' Enrico glared at him with those beady black eyes. 'You talk to the girl too. I've seen you.'

Pasquale dismissed this with a casual wave of his hand. He had used the exact same gesture once when he was playing Lear. 'Why not?' he said. 'That is how you find out things.'

'What things?' Enrico growled.

Pasquale wasn't sure how much to say. He was aware that he was playing a dangerous game. 'The theatre – it may prove too challenging a project for them in the end,' he suggested.

'You mean they will give up?' Enrico looked interested.

'Perhaps.'

Jiseppu shifted in his seat once again. 'Or we make them give up,' he said.

'And the ownership of the place . . .?' Enrico had a devilish look in his eyes now.

Pasquale gestured. 'There are ways.' He had not really thought about what ways there might be – only that he did not want anything in the theatre to change. But if he could achieve that aim in some other manner . . .

'You must find out those ways.' Enrico leaned forwards so that his face was close to Pasquale's. 'You must go inside.'

'Inside?'

'You have talked to her,' Enrico said. 'Maybe she trusts you – *si*?'

'Maybe.' Pasquale would like to think that he inspired trust more than most. He was nice to people, not an aggressive old lech like Jiseppu or an embittered old devil like Enrico. Pasquale was older in years and he was wiser. He had no wish to threaten anyone.

'So you go inside, you find out everything that is going on and . . .'

'We find a way to stop it,' Jiseppu finished for him. He punched his fist into his own palm.

'*Si*.' Enrico raised his glass.

'Well . . .' Pasquale didn't see how he could refuse. He was a villager of Deriu and he hated the Rinaldis. Faye was a nice girl, but when it came to loyalties . . .

Enrico played his penultimate tile. It was a blank–twelve. Naturally. Pasquale could do nothing. Neither could Jiseppu nor Tomasso – as expected. 'So.' Enrico played his final domino.

'Well played, my friend.' Pasquale got to his feet and clapped Enrico on the back. It was time to return home, his mother would be fretting.

'We will meet here, tomorrow at six,' Enrico said. 'And talk about it some more, eh?'

Pasquale nodded. But what did it really matter who owned the theatre – the Rinaldis or the rest of the town? What mattered was how to stop the restoration, how to keep the theatre exactly as it was now so that Pasquale could still tread the boards, still read the lines, still pretend that she was with him, and that nothing, nothing had changed.

CHAPTER 20

Faye dressed with more care than usual that evening, eventually choosing a simple apple-green linen shift dress that she wore with her brown leather sandals and a gold bracelet bought by her parents for her eighteenth birthday, still her favourite piece of jewellery. Her fair hair hung loose and she kept her make-up light and understated. She didn't want to look as if she'd made too much of an effort, but . . . well, it was a big but.

She was meeting Alessandro for dinner in a restaurant in the old town.

'I have some photographs I would like to show you,' he had said.

Faye didn't know whether the meeting and the photographs were connected to the theatre project or not, but she was keen to go. Not because she was looking for romantic involvement with him, she told herself firmly – though she couldn't deny that he had an effect on her – but she still suspected him of being a bit of a Lothario and she hadn't forgotten what Enrico Volti had told her; besides, as she kept telling herself, this was a business relationship. But he and his family intrigued her. She'd like to get to know both Alessandro and his sister a bit better.

Alessandro was already sitting at an outside table under a pergola, a green vine winding its untidy way through the trellising. He jumped to his feet and grinned as she approached. It was a nice grin, she thought; he seemed more relaxed tonight. He was wearing dark cotton chinos and a loose, pale blue shirt, his hair just long enough to curl over the collar. '*Buona sera*, Faye.'

'*Buona sera*, Alessandro. What a lovely place.' The restaurant was housed in an old building with a candyfloss-pink facade, a bougainvillea the colour of dark red wine clambering up the wall. The entrance was through an archway edged with old grey stone and there were candles and fresh flowers on the brightly chequered tablecloths, both inside and out.

'You look beautiful. *Bellissima . . .*' He kissed her hand, holding it a fraction longer than necessary. His navy eyes gleamed.

Faye smiled at the extravagance of the gesture and the compliment. She hadn't realised men still did that – even Sardinian men.

'Come. Sit down.' He held out her chair for her.

Faye saw that he had already ordered wine and as she sat at the table, he whipped around to the other side to pour some into her glass. 'Thank you.'

'I thought we would try a *Cannonau* tonight, from a local vineyard,' he said.

'It sounds lovely.'

'And you are warm enough – to sit out here?'

'Oh, yes. It's much nicer.' He was being very solicitous tonight, really trying to please. Faye looked around her. She would always prefer to eat al fresco if possible. How often could you do that in England? From here, she could see two tall date palms standing sentinel outside the old chapel at the end of the narrow cobbled street, a small bell tower at the top, a statue of Christ in a niche beside. And next door but one she spotted the swinging sign of the *panetteria*, depicting some of the traditional loaves of bread available inside, where durum wheat and the old kneading methods were still used to this day. Certainly, everything Faye had sampled from there so far had tasted good. The tall houses in the street were squeezed against one another, leaning forward as if to find more room, or to meet their opposite number at roof level; a jumble of peeling paintwork, exposed stone, weathered wrought-iron balconies and wooden doors; ochre merging into mint green into turquoise into hot pink. The street was putting on quite a show.

'Thank you for agreeing to meet me, Faye,' he said. His voice was soft and low, as if they shared some secret.

Faye felt a frisson of anticipation. She sipped the wine. Violets and liquorice. It was delicious. 'I couldn't resist.'

'Ah, yes, the photographs.' He smiled.

'Of the little theatre?' she asked.

'*Si*. Let's order,' he said. 'And then I will show you.' She could sense his excitement and was touched that he wanted to share the pictures with her.

Alessandro chose *malloreddus* to start, a pasta made from semolina and saffron, he told her, and chicken cooked with fennel, olives, and white wine for his main; Faye decided to try the *bottarga*, a type of caviar made from the roe of grey mullet, and spaghetti with clams in a basil and tomato sauce.

While they waited for the food, Alessandro pulled a large brown envelope from the bag slung over his chair with the air of a magician. He held the envelope almost tenderly, before pushing aside their glasses, cutlery and napkins and sliding the contents out on to the table between them. The photographs were in colour, black and white, and sepia, all sizes, some battered and well-worn, others with the print still shiny. He smoothed them out with long brown fingers.

Faye leaned across. They showed the exterior and interior of the little theatre, and actors on stage during various performances. *Il Piccolo Teatro* was almost unrecognisable from the shadowy, dusty place she had been thinking about so much lately; here, it was vibrant, colourful and alive – with props, actors, a background set.

Carefully, Alessandro picked up a photograph from the top of the pile. 'This is my mother, Sofia Rinaldi,' he said. 'Or "Sofia Santi" as she was known in the theatre world.'

Faye heard the love and pride in his voice. She took the photo from him and examined it. There was a bower of flowers positioned behind the elegant woman on stage. Her hair was swept up and she was dressed in full blood-red Elizabethan finery; it must have been a traditional production. 'She's beautiful.' And her son looked like her. He had the same cheekbones, the same dark hair and proud tilt to the head. 'Which play was this?'

'Your William Shakespeare,' Alessandro replied. '*Much Ado about Nothing*. My mother played Beatrice, one of her favourite characters.'

'So you remember her performing?'

'Vividly.' His blue eyes glazed over with the memory. 'My father often allowed me to watch from one of the boxes.'

'How exciting.' Faye thought of her own childhood memory of the Theatre Royal in Brighton. It had been so thrilling to sit high up in the top balcony looking down, to see the lights dim and the curtain rise, to enter this other world. She could only imagine how incredible it must have been to watch your own mother perform.

'It was my father who took most of the photographs,' Alessandro told her. 'He was very proud of her, naturally. He loved to watch her.'

'How did they first meet?' Faye asked. 'Was it through the

theatre?' She handed the photo back to him and felt the light, almost imperceptible, brush of his fingertips against her skin.

'It was, yes,' said Alessandro. 'My mother came on tour here from Italy when she was quite young.'

'And your father owned the theatre?'

'Not then.' Alessandro took a sip of his wine and picked up another photograph. He smiled and shook his head. 'My mother worked with Pasquale de Montis at that time. They were colleagues. They even toured the UK in a theatre company together.'

'Really?' Faye thought of the man she'd heard reciting lines on the stage of the little theatre a few days ago. Even now old Pasquale had a certain presence about him, although he seemed diminished, as if his life had not turned out quite the way he had hoped.

Alessandro was nodding. 'Ah, yes. It was Pasquale who encouraged her to come here to Deriu to work with him. And when she did . . .' He shrugged. 'My grandfather owned the theatre and his son had the love of it in his blood. My mother married him, and the rest, as they say, is history.'

'It's a romantic story.' Faye watched him as he sorted gently through the photographs on the tabletop. She could see how much it all meant to him, how his memories of the theatre had been reinforced by the emotions connected with it, the romance between his parents, their shared love of the place. And she could see why he wanted to recreate its splendour and how hard it was for him to see the theatre project as something that concerned the rest of the community. She let her gaze drift out to the street once more, to the *centro storico* of Deriu, now tinged with pink and yellow in the evening light. But it was a community – and perhaps it was up to her to make him see.

Alessandro continued to flip through the photographs. 'As for me, I could hardly believe that this graceful lady in the fancy costume and make-up was my mother.' He smiled at the memory. 'Not that she was not graceful at home, you understand. But on stage she was transformed. A creature from another world.' He set down the photographs for a moment to pour them both more wine.

His words struck a chord with Faye. She thought about how actors could transform themselves – the magical nature of make-believe. And she thought about the transformation she and the Rinaldis hoped to achieve for the theatre. She felt sorry for Pasquale, who nourished a hope that nothing would change. But everything changed; it had to. Life must move on. Even for those such as Enrico and Carmela Volti who had lost their daughter Giorgia but were still willing to fight for the little theatre. Despite his hostility towards her, Faye felt sympathy for him, too. And who knew how many others there were in this village who had their own memories of *il Piccolo Teatro*. She looked at the man sitting opposite her, still engrossed in the photographs that lay on the table between them. Her loyalty must be to the Rinaldis – she was working for them, after all – but she hoped to be sensitive to other people's needs as well.

Their starter came and went as they continued to pore over the photographs, briefly nudging them to one side so that they had room to eat. Faye's *bottarga* was good; she loved the deceptive simplicity of Sardinian recipes and produce. Alessandro laughed when she mentioned this. 'Did you know that in Sardinia we have more people aged over a hundred years than in any other place?' he asked her.

Faye raised an eyebrow. 'No, I didn't.'

'It is due to our genetics and our diet.' He lifted his wine glass. 'And to our wine, *naturalmente.*'

'Oh, naturally.' She agreed with a smile. She was seeing another side of the man tonight, she thought. A man who was not only proud of his heritage and his family, but also one who knew how to live, enjoy life and have fun. She thought of the secret bay he'd taken her to. Maybe there would be an opportunity to go back there, after all . . .

'*Ah, si.* There is also the pure air.' He breathed in deeply. 'The quality of the water. And the exercise we get from climbing all these alleyways and steps.' He lifted his glass again in a toast. '*A chent'annos.* That is what we say on someone's birthday: "May you live to be a hundred".' He grinned. 'Or more.'

Faye smiled too. She looked back at the photos and spotted a dapper-looking man in Elizabethan dress, cap included. 'Is this Pasquale de Montis?'

'Yes, it is.' But Alessandro's attention did not linger on the photo.

Pasquale and Sofia must have been very good friends if they travelled and worked together for such a long time, she thought. It was nice to see Pasquale not just on the stage of his beloved theatre, but in full costume, taking part in a proper performance.

'After my parents married,' Alessandro went on, 'he did not so often play the main parts, old Pasquale.'

'Why not?'

'I have no idea. Possibly he lost his touch.' Alessandro shrugged. 'Or maybe some other actor came along and took his place, who knows?'

'Poor Pasquale.' Faye felt another wave of sympathy. He so wanted to remember the good old days, and yet the truth was that he had been replaced while still – presumably – in his prime, while his friend and colleague Sofia continued to dazzle – and even married the theatre owner's son while she was at it. 'But your father didn't act?'

'My father – no.' He raised an eyebrow at this. 'Not on the stage anyhow.'

An interesting comment. Faye recalled how quickly Alessandro had understood what she'd told him about her parents, and what he'd said about people pretending. If her parents had only been pretending to love one another – though surely they had loved one another once? – then why had they done so? For Faye's sake? Did this, she pondered, make it easier to forgive?

Faye watched Alessandro's expression as he finally collected up the photographs and replaced them in the envelope with a small sigh. She had the strangest urge to reach out her hand and stroke his dark hair back from his face. If she did that, she wondered, what would he do?

Looking at those pictures he had seemed transfigured – she had glimpsed a younger and happier man, a boy who'd adored his mother and who must have been devastated when she died. Not for the first time, she wondered why Alessandro had not married. He wasn't much older than Faye, she guessed, and no doubt he usually had a beautiful woman in tow, like Jana, from the marina. Had he been hurt by someone? She doubted that somehow; unfortunately, she could imagine that he might be the one doing the hurting. She thought again of Jana. What exactly was their relationship? And was it as ongoing as it had appeared to be?

The waiter put their main courses in front of them and they began to tuck in.

'I thought the photographs might help you see how *il Piccolo Teatro* once was,' Alessandro said.

'Oh, they did. It must have been magical.' Faye appreciated seeing those images first-hand. 'And it will be again.' She hoped. 'It would be great to get some of those photos reprinted for the theatre's living history museum.'

He seemed pleased at this idea. 'I will do that.' And for a few moments they ate in silence.

Faye hesitated to broach the subject, but there was so much more she wanted to know, and seeing the photographs had piqued her curiosity even more. 'Do you mind me asking – how old were you, when your mother died?'

'I was a teenager,' he said. 'Not yet eighteen.'

'It must have been very hard for you.' Her hand slid across the table to rest on his, just for a moment. She squeezed his hand before letting go.

'It was.' He took a forkful of chicken and fennel though he didn't bring it to his mouth. Faye could smell the aniseed of the fennel and the tomato and herbs drifting up from the food. 'She died nineteen years ago, but I still miss her every day.' His voice was choked with emotion.

Her heart went out to him. 'You were close then?'

'Very.'

Faye twisted some spaghetti around her fork. She wondered whether or not to ask what she wanted to ask.

'You are wondering how she died?' he said, after a moment.

'Well . . .' She didn't want to be insensitive. But, 'Yes, I was.' Was that very morbid? She wondered what else might be written on her face; she should take care.

He frowned. Faye could almost feel him withdrawing into himself, into his sadness. 'There is a road. It is not far from here.'

He took a sip of his wine, paused, as if remembering. 'It is called the *via della morte*.'

Faye's eyes widened in horror. 'Have a lot of people died there?' It certainly sounded a road to avoid. 'Why? Is it danger-ous? *Briganti?*' She'd heard that Sardinia's interior had boasted many gangs of bandits not so long ago, though she thought that was in the past.

'*Briganti, non.*' He shook his dark head. 'It is very steep, very high, very winding.' He regarded her intently. 'You have seen something of our island already; you know how things are here.'

She nodded. She thought she knew what was coming.

'There is not always a crash barrier. There are no lights at night. The islanders drive too fast and weave around to get where they want to go.'

Faye speared a *vongole* with her fork. 'But why does anyone even use such a road?'

'You would ask this.' He shook his head. 'But it is not as you would think. The locals, they use the road every day. And my parents, they were on it the night Mama died.'

'Oh, Alessandro . . .' What could she say? 'You mean there was an accident? Your mother was killed on the road?'

'*Si.*' His mouth was a tight line. The atmosphere had changed between them, moved from cheerful to serious, from light to dark in an instant.

'What happened?' Faye whispered.

He pushed the food left on his plate to one side. 'She had been working very hard and was at the end of a long run. They had gone out to dinner in Sassari to celebrate. My father was driv-ing. She was in the passenger seat.'

Faye waited, anxious.

Alessandro took a shallow breath. 'A car was coming towards

them too fast. The headlights were too bright. My father swerved to avoid it. He was too close to the edge. The car went over—' He stopped, clearly overcome.

Again Faye reached out; this time she put her hand gently on his arm. 'I'm so sorry, Alessandro. I shouldn't have asked. Please don't say any more if it's too difficult.' He had spoken with bitterness and she found herself wondering if there was more to the story. But she decided not to ask. What more *could* there be? She shook the thought away. She was no doubt being over-imaginative.

Alessandro swallowed hard and composed himself. 'It was not a sheer drop at that point,' he continued. 'The car skidded, came off the road and turned over. Another car went into it from behind. My father was badly injured: he broke three ribs and his ankle. He had a concussion, too. My mother . . .' His voice broke. 'They think she died on impact.'

There was a heavy silence between them.

'I'm so sorry,' Faye said at last. She put her fork on her plate and pushed it aside. 'How tragic. What a terrible waste.' She paused. 'Your father must have been heartbroken.' That was why he had closed the theatre after his wife's death, Faye recalled.

'Yes, he was.' Alessandro's eyes had filled and he gripped Faye's hand tight. 'We all were.' He sat back and slowly released her hand.

Faye's skin was tingling. She wondered again about Sofia and Bruno. Marisa had told Faye that her parents were a golden couple and even Faye's parents had spoken highly of Bruno Rinaldi. But some of the villagers in Deriu seemed to think rather differently. 'And the other car?' she whispered.

'The other car?' He seemed to snap himself back to the present with some difficulty.

'Who was driving the other car? Not the car that couldn't avoid going into them, but the other one, the one coming the other way with the dazzling headlights?'

Alessandro shook his dark head. 'No one ever knew; it didn't stop.'

Faye supposed it wasn't important. It was an accident, on a road where accidents were commonplace.

They finished their dinner, chatting determinedly of lighter subjects, and finally the waiter brought them coffee. Alessandro told Faye what had drawn him into the trade of boat-building. He had always loved the sea, he said; he even went out fishing with his grandfather when he was a very young boy.

Faye remembered what he had told her about his great-grandfather drowning at sea when the port of Deriu was destroyed by a storm.

'It came to a stage where I was expected to leave Deriu,' he told her as he stirred his coffee, 'to train for a career.'

'By your father?' asked Faye. 'Did he want you to go to university?'

'He wanted me to train as a hotelier,' Alessandro said. 'Like Fabio. The best training, he said, was on the mainland. I could then return and take over his hotel.'

'Oh, of course.' Faye had forgotten that as well as owning the little theatre, Bruno Rinaldi had also owned the main hotel in the village, the one now managed by Fabio. She wondered briefly how Charlotte and Fabio were getting on and what Charlotte would say when she heard about what had been happening here. Faye had rung her a few days previously to tell her that everything was fine and she was returning to the UK for a few days, but would be back. But she hadn't had a chance to say much more – Fabio had come into the room and Charlotte had sounded too distracted for a long story. Things were going well in Italy, she said, but it was full-on, and every single manager seemed to have the ability to drive Fabio bonkers. Faye had laughed and decided to keep quiet. The last thing Charlotte needed was to hear about her adventures in Deriu.

'But you didn't want to run a hotel?' she asked Alessandro. She took a sip of her coffee; the taste was rich and mellow and a heart was etched in the cappuccino foam by a barista who clearly thought their dinner date a romantic one.

'Can you see me as a hotelier, making a business of pleasing people?' Alessandro leaned back to drink his coffee. Once again, he seemed in control; it seemed that he had left his sadness and memories behind. But he had shared them with Faye and she felt she was beginning to know him a little better.

'When you put it like that – no.' Faye laughed.

He grinned back at her. 'I was never cut out for studying, either,' he said. 'The alternative was to take up a trade here in Sardinia.'

'And I'm guessing you didn't want to leave Deriu,' Faye said. Who would? Whatever the shadows of the past, it was still a paradise.

He nodded. 'You are right. There was an old man who worked down near the harbour. He had always built traditional boats and people still wanted them. I was watching him one day and he offered to teach me what he knew. He did not have a son of his own and he did not want the practice to simply die out, as so many other things have on our island.'

'What did your father say to that?' Faye asked, though she could imagine. The family had clearly moved on in status since their days as fishermen.

'He disapproved – very strongly.' Alessandro gave a half-smile. 'My father had very definite opinions about many things.'

Like father, like son, Faye found herself thinking.

'He was an ambitious man. He had worked hard all his life and he thought boat-building too lowly an occupation for his son. He was angry. He even sold the hotel. But for me . . .' He smiled. 'It is a real craft, a real pleasure.' He flexed his long brown fingers and Faye looked down at his hands, at the square-cut nails and hard palms. They were the hands of a manual worker – good, practical hands. 'Worthwhile, for sure,' he said.

'I'd like to see the boats you build,' Faye said impetuously, before she had the chance to reconsider. And he *had* offered to show her the boatyard once before. 'Perhaps I could drop by sometime?'

'Of course.' His navy eyes glinted. 'You are welcome.' He continued to regard her with a close scrutiny that made Faye want to fidget in her seat. 'And what about you, Faye?' He regarded her seriously. 'How did you get to do what you do?'

Faye told him what had attracted her to interior design, how she had enjoyed college but hadn't gone to university until she was thirty. 'Until I was grown up enough to know what I wanted,' she said.

'And are you grown up enough now, Faye?' He leaned towards her. His hand was very close to hers on the table, but he made no move to take it.

'I should hope so.' They had finished their coffee and the restaurant staff was hovering. Faye realised that it must be rather late. She glanced at her watch and the spell – if there was a spell – was broken.

'Time to go, I think.' Alessandro got to his feet.

'You must let me—' Again, Faye reached for her purse and tried to make a contribution.

'No.' Really, the man could look quite fierce when he wanted to. 'I am the one who has dragged you back here to Deriu. And I invited you out tonight.' He softened slightly. 'You must at least let me buy you dinner.'

But how many times, Faye thought.

'How about a nightcap?' He drew her wrap from the chair and placed it carefully around her shoulders. 'Have you had the chance to try our *mirto*?'

'Not yet. But . . .' She found herself thinking once again of Jana. This was dangerous territory.

'Then you should.' He tucked her arm into his and led the way out on to the street. 'We must have *una staffa*, one for the road, as you say.'

Faye knew that she probably shouldn't, but she liked the feel of her arm in his. It was a lovely evening and she wasn't remotely tired. She was also reluctant to leave him, she realised, unwilling for the night to end. 'Alright,' she said.

'Excellent.' He smiled across at her. 'I live only two streets away,' he said.

'I won't stay long,' she assured him – and herself, as well. She had work to do in the morning. But she had to admit to some curiosity. What would his place be like? Would it reflect his personality or be as carefully non-committal as he sometimes was? He had many sides. What would she find out from the place Alessandro called home?

They walked along the cobbled street side by side, in silence now, yet the atmosphere between them seemed very different to their first evening together when he had shown her the little theatre. They had shared confidences since then and now she knew a lot more about him. They had come a long way.

They were approaching *Piazza del Teatro*. 'It is just up here,' Alessandro said. But he stopped walking. 'What is that?'

Faye followed the direction of his gaze. It was the theatre. And then she saw what had caught his attention: a flame seemed to flood over the window of the foyer, the flush of blood orange lighting up the night. She saw the door half-open, smoke gushing out, the silhouette of a man staggering inside . . .

Faye raced towards the theatre, but Alessandro was already ahead of her, his hand on his mobile, shouting into it. 'Fire! *Il Piccolo Teatro. Venite, veloci, veloci.* Quickly!'

'Stay here,' he ordered Faye. And then with an almost primeval yell, he ran inside.

CHAPTER 21

Pasquale was in his bedroom on the other side of the piazza when he happened to glance through the window across the square at *il Piccolo Teatro*. He never went to bed early, not anymore; when he did go to bed, he slept badly. This night, all was quiet, all was still, the moon was almost full . . .

The hairs on the back of his neck stood up. For a moment he thought he was seeing things – an orange glow through the window of the foyer, like a reflected sunset, some trick of the light; but it was far too late for sunset.

Even as he watched, the orange glow seemed to flicker. As if something were alive in there. *Per l'amor di Dio* . . . Pasquale froze, just for a second. And then he ran down the stairs and out of the house like a man possessed. 'Mama!' he yelled with all his might. 'There is a fire. *Il teatro!*'

He raced up the stone steps, half-stumbling, wrenched at the door, but it was locked. Locked! How could that be when the place was on fire? *In God's name* . . . He thought he saw smoke curling from the gap underneath the old wooden door. He imagined he could feel the heat.

'*Focu! Agguidu!*' He pushed the urn aside and sent it tumbling; grappled in the darkness for the key. Now he could smell the smoke, now he knew he was not mistaken. He shouted again: 'Fire! Help!' Why had no one else come? Why were the streets so deserted tonight? Trembling, Pasquale shoved the key into the lock and turned it. He wrenched open the door. The oxygen would fan the flames, but it was the only way to get inside.

The smoke hit him first – thick and acrid, filling his eyes and mouth. He coughed, pulled his collar over his mouth and charged in. There was no time to lose, no time to think. It was bad, he saw at once, but not as bad as he had feared. It was a localised fire; it did not seem to have progressed further than the foyer. Thank God for the door that separated the foyer from the auditorium. Thank God. He pushed forwards through the heat and the smoke, feeling them searing at his skin and hair with grit in his eyes and throat.

He had to put the fire out before it spread any further. He knew there was a fire extinguisher on the wall outside the box office, if he could only reach it. He pictured it in his mind's eye; the smoke was thickest there. The flames were coming from the box office itself, leaping up now with a life of their own, greedily stroking the chair, the desk, the ticket machine – everything in their path. The place must be tinder-dry. The crackling heat of the fire was deafening. He put his hands over his ears. *Come on . . .*

Pasquale pushed his way by feel through to where he sensed the extinguisher must be. It was there. He grabbed it from the clip. It was heavy and hot, of course – everything was hot – but he didn't think about that. He grabbed the lever; he twisted and pulled. Nothing. He tried once more. Screamed at it. It was no good. The bastard thing would not work. He could cry with frustration. He threw it down. Water. He must get water.

The stopcock was switched off, he knew that, and it was at the back of the building. It would take too long. *Think, man . . .* The fire blanket. He had almost forgotten. His father's face flashed in front of him. Procedures. *We are the background cogs, my boy . . .* It was inside the box office, not in the desk but under the till. He charged in, flames scorching his face, his hands, his hair. His hands were over his eyes now. He couldn't think, could only act. He breathed in the dust, the fumes, the sickly heat. There was a stabbing pain in his chest. It seemed to be taking so long, and yet he had only been inside the building for seconds. The fire was beginning to grasp hold but it hadn't gone any further yet. Even so. He had very little time.

He grabbed the blanket from the shelf – thank God he knew where everything was kept, thank God nothing had changed since his father's day. At least on the outside. He fumbled the blanket open with fingers that seemed to no longer work as they should. Threw it over the worst of the blaze around the box office desk.

He heard a man shouting and all of a sudden, Alessandro Rinaldi was there, pulling him out of the building. He tried to shake him off, go back to the blanket, but he succumbed, he couldn't breathe. The girl, Faye, was there too. Mama had hobbled over with a bucket and they were filling it from the fountain.

Alessandro went back in, beating at the flames with his jacket. Pasquale took in the first bucket and passed it to him, watching him throw it over the fire, grabbing it back to get more. He emerged from the building a second time. More of the townspeople seemed to appear as if by magic, with buckets and water and wet towels and sheets. Enrico Volti was there – Jiseppu and Tomasso too – and many more. They formed a human chain, passing buckets and towels from one to the other; even his mother was doing her bit, refusing to be left out of proceedings.

'We are winning,' Alessandro shouted at last. 'Keep going!' His face was blackened and his shirt torn, but he was still going in again and again.

Finally the fire engine arrived and took over. In seconds the hose was on and a jet of water was gushing into the foyer of the little theatre. Pasquale let out a soft moan. It was a nightmare. A complete nightmare. He thought of that conversation they'd had in the bar just a few nights ago. What did it matter who owned the theatre? They had almost lost it.

Thirty minutes later and it was all over. The fire was extinguished and the townspeople had gone back to their beds. Pasquale sat huddled in a blanket. He didn't want to leave the steps of the theatre, not yet, although his teeth were chattering and an ambulance had been and gone. He'd refused to go to hospital. 'There is no need,' he'd told them. 'I will stay here.'

'Are you alright, Pasquale?' Faye came to sit beside him on the steps. She always seemed to be around when she was least expected, he thought.

'Cold,' he said. But his burns were not severe. He knew he must go back home. His mother was waiting to take a proper look at them; she had told him she was preparing her special poultice.

'You're probably in shock,' Faye said. 'You should go back home and drink some hot, sweet tea or brandy or something.' She looked as though she could do with some herself.

'I will be fine,' he said. 'But how is the theatre?'

'Not too much damage done apparently.' She looked up to where Alessandro was still talking to one of the fire officers. 'Thanks to you, Pasquale.'

It struck Pasquale that he had performed a heroic act. He hadn't even thought about it; just done it. Was that how his father had felt back then? But it was different, of course. And in a way he had still failed the little theatre for it to happen in the first place. 'It started in the box office,' he said.

'Do you know how?'

He shook his head. For one ghastly moment when he was fighting the flames, he had imagined that Enrico Volti . . . But no, it was impossible. The man did not want to destroy the little theatre. Why would he? He frowned. 'I saw some kids hanging around earlier.' The same ones he had chased off some days before.

'Maybe they go in there to smoke,' Faye said. 'A cigarette end not put out properly could easily have started a fire.'

Pasquale nodded sadly. He should have been much fiercer with them. He should have guessed what they were up to.

'And I suppose everyone knows about the key.'

Pasquale looked down. 'It is my fault,' he said. 'I was not careful enough. I should have looked after *il Piccolo Teatro* better.'

'Hey, you're not the caretaker now, you know.' Faye was trying to help, he knew.

He had never been the caretaker, but he was self-appointed. He thought of it as his legacy. And the truth was that he felt guilty, so guilty. He had not protected the theatre as he had sworn to do. He had let it down, let his father down.

'Lucky you saw the blaze, old fellow.' Alessandro was beside them now. He looked tired. He ran his fingers through his dark hair and Pasquale could see that some of it was singed from the fire. His own too, no doubt. There was no word of thanks from Rinaldi though.

'Lucky you passed by,' Pasquale growled. And it had not escaped his attention that these two were together – again.

'And lucky the fire was confined to the box office,' Alessandro added.

'The main theatre is unharmed?' Pasquale asked, trying to still his shaking. That was the most important thing.

'Thanks to the marble floor,' Alessandro said. 'No doubt that helped stop it from spreading.'

'*Si.*' Pasquale nodded.

'Faye.' Alessandro turned to her. 'I'll see you home, shall I? You must be exhausted.'

'Yes, please, it's been quite a night.' Faye turned back to Pasquale. 'You should go home, Pasquale,' she said. 'You can do nothing more.'

Did he not know it?

'Do you think it was arson?' he heard her ask Alessandro Rinaldi as they walked away, her hand linked through his arm. She seemed very comfortable with him. It made Pasquale nervous. He shuddered. Everything was making him nervous. He thought of all the theatre meant to him. It was a bad time.

'I do not know.' Their voices faded as they walked away.

Pasquale slowly got to his feet and made his way back to the house. His mother was waiting in the kitchen, tutting and clicking her tongue in that way she had. 'Sit, sit.' She motioned to the chair. A bowl of the poultice was already made up on the table beside it. 'I need to see to this.'

'Thank you, Mama.' Pasquale guessed that when she had mentioned arson, Faye was thinking of Enrico Volti and certain other townspeople, rather than the kids he had told her about. But he was sure that she was mistaken. He flinched as his mother applied the poultice. After the first shock, however, it was cold and soothing.

'Baby,' she said. And her voice was tenderer than it had been for a long time.

Pasquale was fairly certain it was not Volti. Time would tell. But no one in Deriu wanted to see their *piccolo teatro* burn down. He closed his eyes as his mother's poultice worked its magic. Did they?

CHAPTER 22

'If not for him . . .' Faye let her voice drift into the darkness that enveloped them. She knew that Alessandro was not Pasquale's number one fan, but he should at least acknowledge what the older man had done and thank him properly.

'I know.' He squeezed her fingers. 'He surprised me tonight.'

We never know what we're capable of, thought Faye, until we're tested.

In the quiet of the night, the echo of their footsteps on the cobbles was loud and hollow. Everything around them was so still. The entire village seemed to have gone back to sleep as if nothing had happened. And yet when it came to it, the towns-people had all rallied to the rescue. Faye thought of the people who had hurried to the square carrying buckets, who joined the chain and helped put out the fire. They were the same people – some of them – who sent hostile glances her way when she was walking by the river or through the town going about her business, which they clearly saw as their business. She tried to pass the time of day with them on occasion; she smiled and did her best to be friendly. Some of them responded. But others, like Enrico Volti and his cronies, continued to do their best to make her feel unwelcome in Deriu. She couldn't blame them. Even so, despite the dispute surrounding the ownership of the the-atre, everyone had wanted to have a part in saving it.

'He has always had a lot to live up to, poor old Pasquale.' Alessandro sounded thoughtful.

'In what way?'

'Did you not know?' He dropped his voice almost to a whisper. 'But then why would you? His father was the hero of our village. Long before my time, of course, but folk here still talk of it.'

'His father? Wasn't he the caretaker of the theatre?' Faye was surprised. From what Pasquale had told her, she hadn't visualised him as a hero.

'The very same.'

'What did he do?'

He moved a little closer. Their footsteps were in synch and he was still holding her hand, which was threaded through his arm. They might be two friends simply negotiating the cobbles in the darkness. But they were so close they might also be lovers. Faye shivered.

Alessandro squeezed her arm. 'Are you cold?'

She shook her head. Not cold, no. She rather thought she was still in shock from the events of the night, like Pasquale. But she also knew that the night wasn't over. She was still here, with this man, walking through the old town, the tall houses looming on either side of the narrow street, the moon a mottled ivory, the silvery stars speckling the clear sky.

'He saved many of the townspeople's valuables. He hid them in the little theatre when the Fascists came to Deriu.' His voice was low. 'And when the Bertelli family were scared they would all be taken prisoner, he hid them in the theatre too.'

'Really?' Faye was captivated. 'That must have been so dangerous.' She remembered Pasquale telling her his father was good at saving things. This must have been what he meant.

'Very dangerous, yes.' They came to the main road and crossed. The new town was deserted too; there was no traffic on the road and the boats moored in the river gently dipped and swayed in the breeze and current, as if to a tune only they could hear. 'It was in 1942,' Alessandro continued. 'Senor Bertelli was working for the Resistance movement. That was why they were after him, I suppose.'

Faye glanced across at Alessandro but his features were in deep shadow. 'So Pasquale's father was a Resistance fighter too?'

'Yes, he was. Many people were. They did not agree with what was happening in Nazi Germany. And plenty of people in Deriu and on the rest of the island did not like the direction in which things were going with Mussolini.' He shook his dark head, his gaze shifting out towards the river. 'In the 1930s the Fascists banned our *cantadores* because the content of their public performances often criticised the Church and the government and was deemed to be subversive. And during the Second World War we suffered much bombing on our island, especially in Alghero and Cagliari.'

Faye nodded. She could imagine. 'What were the *cantadores*, Alessandro?'

'Storytellers, poets; often the shepherds, in the old days.' There was a half-smile on his face but he still looked exhausted. Faye thought of the way he had run into the theatre when he saw the fire. If she'd had any doubts about how much he cared for the place, she certainly had none now.

'They say that the most satirical and powerful of them all defeated the Devil himself in a war of words.' He shrugged as he caught her eye. 'Okay, but it is an important tradition on our island,' he added. 'And it was not only our culture that the Fascists attacked.'

'They were violent?'

He nodded. 'Some of Mussolini's men were vicious brutes by all accounts. Many of our people were killed.'

But how many were courageous enough to be actively resistant? 'Pasquale's father must have been a brave man.' Faye wondered why Pasquale had not told her about his father and the Fascists. He must be proud of what he had done.

'He was.' Alessandro slowed down as they reached the bridge. 'At least, so they say. I never knew Luigi de Montis myself, of course. My grandfather did; he always said that he was a fine man.' He paused for a moment, his hand on the rail, looking down at the slinky water below. 'But the real tragedy was that Luigi de Montis was killed for his actions.'

Faye stared at him in the darkness. 'The Fascists found out what he'd done?'

'Not officially.' Alessandro turned to her. He sighed. And then he smoothed her hair from her face, so gently. She looked back at him, trying to keep her focus on the conversation rather than his touch. 'But he was suspected of anti-Fascist collaboration. He was questioned, tortured, and . . .' His voice stopped as if he was imagining the awful reality of what he was describing.

'And?' Though she wasn't sure she wanted to hear.

'Eventually, he was taken to the main square. They shot him in the head.'

Faye gasped. 'Even though they had no proof?'

His hand strayed to her face. He stroked her cheek. 'Dear Faye, the Fascists did not need proof to kill a man.'

'But . . .' Of course he was right. She had some idea of how things had been. But his words were so stark, the situation so real. These events had taken place right here in Deriu.

'He was killed as a warning.' Alessandro's expression was grim.

'And the Bertellis? The people who were hiding in the theatre?'

'The story is that before he was captured, Luigi de Montis got them out and away into the mountains.'

'So they escaped and Pasquale's father got shot for his trouble?'

'It seems so.'

'Oh, God.' It was a horrific story. Faye could see that this was yet another reason why the little theatre was so rooted within the identity and history of Deriu. It did more than just entertain the people, it took part in the Resistance, protesting against cruelty and wrongdoing; it had played its part in the fight for freedom and it had possibly even saved lives. The Church had a reputation for hiding prisoners, but in this case it had been the theatre. A thought occurred to her. 'How old was Pasquale when his father was killed?'

'Five or six, I believe. Certainly very young. It happened in 1945.'

Her breath caught. 'Did he witness his father's death?' That might explain a lot.

'No, but his mother did. She screamed and she wept, but it was no use. Her husband died in her arms.'

Faye could only imagine how this might have affected both Pasquale and his mother. 'Leaving Pasquale with a lot to live up to, as you say,' she murmured.

She was quiet as they left the bridge and walked on. They reached Fabio and Charlotte's house but lingered by the steps, not speaking, not touching. He had stroked her hair and her cheek, but what did that mean? Anything? Nothing? She didn't know. But despite the late hour and the recent drama she was unwilling to leave him and go inside.

'Faye . . .'

She looked up at him, taken by surprise at the tone of his voice. He sounded . . . tender.

'Yes?' she whispered.

'I cannot pretend.' His voice was so soft that she could hardly hear him.

'Alessandro?'

'You have come here to Deriu and yet you see, I had no intention . . .'

'No intention of what?' But she thought she knew.

He bent his head and kissed her mouth. They were standing so close that it was the smallest of gestures, just a brush of the lips. There was a pause, a beat of dark silence. Faye felt the desire flood into that pause. And then her hands were on his shoulders, his arms around her waist and he was kissing her again, with passion this time. Taking her breath away.

Faye closed her eyes. He smelt of wood oil and lemons and of the fire. For that moment, she wanted nothing more than to be in his arms – now and all night, holding him. She was shocked by the strength of it. When at last he drew away, she clung to him. She didn't want to look at him, half-scared of what she might not see in his eyes. But still she felt as if she couldn't let him go.

'Alessandro,' she said again. And she pushed aside the voice that told her to take care, that this man might not be trustworthy, that he might not even be free.

'It has been a long night,' he said. He drew back and looked into her face, half-searching, half-smiling. 'I must leave you.'

'Yes.' He was right. This wasn't the time – how could it be?

Though she guessed her eyes were saying something else entirely.

'*Ciao, bella Faye.*' He leaned forwards again, dropped a kiss on the top of her head, and moved away, one hand raised in a wave that seemed so casual it hurt.

Stupid girl, Faye thought. How idiotic, how naïve to let herself get so carried away by a kiss. She exhaled slowly. Instead of watching him walk away, she ran up the steps and let herself into the apartment, closing the door firmly behind her. Slowly she mounted the stairs to her bedroom and looked out of the window into the night that had become early morning. Alessandro was standing on the bridge, looking back. She hadn't switched a light on; she knew he could not see her. But it made her heart jump to see him gazing her way.

At last he turned and walked towards the old town, and in a daze, she went to the bathroom to wash her face and brush her teeth. The scent of him was still with her. Burnt smoke seemed to hang in the air. She opened the window. If he had wanted to come inside, she would not have stopped him. It had been as much as she could do not to ask him. All through her life she had never been one to do the pursuing – she was old-fashioned enough to believe it should be the other way around. And yet . . . he had kissed her and not asked for anything more. Why not?

She switched out the light and left the curtain open so that the cool air could reach her and she could still see the reassuring fullness of the moon high in the sky. She felt excitement and fear and a churning in her stomach that she had not felt for a long while. Was it the effect of a handsome Sardinian man, a few glasses of wine, an adventure, a kiss? Was it – could it be – a beginning? Should she step back, step forward or stay right where she was?

Faye shook herself. She mustn't read too much into one kiss. They were very different, her and Alessandro, and from very different places. She hardly knew him, not really.

But as the night dissolved into morning and the thin pink light of dawn slipped into the bedroom where she lay, Faye couldn't sleep for thinking of him. He might as well have come into the apartment with her, because he was there. And so it must be the start, mustn't it? – of something.

CHAPTER 23

Ade was driving. He switched on Radio 2. He was looking for safe background music that would allow him to think. He'd realised, once he'd stopped commuting between West Dorset and Exeter every day, that driving was an integral part of his life. Hardly surprising since he'd done so much for so long. But he'd never quite grasped how important it was nor how much he'd miss it. Strange that. He had timed this journey so that he'd arrive mid-afternoon. This would give him the opportunity to take a walk around, get his bearings. To remember. And then . . . that's where his thought process stopped. He couldn't get beyond it.

He had to do something, go somewhere. Wasn't that the point? He had finished work, left Molly, and given up his home. Wasn't that what it was all for? To go somewhere? But he had dithered. He had stayed in Exeter and dithered. He thought about what Molly had told him and he could still make no sense of it. He thought of the travel agency where he had first met Nina. He walked past it for the first time in years, gazed unseeing at the holiday offers. He didn't want a holiday. He wanted a different life.

Then one evening, he saw Jane. He knew it was her. He was coming out of a bar (Ade was aware that he was spending too many evenings in bars) and she was coming out of the cinema opposite, caught in a flurry of people, but head and shoulders above most of them. She was older, of course, more than twenty years older, but he recognised her by her height and the balletic way she walked, by the brightness of the red scarf she wore around her neck. Jane had always been the kind of woman who got noticed. Nina had been, too, though for different reasons.

Nina had adored Jane. Ade had always felt a little shamed by her. He'd never known exactly what she was thinking – he'd never known what any woman was thinking – but he suspected it ran along the lines of *he's nice but he's married; I don't trust him because he's very likely to hurt my closest friend*. And Ade had to face it – he had. He had hurt her, even though Nina had been the one who said goodbye.

He was surprised to see Jane coming out of the cinema. But why shouldn't he see Jane here? Nina's best friend had always lived in Exeter.

She was with someone. The old Jane had been single, like Nina. Ready to distrust, he'd often thought, and quite rightly. This new Jane was softer, he could see that at once. The man was older than her and taller; he wore jeans and a battered brown leather jacket. As Ade watched, he slung an arm protectively – possessively? – around her shoulder. And she smiled up at him in an un-Jane-like way.

Ade slunk back into the doorway of the bar before she saw him. What could he say? *Remember me? I'm the guy who had an affair with your best friend and ended up staying with my wife after all?* But at the same time he wanted to talk to her. What could he do? He could still see them walking down the road away from him on the opposite pavement. He decided to follow them at a safe distance. He'd have no hope if they hailed a cab or hopped on a bus, but they might just be walking home. And then at least he'd know where to find her. If he found her, he could talk to her . . . But Ade didn't let his head get that far.

He got lucky: they carried on walking. Once, they stopped to kiss and Ade stopped too, looking the other way out of politeness. He felt like some scruffy private detective attempting inconspicuousness, trying to look like an ordinary man on his way home, rather than someone skulking and spying. But he also felt a flutter of adrenalin. He'd never done this before.

They walked for twenty minutes and then turned down a small terrace of houses. They went single file up a narrow garden path and Ade halted a good distance away. He watched her get out a key and let them both in the front door. Although her companion seemed at home, Ade had the feeling it was Jane's house. He stayed there for a few moments, avoiding the lamplight, remaining in the shadows, trying to merge into the shape of a nearby hedge, and feeling a bit ridiculous now. He thought of Molly. Come to think of it, when hadn't he? He found a ballpoint pen in the inner pocket of his jacket and wrote down the number of the house on his hand. Not that he'd forget. When they'd disappeared inside and lights came on, he walked back to the flat he'd rented. What now?

Two days went by before he plucked up courage to return. He strolled up and down the street a few times, forced himself not to look in the window. He bought a paper from the shop on the corner, sat in a nearby park to do the crossword. He didn't venture up the cracked concrete pathway, had no intention of knocking on the door.

The next day he was back. What did he want from her? He decided not to think about that. He hadn't gone out looking for her; he had just seen her. And now, he would either run into her or he wouldn't. By hanging around the area where she lived he was increasing the odds, that was all. He stopped to retie his shoelace outside her neighbour's house and had a coffee in a café nearby.

The third time he walked past the house she opened the front door.

'Hello, Ade.' She didn't seem surprised to see him.

'Jane!' He staggered back as if in shock, but she just laughed at him. He'd forgotten that about her.

'I thought I'd save you the trouble,' she said.

He blinked at her. Rumbled, he thought.

'I've seen you hanging round. Coffee?'

Over coffee, they exchanged news of their lives over the past twenty-odd years. Jane had been married and divorced. *It happens*, she said. She had two kids of sixteen and eighteen respectively, both still living with her at home. And she had now met a man who she thought might be 'the one'.

Ade remembered the way she'd looked up at him outside the cinema. 'Do you think there is?' he asked her. 'A "one"?' He'd told her that he'd split up with Molly, not adding how recently this had been. Neither of them had mentioned Nina.

'You're thinking of Nina,' she said.

He met her direct blue gaze. Shrugged. It was never resolved. It had always bothered him, the lack of a proper ending. A proper ending was what happened when a relationship came to its natural conclusion. It wasn't what happened when you found out that not only was your wife pregnant, but that she had lost the baby and needed your support and that you would be the biggest bastard in the world if you didn't go back to her. It wasn't what happened when the desire for the woman standing in front of you was greater than life itself and it wasn't what happened when she was the one who said: 'I can't do it, Ade. You can't do it.' And walked away.

'I often think about Nina,' he admitted.

'Still?'

'Still.' Molly had been right about that. Nina's flame of red hair, Nina's wild green eyes and pale, milky skin. Over the years he'd wondered how much of it was fantasy and how much was due to his own dissatisfaction. But, whatever, yes, he often thought about Nina. It wasn't a crime. And it wasn't just her looks, either. It was much, much more than that – it was how Nina had made him feel, the freedom of her.

Jane laughed. 'Yeah. I didn't think you were stalking me for any other reason, Ade.' She put her hands on her hips. 'Why didn't you just come knocking on the door and ask me?'

He thought about this. 'Because I'm a coward?'

'But at least an honest coward.' She leaned forwards to pat him on the arm. 'I can't help you though,' she said. 'We lost touch.'

'You did?' Ade swirled the contents of his coffee cup around. He was surprised.

Jane looked down and then back up at him. 'She didn't get on with my ex-husband. I had less free time. She moved away. You know how it is.'

'Yeah.' Though he didn't, not really. In Ade's experience, men didn't have the same need to be part of a group, to share confidences. Perhaps they thought it wasn't macho enough. He had the guys from work of course, and a few blokes from the golf club – men he could call for a game of tennis or a beer – but not friends. He'd never tell them his problems or ask for advice – not of a personal nature, anyway. It was a surprise to him that female friendship – which seemed so solid and so intimate – could dissolve so easily.

'Did she get married?' he asked Jane. He had often wondered about this. Nina had been such a free spirit, but equally, she'd had a lot of love to give. Ade had a sudden recollection of her slowly taking off all her clothes, one by one, when they were in her flat one Friday lunchtime. When she was completely naked, she had come to him pressed herself hard against him. Drawn back. 'Now, you.' She had watched him as he did the same. It was the confidence of her that had shocked him. She was so secure in her own skin, so sure of what she wanted. She flung caution and safety – all the things that he hated in his life – to the wind that blew through her flame-red hair.

'Yes, I think so. But that was later.'

Which didn't mean, Ade told himself, that they were still together now. 'Where did she move to?' he asked casually.

Jane looked as if she didn't want to say. 'Cornwall. Somewhere by the sea.'

Ade nodded. 'I just wondered if she was happy.' He got up to go. 'That's all.'

'Yeah.' Jane grinned. 'But remember, Ade, you have to go forward in life, you can't go back.'

'Right.'

As he left, he glanced down at the hall table. *Mrs Jane Francis,* he read on an envelope she'd left there on top of a pile of other post. He turned to her. 'What happened to your husband?'

'Steve's still around,' she said. 'It was an amicable split.'

'That's good.' He nodded. 'Especially for the kids.' There was a framed picture of them in the hall too, on the wall by the stairs. The girl looked like her mother, only her hair was more strawberry blonde; the boy had dark hair and a sunny smile. 'Nice,' he said. He thought of Faye. *Sorry, Faye.* He'd turned his daughter's life upside down. She was an adult, yes, but he'd done a bloody good job of destroying her memories.

'It was good to see you, Ade,' Jane said as he walked out of her front door. 'Have a nice day.'

A nice day, he thought. He should be making plans. He should be researching, deciding where to travel to, what he was going to do next in his life now that he was free. Not dwelling in the past like this, thinking of a woman he had once loved.

When he got back to the flat he looked up Jane Francis on Facebook, scrolled through a list of her friends. It was too easy these days. He'd never seriously tried to find Nina before – there was no point. But of course he'd occasionally looked her up. He'd put her name into Google, had a cursory glance through Facebook and Twitter, although he half-hoped she hadn't fallen prey to social media. Nothing. He knew she'd left Exeter simply because he knew she wouldn't want to stay. She'd left the travel agency almost immediately after they broke up and after a while Ade had stopped walking past the place – he was only torturing himself. He guessed she might have gone travelling because that's what they'd often talked of doing during those all too short lunch hours, those stolen times after work before the drive back to West Dorset. But he didn't know where.

There was a Nina on Jane's friends list and Ade knew immediately from the picture that it was her. It wasn't a picture of Nina though, it was a picture of a place he recognised, a place they had visited together. 'So that's where you are,' he murmured. She was listed as Nina Temple. He stared at the name. Her married name, presumably. Why had Jane tried so hard to protect her? Because she wasn't married any longer? Her profile was private and no, he didn't want to ask her to be his friend. It was a small village: he'd go there and he'd find her. Why not? What harm could it do?

Ade drove into the place, past the shops, and parked down by the sea where he had parked when he had come here before with Nina. He knew it wasn't that simple and he wasn't at all sure what he would say to her if he found her. But he had to try anyway. He switched off the radio. Exhaled. A path by the river wound through to the next village and you could climb the cliff for stupendous views of the red shoreline and bank of trees above. *I could live here,* Nina had said. He remembered. And now, he rather had the feeling that she did.

CHAPTER 24

The following morning, Faye dragged Charlotte's bicycle out of the garage, packed a bag with beach stuff, slung it into the basket and took the winding road along the coast towards the next village. The scents of juniper and rosemary threaded through the salt air that clung to her skin and hair as she rode; the ocean was by her side, sunlit and blue, throbbing with light. Forget work. She needed to get away from Deriu for a while.

In the small harbour, beside another white-flowered myrtle tree with reddish branches and shiny emerald leaves, a fisherman was bent double, crouching over his net. Faye leaned the bike against the harbour wall in front of an ancient and rusty three-wheeled Ape and padlocked it. She turned. '*Bon giorno, Signor,*' she said to the man.

He replied with a friendly enough grunt and a smile that revealed gapped teeth stained with nicotine.

'You have had a good catch today?'

He nodded. 'In the morning I go out with spears.' He pointed to a wetsuit drying on a nearby rock, next to a weight belt with knives, a spear and a tangle of ropes and clips. There was a plastic box too, washed out and empty of fish.

'What did you catch?'

'A big brown chernay – a groper. Some bream and snapper.' Faye caught most of his Italian and looked suitably impressed.

'You are a tourist?' He stopped his work for a moment, straightened his back and looked at her. His face was weathered by sun and wind and his brown eyes seemed to hold a complete well of Sardinian history within them.

'I'm working in Deriu,' she said, rather proud of this. 'So I'm here for a few months.' She hoped.

'Very good.' He nodded again and returned to his work.

Faye watched him for a few minutes. He seemed so content. What was it in life, she contemplated, that could give that peace, that contentment? Was it living every day for itself, in the present? Was it being mindful? Being aware of the world all around, of nature? Or was it the old life that most people had lost in these times of stress and modern technology? This sense of tranquillity seemed so elusive sometimes.

Moving on, Faye watched some goats wandering on the slopes of the mountain beyond the beach; independent and footsure, they tripped daintily to reach the tastiest treats of *maquis*; no ledge seemed too high or too narrow. The muted clang of goat-bells echoed around the bay.

Faye walked down through the juniper trees to the tiny cove where the waves crept stealthily over pale rocks before fizzing into retreat. She stepped over a knot of tangled fishing line. There were a few people around but the place was much quieter than Deriu; it made Deriu seem almost like a city in comparison. Lying down her bag and towel, she slid out of her sundress to the bikini beneath and walked along the sand towards the ocean. And yet Deriu had suddenly become oppressive. Was that because of the fire, the theatre, or Alessandro Rinaldi's kiss?

At the water's edge she found an orange starfish caught up in some strands of sea-grass. She untangled it and admired its perfection before putting it gently back in the water. She didn't know why she was feeling so tense, but as she let the tide swirl around her toes and ankles, the soft water calmed her. She stepped through the gentle waves – the beach was shallow and gradual and it took a long time before the water reached her waist. Then she slid under the surface and headed out to sea in the channel between the camel-coloured rocks. In the distance the horizon was pink and blurred.

As she swam, she thought about things. About Alessandro, for starters. Had that kiss been a challenge? And now, in the light of day, did she want to take it further? Yes, she thought, feeling the dimple of desire once more. *Yes, please*. She thought about her parents. Had she done all she could? She wasn't stupid, she knew that people grew apart. She also knew that it was impossible to think about what was happening between them objectively, simply because they were her parents. And finally, she thought about the theatre project.

Before the fire, she had been busy. She'd done a lot more research into other multi-purpose venue projects and sketched plenty of ideas that she planned to show to Marisa and Alessandro at their next meeting. She'd also prepared mood boards and studied pictures of other theatres in Sardinia, both old and new. The little theatre would recover from the fire so now they must get down to thinking about budgets. The concept had been agreed upon but Marisa and Alessandro had been evasive about money so far; she would have to pin them down.

She didn't know how far out she'd swam until she turned; the beach was tiny now in the distance and the rocks had long since disappeared. The mountains were a wild and shadowy haze of green and grey, with raggedy clouds hanging over them like untidy topknots. She was way out of her depth. Faye pushed down the flare of panic. She hadn't meant to come this far; she hadn't meant to get in so deep. She must get back. She struck back to shore in her usual steady breast-stroke. Forced herself to stay calm. One length at a time. At last she reached the rocks, arms trembling. Gratefully, she grabbed hold, hauled herself out of the water and rested for a moment. She was exhausted. She needed to gather her strength before she could swim the final stretch into shore. And she must get back to Deriu, she thought. She couldn't forget about work. It wasn't just about the theatre; there were other things to do.

She would start by getting out her laptop, going online and looking for a job, she decided, as she eventually cycled back along the coast road. She had stayed on the rocks for half an hour until she'd stopped shivering in the heat of the sun. She'd swum back to the beach and dressed quickly, sud-denly wanting to be gone. She was staying here on the island for a few months, yes. There was plenty to occupy her with the plans for the little theatre. And she didn't want to leave, not yet. But there was something else . . . she needed to feel she could.

Later, Faye walked through the streets of Deriu in a golden afternoon light to see Pasquale. She wanted to check that he had recovered. He wasn't a young man. Last night must have been quite an ordeal. She didn't go into the little theatre as she passed, though she glanced across the square at the closed door, black-ened from the fire.

Pasquale's mother answered her knock. She looked small and fierce and was almost entirely wrapped in black although it was very warm outside. Her dark eyes must once have been sharp but they had grown milky with age and her face was so brown and leathery that it hung in dry folds from her bones like a date. '*Si?*' She looked Faye up and down appraisingly.

'I've come to see Pasquale, *Signora*,' Faye told her. 'How is he?'

The old woman hesitated and then seemed to reach a decision. 'Come, come.' She spoke in Italian and beckoned her in with a bony hand.

'Thank you.' Faye followed her inside to an old-fashioned kitchen with a grey flagstone floor, an old wooden table and an ancient range with cooking pots and utensils blackened from years of use hanging from hooks next to the chimney.

'Sit, sit.' Pasquale's mother pointed to a wooden stool and sat down on the other side of the table, on a rickety high-backed chair where she must have been peeling vegetables. She picked up the small sharp knife and a carrot. 'Pasquale!' she yelled in her brackish voice.

Faye jumped.

'Coffee, *Signorina*?' She gazed at Faye inquisitively. As if, Faye thought, she came from another world. Which she did, really. This elderly matriarch was from the old world that still existed in patches in Sardinia but was otherwise mostly extinct.

'If it's not too much trouble,' Faye said.

The old woman shrugged. '*Non.*' She got to her feet, shuffled to the other side of the room and busied herself at the stove.

'How is Pasquale?' Faye asked her.

'Men have survived worse.' She clicked her tongue. 'His father, for one.'

'Alessandro Rinaldi was telling me about him,' Faye said. 'He was very brave.'

'Or very foolish,' the old woman snapped. '*Biadu quie ischeddat in palas anzenas.*'

Faye frowned.

'Wise men learn by other men's mistakes, fools by their own,' she repeated in Italian. '*Si*.'

Faye considered this. 'But you must have been proud of him.'

'What point in pride when the man is gone?' The old woman spooned coffee grounds into an ancient and battered percolator. She put on the lid and twisted it tight.

She had a point. 'It must have been a hard time for you, *Signora*,' Faye said.

'It was.'

Faye struggled with what to say next. 'But at least you still have Pasquale,' she tried.

'Not half the man,' his mother responded.

Faye was a little shocked. Didn't she care for her son? And besides, Pasquale had been a hero last night. If not for him, the fire could have taken hold, she and Alessandro might not have seen the flames, and the entire theatre could have burned down. But her thoughts were interrupted as Pasquale entered the room.

'Oh.' He stopped short, clearly surprised to see her. 'Good afternoon, *Signorina* Faye. You have met my mother, Dorotea? How can I . . .?'

'I called in to see how you were doing – after last night, I mean.'

'Oh, thank you. That was thoughtful.' He seemed almost embarrassed. 'But you see –' he spread his hands – 'they were surface burns only. Mama's poultice has done its work.'

His skin was reddened and blistered in places, but Faye could see no serious damage. His mother's poultice must indeed be a miracle cure. 'Good. I'm glad about that.'

Pasquale's mother poured the coffee into tiny cups and the

three of them sat around the kitchen table drinking the strong and bitter espresso. Faye wondered if Pasquale had heard what his mother had said about him being half the man. And she wondered how many times his mother might have said it before. Had Pasquale had to listen to it his whole life? No wonder then, if he felt inadequate.

'And you, *Signorina* Faye?' Pasquale asked politely. 'How are you?'

'Oh, I'm fine.'

'And Alessandro?'

'I think he's okay, though I haven't seen him today.' She felt a ridiculous blush curl over her neck. 'I expect we're all a bit shell-shocked by the whole thing.'

Pasquale didn't reply and Faye thought she should say something more. 'He is grateful,' she said. 'He really appreciated what you did last night. But . . .' But what? But he was too rude or churlish or proud to thank Pasquale for it?

Pasquale nodded. 'You are good to defend him.'

She felt the flush deepen. 'I'm not defending him, not really.' Faye was conscious of Pasquale's mother glancing with knowing eyes from one to the other of them. She was still peeling and slicing vegetables, dwarfed by the tall chair she was sitting in. It looked as if she was preparing enough food for twenty, not just her and her son.

'To act as his messenger then.' Pasquale smiled as if to soften his words.

'I just wanted you to know.' But Faye couldn't help wondering what they all thought of her − the English girl who had come over here and immediately fallen for the charms of Alessandro Rinaldi. She hadn't exactly made it difficult for him.

'But you see −' Pasquale glanced at his mother but she

continued to slice a fat shiny *melanzane* into rings – 'you have come to this village a stranger. You do not know what has happened here. There is a history.'

'What sort of a history?' Faye leaned forwards. This was exactly what she would like to know.

He shook his head. 'It is not for me to say.'

'Then how am I supposed to find out?'

'He was in love with the boy's mother,' the old lady interjected. She took a pot from the centre of the table and salted the aubergines, rubbing the coarse granules between her leathery old palms.

'Who was?' Faye was confused. Which boy were they talking about?

'Him.' She nodded at Pasquale.

Pasquale looked down at the table.

'The boy's mother?'

'Sofia Rinaldi.' She almost spat the name. No love lost there then.

'Mama,' Pasquale pleaded.

But she was on a roll. 'She is the reason he has had no life.'

'I have had a life.' He sat up, squared his shoulders, a flash of defiance in his eyes.

'No woman, no children, no home of his own.' The old woman's voice was oddly hypnotic. 'No one to continue the family name.'

'*Menzus a sa sola qui non male accumpanzadu,*' Pasquale muttered.

Faye translated this as 'better to be alone than in bad company'. But who was bad company?

'Pah.' Dorotea de Montis picked up a red pepper and the sharp knife and began to slice it into strips. She glanced across at

239

Faye with her black, penetrating eyes. 'He wasted his whole life waiting for that one.'

Faye blinked at her. It made sense. She remembered what Alessandro had told her about Pasquale and his mother working and touring together, Pasquale persuading her to come back to Deriu. Except she had married the theatre owner's son. 'You always loved Sofia?' she asked him gently.

Mournfully, he nodded. 'But she met Bruno Rinaldi and that was that.'

'That is when you should have moved away.' The old woman swept the vegetables to one side of the pitted wooden board with the edge of her hand. 'Instead of staying to have your nose rubbed in it. Seeing them together every day, knowing what you had lost. Unable to forget, to move on . . .' Her voice carried on what Faye guessed to be a familiar route.

'I could not leave you, Mama.'

'You left me once – to go to England with her.' She looked up and their eyes met.

Faye was beginning to feel more than a little uncomfortable. So this was the history. And perhaps this explained why Pasquale had no longer been given the leading roles in productions at the little theatre. Very likely Bruno Rinaldi had known how Pasquale felt and he might have been jealous. They were rivals for Sofia's affections, after all. It also explained the air of sadness that Pasquale seemed to carry with him and why he had never married. But why did Alessandro not like Pasquale? Did he know how Pasquale had felt about his mother? Had something happened between them?

'How did you first meet Sofia?' she asked.

'At a production in Sassari. Then again in Cagliari. She was only eighteen.' His voice changed, became almost musical. His eyes lit up at the memory.

'Pah!' His mother exploded. 'Listen to him.'

'But not in Deriu?' Faye probed.

He seemed to know what she was thinking. 'Sofia did not come to Deriu until after we had toured in England,' he said. 'I had been hoping . . .'

'That she would settle down with him,' his mother mocked. 'As though a woman like that would ever look twice at him. That she would choose him rather than—'

'Bruno Rinaldi was a womanising bastard.' Pasquale spoke quite matter-of-factly, as if he were commenting on the weather.

'Oh?' Faye said weakly.

'He tried to fuck everything that moved.'

Faye gave a little gasp. She looked at Pasquale's mother but her face remained inscrutable. Faye had wanted to know the history, but was it really necessary for her to hear all this?

'Which is why I tell you to be careful of Alessandro Rinaldi,' Pasquale said. His eyes darkened once again. He leaned forwards across the table.

'Alessandro?' She thought of that kiss. Couldn't help but think of that kiss.

'He is like his father before him,' Pasquale said. 'I have seen it. You are a kind young woman, Faye. I am not your father. Naturally, I am not your father. Nevertheless . . .' He eyed her gravely. 'I do not wish for you to be hurt.'

CHAPTER 25

The walk around the village brought back memories, but not quite the kind Ade had been expecting. He saw a couple of wild ducks on the water and he passed the old mill where they'd had a cream tea that time. It was late afternoon and the light was bold and yellow, but it didn't make him feel optimistic somehow. He tried to listen out for Nina's teasing voice, but instead he found himself hearing Molly's tears. How had she known he was seeing someone? Ade thought back. He had never allowed a trace of Nina to stray into his home life. No unexplained receipts, no undeleted text messages, no lipstick on his collar or pictures on his phone. And if she had known – why hadn't she confronted him about it? Worst of all, and he suspected his mind had been saving this one for a rainy day, had Molly's knowledge of his infidelity somehow brought on the miscarriage? Was Ade responsible for the death of his unborn child? He thought of what she'd said about shared grief. Had Molly never forgiven him for that?

Ade asked about Nina at the Post Office but the woman behind the counter just looked blank. Wasn't everyone in a small village supposed to know everyone else? Apparently not. He asked in the butcher's shop, too, but the florid-faced man shook his head cheerfully and brandished his meat cleaver. 'Never heard of her,' he said. 'Sorry.' Ade took stock. Maybe he'd made the wrong assumption. Just because Nina had a picture of the place on her profile didn't mean she actually lived here. Perhaps he should go back to see Jane. He didn't ask himself why it was so important to find her. He only knew he had to.

He stopped for coffee in a bohemian-looking establishment called the Yellow Brick Café. Bowls of salad nestled under the counter with flatbreads, dahl, couscous and home-made brownies. There was locally ground coffee, fresh apple juice from a nearby orchard and big wooden tables with jam jars of meadow flowers on each one. Maybe someone in here would know Nina? He could imagine her coming to this café easily enough.

Ade ordered his flat white and took it to a table in the corner. He touched the indigo forget-me-nots in the jar with his fingertip and found himself thinking about how relationships began. How random it all was. He had first gone into the travel agency one lunchtime just to talk about all the places he secretly longed to visit. He thought it would get it out of his system; he thought that for a while he could pretend to be someone else – someone who had no responsibilities, who could simply give in his notice, up sticks and go. He imagined that by the time he left the travel agency that day he would have had his fix; he would be ready to return to the real world. But it hadn't happened. Instead, she had talked and he had listened. He had fallen under the spell of the girl with the blazing hair as she spoke of far-flung places, of India, Thailand, Bali and Vietnam. He could see the light of them dancing in her eyes.

'Will you be travelling alone?' she had asked him.

'Yes,' he said, without hesitation.

'How exciting!' And her eyes had shone.

In that moment, Ade was doomed. He wanted to be that exciting. He could have been that exciting, if it hadn't been for his life with Molly. And so when he left the shop, he knew he would return.

Ade stirred his coffee. He sighed, and recalled the night that he'd spent so long in the travel agency that they were about to shut up shop around him. He'd asked Nina if she wanted to go for a drink, not wanting to stop listening to her, not wanting to stop imagining, so desperately wanting to be the man she thought he was. He thought of how the drink had led to another and how they had spun so easily into intimacy from the touch of a hand. Eventually he had told her he was married and he could tell from her eyes that she already knew.

'So you won't be travelling alone?' she'd asked him.

'I won't be travelling at all,' he said. But in some ways he already had.

Ade had phoned Molly that night and told her he was tired from working late and that he'd decided to spend the night in Exeter at the home of one of his colleagues. That was how easy it had been — at least, at first. He had spent the night making love to Nina. It was exhilarating. It had felt like freedom.

'Hi.' She slid into the seat opposite him here in the Yellow Brick Café as if he'd summoned her with his thoughts.

'Nina!' Ade stared at her. 'How . . .?'

'It's been a while.' She smiled, but he saw the wariness in her eyes.

Ade swallowed, shifted awkwardly in his seat. She'd changed, of course. Her hair was short now and it suited her; it accentuated the delicate bones of her face, her wild green eyes. There were fine lines around her mouth and on her brow; she'd put on a little weight. But he'd recognise her anywhere. 'It's so good to see you,' he breathed. She was still a flare from the past. She still lit up the room. He could even smell her perfume; the same floral note with musky undertones, some sort of heady jasmine though he'd never known its name.

'How are you doing, Ade?' She rested her chin on her cupped hands – a gesture he remembered from before – and watched him. He wondered what she was thinking about him, how damn old he looked.

'Alright,' he said. 'I'm fine. And you? I can't believe you're here.'

She raised an eyebrow. 'I usually am.'

'Oh?' He was confused.

She laughed – the same sound that he remembered, a note of wickedness in it. That had always been part of the attraction. 'I thought someone must have told you. This is my place.' She looked around her proudly. 'The Yellow Brick Café. I run it with Petra.' She nodded towards the dark-haired woman at the counter.

'Oh, my God. I had no idea.' And he'd walked right in. He could see now, how someone like Nina could so easily have created the look of this place; mismatched crockery and chairs, fresh wild flowers, locally sourced food, the relaxed and laid-back style. 'I just happened to come in here for coffee.' He shook his head. 'Did Jane . . .?'

'Tell me you were coming? No.' She smiled. 'As a matter of fact, she thought she'd thrown you off the scent.'

'She was always protective of you,' he said.

'Someone had to be.'

A good point. 'I'm glad you're still friends,' he told her.

'Of course we are.'

He had been right: friendships like theirs were the lasting kind.

'So how did you find me?' she asked.

Ade tapped his nose. 'Good detective work,' he said.

'Is that right?'

'No,' he admitted. 'I found you on Facebook.'

'Ah.' She was still looking at him speculatively. 'Why did you want to see me, Ade?' she asked. 'After all this time?'

He thought he saw something in her eyes then – the hurt perhaps, that she'd once felt. She covered it up though; her expression became non-committal again. But it made him pause. 'It just seemed important.' He couldn't answer the question – because he wasn't sure himself.

'To relive the past?'

'No.' Not exactly. Whatever the real reason, he was pretty sure it was an entirely selfish one. Who was the man he had been when he was with Nina? Did she know? Could she tell him? He leaned closer to her. 'What have you done with the last twenty-something years, Nina? Have you been away? Got married? Had children? I always wondered.'

She narrowed her eyes. 'Yes, to all of those,' she said. 'I spent six months in India. I went to Thailand and Australia.' She threw him a look of challenge. *I did it,* she seemed to say. *Did you?*

Ade thought of the travel agency she'd worked in. Of course she had. He'd always known she would – that had been the biggest attraction of all. 'Tell me about it,' he said. Just like before.

'India was the best.' She went on to tell him about the beaches in Goa, her first sight of the Taj Mahal, how she'd fallen in love with Darjeeling.

'It sounds incredible.' But it wasn't just like before. He had been a dreamer then, Ade could see that much. And maybe he still was, but he was older now, and wiser. He looked at the woman sitting opposite him and thought of the girl she had been. They were so different, Nina and Molly. Nina was a natural explorer just like Ade had wanted to be. And he could have had that life.

'It was incredible.' Nina's eyes were full of the memories. 'Then I came back here, met a guy, settled down, had a couple of kids.' Like you do, her expression seemed to add.

'Are you still together?' Ade didn't even know why he was asking. Nina was herself and yet she wasn't the woman he'd been carrying around in his head. She seemed like a stranger. So who was the woman in his head? Ade shook himself as if she might jump out and take off her mask.

'We're still friends,' she said. 'But I'm on my own now.' She paused. 'How about you?'

Ade wondered what she would say if he told her the truth. If he told her that part of him had always wanted to find her, to rediscover what they'd once had, to sweep her up and away as if the last twenty-four years hadn't happened. That part of him had never forgotten how she had made him feel. That was one truth. The other truth was that the second he saw her he realised that this wasn't an option. Nina wasn't the woman of his fantasy. The woman of his fantasy probably didn't even exist.

'Molly and I have gone our separate ways.' He felt the loss as he said it. It was still hard to accept, still hard to say. And he still didn't truly understand how it had happened at all.

Again she arched an eyebrow. 'So you thought it was time to come and find me?' She sounded bitter. He couldn't blame her for that.

'It's not that,' he hedged. 'I wasn't sure what I wanted to do. I wanted to go back to a moment in time when I had a choice. The moment . . .'

'Before you found out your wife had had a miscarriage,' she said.

He flinched. 'I suppose so.'

'But Ade, you did have a choice before that,' Nina said. 'You always had a choice. We all do. But you were dishonest. And you left it too damned late.'

He thought about this. It was true. He had felt trapped by Molly, confined, and resentful too. Nina had seemed like a burst of winter sunshine. He had mistaken Nina for all the places she sold holidays to. He had thought that with her he could be the man he was meant to be. But even back then there was a big part of him that hadn't wanted to leave Molly – and not just because of Faye. Maybe Nina was right: he had made a decision, and that decision had been the right one – taken in context. What a bloody mess, he thought.

'Women know what they're getting into when they get involved with a married man,' Nina said. 'They know it's going to be painful whatever happens.'

Ade frowned. He recognised that he didn't much like the man who had been unfaithful, the man who had let go of his loyalty so easily. 'I thought, if I saw you again . . .'

She shook her head, misunderstanding. 'I'm not interested, Ade. You always pretended to be someone you weren't. You were a selfish man then and you haven't changed.'

Ade blinked at her. He hadn't meant that. He wasn't asking her to go back with him, to go away with him. 'I didn't . . .' His voice faltered. He had the feeling that anything he said would be misconstrued.

'You didn't want to resume a relationship that ended twenty-four years ago?' She laughed, but it wasn't a pleasant sound. 'I should think not. For all you knew I was twenty stone and married with five kids.'

'That wasn't—'

'But you wanted to see how the land lay.' She waited, still watching him.

Ade tried to dig deep. It was a new experience, he realised. Was she right? Was that it? No, not really. 'I felt as if I couldn't move on,' he said. 'Until I saw you.'

Nina leaned closer. 'How do you think I felt back then?' she asked. 'How do you think I felt about moving on?'

'I know.' Ade felt his shoulders slump. 'And I'm sorry.'

She shook her head. 'Sometimes, Ade,' she said, 'we have to be grown up enough to get on with it alone.'

She was right, of course. And he hadn't been grown up. Not then and probably not now. 'I loved you, Nina,' he said. Because he had. And because he wanted her to know.

'And I loved you.' But she was still shaking her head. 'But it wasn't just about us, was it, Ade? It was about Molly — your wife — and it was about your child.'

'Yes, it was.'

'You loved them too.'

'Yes. Yes, I did.'

'And that's the thing you've never grasped, Ade.' She leaned back in her chair.

'What?'

She wasn't smiling. 'Life. It isn't always about you.'

Ade thought about what she was telling him. He looked into her face and he could see now, how much he had hurt her back then. He'd thought so much about his own sacrifice that he hadn't seen that, not really. There she had been, something fine and new, someone who represented what he imagined he'd lost and that elusive thing that he wanted to find. The truth was that he'd spent too long thinking about what he was missing and not enough time thinking about what he had. And she was right.

He'd thought far too much about himself. He had pretended to be something he wasn't. He had been a selfish, unfeeling bastard.

'Do you still love her?'

Ade remembered that Faye too had asked that question. He thought about what Molly had said about not being able to share things with him. And what he had thought about falling out of love. 'I don't know,' he said again.

'For God's sake, Ade.' She shook her head in despair. 'What are you going to do?'

Ade looked into the distance behind her. He felt bruised by the home truths Nina had given him. But he also felt as if a burden had been lifted. The fantasy woman had finally jumped overboard and out of his head. He'd learned an important lesson. 'I'm going to give it a lot of thought,' he said. 'I want to do the right thing.' Whatever it was.

Nina leaned towards him. 'About time,' she said.

CHAPTER 26

Faye had arranged to meet Marisa and Alessandro in the little theatre on Saturday afternoon in order to bring them up to speed with developments. The Rinaldis had employed a couple from the village to clean and work on the foyer and box office area most affected by the fire. They had tried their best. The desk, chair and a few other small things too damaged to be mended had been thrown out and the theatre foyer was looking – if not quite back to its former self and somewhat blackened around the edges – at least more presentable. In shock, thought Faye, like they all were. Not to mention Faye's sense of anti-climax thanks to Alessandro Rinaldi.

Marisa arrived soon after Faye. On the exterior she seemed calm, but Faye knew she was as shocked and upset as her brother had been when he discovered the fire. She joined Faye in the foyer. 'I feel so terrible that I was not here,' she confessed. 'Living over by the river – I had no clue it was even happening.'

'How could you? And there was nothing you could have done,' Faye reassured her. 'It was just luck that we happened to be passing.'

'Ah, yes. That was fortunate indeed.'

Faye didn't miss the sharp look Marisa sent her way. She must be wondering what – if anything – was going on between Faye and her brother. If their dinner date had been purely professional then Marisa would have been invited to come along. And if not . . . Faye decided not to mention it. Not that there was much to say. She hadn't met Alessandro since the night of the fire, and Faye wasn't sure how she'd react to seeing him.

After the warning she'd had from Pasquale, Faye had done some soul-searching. She liked Alessandro; she liked him a lot. But she wanted to know a bit more about him before their relationship progressed any further. And most of all, she wanted to know whether or not there was someone else in his life. She thought of Jana and the way she'd reacted when she saw Faye with him in the marina, that possessive hand on his arm. Jana could be the reason Alessandro had never had any romantic intentions towards Faye, why he had decided not to take that kiss any further. And Jana could also be the reason why Pasquale had warned Faye away from him. Until Faye knew that Jana was no longer in Alessandro's life, she would keep away. It had, after all, only been a kiss.

Only a kiss, but she had continued to wait for a message from him. He had her number. He had told her he could not pretend, he had kissed her, he had stood at the bridge looking back at Fabio and Charlotte's house, towards her. But . . . nothing.

Faye tried not to care. She got on with her work, she sent texts to both Alessandro and Marisa about the little theatre, she rang her parents and Charlotte. She was tempted to ask her friend about Alessandro Rinaldi's love life but she decided against it. She didn't want Charlotte dropping any hints to Marisa and she didn't want her to worry about what might be going on in Deriu. Most of all, she didn't want to be taken for an idiot. It was something and yet it was nothing. Alessandro answered her brief texts concerning the project with no hint of what else had passed between them, no note of intimacy, and no acknowledgement of that kiss. Faye didn't know what to think. Could she have got it all so wrong?

Yesterday afternoon, she had been back at the theatre, meeting with the builder and doing more sketches. On the way home that evening, she took a different route, past a bar she hadn't noticed before. It was called *Bar Portici* — the neon sign was bright red and the atmosphere inside was raucous. Everyone was watching a football match, she saw. The bar was full and everyone seemed to be talking — or shouting — at once. Fists were raised, glasses were slammed down on the bar; it looked as if the wrong side had scored. Everyone's attention was focused on the TV in the corner. And in the other corner . . .

She saw him, sitting at a table with a small group of people — two men and two women. Faye quickly ducked out of sight — the last thing she wanted was for Alessandro to see her, to imagine that she was stalking him. She was pretty sure it hadn't been Jana sitting at the table by his side, but what did it matter? This was his life. Faye was a stranger here in Deriu, and seeing Alessandro in the crowded village bar had brought that home to her more than anything.

As for that kiss . . . by now, Faye was beginning to think she had imagined it. But she couldn't have. She was able to recall it far too vividly for that.

'Did the builder turn up yesterday?' Marisa asked her.

Faye tried to get her mind back on track. 'Yes, he did.'

'That is one good thing at least.' Marisa opened the door to the auditorium and they went inside. It was as tranquil as ever, seemingly oblivious to the fact that it could so easily have been destroyed. 'Did he give you any idea of costings for an extension?'

'It's too early; it's impossible for him to tell without interior plans.' Though Faye had tried to obtain a rough ballpark figure. She was conscious of her own inexperience, added to the fact that she was dealing with a different culture, a different language and a different way of doing things. She knew they could guess at a price, but no one wanted to commit themselves at this early stage.

They walked up the centre aisle along the moth-bitten red runner of carpeting and sat down in two faded red seats at the very front. Faye pulled her sketch pad and project notebook out of her bag.

'And the structural engineer?' Marisa asked. She glanced at her watch. She was clearly irritated by the fact that Alessandro hadn't yet put in an appearance. Faye was more worried about how she would react when he did.

'I'm still waiting for him to let me know when he can come.' Faye didn't want to go too far without knowing what could be achieved structurally and how much it might cost, so she had approached three structural engineers. The first had said he might be able to come over next month, but couldn't quite say when. Number two was off on holiday for three weeks and was vague about future commitments. Number three hadn't turned up at all. This, Marisa had already told her, was perfectly normal in Sardinia. It seemed that Alessandro hadn't been joking when he'd said that even the planning of their project would be time-consuming.

And where was Alessandro anyway? Faye was being paid a freelance retainer but she had no idea how long she'd be staying. Now that she'd applied for a couple of jobs, she might have to go back to the UK at some point for interviews, though there was nothing definite so far.

'But the builder seemed to think our ideas for the extension were do-able,' she went on. Her meeting with him had been a feasibility study as much as anything. 'And he had a look at the dressing rooms and the costume room.'

Marisa seemed to give a small shiver. 'What about the floor?' They both looked down. 'Could we save this marble?'

'I think so, yes.' The cost of laying a new marble floor would be prohibitive and besides, Faye adored the aged look of the mottled old marble that was here already. It was crumbling and cracked in places, but that was part of its charm.

'Good.' Marisa nodded her approval.

'He found quite a lot of damp here in the auditorium though.' Faye pointed to a patch of black mould on the ceiling above them. 'So that will have to be treated.' She surveyed the decorative stucco in the centre. 'And all the mouldings and sculpture need restoring, as we already know – but that's a specialist job.'

'Do we have a restorer coming to take a look?' Marisa gazed up at the four medallions design on the ceiling. They must have been vibrant once, but like everything else in the theatre, the designs had faded and crumbled with time.

'Yes, he's coming to give us a quote next week.' Faye had managed to get hold of a man who had done some similar work on a theatre in the south of the island.

Marisa smoothed back her dark hair. 'What would we do without you, Faye?'

Faye smiled. 'I appreciate you giving me the chance.' It was a big project, but when she took it step-by-step, it was not as daunting as she had first imagined. However, that didn't mean she'd be staying to supervise things from start to finish. It was much too big for that.

'And what else is there?'

Faye laughed. 'A lot.' Marisa needed to know the full extent of what had to be done, which was what this meeting was about, really. But Alessandro needed to know too.

'Such as?'

'New toilets, with disabled access. A ramp for the entrance, too. All the structural rebuilding we've already discussed. Rewiring. A new box office. Refitting the window in the foyer and replacing the others.' She was ticking off the items on her fingers. 'The new seating, emergency lighting and fire alarm systems.'

They exchanged a glance. Faye wondered if Marisa had had any idea of how much there was to do or the time it would take. Not to mention the cost – though she had to.

'I've made a list of everything we've discussed here. It's a project book.' Faye showed her. 'With columns for approximate costs and so on. I was going to do a spreadsheet, but—'

'I'm glad you didn't.' Marisa looked at her in some alarm. 'We tend to use the more traditional methods here on the island.' She took the book, her gaze skimming over the notes and figures. 'Oh, Faye,' she said softly.

Exactly. 'We do need to discuss the budget,' Faye reminded her. 'You said you'd talk to Alessandro?'

'I did. We can go to around a hundred thousand euro, he thinks.'

Faye knew this wouldn't be enough. 'Could we apply for a grant?'

'Alessandro thinks so. In fact, he's spoken to someone already.' Marisa recrossed her legs. 'It's not official – but we hope we can double the money. Other buildings have attracted sponsors and lottery money. Why not ours?'

'Then I suppose we could go ahead in principle.' Faye glanced at her watch. Alessandro was now forty-five minutes late.

'I'll try and get hold of him.' Marisa pulled her mobile out of her bag but after several rings she gave up. 'He's not answering.'

'Should we carry on without him?' Sardinian unreliability was hard enough to deal with, but where Alessandro was concerned, it was a lot more than that.

'Let's give him another ten minutes,' Marisa said.

Faye got to her feet. 'Did you always love this place, Marisa?' She ran her hand over the balustrade that separated the orchestra pit from the stage. She thought of what Alessandro had told her when he showed her those old photographs, the night of the fire. 'Even when you were a young girl?'

'I adored it.' To Faye's surprise, Marisa sprang to her feet and ran lightly up the steps and on to the stage. Behind her, the shroud of the dusty lilac curtain was drawn. 'I longed to be part of it – to be an actress like Mama.'

'You did?'

'I used to have dancing lessons.' She took a few steps across the stage and performed a perfect pirouette, spinning on one foot, the other foot touching the knee of the supporting leg.

'Very good.' Faye gave a little clap and Marisa put her hands together and gave a curtsy. 'So what made you change your mind?' She certainly had the right physique for dancing – she was slender as a wand, extremely light on her feet and like most Italians, her hands were almost as expressive as her eyes.

'I did not change my mind.' Marisa's expression darkened. 'It was Mama who made me do that – back when I was fourteen. That and—' her voice broke.

'Didn't she want you to act?' Again, Faye was surprised.

'Mama was an actress, yes,' Marisa said slowly, 'but she was not keen on the acting world. There was little reward in it, she said. It was not what she wanted for me.' She pulled a sad face.

'She said I was too young to think of it. She said I should study and have more choices and find my own way. If I still wanted to do it when I was twenty-five, then . . .'

'But you didn't?' Faye sensed that there was a good deal more that Marisa wasn't saying.

Slowly, Marisa walked back down the steps. 'By the time I was twenty-five my mother was long dead,' she said. 'So I could have done it. But there were other considerations. I . . .' Her face closed. 'It would have upset my father.'

Faye was pretty sure that this wasn't the only reason, but she didn't want to pry. 'But teaching is a vocation, too. It must be very rewarding.'

'Yes, it is, and I love it.' Marisa's voice softened and she smiled. 'I took a different path and it is a good path.' She sighed. 'At twenty-five I was a very different person from the young girl who only wanted to act and dance.'

Faye wondered if she was at all resentful about that. Had she forgiven her mother? Did she still, somewhere inside of her, long to act, to dance? Alessandro had told her that their mother had started touring when she was still quite young; clearly for some reason she hadn't wanted that life for her daughter. Faye glanced again at Marisa, thought she saw a kind of wistfulness in the dark brown eyes. It was interesting that Bruno Rinaldi had tried to force his will on his son and Sofia Rinaldi had tried to force her will on her daughter. Together, they must have been quite a powerful pair. 'You don't regret it now?' Faye asked her. She went back to her sketchbook. She had already done several rough drawings of the stage and orchestra pit. Doodling really, waiting for different ideas to strike her. 'You don't think you'll ever go back to it?'

'I have regrets, yes.' Marisa looked up and now her expression was so sad that Faye wanted to reach out for her, to help her in some way. 'But as I said, I am no longer that girl and these days I do not even want to think about her.' And once again her expression was shuttered, giving nothing away.

She was more like her brother than Faye had appreciated. She turned over a new page of her sketchbook. And she couldn't help thinking that there were many secrets in the past lives of the Rinaldi family, secrets that they would not wish anyone to know. She thought of what Pasquale and his mother had told her a few days ago. Pasquale seemed to want to protect Faye – almost as if he saw himself as some kind of father figure – and Faye had to admit to being touched by his concern. So perhaps she should be relieved that Alessandro seemed to have taken a few steps back from her?

'Will you stay here in Sardinia, Marisa?' Faye remembered her long-distance boyfriend in Rome.

'I think not. When this job is done –' Marisa's expression brightened – 'I will go to join Leo. He says there is too much that keeps me here – first my father, then the restoration of the theatre. But in fact . . .'

'In fact?'

'In fact,' she said, 'I cannot wait to leave.'

Faye was surprised by her vehemence and about to ask more, but at that moment the door to the auditorium was flung open and Alessandro strode in. Faye swallowed to get rid of the sudden lump in her throat. It had been five days since they had seen each other and it felt like five months.

'Alessandro!' Marisa tapped her watch. '*Sei in ritardo*. You are late. Where have you been? Did you forget our meeting? Or the time?'

Alessandro's dark brows were knitted in a frown. 'I am here now,' he said. He did not even look at Faye.

But she could feel his anger. It seemed to be simmering inside him; the tension could be cut with a knife. Faye looked from one to the other of them. Sardinians were so volatile. Perhaps he should have stayed away. It was easier to deal with Marisa – there was no other agenda, no seductive invitations for dinner or nightcaps of *mirto* to distract her from the business in hand. Marisa could handle her brother in her own way – she was probably used to his fiery temper.

And he wouldn't even look at her. 'What's wrong?' Faye asked. He seemed a very different man from the one who had kissed her five nights ago. She supposed she should be thankful that it had just been a kiss.

'Nothing.' He still refused to meet her eye. 'I apologise for being late. Now, shall we proceed?' He grabbed a seat.

Marisa and Faye exchanged a glance. Help, she thought. But what could she do?

She put on her professional hat and proceeded to give them both a full update, including the figures in her project book. If he wanted to play it that way . . .

'What do you think?' Marisa asked him when Faye had finished.

'I do not know what to think,' he muttered. He tore his fingers through his black hair. He looked terrible – there were dark shadows around his eyes as if he had not slept and the ends of his hair were still singed from the fire.

Faye was conscious of a feeling of foreboding deep in her gut. What now?

'Is it too much?' Marisa asked him. 'Are we being too ambitious?'

'Perhaps.' His voice was clipped.

Faye took a deep breath. They had already agreed all this. 'Is it the money?' she asked. She supposed it wasn't too late to pull back, to reappraise. They didn't have to build the extension and they could economise in other ways if they had to.

'The money,' he said. '*Si*. And the people of this town . . .'

'I thought you'd sorted out the ownership dispute,' Faye said. Rather sharply, she had to admit.

He didn't reply. 'And the fire,' he said.

'The fire?' whispered Marisa.

'Darling girl.' Alessandro's expression changed and he grabbed hold of his sister's hand. 'Was it a sign?' he asked.

'A sign?' Marisa stared at him.

'Everyone is talking about it. On the streets, in the cafés.' He began to gesticulate with his hands. Almost wildly, thought Faye.

'Isn't there an official investigation?' she asked.

'*Si*. They say the fire was probably caused by a cigarette.' He let go of Marisa's hand, finally looked across at Faye.

She thought of Pasquale. 'I heard there were some kids hanging around outside.'

'Perhaps. But what if we are not meant to bring the theatre back to life? What if—?'

'Alessandro—'

'I do not know what to do,' he said. He put his head in his hands.

About what? Faye was at a loss, once again out of her depth. She wouldn't have put Alessandro down as superstitious, but she was aware that superstitions were still powerful here in Sardinia. Was there something else? She had the strongest urge to go and put her arm around him, to try and reassure him. But the way he'd been acting since walking into the theatre this afternoon was telling quite a different story and she just couldn't do it. She looked at Marisa, but she seemed as bewildered as Faye.

'What is it, Alessandro?' Faye asked again. 'What's—?'

He smacked his fist down on the chair arm. Dust danced in the air. 'It is this place,' he said. 'This damned place – and the people in it.'

'The theatre, you mean?' Faye didn't understand this turn-around. He loved the theatre. He'd always loved the theatre. Wasn't that what this job was all about?

'Deriu,' said Marisa. 'Deriu?'

'Alessandro, if you've changed your mind . . .' Faye let this hang. She was thinking about the theatre but he would understand the subtext. *I cannot pretend*, he had said. And the kiss hadn't seemed a pretence either. But if he had changed his mind about any of it, she would return to London and forget that the little theatre in Deriu even existed. Forget him. Faye twisted her hands together. She didn't want to, she realised. She wanted to finish what she had started – at least as far as the theatre was concerned. She wanted to see this through.

'No.' At last he raised his head. He shot her a sad glance. 'I have not changed my mind.'

Relief flooded through her. 'Then—'

'But I need time,' he said.

'You have that.' Faye looked down at her project book. It would be months before the project was off the ground.

'For what, Alessandro?' Marisa asked. 'Why do you need time?' Their eyes locked. 'Do you not want this?'

'I want it,' he said. And there was no mistaking the passion in his voice.

'Have you changed your mind about the nature of the building?' He was her client, but Faye wanted some answers.

'No.'

Again Marisa and Faye exchanged a glance. 'Then what is it?'

'I need time to think,' he said. 'To work out what . . .'

'Alessandro—'

'Leave it, Marisa.' His voice deepened. Once again, he seemed angry. 'Just leave it, will you?' And before they could say another word, he was on his feet and heading out of the auditorium.

Faye watched his retreating figure, winced as he slammed the door. 'What should we do?' she asked Marisa. She must know him better than anyone.

'We go on.' Marisa sat up straighter. There was a light of determination in her dark eyes. 'We continue without him. And in the meantime . . .'

'Yes?'

Marisa's voice was steady. 'That was not my brother speaking.'

'So?' What was she saying?

'So we find out who has got to him and we find out what has happened.'

'You make it sound very easy,' Faye murmured.

'It is not.' Marisa spread her hands. 'But right now, that is all we can do.'

CHAPTER 27

Molly was bent double trying to read the temperature dial on the water tank. She needed her glasses. Damn. She backed out, went to fetch them.

Yesterday, the shower had been scalding; today, it was freezing. And there was no controlling it. It was a minor practicality, but it reminded her of what happened in a marriage and that made her cross. Yet another thing, she thought. And she had imagined she was done with anger tonight.

At which point did it happen? At which point did one partner – Ade – start to be the one who always took the rubbish out, while the other – Molly – always prepared breakfast? At which point did she take over the paying of the household bills and not bother to learn how the plumbing worked? Molly swore softly. An unspoken agreement. Role-play. Division of responsibilities. Call it by any name, but at which point did it become dependence? She had to face it: she had been that kind of wife, the kind who depended on her husband; she relied on him for all things practical, certainly, but even for bringing home a living most of the time. She stopped short. The creative writing class tonight had made her think. Why had she done it?

She had always kept the house nice – a word that, quite frankly, made her want to scream. These days she felt more like sweeping all the ornaments off the bureau and crushing

264

them into pieces under her feet. Which was hardly wifely behaviour – nice or otherwise. She had baked cakes and prepared dinners – millions of dinners over the years, one could count them like sheep before bed: a cottage pie jumping over a fence, a beef stroganoff following close behind – and she had continued making love with a man who had been unfaithful to her. Though she had to admit that the frequency had diminished over the years.

Molly found her glasses and crawled back into the airing cupboard. How much of that wifely behaviour had happened because she was playing a part and how much because of love? Truth was, Molly thought, she had played the role of a certain type of wife to perfection. An accommodating wife, a passive wife, a wife who had no clue her husband was having an affair. What century did she imagine she was living in?

Molly altered the dial. They – she – would probably have to get a new shower unit. Doing so would give her a semblance of control in her life – or of the temperature of the water in her shower, at any rate. Why had she become some sort of cliché of a wife? Ade had never asked her to do that; in fact, she rather guessed that he despised it, even if it did make his life more comfortable.

She knew why: because she was angry with Ade, and because she had decided not to tell him her secret. Anger. Jo, her tutor, had been so right.

Molly crawled back out of the cupboard. She'd try the shower again tomorrow. And then get help. She'd already called the very pleasant man who apparently held the solutions to all heating and plumbing problems at his fingertips, but got only his answer machine and he hadn't called her back. Clearly his fingertips were busy elsewhere. She could try someone else. She could even knock on her neighbour's door – Doug was both sympathetic and obliging (Molly had decided these were now her two favourite qualities in a man) and she was confident he would take a look; she only had to ask. But she wouldn't call Ade. Molly took a deep breath from her belly. Whatever else she was, she was not that kind of wife – the separated-from-her-husband kind of wife who still expected her ex to sort out matters practical and domestic. Besides, she wouldn't give Ade the satisfaction of being needed.

Molly turned her attention to the boiler, which seemed to be lit and functioning. Hmm. Which had precedence – boiler or hot water tank? Did one do the dictating or did they work side by side in some sort of harmony? Who controlled the water temperature? She turned the dial experimentally and studied the list of faults inside the flip-down lid that she had never considered flipping down before. It could be anything, really. It all looked very clever. But the diagrams didn't seem remotely connected with plumbing issues and they didn't help much at all. She was not mechanically inclined, she reminded herself. She never had been. But she could be; she'd just have to work at it. She went to the kitchen to try the taps.

She missed Ade. Molly gripped the edge of the sink. Waited for the feeling to abate. That wasn't to say that she wanted him back. She didn't. Molly breathed in, held the breath, exhaled, slowly moved away from the kitchen sink. She couldn't continue the charade any longer. When he had told her that he wanted to go away, when she had seen how much he wanted to go away, something inside her had snapped. Everything – all these years – suddenly seemed so futile. What was the point? Where had the point been in fighting to keep him, back in the day, when she'd first known he was seeing another woman?

What had her fight, her silence achieved? It had kept him with her; it had stopped Faye from being brought up in a 'broken home', as everyone insisted on calling it these days. But it had only delayed the inevitable. One day, Ade would leave. She'd known it. And until he did, his disloyalty would lie between them, unacknowledged, festering, a wound that would never leave a scar because it could never even begin to heal.

Molly returned to the sitting room. If Jo were here, she would tell her to write that down. And it was true that since she'd started the creative writing class, she'd begun to think more metaphorically, more laterally. But all it seemed to be doing was making her angry.

Kathryn had called in for a cup of tea after work and, uncharacteristically, Molly had not yet removed the signs of her – the dent in the cushion on the sofa, the slight scuff of mud under the coffee table, the tray and empty cups, the plate of biscuits. Kathryn had chatted about work and the family, they'd discussed their mother's health ('she seems fine, she got over that last cold really quickly') and then finally, just before she left, she said what she had come to say. Molly had been waiting. 'How are you managing, Moll? Are you okay? I mean – really okay?'

'Yes.' Molly was so used to fixing a smile on her face that she hardly had to try anymore. It almost jumped there of its own accord. 'It's really quite a relief.'

'A relief?' Kathryn frowned.

'I don't have to worry anymore.' Which was true, Molly realised.

'About what?'

'About when he's going to leave.'

What she didn't say, Molly thought, as she plumped the cushions, was that when Ade left, the emptiness returned. She

267

fetched the dustpan and brush from the cupboard under the stairs, carefully flicked the mud into it and took it outside. Not loneliness, that was different. Molly flipped the dustpan over. The mud stuck. She flicked it with her finger. *Out, damned mud.* She was becoming Lady Macbeth.

She felt the emptiness most at night in her head, sometimes in her whole body. And when she slept, she dreamt of her father. In her dreams he was already frail, out of the hospice and back at home. 'Damned if I'll die in that place,' he used to say. The cancer had taken over his body and now it was attacking his optic nerve. He was in constant pain and close to death. It was just a question of when.

Most of the care fell to Molly. She was doing her A levels and working quite a bit from home. It was a duty she had willingly taken on. Her sister was too young at not yet thirteen; Molly and her mother tried to shield her from seeing too much. Luckily, Kathryn seemed to have an ability to compartmentalise her life, to shut her dying father into a detached part of her brain that didn't affect her school and social life. She was selfish, Molly supposed. She was entitled to be selfish at not yet thirteen.

As for Molly's mother, she tried her best. But her mother had been a clichéd wife, too – even more so than Molly; she had embraced the stereotype with open arms. She expected her strong, handsome husband to protect her for the rest of her days and when he failed to do so . . . When he got sick and weak and when she knew she was going to be left alone . . . Molly's mother couldn't cope. She stopped looking after herself properly; she stopped looking after her children. She sobbed herself to sleep every night and even though he was in a separate room at the other end of the house her husband probably heard it. When Molly's father had said that he wanted to come home, Molly knew how it was going to be. And that was the first time in her life, she thought, that she got angry.

Anger was still on her mind. Although Molly had decided to give up the creative writing class, she hadn't – not yet. And so, after Kathryn left, she gathered up her notebook, her neatly ordered file of tutorial notes and her pens and drove down to the community centre.

Jo told them that this week they were thinking about character emotion. And not just thinking about it, she said, but feeling it, too. It was a practice in empathy – one of the qualities most needed by a writer. Molly wondered if she should have stayed at home.

Jo was fond of doing random 'consequence' exercises and this was one of them. To start, everyone had to think of an emotion.

Molly didn't want to get in too deep tonight – not after Kathryn's visit. 'Joy', she wrote on her piece of paper. She was already rather looking forward to that one. Jo would ask them to pick a colour and perhaps a song that went with it and Molly would choose yellow and write about Donovan or The Beatles, about spring and primroses. More 'hope' than 'joy', but hoping for joy was positive at least. She added a little doodle to the three letters she'd written and smiled around at the group.

'Fold your piece of paper and pass it on three places,' said Jo. 'What you get given is what you'll be writing about.'

She should have guessed. Molly sneaked a glance to check who was sitting three seats away. Malcolm: he of the dark eyes and complex sentences, he of 'why use three words when thirty will do?'

She unfolded the paper he passed to her. 'Anger,' she read. For the love of God.

Molly hadn't realised she was angry with so many people. She was angry with her mother for not being stronger when her father was ill; she was angry with Kathryn for being young and selfish. She was angry with Ade for being unfaithful to her, for being so caught up in his infidelity that he didn't even realise that she knew, for making her pregnant when he was probably already screwing someone else, for making her second best, and then for the miscarriage of the baby she had lost. She was angry with Ade for so many things that her head hurt and she had to stop writing. And she was angry with her father for what he had asked of her. And for leaving her too soon. Molly might have been her father's sweetheart, but ultimately, he had always protected his wife.

Anger, thought Molly now. It was red and boiling. It was sulphurous; it steamed and bubbled and it had to get out or it would fill a person right up like a witch's spell. It wasn't an emotion that belonged to a perfect wife, not even remotely. Molly had always held it back. But now she had found her voice. It was as if Jo had given her permission.

'What we want to write about isn't always what we need to write about,' Jo said in explanation. 'Sometimes there's something within us that we should express.'

Too right, thought Molly.

They had gone around the group, some reading, some not. When it came to Molly's turn, she looked at what she'd written in horror. Where had that all come from? Her wrists and hands were aching. She shook her head. Tore the pages out of her notebook and screwed them together into a tight ball. Of anger, she thought.

Jo nodded. 'You can set fire to them if you want.' Her eyes gleamed as she looked around the group. 'Take control of your life, your emotions.'

Molly wondered how putting a match to what she had written would help her take control of her life. If only, she thought.

Jo fixed her with a look that seemed to know the exact contents of the pages screwed up in her palm. 'Other people can control us, but so can the emotions that direct us,' she said. 'But we can choose to take control by letting those emotions go.'

Back at home, Molly picked up her bag from the table and plucked out the Anger Pages, carefully, as if they might infect her still further. She placed them on the grate, took a box of matches from the drawer. She lit the match, put it to the paper, watched that anger burn.

CHAPTER 28

Faye was walking to the castle. She'd been there once, but the place still drew her. She felt that its perspective – looking down on the town as it did – might let her get to know Deriu a little bit better. She wasn't sure, but she sensed that since the fire, the people of the town viewed her a little differently. She was still an outsider, of course, but she had been part of the effort to save the little theatre; with some of the townspeople at least, she had established a fragile bond.

At the outskirts of the old town, a woman sat outside her house on a wooden chair perched at an angle on the uneven cobbles of the street, a piece of lace embroidery in her lap. She wasn't sewing though; she was looking straight ahead, deep in thought. Faye was about to smile, say, 'good day' and pass by, when she realised who the woman was. She paused. 'Carmela, *bon giorno, Signora.*' She couldn't help looking from side to side as she spoke, half-expecting Enrico's glowering face to appear from behind the branches of the little tree growing in a pot by the door. He was one person who hadn't given up on the hostile glances sent her way.

'*Bon giorno, Signorina.*' To Faye's relief, Carmela returned her smile. 'You are well, my dear?'

'Very well, thank you.' Apart from the not-knowing, that was – what Alessandro had on his mind, what was happening, whether there was still a job here for her to do. 'And you?'

'Yes, yes, life goes on.' Carmela got to her feet, catching the wisp of lace in her hand. To Faye's surprise she came up close and gripped her arm. 'Come in – yes, why not?' she asked her. 'Just for a few minutes. For a small drink? An aperitif, hmm?'

Faye was tempted. It was a bit early for alcohol, and she'd put away more than her share of a bottle of white wine last night as she and Marisa drowned their sorrows and tried to come up with a plan, but she was curious to see inside the Voltis' house. 'Is Enrico at home?' she asked. She didn't want to take the risk of running into him.

Carmela laughed mirthlessly. 'No, he is not. You are quite safe, my dear.' But her eyes remained sad and thoughtful. 'Who knows where the man goes? Not me. He goes out, he drinks, he plays cards and dominoes, he gambles. He can never rest, no, no.' She crossed herself. 'There is no rest for Enrico.'

'Just for a short while then, thank you.' Faye followed her inside. She sensed that Carmela was lonely. She'd seen other women in Deriu chatting to one another outside their houses or at the market, but Carmela seemed more solitary – holding herself apart from the rest of the villagers. Maybe because of her loss, thought Faye; maybe her sadness had made her more insular, more drawn in on herself.

The house was small but homely, the hallway dark with wood panelling and pictures on the walls of saints and other religious paraphernalia. Carmela bustled into the kitchen and Faye followed behind. There was a faint aroma of cooking, the hint of fresh coffee still hanging in the air. Carmela reminded Faye a little of Pasquale's mother, although Carmela was not ancient at all; she wasn't much older than Faye's parents. And although the kitchen was simple, it was not quite so old and ill-fitted as the small house in *Piazza del Teatro*.

'Does Enrico have a job?' she asked Carmela. She seemed to remember Pasquale telling her that the Volti family had been involved with the mining industry. And hadn't he also said—?

'He worked in mining,' Carmela confirmed. 'We had money once. We did not live like this.' She gestured around her. 'Now, he works as a handyman in the village – but most of the time there is no work, of course.'

Faye nodded. She wasn't sure what to say. This family had known so many losses. No wonder Carmela was so sad. No wonder she did not seem to belong.

She watched her take down a small bottle from a shelf in the larder. She poured some thick, oily liquid into two tiny, ornate glasses and passed one to Faye. '*Mirto*,' she murmured. '*Salute*.'

Ah, so at last she was going to try the traditional Sardinian liqueur – served at any hour of the day apparently. '*Salute*,' said Faye.

She took a sip of the smooth, syrupy liquid. It was heavy and sweet with a faintly herbal tang. And powerful, she thought, blinking from the hit of alcohol. Purple myrtle berries mixed with honey and pure alcohol, Marisa had told her, that was about it. It was also supposed to have restorative and medicinal qualities, which Faye felt rather in need of this morning.

Carmela swallowed her *mirto* in one. She exhaled noisily and looked Faye up and down. 'Your mother and father, they are in England, *si*?' she asked.

'Yes, they are.'

'You are close with them?'

'Yes, I am.' Faye didn't want to dwell on her parents' situation and certainly not with Carmela. Apart from anything else, she was clearly a religious woman, and would surely not approve.

Carmela put her glass down on the kitchen table and seemed

to come to a decision. 'You must see my daughter's room,' she declared.

'Oh . . .' The daughter who had disappeared. Giorgia Volti. How could she refuse? Faye took another gulp of her *mirto* and followed her.

'Come.' Carmela beckoned her back into the hall and began to climb the narrow stairs with Faye close behind. There was no carpeting and it smelt musty and damp. Maybe Carmela asked all visitors to see Giorgia's room, Faye thought. Maybe it made her feel better in some way, this simple act of remembrance.

Carmela softly opened the first door on the left at the top of the landing and stood back.

Faye remained on the threshold. The room was immaculate. And it didn't smell damp in here at all. On a wooden dressing table, a delicate square of lace had been placed, a hairbrush and comb positioned carefully across it. There was a narrow single bed, made up, with a shiny satin counterpane in pale blue and a dark wooden headboard. In the corner stood a small wardrobe and a desk. On the desk were some exercise books, a textbook and a pen.

'Her school books,' Carmela said proudly. 'It is all exactly as she left it.' She blinked. 'I come in here to dust every day. I open the window to keep the air fresh for her.'

Faye saw the tears in her eyes. 'I am so sorry, Carmela,' she said again.

'We wait,' Carmela told her. 'We wait and we keep it untouched, you see. Because we do not know what happened to our sweet Giorgia and so we live in hope that one day she will return.' She clasped her hands to her breast. 'Or at least, that one day we find out the truth.'

Faye nodded. There was a lump in her throat and she hardly

dared trust herself to speak. It was seeing it, she supposed. And witnessing such love in a mother for her daughter, such hope against all odds. And she thought of Enrico Volti, out drinking and playing cards, no doubt trying in his own way to forget. She felt a deep stab of sympathy for the man. He was difficult and unfriendly, and he had a nasty temper. But to lose a daughter . . .

'Did the police investigate Giorgia's disappearance at the time?' Faye asked, since Carmela seemed to be waiting for her to say something.

'For many months, yes.'

'And they found nothing?'

Carmela shook her head sadly. 'And so we are not able, you see, to say goodbye.'

Faye's heart went out to her. 'Can I ask . . .' she hesitated, not sure how to put it, 'why Enrico doesn't like the Rinaldis?' Surely not just because Giorgia had loved the theatre?

'Folk always said that Bruno could not be trusted with a pretty girl,' Carmela said, carefully. She held Faye's gaze.

'But didn't the police——?'

'In Sardinia,' Carmela said crisply, 'other factors can govern the law.'

Faye digested this. Had she understood correctly? Was Carmela now accusing the late Bruno Rinaldi of corruption? Of paying to cover up a crime? 'But . . .' She thought of the picture Alessandro and Marisa had painted of their parents – so golden, so much in love.

'In Sardinia,' Carmela continued, 'what you see is not always what you get. And eagles do not catch flies.'

'I think I understand.' Though Faye didn't – not really. *Eagles do not catch flies?* What she did see was that the Voltis craved some sort of resolution – and deserved it. They wanted to know what had happened to Giorgia because not knowing was so much worse. They needed to put her memory to rest. As Carmela had said – they needed to be able to say goodbye.

Faye followed Carmela downstairs, finished her drink and thanked her for the *mirto*, and for showing her Giorgia's room. She felt honoured that she had done so. It made Faye feel like less of an outsider. As she left, Faye put a hand on the woman's bony arm. 'Take care, Carmela,' she said.

Outside the house, Faye paused to admire the little tree by the door. It had red fruit that was just starting to ripen and white flowers beginning to emerge.

'It is the *corbezzolo* tree.' Carmela nodded. 'We make a liqueur from it, and honey too. *Miele Armaro*. Bittersweet – it is not for everybody.'

'It's very pretty.' The strawberry tree – she had tasted that honey at Marisa's apartment and loved it. Bittersweet was a bit like Sardinia itself. And it just about summed up the Voltis, too. And others she didn't even want to think about.

'It is a symbol of hospitality, *Signorina*,' Carmela added.

'Thank you for yours, *Signora*.' Faye smiled.

As she continued walking up the narrow streets of the old town towards the castle, purposefully avoiding the street where *Bar Portici* was situated, Faye decided to phone her mother. She hadn't heard from her for a few days and Carmela's words had made her think. Whatever was happening between her parents, whatever the reasons behind their separation, what was important was Faye's love for them. They were both healthy and they were both there for her. That was all that mattered. Now she had to be there for them.

She tapped into her favourites and found the number, waited for the call to go through. 'Mum?'

'Faye, how lovely. How's it going, darling?' her mother asked her. Faye hadn't yet had the chance to tell her about the turn events had taken in Deriu.

'I'm not sure that it is. Going, I mean.' It was market day and the piazzas were crammed with stalls. Faye lingered to gaze at the luscious-looking vegetables – sleek, shiny aubergines, fat red peppers, the purple-grey buds of artichokes and baskets of richly green-leaved spinach and feathery fennel; and the fruit – ripe figs full of sweet oozy flesh, shiny lemons and oranges that were globes of pure sunshine. On her way back down she'd buy some grapes, she decided – the grapes from Sardinia were the biggest and sweetest she'd ever tasted.

She explained to her mother what had happened at the last meeting with Alessandro as she moved on past the fish stall and the meats. There was suckling pig and lamb and she recognised mullet next to the usual lobster and langoustines and a range of other fish she couldn't identify. The air was ripe with market day.

'What would you do, Mum?' she asked. 'I want to get on with the job. I'm committed to it, but . . .' She let the words hang, walked up the next few steps of the cobbled street. What was the point of designing plans or even hassling the structural engineer if Alessandro Rinaldi had changed his mind?

'You don't know what's going on?' her mother said.

'Not at all.'

Nor how he feels . . . But Faye left these words unspoken. She reached the next piazza where the market was full of handicrafts. There was coral jewellery as far as she could see: coral earrings set in gold, jagged coral necklaces, ornate coral brooches. There were also cork bowls of all shapes and sizes, leather bags and jackets and quirky, hand-carved walking sticks.

Colourful bunting had been tied from house to house across the street and the sun burned down on peeling paintwork and wrought-iron balconies.

'I can see the problem,' her mother said. 'You have to find out.' There seemed to be a new determination in her tone that Faye hadn't noticed there before.

'But how can I?' Faye was asking herself as much as her mother. Marisa had said they should continue to go forward, but wasn't that pointless if Alessandro was not on board? And even if he came back on board – how long would it be for? He seemed to make a habit of going back on his word. A habit of changing his mind.

Danger signs . . . shouldn't she be paying them more heed? Faye walked on down the cobbles. Bougainvillea had wound its way around drainpipes and doorways; washing fluttered from terraces and upstairs windows. It was getting towards lunch-time and the fragrance of roasted peppers, tomatoes and garlic was beginning to waft its familiar path from the kitchens of the houses out into the street. Faye sniffed appreciatively. The Sardinians took their lunches seriously; Charlotte had told her the ritual often lasted three hours or more at the weekends, with the full courses of *antipasto, primo, secondo* and no doubt *alla sarda* to finish – sheep's cheese and a *digestivo*.

Danger signs . . . Faye heard the low clang of the church bell in *Piazza del Teatro* a couple of streets away, which sounded today like a moan of distress. She had to admit that she was disappointed in the direction things had taken. At first, she'd felt unsure and unprepared for this project, but as their meetings had progressed, as she'd begun to draw, get ideas, and form the concept and the plan, her enthusiasm had swept away her misgivings. Best of all, Marisa and Alessandro had seemed to have confidence in her, they had wanted her to take on the design despite her inexperience. They had thought she could do it. She'd jumped in too deeply too quickly, she supposed, both with Alessandro and with the theatre. And now this.

'There's only one way of finding out,' her mother said. 'And that's by asking him.' Her voice was soft but sure.

'Is that what you'd do?' Hardly. Faye thought of her mother's closed expression when Faye had asked her about her parents' marriage.

'Probably not.' She chuckled and Faye had to join in. 'But that doesn't mean it's not the right advice. If you don't talk to the man, how are you going to find out anything?'

This was true, but: 'He might just tell me what he thinks I want to hear.'

'Yes. Or he might tell you what you don't want to hear. But at least he'll tell you something.'

'Mmm.' Faye smiled at a little girl lingering in a doorway. She smiled back, all white teeth and big brown eyes, and then shyly ran back inside. Faye knew that her mother was right, of course. Marisa had suggested they give Alessandro more time. She must think she could use her sisterly powers of persuasion to bring him back on board. But Faye had her doubts. Besides, she didn't want him to be persuaded to do anything against his will. What was that worth? Nothing. She wanted him to want it of his own accord, and there was a limit to her patience.

'Do you trust him, Faye?'

Faye thought of what Pasquale had told her, of Enrico Volti's dire warning, of Jana's possessive hand at Deriu Marina . . . 'I'm not sure,' she admitted. She passed two women sitting chatting outside their houses and smiled and nodded hello. They nodded back. Was it her imagination or did they seem a bit more friendly? She thought of the way Alessandro's dark hair curled around the nape of his neck. The intense navy of his eyes. The tilt of his mouth when he smiled.

'I want to trust him.'

'Do you like him?'

'Yes.' Faye had been trying not to think about this. She did like him. That was the problem. Because why would someone say he couldn't pretend and hold her and kiss her, then . . . It made no sense. Their short texts had become utterly businesslike and horribly polite before petering out entirely since that meeting in the theatre. It was as if that day on the beach and that night of the fire had never existed. She peered down another narrow street as she passed; some of them were little more than alleyways. Each one contained more colourful houses of ochre or peppermint, and in each one there were children playing outside or women sitting gossiping and peeling vegetables for the next meal with a backdrop of the mountains or the sea.

'Faye . . .'

She caught a quick breath. 'Yes?' The scent of lemons was sharp in the air. She was up quite high now; she paused by a ledge where a prickly pear was outlined against the summer sky. From here she could see a jumble of orange roofs and flower-laden terraces; vines twisting around wooden pergolas, purple jasmine blossoming in a blue haze.

'Do you *really* like him?'

'Yes.' What more could she say? She'd heard the warnings and she knew she should probably heed them. But something else was pulling her towards him. It was infuriating. 'Some people here don't seem to like him very much though.'

'Oh?'

Faye walked on towards the castle. She wanted to get up high today – as high as possible. The steps were wide between the dry-stone walls, the pathway towered above an olive grove and she could almost smell the olives ripening in the sun. Faye thought of her conversation with Carmela. 'They say his father was a terrible womaniser and that Alessandro is the same.' She wouldn't tell her mother what else Carmela had said. She didn't want to think that this was true. But why should the people of Deriu lie to her?

Faye registered her mother's sharp intake of breath.

'What is it?'

'A terrible womaniser? Bruno Rinaldi?' She sounded shocked. But of course, he had spent the whole weekend of Charlotte and Fabio's wedding at her parents' place. 'What did you think of him, Mum?' Was he as charming as his son, she wondered. Marisa and Alessandro thought that Bruno and Sofia had been a devoted couple. But look at Faye: didn't everyone want to think this about their own parents? From what Carmela had said, it had all been a charade. Bruno Rinaldi was not safe to be left alone with a pretty woman, apparently.

There was a pause. A long pause. 'Mum?' Faye's brain went into overdrive. Something from the past seemed to click into place. Something that had happened after Fabio and Charlotte's wedding. She tried to think what it was. Something about her mother. Around her the air was still; the gnarled olive trees old and wise as time itself. She recalled her mother's reaction when Faye had first told her she was going to work on the little theatre. 'Did you like Bruno Rinaldi?'

'Yes.'

'Did you *really* like him?'

Her mother didn't deny it. 'He was lonely when he came here,' she said. 'Everyone thought of him as a successful businessman who had it all. But he didn't have it all, not any-more. He was suffering from grief. He missed his wife terribly.'

'And?' she said. Surely not. Surely not her mother . . .? Faye continued up the hill. She couldn't stop now; she felt that she was finally getting somewhere.

'And I recognised a kindred spirit,' she said. 'Someone else who was grieving. Someone else who was lonely.'

'Lonely . . .?' echoed Faye. But she'd had Faye's father – hadn't she?

'I found myself alone with him, talking to him . . .'

'Where was Dad?' Faye's voice sounded strangled. She had asked her mother to talk to her but she didn't much like what she was hearing. And about Bruno Rinaldi, of all people. Sud-denly, everything that was happening with Alessandro seemed so much more complicated.

'Around. At the wedding reception. I'd left early because I had a headache. Bruno . . .'

Faye waited.

'Well . . . sometimes it's easier to talk to a stranger,' her mother said.

Faye took a deep breath. She wanted to ask more but she didn't dare. At least this confirmed it – her parents hadn't been happy for a long while. Her mother had needed to confide in a total stranger. Was that all it was? Or had there been more? Of course not, she told herself firmly. Her mother was absolutely not the type.

'I'm at the top of the hill now,' she told her mother instead. At last she had got to the old castle, which looked down at the terracotta rooftops of the town below. It was still impressive, although only the original towers and outer walls had survived. From her guidebook, Faye had learned that some rebuilding had taken place in the 1300s when the main tower of light ochre trachyte was added. Which Faye found interesting – if one considered restoration in terms of redesign, was it a blend or a complement, or a combination of the two?

'Lovely,' said her mother.

'It is.' Faye paused on the ramparts, catching her breath, taking in the sight of the clutter of stone houses that made up the *centro storico* and the seventeenth-century *Cattedrale della Immacolata* near the waterfront with its multi-coloured mosaic-tiled domed roof. The backdrop of the mountains – the green tinged with gold now that it was summertime – led down to the river and through to the sea.

'Have you seen Dad?' Faye began to walk around the ramparts. Although there wasn't too much left of the original castle, the old chapel with the mediaeval frescoes depicting the Last Supper, which she'd seen on her first visit, was still intact. She didn't go in this time; she stayed on the ramparts. She'd walk all the way round, she decided, until she arrived once again at the steps that led back down to the *centro storico*.

'No.'

Faye sighed. 'What would you do? If he came to you? If he tried to talk to you? Would you forgive him? For whatever it is he's done to you?' Because she knew, even without them telling her, that was where it must have started.

'All marriages have their ups and downs,' her mother said. Which wasn't an answer – not really. 'But when you're not honest with each other it creates a pattern for the way you live.'

Faye thought about this. It was something she'd never considered – that her parents weren't honest with each other. She'd always taken their honesty for granted. She'd trusted them.

'Your father and I lived in that pattern for years,' her mother went on. 'I don't think we could go back and live in it again. Things have been said. It would be impossible.'

'But couldn't you create a new pattern?' Faye pressed.

'Without unpicking the old?'

Faye was transported back in time by her mother's words. She thought of a cardigan she had knitted herself years and years ago. Her mother had taught her to knit when she was a girl, and she had gradually progressed from holey, twisting scarves to doll's clothes, bobble hats, and finally a bright blue cardigan in moss stitch. She had almost finished the left front – the last piece of the cardigan – when she realised she'd made a mistake, way back. There it was – a line where there were plains instead of purls, and purls instead of plains. She'd gone wrong and stayed wrong for two rows, before straying back once again to the right pattern. And it showed. She had almost cried with frustration; it had taken her so long to get this far.

Her mother had told her she should take it out. 'You'll always see it,' she said. 'You'll always know it's there. If you take it out and start again, you can make it perfect.'

Her father had listened to the knitting discussion between his wife and daughter and he had laughed. 'Leave it be,' he'd said. 'Life's too short.'

'But it's a mistake.' Faye's mother had felt quite strongly about it, Faye could hear it in her voice. 'You can see it.'

'Life's full of them,' he'd said. 'You can see them too, but it doesn't matter. We're only human.'

Faye must take after her father more than her mother – either that or she was lazy – because she hadn't unpicked the left front of her cardigan. She had finished it, and at the end had to concede that her mother was right – she was conscious of the flaw and half-wished she'd gone back and started over. After a while though, the mistake didn't matter; she hardly noticed it, it had blended in – it was as much a part of the cardigan as the black, shiny buttons or the neat rows of rib on the buttonhole band. It was what it was and she loved it – warts and all.

Still, Faye knew that an old cardigan wasn't the same as her parents' marriage. 'It might be worth a try,' she whispered. She hugged her mobile to her ear as she made her way back down through the olive grove.

'I know it's hard for you, my darling,' her mother said. 'But nothing lasts forever, you know.'

Like Faye's cardigan. It had been consigned to the bottom of a drawer after its first winter, sent off to a charity shop after its third. But it was easier to move on from a cardigan than a marriage. 'So you couldn't go back to the pattern you had before? Too much would unravel if you tried to take out what went wrong?' Faye was trying to follow the analogy through. This was life. A mistake couldn't be undone. It would always be there.

'Something like that,' her mother said. She sounded sad.

'Did you stop loving Dad?' Faye had asked her something similar before, but her mother hadn't given her a proper answer. She stopped at the same ledge, by the same prickly pear, and looked down again towards the river.

'Sometimes love isn't enough, darling.'

'But did you?'

'I was always scared,' her mother said. As if she'd just realised it at this moment. 'Don't be scared, Faye. Talk to your Alessandro. Be brave. Talk to him and find out what's going on. Then you can decide.'

Faye wondered how much they had been talking about both of them. She felt the mid-day sun hot on her bare arms and legs, noticed the way the river twisted and curled like a comma before it reached the sea. 'What were you scared of, Mum?' she asked gently.

She heard her mother's hesitation, but this conversation had been about bravery and honesty and her mum would know she couldn't stop there. 'I was always scared of losing him, Faye,' she said.

CHAPTER 29

Faye rode Charlotte's bike down to Deriu Marina. There was nothing else for it. Her mother was right: it was no use waiting for Alessandro to contact her. She would have to go to him. And not only go to him, but get some answers too.

She leaned the bike against the harbour wall and took a moment to regain her composure. She looked out over the rocks and the boats and ships in the harbour, towards the dark mountains draped with mastic trees and to the open sea beyond. She straightened her shoulders and steeled herself. For battle, she found herself thinking. She made her way over towards the small boatyard Alessandro had shown her when they came here before. Before. It seemed like years ago.

She spotted him immediately. He was outside the boatshed in the yard, working on the hull of a wooden boat, dressed in faded shorts and a blue tee shirt splattered with paint. She watched him for a moment before he had a chance to realise that she was there. He seemed content in a way she'd rarely seen him, his brow clear, his focus exclusively on the boat he was working on, his brown hands sanding the wood in long, smooth strokes before sweeping the dust away. Faye felt a shot of warmth flood through her. He was a difficult man and there were things going on in that head of his that she could only guess at, but watching him now, working on the boat, engrossed in the activity, she felt that pull of attraction once more.

As she watched, he straightened, brushed his palms on his shorts and looked around. He saw her standing there.

Faye felt herself flush. Damn it. Once again she'd lost the initiative. But she moved forwards to meet him. 'Hello, Alessandro.'

'Faye.' He frowned, but he didn't seem surprised to see her. He drew a rag from his pocket, wiped it ineffectually across the bench beside him. 'What brings you here?' He sounded casual but she sensed an undercurrent of tension.

'Don't worry,' she said. 'It's not a social call.' She could read the signals – that he wasn't interested, that he regretted what had happened between them.

He raised an eyebrow. He rubbed his hands with the rag but they looked even more wood-stained than before. 'Then . . .?' He let the question hang.

'I'm sorry to disturb you,' she said stiffly. Perhaps she shouldn't have come, but this was business. And like her mother had said – she needed to know. 'But we have to talk.'

'We do?' For a moment that navy gaze seemed to latch on to hers once again and for a moment he seemed the same man she'd had dinner with, fought the fire with; the same man who had walked her back to Charlotte and Fabio's house. And then he glanced away into the distance and that man was gone.

'Yes, we do. About the theatre project,' she clarified.

He shrugged. 'Very well. Would you like to sit?' He indicated the paint-stained bench. 'Or we could walk?'

'Let's walk.' Faye didn't relish the thought of having this conversation sitting side by side on a bench. It wasn't going to be that cosy; his casual attitude was already making her blood boil.

'*Eh, va bene.* One moment, please.' He stepped over to an out-side tap, rubbed his hands under the water and shook them dry.

Faye looked away. Courage, she thought. She glanced through the window of his workshop. She could see the hull of another boat inside – a wooden one, in the early stages of being built – and a bench running the length of the workshop with various traditional and power tools laid out on it. Shelves held tins of paint or varnish and in the corner were some metal steps and a stool. She could smell the scent of the boatyard too – the scent that also clung to Alessandro's skin and clothes, of wood resin, oil and varnish.

He pulled some keys from the pocket of his faded denim shorts and locked the double doors of the workshop. '*Andiamo.*' He indicated the path that ran alongside the marina beach. 'Let's go.'

Faye took a deep breath and followed him. He could be as cool and casual as he liked but he wasn't going to escape her questions this time. She looked around. The beach was made up of dark sand that reflected the rugged cliffs. Holidaymakers were sunbathing, playing bat and ball and swimming in water so calm it looked more like a dark blue haze. It was still only 11 a.m. but it was hot. Faye adjusted her sunhat so it covered more of her brow. She'd love to be in the water too, but first she had to do some straight talking with this man.

'What can I do for you, Faye?' He half-turned towards her but didn't meet her gaze. His voice was cool. Had he really forgotten everything?

'You said that you needed some time to think about the the-atre project,' she reminded him. The path was narrow and lined with myrtle and blackthorn shrubs; they could walk side by side but it meant close proximity. Faye tried to pull herself inwards so that she didn't brush her arm against his. She was sharply conscious of his nearness, his physicality, the scent of him.

'Yes, I did.' He glanced across at her, raised his eyebrows once again. 'Do you find that unreasonable?'

'No. That is . . . yes. I mean . . .' She tried to stay calm. 'I need to know the reasons why.'

He half-turned again. 'Need or want?' he asked. His voice wasn't unkind, but it was carefully neutral. Did that take any effort, she wondered. She could see that this wasn't going to be easy.

'Both.' Faye kept her voice firm and, she hoped, businesslike. If he could be neutral, then so could she, even if it killed her. 'It simply isn't fair.'

'Fair?' he echoed. He almost sounded amused by this.

Faye felt a flush of irritation. 'You may not be aware of it, Alessandro,' she said sharply, 'but I'm right in the middle of dealing with the structural engineer and builders. I've started drawing up some plans that I've had to put to one side. I have no idea how long it's going to take you to make up your mind, or even why you changed your mind in the first place, and—' She broke off, looked further out to sea, where the sunlight was shimmering over the barely rippling blue ocean, and tried to find her inner calm.

'And?' He pushed a bramble out of their way. He didn't sound amused any longer. His mouth was set in a tight line.

Now you're angry, she thought. Well, be angry. She didn't care as long as she got those answers. 'And I can't help thinking that whatever you decide, you might change your mind,' she said. 'Again.' She tried to get her breathing to return to normal but it was even harder now.

'I see.' His words were clipped short.

But did he? They continued walking along the sandy path and Faye could feel the tension in him now. It was in the set of his shoulders, the tight swing of his arms, the closed expression on his face. She waited. They had gone halfway around the semi-circular arc of the bay and now were heading towards the lookout tower that stood high on the headland beyond.

'I realise that this situation is not ideal. And also . . .' He hesitated. 'Unfair. But, you see, Faye . . .' As he spoke her name, he let out a sigh and at last she felt some of the tension release. 'It is not a question of me changing my mind.'

'Then what is it a question of?'

He didn't reply to this. 'Did Marisa send you?' he asked instead. He stopped walking and turned to her, his eyes intent.

'No, she didn't.' Faye stopped walking too. She looked away for a moment, saw a dragonfly with gorgeous green iridescent wings skim over the water beyond the rocks. 'This is for me.' She stared back at him. 'I need to know for myself. Either you're employing me – or you're not.'

His eyes seemed to soften. Gently, he took her arm for a moment and led her on down the path. It seemed so natural for him to touch her and yet Faye was so conscious of that touch, of the heat of his skin. 'We are employing you, yes, of course,' he said. 'Do you need more money?'

She stiffened and pulled her arm away. 'This has nothing to do with money.' How could he even think that?

'What then?' He put his head to one side. 'You are unable to hold things up for a week or two, to let me sort out certain matters?'

Put like that it almost sounded reasonable. But . . . 'What matters?' she pressed. 'What's the problem, Alessandro? Why can't you tell me? If I don't know what's happening, if I don't know what's going on—'

'I thought you wanted a holiday in Sardinia?' His voice was tender, but Faye felt that was below the belt. She glanced across at him. He was trying to placate her, still determined to give nothing away.

'I did.' The path was greener now. Faye recognised juniper and tamarisk trees. Her parents had tamarisk in their garden in West Dorset; they were dusky pink and feathery and bent with the wind. The beach was wilder on this stretch. White cistus and wild lilies were growing freely in the sand and she could smell the lemon and peppery scent of the thyme that grew freely on the slopes of the hills.

'But not anymore?' Was it her imagination, or had his tone changed? He still sounded guarded, but something told her she was getting through to him at last.

Faye raised her face to the sky, felt the warmth of the sun on her skin. 'I'm working now, Alessandro, that's the difference. I've accepted a commission – from you and Marisa – and I want to get on with it. I need to know what's happening. To keep me dangling like this is unprofessional.'

'Need or want?' he repeated. There was a slant of humour in his eyes now but his expression remained serious.

'Both,' she said again. 'And to be honest I'm fed up with you playing games.' Games with the project and games with her heart.

'Oh, Faye . . .' He led the way into the maquis which was thicker and greener now, almost blocking their view of the sea. 'I am not playing games.'

There was no answer to that. Because if he wasn't playing games—

'This is not a personal concern?' He stopped walking, turned and put his hands on her shoulders. 'Or is it, Faye?'

She flinched. 'You tell me.' How could he even ask her that? Of course it was also a personal concern – she longed to know how things stood between them. But that wasn't what she was here for, at least not entirely. She was here because she needed to know what was happening with the little theatre. That, she told herself, was her primary concern.

'I cannot help hoping that there is.' His voice was low.

'Is?' Her knees were almost buckling – it must be the heat of the sun, she thought.

'Is a personal concern.'

She stared at him. What was she supposed to make of that? Did that mean that he didn't regret what had happened between them? That he hadn't forgotten? That he felt something for her after all? If so, he had a funny way of showing it.

He was smiling. 'Relationships are complicated, Faye,' he said, 'are they not?'

She nodded.

'Look at your parents. They stayed together when perhaps they might have been happier apart.'

'Perhaps.' She didn't want to admit that.

'People find it hard to leave,' he murmured. 'In a relationship, there is security as well as love, I think. It is too difficult sometimes, for people to say goodbye.'

Faye couldn't work out what he was trying to tell her.

'And as for the little theatre . . . I understand your frustration,' he said. 'But there are complications which I must deal with.' He spread his hands. 'I have no choice. I am simply asking you to be patient. To give me—'

'Time, I know.' She looked away, over his shoulder. There

was a leaf caught on the sleeve of his tee shirt and she wanted to brush it off.

Slowly, he nodded. 'If I could tell you what is going on, Faye,' he said, 'I would.'

She waited.

'If I could make things different . . . give you a decision here and now, I would.'

Faye was almost ready to give up on this conversation. She was getting nowhere. And she was no longer sure whether they were talking about the little theatre or their relationship or both. A gull shrieked above them, and seemed to plummet from the cliff top. Faye took a deep breath of the sea air: fresh and salty, it mingled with the rich sweetness of the flowers of the maquis.

'If I could do or say more . . .' He seemed to move closer towards her and then he snapped away. He shook his head. Swore softly.

Faye sensed a further breach in his defences. 'Is it about the ownership of the theatre?' she asked, carefully. 'Has something else happened with Enrico Volti that you don't want to tell me?' Because Enrico was intent on causing more trouble, she was sure of it.

He shook his head once more. 'If only it were that simple, Faye.'

Faye noticed the beads of sweat gathering around his eyebrows. 'Is someone threatening you, Alessandro?' This sounded melodramatic and slightly ludicrous, but it was the only thing she could think of, and here in Deriu, she had to admit that it was a possibility.

'Not exactly.' He hesitated. 'But if I am honest – it may be that I am no longer free to move forward with the project.'

Faye stared at him. 'Why not?'

He shook his head. 'I cannot tell you.'

She rubbed at her temples. The sun was getting hotter. 'So you'll just give up?'

'Give up?' He looked startled at this.

'Give up on your dream, on your sister's dream, what you wanted to do for your mother's memory?' How could she get through to him? 'You'll let someone or something stop you from doing what you want to do or having what you want to have? Just like that? Without even fighting for it?'

He didn't reply, but his navy eyes narrowed.

'I expected more of you,' said Faye. She looked away, back towards the shimmering ocean. She didn't want to see the hurt in his face, didn't want to dwell on the fact that his shirt was exactly the same colour as his eyes, as the ocean.

'You do not understand.' His voice was heavy now. He really did sound defeated.

'I might, if you explained it to me.'

But he wasn't looking at her now. He was looking out to sea, thinking of something or someone quite different. *And what about us,* she wanted to say; *what about that night, that kiss?* But of course, she didn't.

'I know I am asking a lot,' Alessandro said after a moment. 'I know that you want to do your job and that Marisa is impatient. I know that you have no reason to trust me—'

'No, you're right, I don't.' Faye was still cross with him. If it had only been about the theatre project she might have been capable of more professionalism. But it wasn't and there was no use pretending. She'd had hopes of so much more.

He drew back as if she had slapped him. 'I am trying to do what is right,' he said softly.

'Right or wrong,' said Faye, 'you need to make up your mind,

Alessandro. Let me know when you have – but don't take too long.' She turned around. She'd had enough of this.

'Faye . . .'

She ignored him. It was easy for him to talk of trust. But what about trusting her and telling her what was going on? It was all a bit one-sided.

'Faye.' He followed her as she stalked back through the maquis, down the path. Her eyes had filled with tears that she was trying to hold back and she almost tripped on a rock jutting out of the sand. He grabbed her arm to stop her falling, pulled her none too gently round to face him. 'It is not what you think.'

She wrenched her arm out of his grasp. 'Then what is it?' she challenged him.

His face was very close; those eyes, that mouth. She didn't move any nearer. Again, she watched him. Again, she waited.

He pulled her to him in a sharp, sudden gesture, let out a small groan, held her face in his hands and kissed her with such force that her knees almost buckled from under her. Just as suddenly he drew back; he let her go.

Faye tried to catch her breath. She'd hardly had time to respond, certainly no time to stop him. Who the hell did he think—?'

He put a fingertip to her mouth, gently traced a line over and around her lips. 'I will sort it out, Faye,' he said. 'I promise. But it is as I said. You have to trust me.'

Could she trust him? Faye's emotions were tangled as she wheeled Charlotte's bike away from Deriu Marina. He had said he would sort it out. He had said he would have an answer for her in a week. She couldn't walk away from the project – not at this moment in time; it certainly wouldn't be fair on Marisa. And she wasn't sure she could walk away from Alessandro Rinaldi either. He had this way of getting to her, of giving her hope. And no matter how much she tried to push it to the back of her mind, she still hoped, still responded when he touched her, when he kissed her.

Faye sighed. She supposed she'd have to give him that week.

As she got to the bridge, she swung on to the bike, put her foot down and paused for a moment, looking back at the boatyard. Alessandro had returned to work already, head down, sanding the boat hull. It was too far away to read his expression.

Someone must have shouted to him because as she watched, he looked up, shielding his eyes from the sun. That someone was going into the boatyard now. A female someone. Jana – Faye recognised the swing of the long dark hair, the olive skin, the flash of jewellery. Alessandro straightened up. Faye couldn't interpret his body language, but there was no need. Jana launched herself at him, flung herself into his arms. And he was stroking her dark hair and holding her.

What a fool she had been. Faye turned around – she couldn't watch anymore, she didn't have to. She pushed herself off and rode over the bridge, back towards Charlotte and Fabio's house. Her eyes were watering – from the sun or the wind in her face, not tears. She understood now what he had been trying to tell her earlier when he'd talked of security and how hard it was to end a relationship. Because he was in one. He had Jana and Jana had him. He might have been tempted by Faye – for a moment or two – and imagined himself to be a bit of a Casanova . . . Her lip curled. He had made a play. And she had been right; it was just a game. Faye meant nothing to him. Now, it was clear as day. Pasquale de Montis had been right too, and Enrico Volti, when they had warned her about Alessandro Rinaldi. She should have listened.

Thank God it had gone no further. Thank God it had just been a kiss, two kisses, a brush of the hands, an embrace . . . Faye shuddered as she arrived back at the riverside house. She had been a fool. But she wouldn't be a fool any longer.

CHAPTER 30

Ade had arranged to Skype with Faye. He set up his laptop, got a beer out of the fridge and called her. 'Hello, love?'

'Hi, Dad.' The video came on. She looked tanned but tired.

'How are you doing? Still loving Sardinia?' He hoped she wasn't working too hard. She hadn't said much, but this job she was taking on must feel like a huge responsibility to a girl fresh out of university. And Ade felt guilty. He and Molly had added to Faye's problems. Their timing had been appalling.

'Oh, yes and no.' She gave an unconvincing grin.

Ade frowned. Something must have happened since they'd last spoken. 'Is everything alright, love?'

'Well . . .' He saw her hesitation. 'I really like it here – in some ways. But the job's been put on hold. To be honest, Dad, I'm not exactly sure what's happening.' And her voice seemed to wobble slightly.

Ade scrutinised her more carefully. 'Oh?' She certainly looked a little bit lost today. He wished he was with her right now so he could give her a big fatherly hug. It was so hard when your child grew up, when they became an adult. Part of Ade still wanted to sort everything out for Faye, wanted to be the one she always turned to. It was a hard lesson, appreciating his daughter's independence, learning not to be the ultimate problem-solver that he wanted to be as a father. And yet here he was – not able to even solve his own problems.

'I'll know more in a week or so.' She gave a little shrug, but she sounded fed up and Ade thought he could see behind it. Unless he was no longer as close to his daughter as before.

'And how about you, Dad? You look a bit tired. What's happening your end?'

'Yeah, well . . .' That was a question and a half. He knew that he was looking weary. Old, more like. For more years than he cared to recall, his hair had been gold tinged with white. Now, suddenly, it was white tinged with gold – he could see that on the video cam. He looked blurred around the edges. He felt blurred around the edges.

Ade thought about his meeting with Nina – he'd thought about it a lot. Her words had been hard to take, but of course she'd been right about most things. Ade was beginning to realise that he'd made more than a few mistakes in his life. And where should he go from here? He still had no bloody idea. 'Nothing, really. I'm still in Exeter,' he said. Because of course he wasn't going to tell Faye about Nina.

She raised an eyebrow. 'You've finished work though?'

'Yes, I have.'

'So . . .?'

Ade knew what she was thinking. Was Exeter his new base? Why was he still there when he loved Dorset so much? And where was he going? Wasn't the world supposed to be his oyster?

'This is the flat I'm living in at the moment,' he said, to distract them both. He spun his laptop around so that she could see his surroundings. There was a coffee cup on an empty table, a stiff-looking sofa and a TV in the corner. The carpet was oatmeal. No rugs, no cushions, nothing personal.

'Hmm,' she said. 'It looks . . .'

'I know.' Bleak and empty. Nothing like a home at all. 'I left everything back at the house,' he said. What was he even doing here? He couldn't go back to West Dorset, though. Molly had been clear enough. That was one place definitely out of bounds.

'How long are you planning on staying in Exeter, Dad?' Faye's voice was non-committal but curious.

Ade knew why. Last time they'd spoken he couldn't wait to leave, was full of plans to buy a camper van and go off travelling. She had been cross with him. 'Aren't you a bit old for that sort of thing, Dad?' she'd asked him, though he was only fifty-six and the average age of camper-vanners was probably more like sixty-five. There was a difference, of course, between motorhoming for the retired and old hippie camper-vanners of the VW Classic variety; Ade liked to think that he was somewhere in the middle. 'I've worked hard all my life,' he had told her. Why shouldn't he have the chance to do what he'd always wanted to do?

Now though, something was holding him back. After everything that had happened, it seemed selfish and irresponsible to go and leave it all behind.

'I don't know,' he said. He knew he sounded forlorn. 'I'm not sure of anything much at the moment.' Which was the most honest thing he'd said for a while.

'Oh, Dad.'

And here he was, laying even more problems at his daughter's feet. Now he was making her worry about him.

'I was looking forward to early retirement,' he confessed. 'But now it's here . . .' He laughed, but it sounded forced even to his own ears. 'And now that your mum and I . . .' His voice trailed. 'There seems to be so much time. And I don't know quite what to do with it all.' He'd been plunged into life as a single man again. A single man with no job and no home. It had been a shock.

'Are you having second thoughts about going travelling?' Faye asked him. 'Is that it?'

'Yes and no.' Ade realised belatedly that he was echoing Faye's earlier words to him. 'I've wanted to do it for so long. It seems a bit pathetic that now I've got the chance I'm not even getting on with it.'

'So why aren't you?' she pushed.

He laughed. 'Good question, love. Why aren't I?' Where did he imagine his responsibilities lay? With Molly? With Faye? With himself, perhaps?

She laughed with him, which was a relief. 'Where would you go, Dad? If you could choose anywhere, I mean?'

He didn't need to think about it. 'I've always wanted to go to Australia.'

She went quiet.

'Faye?'

'Australia's an awful long way away, Dad,' she said.

'Yes, it is.' And Ade felt something pulling at him deep in his belly, some sort of sense of imminent loss. But he didn't have to lose anything, did he? He could come back. 'How about Sardinia then?' he said. It was just the sudden need to see her, he supposed. There was something not right with Faye – he could see it in her face. She was trying to laugh and smile, but she was hiding some inner sadness, he was sure. He was her father. He'd messed up so many times before. Now, he wanted to try and make it better.

'You want to come over and see me?' Visibly, she brightened.

'Well, if the job's been put on hold . . .' He let her have a think about it. Hopefully, she wouldn't see this as taking sides. He was pretty sure Molly wouldn't mind. Faye was their daughter. And anyway, what was happening between Ade and Molly – it wasn't a battle; it wasn't a question of sides. 'You might have the time to show me around a bit.'

'I'd love that.' And he could see that she meant it.

'Really?'

'Really. I'll have to check with Charlotte, but I'm sure she won't mind.'

'And I'll check the flights.' Ade felt a rush of anticipation at seeing her. It would give him a break from all this soul-searching, and it would also be a chance to review things and decide what he really wanted to do. He could talk things through with his daughter, spend some quality time with her, see if he could help with whatever was bothering her.

'Brilliant.'

'I'll get back to you as soon as I can, love,' he said. 'I'll get there as soon as I can.' And Ade felt more hopeful. More hopeful than he had for quite a while.

CHAPTER 31

Pasquale gently opened the door of the auditorium and strolled up the centre aisle towards the stage of the little theatre. He felt an undeniable sense of pride. He turned from left to right giving a slight nod to the audience on each side. He had, after all, saved the little theatre from burning, from what could have been total destruction.

He shuddered. The very thought made him sick to his stomach. His little theatre gone . . . But thank the Sweet Madonna, this had not happened. There was some fire damage naturally – but the heart of the theatre, his secrets and his memories, remained.

He sat on the stage for a moment, absorbing the sense of tranquillity he'd always found here. There might be little enough peace soon enough. He sighed. What was happening now with this project the entire village had once seemed to be talking about? All had gone very quiet; he hadn't even seen the *Signora* Faye here in the theatre, scribbling in that book of hers. Had she taken heed of his warning? Probably not. The young always imagined they knew best; they would always go their own way.

His head slumped towards his chest. How would he feel if builders came in to desecrate the place? What would he do? Pasquale shrugged and slipped off the stage. Now, after all that had been said, he sensed that it was up to Fate to decide. One thing he had learned in life was that you never knew what it would throw at you next.

Pasquale climbed the steps on to the stage and used the pulley to raise the lilac curtain. All the time he had been touring in Europe with Sofia and the repertory company, he had held Deriu and this theatre in a special place deep in his soul, alongside his most precious memories of his father. Indeed, the theatre was inextricably bound up with his father and his father's heroism – it always would be. He strode on to the stage. He hoped it was not too vain to imagine that he, Pasquale de Montis, had now also played his part.

The touring too had been special. Sofia was young and growing in experience. She shone. But still she deferred to Pasquale in so many things and he was grateful for that. She would ask him: 'What emotion should I be portraying here? It is complex, *non*? She wants to save him, she loves him and yet she is remembering what happened between them at their last meeting . . .'

And she would fix her beautiful almond eyes on Pasquale and he would clap his hands in delight. 'That is it. You have it. That is perfect.' Because she had captured an expression, an emotion that was exactly right. That was what had made her a great actress. What made her a remarkable woman, though, was that she did not know it.

'Pasquale – is this make-up right?' she would call as he hurried to her dressing room to inspect. 'And in that final speech, should I put my hands out, or clasp them to my heart?'

Pasquale was not directing, but she seemed to have high respect for his judgement. If an audience was restless, it was Pasquale she ran to for consolation. If an audience gave a standing ovation she would celebrate with him. How she would sparkle . . . Her successes were his own and vice versa, because invariably they were playing opposite each other. It was his arms she fell into when she must faint or die; it was his lips that brushed against hers in a love scene. A love scene . . .

'My bounty is as boundless as the sea, my love as deep; the more I give to thee.' He sensed the hush of his imaginary audience; he felt their emotion. Playing Romeo to Sofia's Juliet had been the climax of his career.

If only he too could have died when she died. 'Goodnight, goodnight! Parting is such sweet sorrow, that I shall say goodnight till it be morrow.' God knows in those days after her death, he had wanted to. It had been a mad and terrible time. If only they could have been star-crossed lovers to the end of their days . . . He beat his chest with his fist and gazed out beseechingly into the auditorium. 'Oh teach me how I should forget to think . . .' Enough.

Pasquale left the stage. He stood in the wings for a moment. Thought of the Resistance and the Bertelli family scurrying through. His father's voice. '*Andiamo*. Hurry. Hurry.'

His mother was right, of course. He had always loved Sofia. From the first moment he saw her on stage at the Civic Theatre in Sassari . . . It was a love that had been strong enough to persuade him to leave his mother, the theatre and Deriu. He'd left because Sofia wanted to go to England. Where Sofia went, Pasquale would follow. And yet he had persuaded her to come back here to Deriu – and that had been his downfall.

Pasquale went backstage down the narrow corridor that led to the dressing rooms. The paint on the walls was peeling. Dust was thick on the skirtings; each layer representing a passage of time that would be no more. He walked into the first *camerino*, dressing room, hesitantly, almost feeling that he should knock on the door. But his Sofia was in there no longer. He could picture her though, sitting in front of this same cracked mirror, letting down her dark hair, giving him that look as he stood behind her gazing at her reflection. 'Was I good tonight, Pasquale? Did I do well?'

'Yes, my love,' he would sooth. He would rub her shoulders, knowing that her neck was aching, relishing the pleasure of touching her soft skin, her perfume an intoxicating cloud around him. 'You were perfect.'

He had persuaded Sofia to come to Deriu because he thought being here, in his hometown, would make a difference to the way she viewed him. Here, he was sure, she would turn to him one day and beg him to take her in his arms when they were not on stage, when they were simply Sofia and Pasquale; they would go from friends to soul mates and then lovers.

But it did not happen.

Pasquale left the room. He knew it was silly – his mother would doubtless make some acid comment about him living in the past – but he liked to wander around, checking up on everything, seeing that it was all just so. *Il Piccolo Teatro* was old and practically derelict. It had even suffered a fire. Pasquale's imaginary audience was the only one who ever came here now. Still . . .

He had gone to the bar to play dominoes, kept his ears pricked for gossip of how the fire might have started. But now the fire officers had carried out their investigations and they were satisfied; it had been as he suspected – a cigarette end not extinguished. Kids. And if he ever saw them loitering near *il Piccolo Teatro* again . . . He would not be responsible for his actions. Pasquale liked to think that just as his father before him, he was the caretaker of the place; he liked to think that he looked after its heart, its soul.

What did happen when he and Sofia came to Deriu was

something Pasquale had not envisaged. Sofia settled into Deriu immediately – she might have been born here. People befriended her. She was looked up to, almost as a queen, and for a short while, Pasquale was looked up to as well. Despite his lowly beginnings and somewhat menial caretaker's job, his father had been the village hero. And now here was his son, Pasquale de Montis, an actor, even celebrated in a small way, and the consort of the woman who had somehow immediately won the hearts of the people of Deriu.

Pasquale reached the costume room at the very end of the corridor. This, more than any other area of the theatre, took him back into those memories of the past – some good, some bad. In here, racks of dresses, suits and shawls still hung on rails against the walls; lavender silk, black satin, brocade in yellows, blues and purples shot with red or platinum, shimmers of gold and silver brushed one against the other; dusty and faded now with time, but a visible reminder of those players on stage, those times of *il Piccolo Teatro*'s heyday. In here, women had pinned, stitched, refitted and altered garments for performance after performance. There was still an old sewing machine on a treadle, pushed into the corner with a covered stool tucked beside it and a tattered brocade chair for the comfort of whoever might be waiting. Why, Pasquale had sat there himself, many a time.

He shook his head, felt the slump of energy that was commonplace these days. He could not avoid catching sight of himself in the gilt-edged mirror, though if he tried harder he could see Sofia turning from left to right, head tossed back, laughing, spinning around in a graceful twirl. And he wanted to see no more.

He could not stay in this room. Quickly, Pasquale left, shutting the door behind him. All was as it should be. Nothing had changed. But the memories were too painful. They alone could never be discharged.

Pasquale and Sofia were halfway through the first run of the first performance at the little theatre in Deriu when it happened. He went to her dressing room after the show — he always went to her dressing room; they would talk and laugh and run through their performance together, to see if anything could be improved or to congratulate one another on how well it had gone. But on this night he went to her dressing room and there she was, sniffing appreciatively at a huge bouquet of roses.

'Ah, an admirer.' He gave her an arch look. Of course this had happened before — it was yet another thing that they had always laughed about.

But this time she did not laugh. 'They are from Bruno Rinaldi,' she said instead.

'Rinaldi?' Of course he knew Bruno Rinaldi — his father owned the theatre. His family was one of the oldest in Deriu — some said they were Deriu.

'I am going to meet him for dinner,' Sofia said.

'Of course you are.' Pasquale tried to make a joke of it. 'His father employs us. You must be nice to him, Sofia, eh?'

'I will be.' But she didn't laugh. Her eyes had a dreamy quality that he'd never seen in them before. She was somewhere else, he realised. Already, she was somewhere else.

Pasquale retraced his steps back to the dressing rooms. And that had been the start of the greatest love affair in Deriu, as some called it. Within days, Bruno and Sofia were inseparable. She no longer asked Pasquale what he thought about her speeches, her performances, her costume. She no longer met up with him at the end of a performance. They still saw one another, of course; they still worked together. But in the following show, Pasquale did not get to play the lead opposite Sofia. Nor the next, nor the next.

And gradually, something else happened, too. Pasquale was not regarded in the same light as he had been when he first returned to Deriu with Sofia. People still remembered his father as a hero, yes, they always would. But Pasquale could no longer bask in the shadow of his father's bravery. Just as he was no longer given the main parts to play, so the people of Deriu seemed to lose some respect for the man who was bullied by his mother, who had so easily lost the woman he loved, who was no longer the leading actor on stage.

With increasing desperation, Pasquale waited for the infatuation between Sofia and Bruno Rinaldi to fade, to end. But it did not fade; it did not end. Sofia Santi married Bruno Rinaldi and when his father died, it was Bruno Rinaldi running the theatre and Sofia, the Queen of Deriu, by his side. Everyone said that it was meant to be. For a while, at least, everyone adored them. But Pasquale's heart was broken.

They had children. Pasquale had never taken to the boy. But Marisa reminded him of Sofia and what he had lost. Why had Sofia been so against her daughter following in her footsteps on the stage? He could never work that out. Had Sofia and Pasquale's days together in the theatre – those blissful, halcyon days – been so bad? He hoped not. He would live them again, every single one, if only he could.

Slowly, he descended the stairs and returned, past the dressing rooms, back to the stage. Nevertheless. His claim to the theatre, he believed, was the longest. It wasn't *il Piccolo Teatro* who had taken Sofia away. It was that bastard Bruno Rinaldi.

Pasquale knew in his heart that he should have left Deriu – his mother was right about that. But he found he could not. And besides, he did not want to run away. He had to look after his mother – he was all she had and she was growing old. And he still belonged in Deriu; nothing had changed there. But even worse – he could not stop loving his Sofia. She was not his Sofia, never had been his Sofia; she had betrayed him. But love was not a switch one could turn off and on at will. And so.

'Thus with a kiss I die . . .'

And so Pasquale had stayed. Now, his bonds to the little theatre were as strong as they had ever been. Now, he supposed he would stay in Deriu until his dying day.

CHAPTER 32

Faye was surprised when the text arrived. With her father here, she had almost managed to put Alessandro Rinaldi and the little theatre out of her mind. Almost, but not quite. It seemed they had both crept further into her consciousness than she had been aware. For days, her lips had felt bruised by his kiss; her romantic notions totally dashed by that vision of Jana throwing her arms around Alessandro's neck as she arrived at the boatyard that day. Faye's father's visit had been good for her though; it had happened at exactly the right time.

She glanced at the text. Now she would find out whether or not Alessandro had sorted out what he had promised and if the project was going ahead. *Trust him*, he had said. That had become difficult. But she'd promised to wait a week. After that, she'd go back to England and start again. She had no choice. She had committed herself to the project, but if it wasn't going to happen, then she'd just have to un-commit herself. She couldn't put her life on hold forever.

Faye's father was leaving the day after tomorrow and she would be sad to see him go. He had hired a car from the airport and together they had explored more of the island. The Costa Smeralda on the east coast of Sardinia had the most spectacular scenery, but the west coast was less touristy and more rugged and she secretly preferred it. One day, they drove to the historic

Catalan fortified city of Alghero where they ate a delicious lunch of *aragosta alla catalane*, lobster with tomatoes and onions; another day they ventured further, to the northwest promontory of Capo Caccia where swifts and peregrine falcons nested in the crevices of the precipitous cliffs and it was possible to walk down 656 steep steps to the stunning caves of the *Grotta di Nettuna* – if they had the energy, Faye's father said, and they did. Another day, they headed south to the ancient site of Tharros to see the Nuraghic settlement there and Faye was delighted to spot a blush of flamingos and some purple herons in the marshland around Oristano. They ate *fregola* pasta and seafood in beach bar restaurants and Sardinian *gelato* as they strolled along cobbled streets and sea front promenades. For the first time since she'd arrived in Sardinia, Faye was feeling like a tourist and she was enjoying it.

She could see that her father was especially fascinated by the *nuraghi;* there was such an air of mystery surrounding these ancient villages that flourished in Sardinia from 1800 to 500 BC; apparently there were seven thousand sites, ranging from a single tower to the remains of a complex village with burial chambers, towers, ramparts and ordinary dwellings. Faye had to practically drag him away from the settlement. No traces of written language had ever been found, but there were bronze figures and other finds on display in various archaeological museums.

Faye's favourite trip, however, was to the ancient village of Nora, to see what was considered to be the first Roman theatre (amazingly still almost intact) in the first pre-Roman settlement in Sardinia. The little town on the south coast – apparently part of it sunk and already under the sea – was surrounded by mountains and pine trees; there was a soft breeze and an undeniable sense of history. They stood at the perfectly straight *crocevia* crossroads. To the east stood the clearly identifiable Temple of Aesculapius, and to the south, the *Terme A Mare* – Spa by the Sea – complete with rectangular bathtubs, the remains of furnaces and brick pillars that once supported an upper pavement with underfloor heating. They walked around the remains of the houses, peered at the black and ochre tesserae mosaics and admired the complex vaulted system of sewers that led to the sea. Standing together under the pine trees, Faye and her father listened as their guide talked about the theatre, which had thin bricks, vaulted archways and niches reminiscent of the Colosseum in Rome. Faye felt a strong sense of connection – to this place, to the past, to the theatrical tradition of this island that had lasted so long. She wanted to be a part of that tradition, too.

They hadn't talked much about Faye's mother or her parents' separation; Faye wanted to, but she also only wanted her father to talk about it when he was ready. He seemed calmer and refreshed. She hoped that whatever demons he was struggling with, he would find a way of dealing with them. Neither had she told him exactly what had happened with Alessandro Rinaldi, though she had admitted to being upset that her first interior design project might come to nothing after all. She had the feeling that her father might have sensed some of what had gone on here in Deriu. He was certainly alert to the occasional hostile look that Faye still received; she could almost feel him bristle. There was a new closeness between them, a bond renewed.

The afternoon Faye received the text, she and her father had visited Sassari to explore the city and take a look at the civic theatre. Faye hoped it might give her some ideas. After her visit to the boatyard she had called Marisa, who had just come back from a weekend in Rome with her boyfriend Leo, and suggested that they hold back on any further work. It could – depending on what Alessandro decided – turn out to be a waste of time. Marisa agreed that Faye should keep it to a minimum, just working on some of the layout options and general elevations, but she was adamant that they carry on and insistent that Faye invoice them at an hourly rate. Faye acquiesced. She knew that Marisa didn't want a hold-up any more than she did. Besides, she couldn't resist visiting another Sardinian theatre.

Predictably, she'd heard nothing from Alessandro, and neither did she want to, though she'd seen him twice. Once from a distance, prowling the streets of Deriu *centro storico* like a hunted animal, once in the bar where she'd spotted him before. Her father had suggested they go in for a beer – tempted by the football showing on the TV screen, Faye suspected – but she had shaken her head, held firmly to his arm and walked on by. Thankfully, her father had made no further comment.

The *Teatro Civico* of Sassari was located in the heart of the old city on Corso Vittorio Emanuele II, the road they were now strolling along in the afternoon sunshine.

'It's really got to you, hasn't it, love?' her father remarked. 'This theatre thing?'

Faye laughed. *This theatre thing* . . . It was true, she supposed. What had started as a situation into which she had been thrown, had become something of a passion. 'I'm going to look into whether I can do any more courses,' she told him. Everyone needed a specialist subject, after all, designers arguably more than most.

'When you come back to England, you mean?' her father asked her.

She nodded. Which might be sooner rather than later.

Her father looked as if he was about to say more but they had arrived. 'Here it is,' she said. The theatre in Sassari had once also fulfilled the function of town hall, as Faye had discovered when she'd Googled it earlier in the week, and in 1947 much of its wooden structure and decoration had been demolished due to severe deterioration. Interestingly, it too had suffered a fire and extensive restoration in 1967 and then again at the end of the century, so that now it was able to house art exhibitions, musical shows, cinema and other cultural events, much as she hoped to achieve for the little theatre in Deriu.

They both took a moment to study the outside. The facade was impressive; there was some interesting sculpture and decorative work. Faye pointed this out to her father and made a note to ask Marisa about the sculptor.

'Shall we go in?'

Faye spoke to the woman on reception who was happy to let them take a look. She glanced at her watch. 'There is a rehearsal at four,' she said. 'You are welcome to go in now.'

'Thank you so much.' Faye loved the decor at first sight: the rich cream of the entrance to the auditorium, the dusky pink of the stage curtains. The designer had achieved a classic feel and impact through simple sculpture and bold garlands on the facades of the tiered horseshoe seating.

'What do you think?' her father asked her. 'It's very grand.'

Faye nodded. It wasn't what she had in mind for the little theatre, but it was impressive.

After their visit to the theatre they went for coffee in a small bohemian bar with modern abstracts on the red walls. 'Can you manage without me tonight?' Faye asked her father. She retrieved her mobile from her bag.

'Of course.' He smiled. 'Have you had some news?'

Faye stirred her coffee. 'Not yet – but hopefully I'll know more tonight.' The text she had received was from Marisa. She got it up on her phone and showed him. *Can you come round to my place this evening? Alessandro will be there.*

He raised an eyebrow. 'Sounds like a warning,' he said.

Faye smiled.

'Have you answered it yet?'

'I will now.' Her father was right. Marisa's text did sound like a warning. But Faye could read the subtext. If Alessandro was there it meant that he had called the meeting. And if he had called the meeting, it meant that he had reached a decision on the future of the design project. *OK, see you later,* she replied. She gave a little shiver.

'Don't worry, love.' Her father's pat on her hand was reassuring. 'Good news or bad news, it's always best to know exactly where you stand.'

'You're right.' She could do it. She could face up to Alessandro Rinaldi and she could carry on as if nothing had happened between them. Faye squared her shoulders and smiled at her father. She was so glad that he had been with her this week. His familiarity and his easy companionship had helped her more than he could know. But was he also aware that he sounded just like her mother? That the two of them were more alike than they thought? And was he also aware, she wondered, of how scared Faye's mother had always been of losing him?

CHAPTER 33

When Faye stepped inside Marisa's apartment that evening, she could see that Alessandro had not yet arrived. She was relieved. It would give her a chance to prepare for him, perhaps quiz Marisa about what was happening.

'Thank you for coming, Faye.' Marisa handed her a drink. 'You may need it.' She rolled her eyes.

'Has Alessandro told you anything?' Faye took a sip of the chilled white Vernaccia, full-bodied and strong.

'Nothing.' Marisa led the way over to the couch and they sat, side by side. 'I had a text from him, that is all. It only said to get you here tonight. That we would have a meeting, the three of us.' She shrugged.

'So you still have no clue why he changed his mind in the first place?' They were close; it seemed impossible she had no idea. And yet Faye recalled Alessandro's inscrutable expression when she had cross-questioned him down in the marina. He was a man of mystery, alright. She had been determined to get some answers and yet if she hadn't turned around on the bridge to look back at the boatyard, she wouldn't have had a clue – and she would never have known that Jana was very definitely still in his life.

Marisa shook her head. 'He would not tell me. I have tried, Faye, but he just looked miserable and said: "Leave it to me".'

That sounded like Alessandro. Faye leaned forwards. There was nothing to gain by it, but she still wanted to know. It was a bit like lancing a boil. 'Marisa . . . can you tell me? How long has he been involved with Jana?'

'Jana . . . Oh, Mother of God, forever. Those two were at school together—'

She broke off at the sharp rap on the door. Alessandro strode in like a whirlwind, bringing with him his usual energy and tension.

Forever. So now she knew. Faye took a deep breath and forced herself to sit back and observe him. He had less of a hunted animal look about him now and more an air of angry triumph. He was wearing faded blue jeans and a button had been ripped from his cream linen shirt. His hair was unruly, and she suddenly noticed a livid scratch on his face and the redness of his knuckles. Oh God. She sat up straighter. There was a wildness about him, almost as if he'd been in a fight.

'Alessandro!' Marisa sprang to her feet. 'Are you okay? What has happened?'

'Do not fuss.' Gently, he pushed her away. 'I am fine.' He eyed Faye from across the room. '*Buona sera*, Faye,' he said. And he took a step towards her. 'Thank you for coming.'

She nodded. Right at this moment, she didn't trust herself to speak. There was something in his eyes, something that was reminding her of that afternoon in the marina. Of course he didn't know that she had seen him with Jana. But she hadn't heard a word from him, either; did he really expect that they could pick up their relationship – professional or otherwise – where they had left off?

Alessandro seemed to want to stare her out. But Faye wasn't playing that game. She looked away from his navy gaze and swallowed hard. 'What's happening?' she asked him. 'Have you come to a decision? Have you sorted out whatever the problem was?'

He smiled grimly. 'Oh, I have sorted it out.' He pulled a brown envelope from the pocket of his jacket. It was folded in two. He crossed the room and flung it on the bureau.

Faye raised an eyebrow.

Marisa was staring at the envelope in confusion. She turned to stare at her brother. 'I do not understand.'

She wasn't the only one. Faye repressed the urge to get up and take a look at it; only it didn't seem quite appropriate.

'Marisa, Marisa,' Alessandro said softly. 'Why?'

Faye watched as Marisa walked across the room. She picked up the envelope but she didn't open it. She looked back at her brother.

'You should have told me,' he said, 'if you were frightened.'

Frightened? Frightened of what? Faye was more confused than ever. She felt as if these two were acting out a tableau in which she had no part to play. Why was she even here?

'No . . .' Marisa's shoulders slumped and Alessandro took three steps towards her, pulled her into a hug.

'It is alright now,' he soothed.

Marisa let out a small sigh and rested her dark head on his chest. Faye felt even more strongly that she did not belong here. But she got to her feet. She still had to know.

Over Marisa's head, Alessandro's gaze locked on to hers once more. 'The show will go on,' he murmured.

Faye took a step closer. 'Meaning?' She frowned.

'Meaning I have sorted out the problem. We will continue with the theatre restoration project as planned.'

'Oh.' Faye wasn't sure what to say. She realised that she hadn't been expecting this. She'd been half-prepared to fly back to the UK with her father the day after tomorrow. 'Just like that?' she asked him.

Alessandro smiled grimly. 'Not just like that,' he said. 'Not just like that at all.'

'But you're sure this time?' said Faye. 'You won't change your mind again? Because otherwise—'

'I am sure,' he said.

Marisa drew away. 'Oh, Alessandro,' she said. 'I did not think . . .'

Think what? But Marisa didn't finish her sentence.

'Is someone going to let me in on the secret?' Faye glanced from one to the other of them. But even as she did this, the faces of both Rinaldis seemed to shut down. Secrets, thought Faye. There seemed to be so many. Alessandro looked at Marisa and she looked back at him, then down at the floor. No one was looking at the mysterious package on the bureau.

'Fair enough.' Faye walked towards the door. She was still a stranger here after all – an employee, nothing more. She was an outsider. She certainly did not belong in Deriu.

'Faye . . .' Alessandro seemed to want to say something more, but glanced back at his sister. 'I am sorry,' he said to Faye. 'For . . .' He fumbled. 'I am sorry,' he said again. And truly – he did look it.

'It's fine.' Faye was trying so hard to look as if none of this mattered a jot. 'I'm glad you sorted out the problem. I'll be in touch.' She couldn't believe how blasé she sounded. And then she pulled open the front door and let herself out.

She exhaled. Shut the door firmly behind her. It wasn't just a question of secrets in the Rinaldi family. Tonight she'd seen a glimpse of something else – something darker. Perhaps this was the darkness that some of the villagers had told her about; Pasquale, Enrico, Carmela – they had all warned her about the Rinaldis.

Faye walked on, breathing in the fresh and balmy evening air, relieved to be out of the flat and away from them. Slowly, she felt a growing sense of calm. No matter. She had wanted to get on with the theatre project and now she could. She would do her job and then she would leave Deriu. Even if Alessandro Rinaldi had been available . . . She let out a small sigh. She wasn't interested in a relationship with a man who kept secrets, a man who had to fight his way out of trouble, a man who could not trust her with the truth. She didn't know what had happened tonight, but of one thing she was sure: Faye wanted no part of it.

CHAPTER 34

The following evening – her father's last night – they decided to stay in and simply enjoy some father-and-daughter time. Faye was preparing pasta with a sweet fennel sausage she had bought from the butcher's in Deriu earlier. Wild fennel – *finocchietto* – was used to flavour so many foods, from biscuits and bread to chicken or sausage, and she loved it. Her father was opening a bottle of Prosecco for a last-night-together celebration.

'This has been so lovely, Faye.' He handed her a glass. 'Here's to the rest of your time in Sardinia, my love.' He raised an eyebrow as he made the toast and Faye had to smile. She'd rather bent his ear when she got back last night – mainly about the Rinaldis and how impossible they were.

Faye wiped her hands on her apron and took the glass from him. 'Thanks for coming, Dad,' she said. 'I appreciate it.' She raised the glass. 'And here's to the next stage of your life, too – whatever it turns out to be.' Stage, she thought. It seemed she couldn't get away from the theatre even when she tried to. But at least now there was a clear road in front of her; now, she could get on with her plans. She took a sip of the wine.

Her father's eyes clouded. 'Whatever it turns out to be,' he repeated. 'It's ridiculous, don't you think? A man of fifty-six and I haven't a clue what to do next.'

Faye leaned over and touched his arm. 'It's not ridiculous.' She returned to slicing the fennel sausage. She could say more – like the fact that retirement was life-changing, and so was divorce. But she didn't want to rub it in. She glanced towards the cooker. The olive oil was hot in the pan and she slid in the rounds of sausage, tossing them in the fragrant oil. 'But do you really not know what to do next, Dad?' He'd always had so many plans.

He shook his head.

'What about Australia?' It was far away, but it would be wrong of her to try and influence his decision, to make him feel guilty about going.

Her father lifted his glass and took a sip of the bubbles. 'I've always wanted to visit Oz,' he said. 'And I thought I would do it. But after spending this time with you here . . .' He eyed her over the rim of the glass. 'Heading off to Australia feels a bit like running away.'

'From Mum?' she asked him. 'From home?' Now was the time, she thought. She couldn't have him here for a week and not even discuss it.

'Yes.' He put down the glass. 'I'm not sure I am such an explorer anymore.' He laughed. 'Perhaps I never was. Perhaps I just wanted to be.'

Faye increased the heat to high and added the fresh tomatoes. 'What are you then, Dad?' she asked.

'I don't know.' He seemed to consider this. 'But someone told me some home truths recently and it's given me a lot to think about.'

'Mum?' She hazarded a guess.

'Not Mum.' He shook his head and Faye thought she saw a shadow of sadness in his eyes.

There was a knock at the door. Her father shot her an enquiring look. Faye shrugged. 'Someone for Fabio or Charlotte probably,' she said. She turned the heat down on the cooker and went to answer it.

Alessandro was standing outside. He looked a good deal tidier and more in control this evening. He was carrying a bottle of wine loosely by the neck in one hand.

'*Buona sera,* Faye.' He gave her a rather shamefaced grin.

'Hello, Alessandro.' No chance, she thought.

'You are cooking.' He sniffed the air and surveyed the apron she wore, which sported a picture of a large chicken. He arched one dark eyebrow. 'Very nice,' he said, though whether he was talking about the chicken or the aroma of fennel and sausage wafting through from the kitchen, she couldn't tell.

'Yes, I am.' She waited. Why not make things difficult for him? Didn't he deserve it?

'I wanted to apologise.' He held up the wine. 'A peace offering.'

'You already did.' She folded her arms. 'Apologise, I mean.'

'I know, but . . .' He let out a sigh. 'It has been a difficult time.'

'I'm sure.'

'And I had a major decision to make.'

Faye leaned on the doorframe and watched him struggle. She decided not to invite him in. 'I realise that,' she said. Even though she didn't know the reasons.

'It is possible I did not handle it as well as I could have.' He half-turned, looked back for a moment towards the river. 'As well as I *should* have.'

'Possibly,' she agreed, standing her ground.

'It was a complex situation. I had to give it some thought. Others were involved.'

'Others?' She knew he was talking about the theatre project, but even so, Jana's face popped into her mind.

He took a deep breath and fixed his eyes on hers. 'There was a threat.'

Despite her resolution to just get on with things and not become involved, Faye's curiosity was once again aroused. 'A threat? Who from?' Though she knew he wouldn't say.

Sure enough, he shook his dark head. 'I know that you think I should tell you everything,' he said sadly. 'But you see it is not possible for me to do that. However, if you did know the full facts . . .'

Her expression said: *Try me.* It was, after all, to do with building trust, even if their relationship *was* only professional.

He spread his hands. 'More than that, I cannot say.'

Faye couldn't say that she was surprised.

'And as for my own feelings . . .'

She waited. She wasn't sure she wanted to hear about his feelings.

'I was trying to keep things clear and separate in my mind.'

Yeah, she thought, men were never good at multi-tasking. But she kept this to herself. 'You're quite right. It's always best to keep things businesslike.' Like hell.

'No. *Si.* That is . . .' He let the words hang, gave her that long look again. He was good; she had to hand it to him. 'Is that how you feel, Faye?'

'Absolutely,' she said. After all, she too had been doing a lot of thinking. 'That's how I feel. As far as I'm concerned, I'm helping you get the theatre project off the ground and then I'm going back to the UK.'

He stared at her. 'You are?'

'I am.' What did he think? That she was going to stay in a

glorious backwater like Deriu for the rest of her life? She had a career to build, other projects to work on. The Little Theatre of Deriu was not everything. And neither was Alessandro Rinaldi.

'But—'

He broke off, his expression changed and Faye realised that her father had come to stand behind her. She stood aside. 'Alessandro, this is my father, Ade. He's been staying with me for a few days.' Which Alessandro would know if he had bothered to keep in any kind of contact. 'Dad, this is Alessandro Rinaldi, my . . . client.' She wondered if her father's face would betray the nature of the things she'd said about Alessandro Rinaldi lately, but he remained cool and self-assured.

'Pleased to meet you.' He was polite, but Faye imagined his protective hackles were raised. The name Alessandro Rinaldi hadn't exactly gone down well with her father this week, she had noticed that much.

'And you, *Signor*.' They shook hands.

There was an awkward pause. 'I'm cooking dinner for my father,' Faye told him. 'Otherwise I'd invite you in for a drink.' Seeing as you've brought the bottle, she added silently. But he would know she was just being polite. He would understand.

'Of course,' he said. 'I am sorry to disturb you.'

Faye took her father's arm just in case he was thinking of disappearing back into the house to leave them alone. 'I'll be in touch tomorrow about the project,' she said. 'Goodnight, Alessandro.'

He gave a little bow of the head, looked up and met her gaze full on for a few seconds. 'Goodnight, Faye,' he said. 'Goodnight, *Signor*.'

Faye was reminded of all the other times they had said

goodnight. Quickly, she shut the door and felt herself enveloped in a fatherly hug. 'What was that for?' she whispered.

'You looked as though you needed it.'

'Thanks.' She broke away reluctantly.

Her father was regarding her thoughtfully. 'You and this Alessandro, Faye . . .'

'Hmm?' He looked uncertain of his ground. Faye realised she'd never discussed matters of the heart with her father. 'Don't worry,' she said quickly. 'There is no "me and Alessandro".'

'Okay.' Though he didn't look entirely convinced.

'But we were talking about you,' she reminded him as they returned to the kitchen. She didn't want to think about Alessandro. She took a restorative gulp of Prosecco before returning to her skillet. Only – why had he come round here exactly? Was the bottle of wine really just a peace offering or had he been planning something more romantic? Faye decided not to dwell on it. She turned up the heat. 'So you don't want to travel the world anymore, Dad?'

'Not on my own,' he said. 'And since I don't have anyone to share the experience with, and I don't want to play golf or do gardening all day, it seems like there's only one option.'

'What's that?' Faye took the garlic and fennel she'd prepared earlier and added it to the pan, along with saffron and a bay leaf. She stirred the sauce.

'I'm thinking of looking for another job,' he said.

Faye stopped what she was doing and stared at him. 'Really?' Now that, she hadn't been expecting.

'Not in banking,' he said quickly. 'I've had enough of that.'

'What then?' Faye tore some basil leaves from the plant on the windowsill and added these to her pan, along with some parsley she'd chopped earlier.

'I'd like to work outside.' She saw his eyes lighten, noticed the way he sat forward in the chair. She recognised the enthusiasm. 'Out in the open – for the National Trust or something like that. Even voluntary work, maybe helping to maintain woodland. Or part-time. Oh –' he smiled – 'you know the sort of thing.'

'Yes, I do.' Faye wiped her hands on her apron once again and put a pot on for the spaghetti that she'd bought fresh from the delicatessen on the other side of the river. She regarded her father thoughtfully. 'It's a good idea, Dad. I can see you really enjoying it. But where would you do this environmental work? In Exeter?'

He shrugged. 'Something doesn't feel quite right about Exeter. I know it's not far away but I do miss Dorset.'

Faye nodded. When she pictured her father she saw him striding out over the cliffs above Chesil Beach. As far as she was concerned, he belonged there. So he missed Dorset. Did he miss Faye's mother too?

'I didn't realise how much I loved the damn place,' he said. He was looking at the fish in Fabio's tropical aquarium as they swam back and forth, their iridescent colours glowing.

Faye put the fresh spaghetti in the pan, twirling it with a fork so that it fit. Again her thoughts returned to her mother. Was she part of his revelation?

'I couldn't wait to retire, you know,' he went on. 'I thought that I'd be free to catch up on everything I missed before.' He looked at her then quickly glanced away. 'But it feels as if what I've been waiting for all these years isn't what I thought it was at all. Funny that.' He reached for the wine bottle and refilled their glasses. 'And what I had . . . maybe it was worth a hell of a lot more than I realised.'

Faye felt a skip of hope. Was he saying what she thought he was saying?

He still seemed deep in thought. 'What has to change is inside you,' he said. 'The way you view things. And do you know, love, I've only just realised that.'

Faye began to lay the table. 'I think I know what you mean.' She paused and watched him as he continued to gaze at the fish in Fabio's tank. Fabio had it bang on. Those fish were certainly therapeutic. 'And have you changed, Dad?' she asked. 'Inside, I mean?'

He turned to face her. 'I'm working on it, love.'

When he had first talked about early retirement and going off travelling, she'd assumed it was just a whim. But now . . . Faye laid the second place setting on the table. She'd changed her mind. Maybe he should still go, still try out some of those things he'd always wanted to do, now that nothing was stopping him. Maybe he should do it – whether it was travelling to Australia or working out in the open in Dorset. 'I just want you to be happy, Dad,' she said. She wanted both her parents to be happy. She'd been thinking of herself, but Alessandro had been right. Part of growing up was about seeing your parents as individuals – not just some generic parental unit. Everyone had their own hopes, fears and dreams, whatever their age. Everyone was struggling to make sense of the world.

'Thanks, love.' He smiled but it was a sad smile.

The spaghetti was done. 'You say you miss Dorset . . .' Faye drained the pasta in a colander. 'But do you miss Mum?' She tipped the colander and tossed the spaghetti with the fennel sausage sauce in the skillet. Because this was the real question in her mind and she needed to voice it. If they no longer loved one another, if they no longer cared, if they no longer wanted to be together, then they were right to separate. Anything else was hypocrisy. She didn't want her parents to have to pretend, for her or for anyone.

Her father let out a deep sigh. 'Yes,' he said. 'I do.'

Then was it possible . . .? Faye tried not to get ahead of herself. 'So –'

'But I reckon I've blown it, love.' He shook his head.

Faye began to dish up the food. She thought about what her mother had said about the cardigan. 'I'm not so sure,' she said. It may have been a metaphor but wasn't that how one got at the truth?

They sat down to eat.

'I've tried contacting your mum,' her father said. 'She said she's fine and that I should just leave her alone to move on.'

Faye almost laughed. That was so like her mother. 'Maybe you should give it one more try,' she said. 'Talk to her face to face.' In person there was less room for hiding.

'We've never been very good at talking,' her father said. 'That was part of the problem.' He took a mouthful of the pasta. 'This is delicious, by the way, love. Well done.'

'Thanks.' Faye paused, twirling some strands of pasta around her fork, thinking about how to word this to make a difference. 'But if you tried a bit harder . . .?' she suggested. She wasn't entirely sure when the role reversal had taken place, when she had started wanting to solve her parents' problems, but she suspected it was when she started seeing them as people.

They continued to eat in a companionable silence. Finally, Faye took the last bit of spaghetti coated in the delicious sauce. It had a faint aniseed flavour that worked perfectly with the caramelised tomatoes and garlic. She could see that her father was still thinking about what she'd said. She decided to be patient.

'I'm not going to lie to you, Faye,' her father said, when he finally put down his fork. 'I haven't always treated your mother as I should. I haven't done right by her and now I've paid the price.'

Faye couldn't say that she was surprised. She'd known there was something. 'She might forgive you, Dad,' she said. 'If you tell her how you feel.'

He shook his head. 'It was a long time ago,' he said. 'And there's a lot to forgive.'

'Did you have an affair?' Faye found the words difficult to say. She found them difficult to even think. But somewhere inside her she knew.

He eyed her seriously. 'I did, yes. No excuses. And you have every right to be angry with me.'

'Why did you do it?' She was angry, it was true. But also sad. And she felt sorry for him too.

'I met someone who made me feel special.'

Faye watched him. She sensed that he wouldn't say any more, and she supposed he was being brave to tell her at all. 'It happens,' she said. 'Everyone makes mistakes.' If that was what it had been – a mistake. She knew that they hadn't been together long before having Faye. He had been young. He had told her that he'd always wanted to travel. Perhaps he had felt trapped. Perhaps he simply hadn't been ready for fatherhood, marriage.

'But at the time, your mother was pregnant.'

'With me?' Faye hadn't been expecting that. She was shocked. He'd had an affair so soon? And when . . .

'No.' He looked down at the table. 'It was seven years later. I didn't know. She had a miscarriage. She – we – lost the baby.'

Faye stared at him. So she would have had a brother or sister? She'd never thought, never imagined. But now she had a memory of that time, of her mother red-eyed and cooking, of her father distracted, of her grandmother comforting her and taking her out to the playground 'until your mother feels better, my dear'. Was that the time?

'Oh, Dad.' She let her hand rest on his sleeve. No wonder. There was so much she hadn't known.

'Which is why your mother won't listen to me,' he said. 'She's buttoned up. I can't blame her. She always has been. She's still cross with me. And now you know why.'

Faye looked at him. He was her father and she loved him. He had given her a glimpse of how things had got so bad between them and now she wasn't sure what to do with it. But . . . 'Then do some unbuttoning, Dad.' She took a deep breath. Thought of how it must have been for her mother when she lost that baby; how desolate she must have felt. She just hoped that her instincts were right. 'Find out what's underneath.'

He pushed his plate to one side. 'Face to face?' he said. 'You really think it's worth a go?'

'Face to face,' said Faye. And she thought again of the cardigan. She was beginning to understand rather a lot. A sister or a brother . . . 'Yes, I do.'

He glanced at her thoughtfully, took a slug of his wine and poured more for them both. Faye realised that she would miss him, miss the companionship of the past week. 'I'm not sure, love,' he said. 'If your mum wants me to leave her alone—'

'Mum's scared,' Faye told him. It was her trump card.

'Scared?' He looked as if he hadn't considered this. 'Of travelling, you mean? Of leaving her home?'

'No.' She leaned towards him. 'I think she's scared of something else – something that goes much deeper.' Faye decided to press her point home. 'And don't you think,' she said, 'that it's time you put the past behind you and discovered what it is?'

CHAPTER 35

Several days later, Faye was at the little theatre with her sketch pad, her laptop, and her measuring tape. A builder had been magicked up too. Since her father's departure, since the night Alessandro had come round to Marisa's with that mysterious brown package, things had really started to happen. All Faye's preparatory work over the past weeks had not been in vain and now she was free to throw all her energy into her ideas and her drawings.

It hadn't been as difficult as she'd expected to continue working with Alessandro. He was polite and friendly enough, but he kept his distance, and he let Marisa handle most of the communications between them. And Faye didn't have the time to think about what might have been. Right now she had a different problem. She'd worked really hard on the plans – checked and double-checked them, in fact – but something didn't quite fit. She couldn't believe that she'd made an elementary mistake in the measuring, but . . . it was possible, and that was what she had to sort out today. After all, she didn't have any practical experience to speak of. It was a big responsibility. Marisa and Alessandro were both depending on her. She knew she had to get it right. She had to complete the plans, sections and elevations and present the builders with a package of drawings that they could follow to the letter.

She made her way across the stage, pausing for a moment to survey the crumbling plasterwork in the ceiling above the auditorium. Some more red paint had flaked from the original fresco and the patches of black mould seemed to have increased in size even since her last visit. What happens after the curtain falls, she thought, and it had last fallen a long time ago in the little theatre. This morning, the builder was checking the joists under the floorboards to see how strong they were, to ensure none of them were rotten and needed replacing. There was probably as much disrepair under the surface as there was on view. The theatre had suffered years of dereliction and neglect – not to mention a fire or two. And it was part of her job to take all of this into account.

A man stepped out in front of her as she walked offstage and into the wings.

'Oh!' Faye jumped.

'I am so sorry, Faye.' Pasquale grabbed her hands. 'I did not mean to frighten you.'

'Pasquale –' *What are you doing here,* she was going to say, but she knew full well. Pasquale was here most days; sometimes loitering in the shadows, sometimes following her round the theatre like a wounded animal. Not that Faye didn't feel sorry for him; she knew he had his reasons for wanting to hang around. But he was always following someone, she thought. First his father when he was caretaker here, then Sofia when he fell in love with her and followed her all the way to England. And now Faye. It was no surprise he had become an actor, where he could – at least for the duration of a performance – command the attention of an audience.

'It's okay. I'm fine. You startled me, that's all.' Faye tried to suppress her irritation. The poor man couldn't help it. He just couldn't bear the thought that his precious theatre would be changed in any way. He was rooted in the past.

'I confess that I was worried.' He let go of her hands, lifted his mournful brown gaze to meet hers.

'Worried?' Faye always tried to be patient with him but she really didn't have time for this. And she had something else pressing on her mind: she had been contacted by a design company based in London – they wanted her to come up for an interview. She wondered how long she could put them off. There would come a point with the theatre job when she would be kicking her heels, waiting for the builders and restorers to do their work; that was the point when she should hand the project over to a foreman and take on another job, another project. And that would mean moving back to the UK. She knew she must do it, she knew she should go . . . but she didn't want to think about it right now.

'Your builder . . .' Pasquale eyed her accusingly. 'He is banging around, moving things.' He put a hand to his brow. 'It is painful for me to witness, you understand.'

Then don't witness it. This was Faye's first thought. She took a deep breath and tried a more diplomatic approach. 'Maybe you shouldn't come here so often, Pasquale,' she said.

He reared back from her, as if she had struck him.

'Only while the restoration takes place,' Faye soothed. 'Stay at home with your mother. Try to keep your distance for a while.'

'How can I?' he muttered. 'When I do not know . . .'

Faye put a hand on his arm. 'I realise that it's difficult for you.'

'It would be worse not to be here.' He looked around at the peeling paintwork on the walls, the patches of damp on the ceiling, the broken tiles underfoot. 'My imagination – it would go crazy.'

Faye sighed. She should tell him to leave but he was a part of the theatre, she couldn't imagine the place without him. And she knew how deeply he felt about it. 'Things change, Pasquale,' she said. 'But change doesn't always mean things get worse.'

He eyed her uncertainly. 'You would say that.'

'Yes, I would.' Change was her business, after all.

'But it is so violent. This ripping up of floorboards, knocking down walls, the desecration . . .'

So he had been into the costume room, seen what the builder was doing in there. Faye frowned. There was such intensity in the feelings Pasquale had for the theatre. It made her feel distinctly claustrophobic. Was this how Sofia had felt? Faye really didn't know what to do with him.

He was waving his arms around now. 'What next? Can you tell me that, eh?'

'Calm down, Pasquale.' Faye fixed him with a steady gaze. She ought to be firm. If he carried on like this she'd have to insist he left. And he'd have to stay away when the building work started – for health and safety reasons, if nothing else.

'How can I be calm?' His pupils flared. 'If I do not even know what is happening to my theatre? How it is to be treated? How it is to be defiled?'

Faye decided that now was not the time to point out that this wasn't his theatre. It didn't matter if he had acted on the stage or his father had looked after the maintenance of the place – it didn't belong to him and rightly or wrongly he had no say in what was going to happen to it. 'Let me show you what we're doing,' she said. Perhaps that was the answer. Instead of trying to shut him out from what was going on, she would include him. It wasn't exactly standard practice but then this project hadn't been standard practice from day one. This was Sardinia, after all.

She led him into the first dressing room that she was using as a makeshift office. She'd brought in a table and chairs and some of her plans and sketches were in here, though she took care to take them home with her every night. She switched on her laptop. 'Sit down.'

Faye showed him the plans and ran through some of the changes that would be made – not in detail, but at least the broad outline so that he would see their intentions. As she'd expected, he was more interested in the structural work that might alter the intrinsic make-up of his precious little theatre than he was in the cosmetic – the restoration of the theatre's original features – or even the changes of use that would make the theatre a cultural arts centre in its own right.

'You have to accept it, Pasquale,' she said when she had finished. 'These changes will benefit Deriu and they will bring *il Piccolo Teatro* alive again by making it a part of the community.'

He nodded sadly.

Had she got through to him at last? Did he understand? Faye put her hand over his. 'Something has to be done,' she said. 'You can't go on living in the past.' She seemed to be saying that rather a lot lately.

Her thoughts slipped to her parents back in the UK as they often did. Had her father gone to see her mother yet? She didn't think so – she hadn't heard anything. Had Faye got through to him? She hoped so with all her heart. Her mother might not forgive him, the two of them still might not want to try again – and even if they did, they might not be able to make it work – but the conversation would be good for them both. Faye knew it was asking a lot to expect them to put the past behind them. There had been so many losses. She thought of her mother's unborn child. And she had the feeling that there was more.

'What is going on?' The voice from the open doorway cut into her thoughts and made them both jump. Faye had heard footsteps and voices from a distance, but she had assumed it was the builder talking to his young apprentice. It wasn't. Alessandro Rinaldi was standing glowering at them in the doorway. And behind him, almost out of sight, was Marisa.

Pasquale got to his feet. He looked so old and fragile compared with Alessandro.

But he glared back at Alessandro nevertheless, held his fists up as if he might have to defend himself. Alessandro's eyes narrowed.

'Hey.' Faye got up too and stood between them. Wasn't it time to bring an end to hostilities between these two? It wasn't Pasquale's fault that he had been in love with Sofia Rinaldi — after all, some might say he'd seen her first. And he had saved the little theatre from the fire that might have seen it burn to the ground. 'Nothing's going on. I was showing Pasquale some of our plans.' There was nothing wrong with that, surely? They were hardly top secret.

'May I ask why?' Alessandro's voice was distant but she sensed that he was holding back his emotions with some difficulty.

She looked straight into the navy eyes. 'The theatre means a lot to Pasquale,' she said. 'As you know.'

'That does not mean he has to approve its redesign.'

This was true, of course, but harsh. Faye gave a small nod of acknowledgement. 'It was more a matter of reassurance,' she said. 'Pasquale was worried about all the changes we're making to the theatre.' Couldn't he see how upset Pasquale was? Where was Alessandro's compassion?

'Reassurance?' Alessandro shook his head. He turned to Pasquale. 'You should stay away from here, old man.'

'He's been part of this place almost his entire life.' Faye's voice was soft. She might be working for the Rinaldis, but she couldn't help sticking up for Pasquale. What was Alessandro's problem with him? She noticed that Marisa hadn't said a word. 'The plans will be public knowledge before long.' Which was how it should be if the little theatre was to be part of the community of Deriu.

But Alessandro only turned to Pasquale. 'It is over,' he said. 'It is happening. Get used to it.' And once again, Faye had the feeling that there was something going on here that she didn't understand.

'Alessandro—' But she broke off when she saw the expression on his face. It had changed. He no longer looked angry – now his eyes just held a look of sadness and regret.

'There is a lot you do not know about Deriu, Faye,' he said. He took a step towards her and then seemed to check himself and hold back. 'There is much you do not understand.'

'So everyone keeps telling me,' Faye replied crisply. She had been made to feel unwelcome almost since she'd arrived. She continued to receive hostile glances from villagers like Enrico Volti and she sensed people whispering as she passed by. She knew that she was an outsider, and worse that she was perceived as working against the community she would in fact like to help. And so far practically the only person who had been completely straight with her was Pasquale de Montis.

Alessandro sighed. 'I am going back to work,' he said. And he shot Faye one of his *why can't you trust me* looks. The answer to that was simple. She thought of the brown paper package. She thought of Jana. Because he wouldn't tell her exactly what was going on.

Alessandro left the room and Marisa went after him. Faye sat down heavily. They were her clients but they were awfully hard to handle.

'I am sorry,' said Pasquale. 'I seem to make him very angry.'

'Don't worry about Alessandro.' Though as co-owner of the theatre, she supposed he had the right to decide who was allowed to come into the building. She was pretty sure that Alessandro wasn't coming back, but if she were Pasquale, she'd make herself scarce for a while. 'But maybe you should keep out of the way for a bit.'

He snorted and she had the feeling that he would carry on exactly as before. 'You see for yourself how he is,' he muttered.

Yes, she thought. She did. 'Right.' She sat up straighter and closed the documents on her laptop. 'I need to see how the builder's getting on.' Which was presumably why Alessandro and Marisa had come here in the first place. They hadn't hung around though, once they'd seen Pasquale looking at the plans.

'Is he still in the costume room?' Pasquale's gaze flickered along the corridor.

'Yes. They're checking the joists.' Faye shut her laptop and made her way over. Yet again, she sensed that Pasquale was following her but she didn't have the heart to tell him to go away.

In the costume room several floorboards had been taken up.

'How's it going?' Faye asked. She stepped inside. All the costumes had been covered with a sheet for now, but they would have to be sorted to see if anything could be salvaged from the glorious mass of silk, satin and brocade. Pasquale hovered in the doorway.

'The joists and woodwork underneath the room are sound,' the builder told her.

Faye looked down into the well beneath the floorboards. The joists were obviously old, but she was pleased at the report. 'That's good news.' She moved over to the other side of the room by the full-length gilt-edged mirror, looked down again into the void.

Something glinted below. 'What's that?' She bent to get a better look.

'A coin?' The builder shone his torch where she was pointing.

'No.' She reached down and picked it up. 'It's a necklace. A crucifix.' It was made of gold, still shiny, only very faintly tarnished. It nestled in the palm of her hand.

Pasquale gasped.

Faye glanced over. His face was white. 'What's wrong?' She looked again at the crucifix in her hand, held it up to the light coming in at the small window. It was most distinctive. The cross was very fine filigree and the Christ's body was solid gold, the arms stretched out almost to the outer edges, which were tipped with coral. Above the figure was a glorious spiked halo of gold.

'Do you recognise it, Pasquale?' She took a step towards him. Again, she held it up, watched his expression. It was clear from his reaction that he did.

He stared at it, silent.

And suddenly Faye understood. 'Did it belong to Sofia?' she whispered. Once again, she put her hand gently on his arm. Poor Pasquale – yet another reminder of the past he had lost, the woman he had never had. It would of course have been easy for any of the actors to lose a piece of jewellery in the costume room where they were always changing in and out of dress. It must have slipped through the gap between the floorboards. It must have been lying there in its dusty hiding place for years.

'Yes.' Pasquale hung his head. 'It did.'

'It's alright.' Faye nodded to the builders and led the way out of the room.

'May I have it?' Pasquale stood facing her now. 'As a memento?' He held out his hand, eyes pleading. But at least he seemed calmer, she was relieved to see.

Faye hesitated. She was tempted. But: 'It wouldn't be right,' she said after a moment. 'I think we should give it to Marisa.'

Pasquale's shoulders slumped.

'It was her mother's, after all.'

Pasquale looked as if he was going to object, but then they heard footsteps behind them. Faye looked up with a jump of anticipation. But it wouldn't be Alessandro. He wouldn't have returned so quickly.

And she was right – it was Marisa herself. She seemed hesitant, her hands twisting nervously together. 'I just came back for a moment,' she said. 'To apologise for my brother.' She gave a sidelong glance towards Pasquale, but already he seemed to have hung back, to fade into the shadows.

Faye shrugged. 'It's okay.'

'He has his reasons.' Marisa seemed to want to say more. 'He is very protective.'

'Of you?'

'*Si*.' She looked down. 'And of Deriu.'

Faye nodded.

'He has had many problems to deal with in the past weeks and months.' She put a hand on Faye's. 'Please do not judge him too harshly.'

'I'll try not to.' Faye smiled. Marisa was such a lovely girl. She could see why Charlotte got on with her so well and why Alessandro adored her.

'So have there been any new developments?' Marisa looked around her.

Faye decided not to mention the problem with the measurements. She would sort that one out herself. 'The joists are sound.' She echoed what the builder had told her. 'And I found this.' She handed her the crucifix. 'Pasquale said it was your mother's.' She looked to him for corroboration but he had de-materialised completely and was nowhere to be seen.

'Mama's?' Marisa frowned. 'It seems familiar. But . . .'

'Perhaps she lost it when you were very small,' Faye said. 'Maybe even before you were born – we found it in the costume room under the floorboards.'

'It's beautiful.' Marisa clutched it tightly in her palm and then opened her hand. The crucifix had made red marks on her skin but she didn't seem to notice. She held the necklace up to the light as Faye had done. It spun around. The gold glistened. 'Will you fasten it for me?' Her velvet-brown eyes began to fill. She put it up to her throat and Faye went behind her to do up the delicate gold clasp.

'Thank you,' she said. She turned around and reached up to kiss Faye on the cheek.

Faye smiled. It must be very moving to receive a memory of the past so unexpectedly. And once again she felt a stab of sorrow for Marisa and Alessandro who had lost their parents so young. Her own parents might be separating but at least she still had them around. Her week with her father seemed long ago already, but it had been a special time.

'I will always wear it,' Marisa said to Faye. 'And please take no notice of Alessandro. He did not mean to be rude. It is only that he has things on his mind.'

Faye nodded. 'I told you, it's fine,' she said. But despite everything, she couldn't help taking notice of him. She'd tried not to, but it didn't work. Even though Faye too had plenty of things on her mind.

CHAPTER 36

As he drove from Exeter to Dorset, Ade thought about what Faye had said when he was staying with her in Sardinia. He began by taking the Topsham Road, which ran parallel with the river Exe. The route was a little longer but more scenic. He would drive down Rydon Lane and join up with Honiton Road that way. A familiar route, but one he hadn't travelled for a while. So much travelling and yet how far had he got, really?

Faye had said that her mother was scared. How did she know that? Could Molly have told her? Ade drummed his fingers on the steering wheel – thought of the girl he'd first seen in the Electric Palace all those years ago; those chestnut-coloured eyes, that shiny dark brown hair and the wide, smiling red-lipsticked mouth. Scared?

It was a lovely mid-summer's morning and the hedgerows were green, the Devon hills and fields still lush from a wet spring and early summer. The sky was clear silver-blue. It felt like a good day to be coming here; a day of hope. Ade had decided not to phone first, that it was best to be casual about it. He could say he was just passing, or more believably that he'd come to pick up some things. After all, most of his stuff was still there: his collection of DVDs, CDs and old albums, as well as his books, his pictures and most of his clothes. And then there was all the stuff he and Molly owned jointly. It was all just stuff – he didn't much mind saying goodbye to most of it. Some they'd chosen together, but mostly they were things she'd wanted more than he had. Perhaps he hadn't cared enough what the house looked like, how it was decorated, what kind of patterned plates they ate from. Perhaps it was the minutiae of life that kept couples together, not the big things.

Outside, Ade thought, as he negotiated the narrow country lanes – as he'd told Faye, being outside was the big thing for him. The hills, the cliffs, the sea. Nature in all her glory. He might actually do it – look for the kind of job he'd mentioned to Faye. And if he couldn't go back to Dorset, then there were other places. Devon, Cornwall? He'd find the right place, he was sure.

It was odd, he thought – this past month he'd said goodbye to a lot: his job, his commute, the fantasy of Nina representing the life he wanted to have and thought she could give him. (He still hadn't quite come to terms with that one, but he knew it was true.) An awful lot of goodbyes. But did he want to say goodbye to his wife as well? He had told his daughter that he missed Molly and it was true. He missed the orderliness of her, the way she'd always made some sense of his life. He missed the way her hair swung when she turned her head, the look that was sometimes there in her eyes, but then was gone before he even had the chance to blink. And this – none of this – really made sense to him.

On the A30 he passed by Exeter airport, which made him think of Sardinia, even though he hadn't flown from here but from Bristol. Sardinia had been a good place to spend some time. He'd reconnected with his daughter – they'd always been close, but when Faye left home they had naturally drifted some way apart. He had tried to take her mind off what she was going through – problems with her very first design project, feelings of insecurity, of being alone. And he had tried to make her feel better about things – including her client Alessandro Rinaldi. It was horribly ironic that he was the son of the man who had apparently got close to Molly when he stayed with them for Charlotte and Fabio's wedding . . . Was it a case of like mother, like daughter? Ade didn't know. But he was confident Faye would work it out.

Just as importantly – to him – Ade had somehow been able to tell Faye things that he thought she ought to know. Ade clenched the steering wheel more tightly. This was a good wide road and he'd always loved the surrounding views of green fields, hills and valleys. And she hadn't screamed at him. She hadn't cried and she hadn't told him how much she hated him. For this, at least, Ade was thankful.

Perhaps it should have been Molly's place to tell their daughter about the child they'd lost – it had been more of a loss to her, of course; the child had been growing in her belly – but Ade didn't think Molly would mind him telling Faye, not now. And Faye, he felt, had a right to know what made up their past. He smiled grimly. If not all of it. She could cope. His daughter hadn't found the man for her – yet. Again, he thought of Alessandro – he was a good-looking bastard, he'd say that for him. His father had been the same. Ade sighed. But Faye led an independent life; she was all grown up. What he had to do now was keep their relationship special. This week in Sardinia had reminded him of that – how special it was. And he had to be there for her too – whenever she might need him to be.

Ade passed the thatched and white-painted Hart Inn. Sometimes he'd stopped here for a quick half on the way home. He was tempted to stop here now for some Dutch courage, but how would it look if he arrived stinking of booze? Not good. He didn't think Faye would approve of that. He thought of Molly. She'd never had the gradual disconnection with her father that he had experienced with Faye; she had lost her father so completely when she was just seventeen. That must have been hard. And he wondered – had he ever given her credit for that loss? Had he ever thought about how it had been for her? How much she had gone through?

While in Sardinia, Ade had done some Internet research on campervans when Faye had gone to meet with the Rinaldis that night. He'd studied eBay and motorhome owner sites. He'd considered different layouts – where the table should be, if a fixed bed was really the necessity some people seemed to think it was. And then he'd looked at the passenger seat and imagined it empty. It would never be Molly sitting there and certainly never Nina. Was his dream of travelling as insubstantial – preposterous even – as his dreams of Nina? He was starting to wonder. Like he'd told Faye, travelling was beginning to feel more like running away.

Ade felt that he was getting close to his destination when he reached the turning for Axminster – he always had. He was still in Devon but this was where the countryside seemed to change. Just a bit further on was Monkton Wyld where he sometimes went walking in the woods and then there was Charmouth where they used to take Faye fossil-hunting when she was a girl.

He replayed his last conversation with Molly in his head. Where had he gone wrong? Where had they gone wrong? Had it been his affair? He supposed so, though something told him it was more than that and Faye had seemed to think so too. What did it have to do with Bruno Rinaldi? Molly had said that she should have taken her chance of a new life – what had she meant by that exactly? Had Rinaldi offered her a new life? Ade gritted his teeth. Had something gone on between the two of them? He tried to stay calm, but he felt a surge of anger, despite the inescapable fact that he'd done the very same thing himself. What had she meant when she talked about getting so close to someone that they learned the heart of her? Is that what had happened? If Molly was scared, then what was she scared of? And had Molly – fallen out of love? Ade couldn't help feeling that he'd missed something. And that was why he was going back – to try and find it. He needed answers. If, that is, it wasn't too late.

Ade drove through the Dorset villages of Morecombelake and Chideock, past the Clock House Inn which had burned down in that terrible fire last year but was being done up again, thatching and all. It was always congested down this road and today was no exception. But he got through the traffic in less time than usual and before he knew it he'd passed the Bridport turning and was indicating right to turn up the old hollow that led to their house – Molly's house, he supposed he should call it now since he didn't officially live there anymore.

It looked exactly as it always did and Molly's dark blue Renault was parked in the driveway – so she was in. He studied the exterior of the house for a few minutes without getting out of the car as if he were seeing it for the first time. The house was long, detached and painted white. It had high hedges and a neat front garden; there were curtains at the windows and a vase of fresh flowers on the windowsill of the sitting room. The house looked cared for. He'd always liked the location – behind the house were fields with sheep grazing and Bothen Hill, smooth, green and undulating. It looked, he thought, like home. Like someone's home, that was. But not his. Not anymore.

In the porch were some red and white geraniums and outside Molly had hung a basket of petunias and other flowers that cascaded prettily in a way he knew she liked. At least, he thought, he knew that much about her. But he hadn't known she was scared. Ade had laughed at her sometimes for the way everything had to be just so, but he wasn't laughing now. He missed that neatness in his life, that certainty. Now, he felt adrift.

Ade got out of the car and went to the front door. He rang the bell although he had his keys in his pocket (he wasn't that insensitive to Molly's privacy) and heard the musical chime in the hallway. He imagined what she would be wearing when she came to the door – a summer dress because it was a warm day, maybe the red and white waisted one that he liked. He imagined her face when she saw him. '*Ade!*' She'd be surprised. He chuckled to himself. She'd invite him in for coffee obviously, they were still amicable enough for that, and they'd sit in the wicker chairs in the conservatory and chat – about the house (maybe something needed doing? He could fix that while the coffee was brewing) and about how Faye was doing in Sardinia. Maybe he'd stay for lunch and the conversation would get deeper. He'd take her hand and . . . *Yes? What would you do next, Ade?*

The door opened. A man was standing there. A man he recognised, though he couldn't think at the moment who he was. He was just so shocked that the man wasn't Molly.

'Oh, hello, Ade.' The man – who was in his shirtsleeves and seemed rather at home – did not seem pleased to see Ade. He scowled. 'What are you doing here?'

The name came to him. 'Doug. Hello. Well . . .' Ade had always been a well-mannered and laid-back kind of guy – he prided himself on it. But hang on a minute. Doug was their neighbour. Molly's neighbour. He lived next door. What was he doing in the wrong house? And why the hell was he asking Ade what *he* was doing here?

He clenched his fists. 'I might ask you the same thing.' He heard his own voice and it didn't sound pleasant at all. Doug was a single man and a bit of a nuisance to tell the truth. He'd often come round to mention that their hedge needed trimming or that they'd left the back gate undone. And it seemed he hadn't waited long to get his foot well and truly in the door.

Doug laughed. His eyes twinkled as though Ade had made a joke. He turned around and called up the stairs. *Up the stairs?* 'Molly, love, your ex is standing on the doorstep.'

Molly, love? Your ex? Doug had a smug smile on his face and he hadn't even moved aside so that Ade could come into his own bloody house. Ade saw red. And before he could even think about what he was going to do, he'd hit him.

CHAPTER 37

'Ade!' Molly was saying his name, but not quite in the way he'd envisaged. She sounded horrified. She ran down the stairs to where Doug was lying flat out at the bottom. 'Ade! What have you done?'

Ade wasn't quite sure. He was still in shock. He'd never hit a man before. Once, in the playground, he'd lashed out when some kid had pushed him too far – called him a fairy, actually, because he'd scored an own goal in a football match which had made his team lose the game – but . . . His knuckles were sore; he rubbed them gingerly. 'I haven't hurt him,' he said. It wasn't as if he'd knocked him out.

He glanced down at Doug to check. His eyes were wide open and angry. He pushed himself up to a sitting position and glared with open hostility back at Ade – hardly surprising really.

'Not for want of trying,' Molly snapped. 'What on earth did you hit him for?' She glared at him too. 'Don't even answer that.' She knelt down on the hall carpet so that she had her back to Ade. 'Doug? Are you alright?'

'Bloody maniac,' muttered Doug. 'No wonder you left him.'

Ade felt the anger rise once again and shoved his hands in his pockets just in case.

Molly half-turned. 'Have you got anything to say, Ade?'

Ade felt about ten years old. 'I shouldn't have punched you,' he mumbled.

'A bit more than that, I think.' Molly turned fully round to glower at him once more. He'd never seen her so animated. What did that mean? Did she care for him? Doug? Their — alright, *her* — fussy old-womanish next-door neighbour?

'Yeah, you're right, I was well out of order,' Ade said.

She didn't look away.

'Sorry, Doug.'

She nodded at this and turned her focus back to the patient who was now rubbing his chin and probably revelling in the attention, Ade thought rather unfairly.

'I'm alright,' Doug said. 'He just took me by surprise, the bloody maniac. That's the only reason I fell.'

Inside his pockets, Ade's fists clenched. Yeah, you went down like a stone, he thought. What was happening to him? Had some long-buried violent gene suddenly leapt into action? Was his body being flooded with post-retirement testosterone? Suddenly it seemed that Doug was the most irritating man on earth.

'Nothing broken then.' Molly's voice was crisp. She got to her feet.

'I could still report him.' Doug followed suit, scrambling up from the floor, though Ade couldn't help noticing that he had to use the wooden banister to help him. He was older than Ade by several years and the same height, though where Ade was lean, he was burly and still a fit-looking man. Frankly, Ade was amazed at his own temerity.

'Fair enough,' said Ade, almost wanting him to.

Molly glared at him again. She turned back to Doug. 'Please don't, Dougie,' she said.

Dougie?

'I really don't think I could bear that on top of everything else that's happened lately.'

Christ. She was almost batting her eyelashes at the guy. Ade hadn't realised she was such a good actress – if she was acting. And if she wasn't . . . *I shouldn't have come here,* he thought. Faye had been mistaken. Molly didn't seem scared of anything.

Doug seemed to consider. 'I'll do it for you, Molly,' he growled at last. 'I'll forget it ever happened. But if he tries anything—'

'Shake hands,' Molly ordered.

Ade had never seen her so forceful. He stuck out his hand. Doug scowled and took it briefly. Ade was gratified to note the slight bruising developing around his jaw line.

'Want me to chuck him out now, Molly?' Doug didn't take his eyes off Ade. Maybe he thought he was going to take another swing at him.

Ade held his breath. Just let him try.

'Stop being childish, both of you. You're grown men – or supposed to be.' Molly had her hands on her hips. She wasn't wearing the red and white dress Ade had envisioned, but a different one, a new, pale blue one in a fitted style that made her look somehow more in control. She *was* more in control, he realised. He could see it in her eyes. Ade wasn't sure how he felt about Molly going out to buy a new dress straight after her husband had left her. Equally, he wasn't sure about her being so in control. She didn't seem upset in the least and she was clearly managing very well without him. He felt more than a little redundant. Shouldn't there be a period of grieving or something? She looked very attractive with those pink spots of anger in her cheeks. And she was wearing lipstick. What had she been doing upstairs? Ade blinked at her.

'You go home, Doug,' she continued. 'And Ade, you can come in and tell me what you want and why you didn't phone to warn me.'

'Warn you?'

'That you were coming.'

'See you later then, Molly.' And with a last doubtful glance at Ade, Doug stomped out through the door.

Ade took another step inside the house. It was ridiculous, but he felt a sense of victory.

Molly shut the door. She turned on him. 'What were you thinking?' she said.

'I didn't think.' For once in his life he had just responded.

'He's our neighbour,' Molly hissed. 'My neighbour.'

'So what was he doing in here? And what were you doing? Upstairs?'

Molly's eyes narrowed. 'Not that it's any of your business, Ade – not anymore – but Doug had kindly come in to look at the hot water tank.'

'The hot water tank?' Shit.

'Yes. And I think he's fixed it. He did all the plumbing in his own house, he told me.'

'I'm sure he bloody did.' Ade hated him even more.

Molly ignored this. 'I managed to fix the boiler myself – it was just a matter of making a few adjustments to the settings . . .'

Adjustment to the settings? Ade gaped at her. This was the woman who didn't know the difference between a pair of pliers and a screwdriver.

'But the hot water tank wasn't so easy,' Molly continued. 'I experimented with the thermostat and checked all the pipe-work, but . . .' She broke off – probably at the sight of Ade's shocked expression. 'Anyway, Doug sorted it. He'd just finished. I was putting the towels back in the airing cupboard.' She gave him a look. 'When you arrived.'

Ade shrugged. 'I didn't know.' He felt a bit of an idiot.

'You didn't ask,' she pointed out.

'It was the way he spoke to me,' he said. 'The way he looked. The . . .' *Intimacy he implied*, he was going to say, but perhaps it was better not to elaborate further.

Molly shook her head. 'Oh, Ade,' she said.

'Sorry, love.'

She glanced at him sharply. So what? He couldn't help it if the old affectionate endearments still tripped from his tongue. And wasn't that what Doug had called her: *Molly love?*

Ade looked around. Everything looked familiar, and yet not the same. 'You're obviously managing pretty well without me,' he said. He had intended this to be a compliment but he saw her bristle. 'Which is great,' he added lamely. 'Really great.'

'What did you expect me to do?' She had her hands on her hips again now. 'Go to pieces?'

'No, of course not.' Though he had kind of expected the odd call for advice. That's how arrogant he was, Ade realised glumly. Molly was clearly perfectly capable. Not only could she function alone (with a little help from Doug) but she seemed to be relishing it.

'What are you doing here anyway?' She bustled past him towards the kitchen. 'I'll make some coffee. I expect we could both do with some.' Which was about the only predictable thing that had happened since he'd got here.

Ade hesitated. He thought of all the things he'd been going to say, his excuses for being here. Something told him they were a waste of time, that he had to be honest now. 'I wanted to see you, Molly,' he said. He followed her into the kitchen. 'I came here to talk.' Ade tried to remember the last time they'd sat down together and done that.

'To talk?' She turned towards him. And there was something in her eyes, something that could be fear. 'Isn't it a bit late for—?'

Ade took her hand. 'I want us to be honest with each other, Molly,' he said. 'I want us to see if there's any chance . . .'

'Any chance?'

He had to say it. He wanted to say it. It had always been there somewhere in his heart and leaving Molly and Dorset had brought it to the surface. Going to Sardinia and talking with Faye had dispelled any final doubts. 'Any chance that we can try again,' he said. Because that was what he wanted. Not just answers, not that elusive something. He wanted to try again.

Ade took Molly down to the beach café at Burton for lunch. It was one of his favourite places. It was built on the rise of the hill so there was a clear sea view. Chesil Beach was golden and magnificent. It seemed to go on forever.

'We can talk later,' he told her. First, he wanted for them to just be. To sit together, to eat, to watch the waves. They had time for the rest. They hadn't sat down and talked for so many years, another few hours wouldn't make any difference.

While they ate fish soup with brown crusty bread and drank glasses of local, chilled ginger beer, he told her about Faye and Sardinia. 'She's doing well, our girl,' he said. He had seen her drawings and her first plans. She had talked about what she had intended to do. Ade had been impressed. She was good.

'And did you meet Alessandro Rinaldi?' Molly asked him. She looked away as she said this, over towards the metallic sheen of the ocean where two rowing gigs were coming into sight around the headland. It was a good day for it, he found himself thinking.

He nodded. 'Briefly.'

'What did you think?'

'There's an attraction,' he admitted. The thought of Alessandro's father reared its head, and he pushed it away. Later.

'Just an attraction?'

He knew what she meant. But Ade couldn't answer that. Once again, he took Molly's hand. 'Let's walk,' he said.

They left the café and walked along the beach towards Cogden. There was a fresh sea breeze and Molly zipped the fleece she was wearing right up to the neck. Side by side, they stomped over the small ginger pebbles of Chesil Beach, watching the thick green waves roll and plunge into shore, leaving their foamy imprint in arcs behind them.

'I did a terrible thing to you when I started seeing Nina,' Ade began. He had to say it. 'I tried to justify it to myself at the time. But when I look back at it now . . .' And he had been looking back. Oh, God, he had been.

'How did you justify it?'

Ade tried to explain. The feeling of being young, being trapped. The responsibility of fatherhood. 'I'm not making excuses,' he told Molly. 'I knew it was wrong. I was an idiot. I hardly ever stopped to think about what it might be doing to you.' He glanced across at her. 'I never meant to hurt you, Molly,' he said. 'I know everyone who has an affair always says it, but it's true.'

Molly gazed out towards the pale grey horizon. Above them, some unexpected summer clouds were gathering. She shivered. 'But what was it I wasn't giving you, Ade?'

Ade had never thought about it like that before. 'You were busy with Faye,' he said. 'You were being a mother. You didn't do anything wrong, Molly.'

'I was young too,' she reminded him. 'I didn't have dreams of travelling, but I did have dreams of getting married, having a baby, having my own home.' She smiled wistfully as if that girl with those dreams was now a very long distance away. 'I pushed you into marrying me, Ade. I have to take some responsibility for what happened.'

'Hardly.' He grabbed her hand and tucked it through the crook of his arm. 'You were pregnant. It wasn't your fault. I would have been a complete arsehole if I hadn't married you.'

She leaned towards him. 'Complete honesty?'

He frowned. 'Yes.'

'I got pregnant on purpose.' She stopped walking. The wind seemed to catch her words and lift them up, releasing them over the sea, over the cliffs and away.

'Really?' Ade stared at her. He hadn't seen that one coming. 'Why?' She had known they couldn't really afford a baby – not yet. She had known that Ade had other things on his agenda. Like travelling. Like . . .

'I knew you'd leave me,' she said. She turned to him and for a moment her pupils seemed to dilate as if she were about to cry. But instead, she laughed. 'I'm right, aren't I? Total honesty, remember. If I hadn't got pregnant when I did, you would have left.'

'Bloody hell,' said Ade.

'Are you angry?'

Ade thought of Faye. How could he be? 'No, of course I'm not angry.'

'And was I right?'

He nodded. 'You were right.' He would have left her; he was already feeling it – the need to be gone, the desire to be a free man again – single and carefree. And being the idiot he was, he might never have tried to go back. Ade glanced across at her profile as she walked on, her dark hair flattened and blown back by the wind, her cheeks pink. Her lipstick had faded now and the fleece she was wearing had entirely spoilt the effect of the new blue dress. But to Ade, she looked beautiful. 'I was a bloody fool,' he said.

She threw him a look. 'You were young. We fell in love. But you didn't want to be tied down.'

So he had been trapped. Ade thought about this as they walked on. The stones scrunched under their feet and the curling foam of the waves fizzed beside them. High above, a seagull shrieked and the breeze seemed to fill his eardrums. He had felt trapped and he had been trapped. But somehow it didn't seem to matter so much anymore.

'That doesn't make it right – what I did,' he said, after a few moments.

'No,' she agreed. 'It doesn't.'

'But if you knew about Nina,' he said, 'why didn't you say something at the time? Why didn't you scream and shout and tell me what a bastard I was being?'

Her pace slowed. 'I didn't want to make you choose,' she said. She spoke so quietly that he had to strain to hear her. 'I was frightened, Ade.'

That he was going to leave. He thought about this too. It was all starting to make a lot more sense. He was beginning to imagine how it must have been for Molly. Having lost her father, she had fallen in love. And yet she could see it all drifting away – again. 'And you didn't forgive me for what I did with Nina.' Ade drew away from her as he said this so he could see her face. It wasn't a question. 'You never forgave me.' Not that he blamed her for that.

'I couldn't.' Molly stared back at him. 'I tried to make things work, but she was still there between us. I could feel her. And . . .'

He realised that her cheeks were wet. She was thinking of their dead child, he knew it. Their baby who had died. Molly had been carrying that child when she found out about Ade and Nina, and then she had lost it. 'Don't think about that now,' he said. He pulled her towards him and he held her dark head against his chest, felt her body heaving with sobs. He didn't think he had ever held her so closely.

'Please don't, Molly.' *But was it my fault?* He wanted to ask this. *Was that my fault too?*

She shook her head into his windproof jacket although he had not spoken.

'Do you think you could forgive me now, Molly?' He drew away from her, lifted her chin. 'For treating you so badly? For everything?' Molly had lived with the knowledge of Nina and Ade's betrayal for all these years. But of course there was more, much more. All the times he hadn't listened, all the things he hadn't said, all the ways he hadn't cared.

'Can you forgive me?' she whispered.

'For getting pregnant on purpose?'

She nodded. 'And for all the other things I didn't tell you.'

'What other things, Molly?' Ade thought again of Bruno Rinaldi. He could take it. Now, he just wanted to know the truth. He could see that Molly was very different from the woman he had always imagined her to be. It amazed him that he could have lived with her for so many years and yet not really seen her, never really known her. Each of the women he had loved – Molly and Nina – had represented something to him that he had blithely connected to his own life rather than to the women themselves. Molly had been the wife who trapped him in a life he didn't want and Nina had been the woman who showed him a way out of it, who represented the freedom he longed for. How selfish he had been. Nina had been right – it wasn't all about him. It was about them too, and he had entirely lost sight of who they really were.

'I didn't tell you about my father,' Molly said.

'Your father?' That wasn't what Ade had been expecting. Was this the something that he'd been missing? Ade tried to read it in her eyes, but he couldn't see for looking.

'I didn't tell anyone about him,' Molly said. 'Anyone, that is, except for Bruno Rinaldi.'

CHAPTER 38

Faye was going through all her plans again that afternoon when a text came through from Alessandro.

I have not yet returned to work. Can I see you?

She read it twice. Texted back. *Yes, OK. I'm still at the theatre.*

What now? She couldn't settle while she was waiting for him. She gave up on the plans and instead prowled from room to room, thinking. She'd checked the exterior measurements and they were correct. And behind the stage were the backstage area, the corridor, the dressing rooms and the costume room . . . She frowned. It didn't make sense. Something wasn't right.

Alessandro found her in the costume room, staring at the window. 'What is it?' he said.

'Oh, nothing.' She'd work it out later. She turned to face him. She was glad to see him, she realised. One thing about Alessandro Rinaldi – he wasn't predictable. She never knew quite what to expect from him. He'd never be boring.

'Let us go and sit outside,' he said. 'I need to talk to you, Faye.'

'Okay.' She followed him down the corridor. What now? she couldn't help but think. Thankfully, Pasquale had long gone and the builders were working in the far dressing room at the moment.

'This place gives me the creeps sometimes.' Alessandro gave a small shudder.

Faye was surprised. 'I thought you loved it.'

'I love the memories.' He glanced towards her. 'But now . . . I have mixed feelings.' They went down the steps by the side of the stage into the auditorium.

Mixed feelings. Faye could identify with that. She followed him up the faded red runner that led to the foyer. She had so many mixed feelings that she hardly knew which way to turn – and they were mainly concerning him.

'Will you wait here?' he asked, when they were outside. 'I will be five minutes.'

'Yes, alright.' Why not? Faye sat down on the steps and watched his tall, rangy figure loping up the street, on a mission. She had no idea where he was off to, but she didn't object to taking a break. And he was right – the theatre could be claustrophobic; it was good to be outside in the fresh air. The sun was hot today and since it was siesta time, the streets and piazza were deserted. A heavy heat seemed to hang in the air like a blanket. The palm trees were still and even the birds had stopped singing. Faye lifted her head, closed her eyes and enjoyed the feel of the warm sun on her face.

'Here. *Ecco*.'

Her eyes snapped open. Alessandro was in front of her, blocking out her sun. He was smiling and in his hands were two cups of iced coffee.

'Mmm. Just what I needed.' She sniffed appreciatively and took the one he handed to her. 'Best iced coffee in Deriu?' she teased. She took a sip. Predictably, it was mellow, cool and delicious. 'Thanks,' she said.

'*De nada*.' Alessandro sat down on the steps beside her,

unwound his body and stretched out his long legs. Despite the heat, he was wearing jeans with flip-flops. His feet – like his hands – were brown. His pale green tee shirt betrayed the fact that he'd been working down at the boatyard before coming to the theatre this morning – it was stained with wood varnish and grease.

'Did you used to sit here when you were a boy?' Faye asked him. She could imagine that. His mother would be on stage rehearsing for some play; his father would be working in his hotel. Alessandro and Marisa would be out here playing by the fountain in the shade of the myrtle tree. She sniffed. The faintly aromatic orange blossom scent from the flowers was still there, mingling with the fragrance of the fresh coffee.

'*Si.*' His blue eyes were serious as he looked at her over the rim of the styrofoam cup. 'Back then the myrtle tree was still young and we used to balance on the edge of the fountain before we jumped in.'

Faye smiled, though she felt a little unsettled by his gaze. 'It's hard for people sometimes,' she said, 'to see things change.'

'You are thinking of Pasquale de Montis.' His lips tightened.

'Not just Pasquale, no.'

'Who then?'

She shrugged. 'Most of Deriu, I suppose. No one really wants me to be here. Everyone seems to want the little theatre to remain untouched.'

'Because no one knows how we will change it,' he said. 'No one knows how it will be.'

'True.' Faye hoped that they would come round in time, that they would see that this wasn't merely a project designed to bring hordes of tourists to their little town, but that it could benefit the community too.

'They cannot see into the future,' he remarked. 'But you, Faye, you are the designer. You do see into the future. You have a vision, *non*?'

Faye considered this. 'In a way, yes.' It was her job to look ahead, to imagine, to plan.

'A vision . . .' He leaned back, still regarding her closely in that way he had. 'But this is only a job to you, I think. In the next weeks or months, you will have other visions, other projects to plan.'

'Yes, I suppose I will.' Faye didn't want to think of leaving Deriu, but of course she must. She had an interview to go to and her career to think of. She had even found a course in theatre restoration and design, which would suit her very well. This had been her first undertaking and it was very special. But soon, she would have to say goodbye.

'And then you will forget us.'

'Hardly.' Faye grinned. He wasn't the most forgettable man in the world.

He grinned back at her. 'This place – it has got to you a little, yes?'

'Just a little,' she conceded. Even the hostile villagers, even this infuriating man, had – not to mention the little theatre itself and the landscape it stood in. It had all got to her; it had all begun to touch her heart.

He swung himself lazily up to standing, walked down the steps and across to the fountain. She watched him break a small twig from the myrtle tree. He brought it back and handed it to her. 'This is Sardinia,' he said.

She sniffed the delicate but heady scent – it did indeed seem to hold the heat and fragrance of Sardinia inside its tiny white flowers.

'The myrtle – she needs a hot summer to produce her flowers and fruits,' he said conversationally.

There were certainly hot summers here in Sardinia. This one was positively sizzling.

'The myrtle is an old tree,' he went on, 'as ancient and wise as the olive. She is mentioned often in Greek mythology.' He pulled some shades from the back pocket of his jeans and put them on as he sat back down.

'Is that so?' Faye's attention was inevitably drawn to the shape of his mouth.

'Yes.' He smiled. 'She is known as a symbol of love and immortality, which is why you will often see a sprig of myrtle in wedding bouquets.'

Faye was becoming more and more conscious of the heat. Her own sunnies were inside her bag in the theatre dressing room. She looked away from Alessandro to the safer view of the skinny houses on the opposite side of the street, whose paint was peeling to reveal the bare render beneath. And inevitably once again she thought of Pasquale. She hoped he would cope with the alterations to the theatre that would be continuing over the summer months and beyond. He wouldn't be able to go in there whenever he wanted to relive those theatrical moments of his; he would have to watch the restoration from across the square. But hopefully he would appreciate the end results and be able to love the new *piccolo teatro* just as much as he did now.

'So what did you want to talk to me about?' Faye asked Alessandro. Lovely as it was to chat to him on the theatre steps with the fragrance of myrtle filling her nostrils and the sun beating down from above, she knew that she ought to get on.

He sipped his iced coffee thoughtfully. 'I wanted to apologise,' he said. 'Again.' He arched an eyebrow. 'And I wanted to explain to you why it is impossible to explain.'

The man of riddles. 'Really, Alessandro . . .'

'This whole thing,' he said. 'The problem I had to deal with, the reason I found it hard to come to a decision, the obstacle to the project.'

'Yes?'

'It concerned my sister Marisa.'

Faye had already guessed that. It was the way he had thrown that envelope down in Marisa's apartment, the way he'd held his sister in his arms that night. 'Are you protecting her from something?'

'Yes.'

'So – she is the one being threatened?'

'Yes.'

'But by whom?'

He shook his head. 'She has no one else to look after her, Faye,' he said. 'I am her brother. She needs me.'

Faye considered this. Was this why Marisa was so eager to leave Sardinia and move to Rome? Leo was there, of course, but was there something else, something that Marisa wanted to escape from here in Deriu? It would mean leaving her brother . . . Faye glanced across at Alessandro, at the dark frown on his face. She could understand his feelings of protectiveness. Marisa was his sister and since their father's death they only had each other, as he had said. Leo was in Rome and Jana . . . Well, Faye didn't want to think about Jana. But it all sounded very cloak and dagger. 'Can't you just tell the police?' she asked. 'Couldn't they help, if it's as serious as you seem to think?'

'That is equally impossible.' He gulped the rest of his

coffee and crumpled the cup in his hand. She heard the ice crunch.

'But Alessandro – is Marisa in some sort of danger?' Here, sitting on these sunny steps, her question sounded wrong and crazy. But although Deriu was a warm and friendly place, although the *centro storico* was atmospheric and the scenery stunning, Faye knew from her short time here that the village wasn't as peaceful as it appeared. There was a dark underbelly to this place, to these people.

'Not any longer, no. I think that now she is safe.'

'That's good.' Faye cradled her coffee cup between her palms. He hadn't really told her anything new, but somehow he had made her feel better. Though it didn't change one thing – that Alessandro didn't trust her enough to tell her the full story. And neither did it change the fact that he had come on to her when he was clearly involved elsewhere.

'And I am sorry for this morning,' he said.

She turned towards him. He certainly looked contrite. 'It's okay,' she said.

'I overreacted.'

'Yes.' Faye thought of Pasquale, poor man. 'But you had a point,' she conceded. 'I shouldn't have shown anyone else the plans. Not yet.'

'Truce then?'

'Truce,' she agreed. It was far easier being friendly with this man than being angry. Especially on a day like this.

He sighed. 'It is very hard, Faye, when you make a promise to someone, and that promise creates difficulties with another.'

'Yes, I suppose it would be.' Faye had no idea what he was talking about. Had he promised something to Pasquale? To Marisa? But it was far too pleasant sitting on the steps beside him, conscious of his proximity, warmed by the sun, drinking delicious iced coffee. She felt wonderfully lazy. She didn't want the moment to end.

'Are you happy, Faye?'

She glanced up at a certain inflection in his voice. It was an odd question. And he looked as if her answer mattered to him. 'Happy with the project, do you mean?' she asked carefully.

His expression changed. 'Of course.'

She wondered whether or not to tell him what was bothering her, about the discrepancy in her plans. On the one hand he might be able to help; on the other, she didn't want him to think her inept. She decided to keep quiet, to try and work it out for herself. 'Everything's fine,' she said. Which didn't really answer his question. But the question was too personal; she didn't trust herself. This man was rather too good at personal.

'And your parents? How are they?' The concern in his voice seemed to caress her. Or was it simply the heat of the sun?

Faye thought about this. Her father had texted her earlier to tell her he was on his way to Dorset. *Good luck!* she had texted back. How would it go? Neither of them had phoned her yet. She wasn't sure if that was a good thing or a bad. But at least it implied that they were communicating and that they were together – at least for now.

'They're talking,' she told him.

He smiled. 'That sounds promising. It is always good to talk.'

'I hope so.'

'And you, Faye?'

'Me?' Faye put her coffee cup down on the step beside her.

'When will you be leaving us?'

Faye blinked at him. 'In a week or two.' Though she didn't want to think about it.

'So soon?' He drew slightly away from her. She couldn't read the expression in his eyes behind the dark shades.

'I'll do my job here first,' she said defensively. She wouldn't let them down. 'I'll get the job to a good point, and then—'

'You will go,' he said shortly.

'I can't stay here the entire time the work's being done,' she pointed out – quite reasonably, she thought. 'I have to take on other work.'

'In the UK?'

What was he asking her exactly? What was he expecting? 'I will fulfil the remit we discussed,' she said. 'I'll still be on board.'

'From a distance.'

'From a distance,' she agreed.

'It is, as you say, just a job,' he said.

Faye reached out. She put her hand over his, which was warm and brown. 'It's not just a job, Alessandro,' she said. 'But I have to work. I have to live.'

'I know you do.' He took hold of her hand, his thumb gently stroking the base of her thumb. 'But it is a shame. We shall miss you.'

It was such an intimate gesture. She watched, fascinated. She would miss them. And Deriu. Faye closed her eyes. The touch of his hand was sending all sorts of deliciously warm sensations careering around her body. She didn't even want to talk any-more. She just wanted to sit here and feel. But – she remembered Jana and abruptly snatched her hand away, eyes opening. 'I have a job interview,' she said. She hadn't meant to tell him this – and certainly not so bluntly.

He was silent for a few moments, absorbing this information. 'I wonder, Faye . . .'

'What, Alessandro?' In the shimmering heat of the afternoon, she was almost beginning to think that this moment was a dream.

'What it is that you want from me?'

Faye had not been expecting that question. She squinted into the sun. He was watching her. What was the point of asking him why he was playing with her emotions when he had another woman in tow, a woman he had been with for years? One who presumably thought that one day he would stop playing the field and marry her? Some men couldn't help it. Apparently his father was the same. There was no point. And every time Faye responded to him, she was further feeding his ego. She shook her head.

There was a silence between them. It grew heavier by the second. Over on the other side of the square, Faye thought she saw someone standing outside the front door of the de Montis house. Pasquale? She wasn't sure. She blinked and he was gone.

Once again, Alessandro unwound his long legs and got to his feet. Once again he let out a deep sigh. 'I should return to the boatyard,' he said.

Faye nodded. And she should get back to her drawings.

Alessandro held out a hand and helped her up. 'I will see you again very soon.' He said this as if it were a promise.

Faye felt the regret as she watched him slowly descend the steps and walk away. He had asked what she wanted from him. But what she wanted from him, she could not have. 'Goodbye, Alessandro,' she said.

CHAPTER 39

They were still walking along Cogden Beach when the rain came. One minute Molly was watching a golden retriever race for a ball, bounding over the pebbles – so excited, she thought, so happy in the present moment, which she supposed they should all be striving for . . . The next minute the sky had bruised and darkened and the rain came bucketing down.

Ade swore colourfully. He looked around them, but there was nothing here. No shelter anyway: Cogden was a nature reserve and it was remote – just sea, a broad expanse of pebbles leading to a steep shelving beach and rugged countryside beyond. In the spring it was a colourful garden of white-flowered sea kale, campions and purple thrift, but most of the flowers had disappeared by now. 'How far have we come?' He looked back towards the Hive.

'A couple of miles.' Molly had put up her hood but her fleece wasn't up to this sort of rain; it was soaked in seconds. She started to laugh.

'What the—?' He glanced across at her in confusion. Then his mouth twitched.

'It's so ridiculous.' Molly bent double. She could hardly speak, she was laughing so much. She couldn't remember the last time she'd laughed like this. Hysteria, probably.

'What is?' But already he was properly grinning in that way

she remembered; rain on his sandy eyelashes, his cheeks wet, fair hair already plastered to his scalp, his shorts to his legs.

'You and me. Our conversation. The rain.' And she started laughing again. It had been the suddenness of it, she supposed; like being caught by a rogue wave. The few people on the beach were scattering, heading back up to the National Trust car park. But Ade's car was parked way back at Hive Beach Café. Molly didn't care. The rain was sleeting down on the sea like arrows. Water, water everywhere. She was loving it down here.

It had been a relief to tell Ade about getting pregnant on purpose, such a huge relief. It was a long time ago, but Molly could feel the burden of it slipping from her shoulders; she'd carried that burden far too long. She remembered how it had happened very well. It was almost unintentional – almost, but not quite. She and Ade had been together for a couple of years. She was still young – coming up to twenty-two. One day she had realised she'd missed two contraceptive pills in a row. She'd panicked, put the next pill on her tongue. And from somewhere . . . *Would it be so awful?* The thought had come. Mightn't it cement them, her and Ade? Mightn't it push him into making a commitment? She couldn't quite admit to herself, not then, that she could already see the restlessness in his blue-grey eyes – so often somewhere else, dancing without her on some distant horizon.

She hadn't taken that pill, or the next. Then she'd come to her senses and started taking them again – only by then it was too late.

Molly held her face up to the rain. Ade was laughing at her. Summer rain was different from winter rain; it didn't lash out or chill you to the bone. It was refreshing almost; a release, she thought.

'Come on, you.' Ade's voice was affectionate. He took her arm. 'Let's head back.'

'Okay.' She liked this new affectionate Ade who seemed to be looking at her in a different way. *Absence makes the heart grow fonder.* Was that it? And if so, would it last? Or would that restlessness reappear one day?

They trudged back along the shoreline, wet shoes making the going hard on the slippery shingle. The rain was easing off now; the pebbles had drunk up the moisture and were gleaming like they did at high tide. And would Ade still be affectionate, Molly wondered, when she had told him the rest of her story?

'So what's this about your father?' Ade's voice was tender still.

Molly gazed ahead to the reassuring contours of the grey-green summer ocean and allowed the memories to come forward.

'It was when he came out of hospital that last time,' she told Ade. 'I think he knew. I think he'd already decided . . .'

'You're brave, Molly, my sweetheart,' her father had said to her as he lay, already ghost-white, in his sick bed. 'Will you help your old dad?'

'I'll do anything to help you, Dad, you know that.' Molly had drawn the curtains because his eyes were weak. *I don't want sunlight,* he'd said. *There's no sun for me, not anymore.* She'd given him water he could sip through a straw because his mouth was so dry. She'd plumped up his pillows to make him more comfortable and put his dressing gown around his shoulders to keep him warm. She was glad that he thought she was brave. But she didn't feel it.

She sat next to him in the dim light and held his hand. It felt like a loose bag of bones, the skin already parched of moisture, of life. The smell of medicine was in the air, metallic and sickly.

Molly hated it. His forehead was glistening with sweat. She reached up and smoothed his hair from his brow. There was no hint of grey. He was too young to die. But there was nothing of him. He had always been a lean, rangy man; now, his cheeks and eyes were sunken, the bones standing out in sharp relief.

'Anything?' he whispered.

'Of course.' Molly leaned closer. She was only seventeen. Other girls her age were out enjoying themselves, breathing in the fresh air, dancing and drinking with their friends, having a good time – a normal time. Molly was nursing her father. She didn't mind. It was better than watching her mother try to do it. Her mother couldn't hold back her resentment, her tears. She seemed to blame Molly's father for being sick, for being unable to leap out of bed and fix the washing machine or put up a shelf. She treated him as though he'd reneged on an agreement, as if he'd let her down. Molly knew it was her mother's way of coping. But it didn't help. It didn't help her father.

'I've had enough,' her father muttered.

'Course you have.' Molly couldn't imagine what it was like. To be fit and healthy one day and to hear the next that your life expectancy was less than a year; to deteriorate week by week, to be so reduced by illness and drugs that you became a weak shadow of the man you once were. She looked at her father and felt the tears spring to her eyes. She held them back though, she always did. It was the very least she could do for him.

'I can't ask your mother.' He fixed his watery brown eyes on hers.

'No?' Molly didn't quite understand. 'What can't you ask her?'

'I can't ask her to help me.'

'Help you with what, Dad?' Like she'd said, she'd do

anything. Only she was getting an uneasy feeling. It was the way he was looking at her. Serious. Pleading. As if this was a big thing. 'What?' she said again. Something was hurting in the pit of her stomach. Something was making her want to run.

'Help me end it, sweetheart,' he whispered. Every word seemed to be an effort.

Molly was silent. She didn't run. He was gripping her hand with a strength that surprised her. She knew what he was saying now, what he was asking. *You can't ask me to do that.* But she didn't say this; it wasn't true. He could ask her and he had.

'Dad . . .' *Please, no.*

His breathing was shallow. 'You're the only one who can.'

Ade stopped walking. 'Jesus, Molly.' His arms were around her, making her feel safe. For a moment, Molly felt that this was all that she wanted.

'I know.' Her voice was muffled into his coat. She trembled.

'How?' Ade asked her. He was stroking her hair.

'He had morphine.' He had directed her every step of the way, urged her on when she hesitated. His body had become used to a small dose of the morphine-based drug that managed his pain; he seemed to know how much it had to be.

'I can't do it, Dad,' she had said at the last moment, her courage failing. She knew he was in pain, she knew he had given up on life, she knew that the only thing in front of him was more pain, more drugs and a certain death. What was there for him to live for? His life had become deeply upsetting to his wife and daughters. They were all hurting – and for what? To see him suffering for a few more months?

'For me, sweetheart,' he said. 'You can do it for me.'

And so she had. In the end it was the most unselfish act. It was her father's choice. She had closed her mind to everything apart

380

from the need to release her father from his pain. His breathing had stayed regular after the overdose, but become very slow and then gradually more laboured. He had stopped talking and after a while he had become unresponsive. She had stayed with him to the end.

'He was right in one thing,' Ade said. 'You were very brave. I never knew you were so brave.'

Molly cried then. She wept into Ade's shoulder as if she had never cried for her father before – although she had, many times. But this time it was different. This time she was crying for the seventeen-year-old Molly who had never quite got over what she had done to the man she adored most in the whole world.

'He should never have asked you,' Ade murmured into her ear as her tears subsided.

Behind them to the east, she could just distinguish the outline of Portland. They were alone on the beach it seemed, the raw wind and salt spray on their skin and in their hair, their bodies closer than they had ever been. Ade was rocking her very gently from side to side as if she were a child. She could feel the comfort of it.

'No.' Though Molly didn't blame him. Not for that, not for anything.

Ade drew away and looked into her face. 'Did your mother know?'

Molly shook her head. Her mother was a lot stronger now than she had been then. She had learned to lead her own life; she had become independent. But back then she would never have coped. 'I think our GP suspected what had happened,' she said. 'But Dad actually died from cardiac arrest. Our doctor signed the death certificate. He was a very understanding man.'

They were both silent for a moment, considering the implications of what might have happened.

'And you didn't tell anyone?'

Again, she shook her head.

'You dealt with it completely on your own?' He held her by the shoulders and kissed her forehead gently. It was a damp kiss from rain-wet lips. 'At seventeen?'

'Yes.' She looked up at him and he wiped a tear from her cheek. Who could she have told about a thing like that? There was no one.

'Oh, Molly, I wish . . .'

'What do you wish?' They walked on, his arm slung around her shoulders now, just like it had been in the old days. Cogden Beach stretched out in front of them, this wide expanse of sand and shingle and sea, the pebbles meeting the path that had crept down from the high cliffs at Hive Beach, crept down into a flat expanse of shoreline interspersed with gorse and sea kale and the occasional clump of bright yellow poppies. From here, Molly could see as far as Golden Cap to the west.

'I wish I'd been worthy of your trust,' he said.

Molly faced him. 'And I wish I'd been honest with you from the start,' she said. She had never allowed Ade to see who she really was, that was the thing. She had never been fully open with him. She had been so busy trying to be the perfect girlfriend, the perfect wife. She had always pretended. If she had trusted him with the truth, she thought, he might not have strayed. If she'd been honest, if she'd been herself, things might have been different. If she had turned to him rather than to Bruno, that time, they might never have grown so far apart.

'Though there's a chance we wouldn't have made it if you'd told me everything back then,' Ade said.

Molly thought about this. A finger of sunlight had parted the clouds. It was soothing, watching the tide roll in to shore and draw back over the pebbles; the flow and the tension of the rolling waves were almost hypnotic; the soft low rumble of the ocean seemed to come from the depths of the sea bed. She had talked to Faye about a pattern of dishonesty that could prevent a person from having an honest relationship. But Ade might have a point. The reason one was dishonest in the first place was usually because you wanted to save something, because you were scared. She had wanted to save her relationship with Ade; she hadn't dared risk losing it. And now? She sneaked a glance at him. It felt good to tell him the truth, whatever happened next between them. By confiding in Ade, by trusting him . . . It was another step towards coming to terms with her past actions, emotions and losses. She remembered what he had said to her. *I've lost our baby too . . .*

Molly took a deep breath. 'Lately, I've been writing about it,' she told Ade.

'About your father?'

'And about us. About the child we lost.' She'd resisted it at first; she had no time for 'therapy' and she certainly had no intention of sharing her experiences with a creative writing group. But it wasn't about that, Jo had told her. It was her story. She would be writing it down for herself. And gradually, it had come. She had started going to these classes because her life felt empty. But they had given her something to think about. She had let honesty in, she realised; she had begun to find acceptance. And in that acceptance, she felt in control of her own destiny for perhaps the very first time. She was who she was. She was empowered.

'And you told him everything?'

She knew he was thinking of Bruno Rinaldi. 'Bruno wasn't a happy man.' Molly remembered the shape of his mouth, the grief in it. 'He saw my unhappiness too.'

'So you talked to him?' Ade glanced at her, then away. Molly knew he would find this difficult.

'Yes,' she said. 'I told him, Ade. All the things I should have told you. About my father, about what I'd done, about how I got pregnant, about you and Nina, about the miscarriage . . .' She sighed. There had been so much. Bruno had listened and nodded and seemed to understand. He had not judged her. He had poured her a drink, put his arms around her and then he had told her his secret.

'And then what happened?' Ade asked. 'You can tell me, Molly.' She could feel the tension in him, but he hadn't taken his arm away from her shoulders. He was holding her as if he were worried someone was going to grab her and run off with her into the sea. It was important, Molly thought, that he hadn't taken his arm away.

'Nothing,' she said.

She sensed his surprise. 'I wouldn't blame you if—'

'I know.' Yes, Bruno Rinaldi was an attractive man. And yes, she'd confided in him and he in her. There was a part of her that had been tempted to do more – she was only human, after all. And they had the opportunity: they were alone in the house and her husband – who had been unfaithful to her – was still out enjoying himself at the wedding reception. 'He kissed me,' she said. 'That's all.' Bruno Rinaldi had kissed her. The memory of it was still there, imprinted on her lips. It had been sweet and forgiving and it would have been so easy to have gone further. But she hadn't. With Bruno Rinaldi, Molly thought, it hadn't been about that. She supposed it had been a different kind of bonding altogether. And that in itself had been an infidelity. She had the feeling that Ade had been brooding about this, that he understood it now.

'So what about us, Molly?' Ade asked. He too was looking out to sea. 'I'd like us to try again. Do you think it's possible? Do you want it, too?' He looked back at her.

Molly searched for the restlessness in his eyes but all she could see was vulnerability. She hadn't seen that before in Ade, she thought. It had been her worst fear realised when he left her. Painful, but also a relief: the worst thing had happened and she had survived. 'Oh, Ade,' she said. 'I don't know – not yet.'

They walked back to the car in companionable silence. Molly knew that she had given Ade even more to think about. But then she had more to think about too.

They drove back to the house.

'Let's have some tea,' Molly suggested.

Ade raised his eyebrows. 'What about Doug?' he said. 'What if he's watching us from behind his net curtains?'

Molly snorted with laughter. She knew she shouldn't have found it funny when Ade had laid him out like that. Doug had only been trying to help her and Ade could have hurt him. But . . .

'I wouldn't expect you to decide straightaway,' Ade said. 'And I wouldn't expect us to go away anywhere, either. It was selfish of me to imagine you'd want to do that, just because I did.'

Molly filled the kettle. 'I've been thinking about that,' she said. 'If Mum's okay with it, I would rather like to go away somewhere for a while.'

'With me?' His eyes widened.

Molly had made a promise to her father to look after her mother. *Don't leave her alone like I have*, he'd said. *Do your best for her, sweetheart*. But how much could one person ask another person to do? Her mother was well, her sister Kathryn wasn't far away and really, wasn't it time Molly felt less responsible for everyone else and did something that she wanted to do?

So she smiled at Ade and took his hand. She wasn't sure about the camper van he had always talked about – she'd have to have a think about that – but she was sure of one thing. 'Yes,' she said. 'With you.'

CHAPTER 40

Later, when she was back at the apartment cooking dinner, Faye's mobile rang. It wasn't either of her parents as she'd half-expected and it wasn't Alessandro as she'd half-hoped. It was Charlotte.

'Hey! How's it going?' Faye asked her friend. It seemed so long since Charlotte and Fabio had left. Sometimes Faye felt as if she'd been living here in their house in Deriu for years. She glanced over at the aquarium to check that all was well. She'd grown used to watching the fish peep out from behind the pink coral, enjoyed being mesmerised by the way they glided so effortlessly and elegantly through the water. It was as therapeutic as meditation.

'Fine, thanks, my love. Fabio's nearly finished the tour and I'm about ready to come home, to tell you the truth.' Charlotte exhaled loudly.

'Are you homesick, sweetie?'

'A bit. There are only so many Italian towns you can look around before they blend together. Beautiful churches, pretty piazzas, turquoise bays. It's all much of a muchness.'

It sounded pretty good to Faye. She had so loved her time in Naples and it had been no surprise to find how much she loved Sardinia too. Maybe one day she would be able to explore the rest of Italy. She hoped so. Her Italian had come on in leaps and bounds since she'd been here; there was no substitute for living in a place to learn its language and its culture – and its people, too . . .

'And none of the places we've been to can match Deriu,' Charlotte added.

Faye smiled. 'I know what you mean.'

'And that's why I rang, my love, to warn you that we'll be back at the end of the week.'

Faye made a rapid calculation. She hadn't yet had a reply from the design company in London, but she thought she'd need at least another week for everything here to be up and running at a level that would allow her to leave. Alternatively, she could take a quick flight back to the UK for the interview, see her parents and then come back to Deriu until she heard whether or not she'd got the job. There was plenty to do here; she could certainly use the time. And she had to agree with Charlotte. Deriu – for all its frustrations and dark dealings – held more appeal than London in the middle of a glorious summer.

She explained the timings to Charlotte. 'I could rent an apartment here until the right job comes up,' she suggested.

'Nonsense. You and I haven't spent nearly enough time together yet,' her friend said. 'You're more than welcome to stay with us for as long as you like.'

Faye accepted with good grace. She was rather looking forward to Charlotte and Fabio's return. She hadn't been feeling lonely exactly, but fish were fish and it would be good to have a friend around.

'And how have you been getting on with Marisa and Alessandro?' Charlotte asked. 'I'm so glad you decided to take on their project. How's it progressing?'

Where should she start? 'There have been a few problems,'

she admitted. Should she tell Charlotte that Alessandro had considered Marisa to be in some sort of danger? She decided not to – she'd only worry. 'But it's full steam ahead at the moment.'

'Marisa did mention something . . .' Charlotte's voice dropped low. 'It's nothing serious, is it?'

'I'm not sure.'

'And Alessandro?' The tone of Charlotte's voice gave nothing away.

'What about him?' If she'd been face to face with her friend Faye wasn't sure she could fool her, but . . .

'How are the two of you getting along?'

'Oh, not so badly.' Faye crossed her fingers.

'He's gorgeous, don't you think?'

'Er, yes, I suppose.'

'Since when didn't you notice an attractive man?' Charlotte laughed. 'He's hot.'

'But taken,' Faye pointed out.

'Ah, the glamorous Jana . . .'

Exactly. The glamorous Jana indeed.

'She hasn't been sharpening her claws on you, has she?'

Faye had to laugh. 'No. She's given me a look like daggers though.'

'It's such a shame.' Charlotte chuckled. 'Alessandro's an absolute poppet.'

That wasn't the first word Faye would use to describe him. Clearly Charlotte hadn't been on the wrong end of his bad temper. 'But perhaps he drives her to it?' she suggested. 'Maybe he has a roving eye.'

'Alessandro?' Charlotte seemed surprised. 'No, he's not the type.'

'You don't think so?' That wasn't what the rest of the village seemed to think. Like father, like son, hadn't they said?

'I don't *think* – I know.' Charlotte seemed very sure. 'Don't get me wrong – our Alessandro always has women running after him and I can't blame Jana for taking offence now and then. But he's a loyal kind of man. And people always talk, don't they?'

'That's true enough.' They certainly did in Deriu.

'Look, Faye, I have to go,' said Charlotte. 'See you soon, okay?'

'Okay.' Faye said goodbye and ended the call. But she remained thoughtful. Charlotte was pretty perceptive. Faye would normally have trusted her judgement. In this case though . . . Alessandro Rinaldi was definitely not a loyal kind of man. A loyal kind of man would never have encouraged another woman, kissed her, made her think that . . . Faye shook her head in despair. Even Charlotte seemed to have been charmed by him.

After she'd eaten, Faye decided to do some work on her drawings. She went to fetch her laptop and then she realised: she had left her laptop bag – and most of her plans and drawings that were inside the zip pocket – in the little theatre. 'Damn.' She'd have to go and get them; she didn't like leaving them there all night, especially since the fire. Fortunately it wasn't far and it was a pleasant evening; a walk would probably clear her head and do her good.

She left the house and walked past the palm trees along the path towards the bridge. As always, the boats moored along the riverbank were rocking gently. A pleasure boat chugged along the river with the sound of dance music drifting from it, away into the dusk. The sky was growing pinker and more yellow; the river darker as if it knew that soon it would be night-time. Some people were dining al fresco at the riverside restaurant; Faye walked past and on to the bridge; thought for a moment of Alessandro Rinaldi and how she had stood here next to him and watched the river as it wound its way towards the sea.

On the other side of the river she struck up a side street and immediately entered Deriu's *centro storico,* which was like stepping back in time. The old stone houses were crammed so close to one another, mortar crumbling, paint peeling, telling the story of times gone by, of past generations who had looked out from their grilled windows and wrought-iron balconies, who had encouraged bougainvillea to snake up pillars and above doorways to explode in a flush of colour over an archway or from a high wall.

Faye nodded hello or said '*Buona sera*' to those she passed chatting in open doorways or watering their geraniums or oleander. She couldn't swear to it, but she had the sense that people were continuing to grow friendlier towards her. Either they were getting used to the idea of the little theatre being renovated by the Rinaldi family or she was finally being accepted by this community. She could smell the food being prepared and cooked in houses and restaurants: the sweet tang of seafood freshly caught that day, the rich sauces of tomato and basil, the deeper, more oily smell of *porceddu*, suckling pig cooked on a spit, one of Sardinia's specialities.

Faye was a street away from *Piazza del Teatro* when she heard raised voices on the street below. She reached a viewpoint provided by some worn green railings and glanced down. She wasn't surprised to see Marisa and Alessandro Rinaldi having what looked like a heated debate with Enrico and Carmela Volti. Enrico was leaning forwards in his habitual, somewhat aggressive, stance, with his fists clenched, and Carmela was openly weeping. Alessandro had his arm around his sister, who also looked very upset, her hands clutched to her throat. All four seemed to be talking at the same time, a Sardinian trait Faye had observed many times since she'd arrived in Deriu.

Faye looked down on the lively tableau. What were they arguing about now? The little theatre, probably. She hesitated, wondering if she should go down there. But she didn't want to interfere. She wouldn't be able to contribute anything and her presence might make matters worse. No doubt she'd find out what it was all about soon enough – unless, that was, they decided not to tell her.

She turned around in a decisive movement, taking the street uphill that led to *Piazza del Teatro*. There was no sign of life in the little theatre. The builder would have gone home by now and all was quiet at Pasquale de Montis' house over on the other side of the square. Faye frowned as she remembered the problem that had been bothering her. When she reached the top of the steps, instead of locating the key, she walked round the side of the building and looked up to the windows. She had been sure she knew this building so well by now. She counted, worked out which window belonged to each room, got to the costume room and stopped short. She hadn't realised how far the window was situated from the outside wall. She thought of her plans. Was that where she'd gone wrong?

Faye returned to the front of the building and found the key under the urn. It had taken a tumble on the night of the fire, but Sardinian urns had been made to last and this one was just a bit more cracked and battered than before. She didn't want to hang around but before she went to grab her laptop, Faye wanted to check on one thing . . . As she inserted the key in the lock, the church bell tolled. And she knew that it was preposterous, but tonight it sounded like a warning. She slipped inside.

She walked through the auditorium and checked briefly that her laptop was still in the dressing-room-cum-office. It was. She put it in the doorway so that she wouldn't forget it when she left this time and walked on to the far room. The layout of the long, narrow costume room was exactly as she remembered, exactly as she had drawn. But . . . Faye went to the window. This was the discrepancy. Outside, the window was five metres from the edge of the building; inside, the same window was much closer to the exterior wall. Which meant that either her spatial awareness had gone completely to pot or . . . She turned around to look at the wall. That it wasn't an exterior wall.

Why would someone have built a partition inside the exterior wall? She looked around the costume room. In the corner, next to the old sewing machine and its covered stool, stood the rails of costumes that had been covered with sheeting. Like most of the rooms in the little theatre, the costume room had been neglected for many years and was unkempt and showing the ravages of time. Cobwebs laced the ceiling, a layer of dust coated the floor and a general smell of damp lay heavy in the air. Could *that* be why a partition wall had been built? As extra protection from the damp? But it must run the entire length of the costume room, and they weren't talking about a gap of only a few inches. This would be one-and-a-half metres wide at least. Why would the cavity be so big?

Faye stared into the full-length mirror on the wall. A confused woman stared back at her. She felt a shiver. For some reason, Alessandro's words came back to her, about the theatre giving him the creeps. She wasn't scared, she told herself firmly. But there was something rather odd going on here. She put her bag down on the old brocade chair and touched the mirror cautiously. Looked at the fixings. It was just an ordinary mirror with a chain. But what was behind it? She grasped it firmly on either side and lifted. It must have been there for decades; it resisted at first and then the chain slipped free and the wall released it in a spiral of dust. Faye staggered back from the weight of it. She leaned the mirror against the other wall. She examined it back and front but there was nothing out of the ordinary. Where it was mounted originally there was a mirror-shaped paler patch of wall rimmed by a thick oval of dust. She touched it gingerly. Nothing out of the ordinary there either. It was just a wall.

But what kind of wall? Faye rapped on it. Sure enough, it sounded hollow, not the dull sound that one would expect from an exterior stone wall. She rapped to the left and the right, high and then low. It sounded hollow all the way along, top and bottom. This was an interior partition wall. So . . . behind it was a void, and quite a sizeable void at that. She felt a rush of excitement. Was it some sort of storage space that had been boarded up? But why would it have been? And if it wasn't storage space, then what else could it be? Why have a room if one couldn't access it? She frowned. It didn't make sense. Then she remembered what Alessandro had told her about the family that Pasquale's father had hidden from the Fascists. Was it possible? Could this be some sort of secret hiding place?

In which case there must be an opening. It had to be possible to get in there – and out. She pushed the wall with the palms of her hands, looking for weaknesses, for something that didn't look quite right or original – a mark, a hairline crack. She didn't really know what she was looking for but if her hunch was right, there must be some sort of entrance. She stood still for a moment, thinking. She examined the wall again. But there was nothing. There was no sign of any device or mechanism, no hint of an opening or a door. The wall looked like an ordinary wall, moulded at the edges and above, completely bare apart from the two old candlesticks on either side that looked as if they'd been there forever. She glanced away, glanced back. But maybe they were meant to look as if they'd been there forever?

She grasped hold of the one on the left-hand side, tried to turn it, to twist it. There was no give in it at all. It was bracketed to the wall and solid. She moved across to the other candlestick. This one seemed looser. She twisted it from side to side until it gave, and then she turned it a full forty-five degrees. She almost stopped breathing. The suspense was loud, hammering in her head. She turned it again. Something clicked. Faye tensed and listened. She stopped turning. Cautiously, she pushed the wall on the right hand side. Nothing. But . . . she pushed again, harder this time.

And it moved. The right-hand side of the wall moved back, just an inch or two, with a reluctant grinding sound. And at the same time the left hand side of the wall came forward in response. She pushed again and both sides moved once more. Clearly, it hadn't been opened for some time – the door was grinding against the floorboards, pushing the dust in front of it like an ancient vacuum cleaner. It was turning as if operated by some sort of centre spindle hidden within the wall. Turning the candlestick had pulled out the locking pin, allowing the door to pivot. One side moved forward while the other went back. The gap on the sides must have been disguised by the moulding. Whoever had created this had thought of everything. The whole wall was the door.

She stood there staring in astonishment as, not a cavity, not a small hiding place, but an entire room was revealed – long and narrow just like the costume room itself, which was presumably why it had been chosen for the purpose. Unless one was looking closely as Faye had been, and taking precise measurements, the incongruity wouldn't be noticed inside or out.

Faye's skin prickled with the thrill of discovery. She took a step inside. This must be where Pasquale's father had secreted the valuables belonging to the townspeople; this was certainly where he had hidden the family of Resistance fighters when the Fascists were searching for them. There were two bunk beds attached to the far wall and an old mattress on the floor. A small table, four chairs, and a tall cupboard stood in the corner. On the wooden floor was a threadbare rug. There was no window, of course, but she could see an airbrick that must have served for ventilation when the room was closed and which would be inconspicuous from the outside.

The family would have been found soon enough if they were sheltering backstage or in one of the dressing rooms. So Pasquale's father (at least, she assumed it was him; she remembered how clever Pasquale had said he was, how ingenious at making things) had sectioned off the costume room and created this room by building the door. It was ingenious. And no one else had known of it.

And now? Faye's mind buzzed with possibilities. This room was a valuable piece of history. It had been used to save a village family from certain death. The little theatre possessed even more historical importance than she had realised. How could it be used, in designer terms, for the theatre's new image? Faye approached the cupboard and opened it. There was a pile of clothes and a thin, worn blanket. She rubbed her arms. There was a strange and dank atmosphere in the room and it felt clammy. She didn't like it. Suddenly, she wanted to get out.

As she moved towards the doorway, she heard footsteps. She froze. They were coming closer. Her first instinct was to shut the door, to shut herself in this space, to avoid detection, just as that family had done all those years ago. Her second instinct was to get out.

But it was too late to do either. Someone walked into the costume room just as she reached the opening in the wall. Faye held her breath. Every second seemed to last a lifetime. She halted in her tracks. She waited.

CHAPTER 41

All the breath seemed to leave her body as Faye sighed with relief. It was only Pasquale.

'Faye? What is happening here . . .?'

'Oh, Pasquale.' She could hug him. 'I wondered who it was. I was so scared when I heard your footsteps . . .'

'I saw the light from across the square,' he said. 'I was sure I had switched it off.' There was an air of confusion about him. He scratched his head, glanced nervously around the room in which she was standing.

'Look what I found.' She gestured to the space behind her. 'Isn't it amazing? A whole room we didn't even know about.'

Pasquale stepped into the doorway and stopped. 'Amazing,' he echoed.

'Do you think this is where your father hid the Bertelli family from the——' She stopped short at his expression. 'You knew about the room.'

'Yes, of course.' He shrugged his shoulders. 'I knew everything. I was with my father all day every day almost until the day he died.'

'Did your father build the room himself?'

'*Si*. Perhaps he saw how things were,' Pasquale said. 'It was not our war and yet we were part of it, is that not so? I was young at the time – I cannot know. But I can imagine.'

'But why didn't you tell me about the room?' Faye asked. Its existence had certainly provided a puzzle for her in the last day or so when exterior measurements had not matched interior measurements. Pasquale could have saved her a lot of time and worry.

He put a brown and bony finger to his lips. 'It is a secret.'

'Not anymore, it's not.' Faye turned around and took another look at the simple furniture in the room. It would have sufficed. With outside help – someone bringing food and water and other obvious requirements – a family could have survived here for months. She turned back to Pasquale. He was still hovering uncertainly in the doorway; he looked as if he didn't want to come any further inside. 'Did Sofia know about the room?' she asked him gently.

He shook his head. 'It was before her time.'

'And Bruno?'

'I doubt it.' His gaze raked slowly over the contents of the room.

Faye got the impression that he hadn't been in here for an awful long time. Perhaps he had almost forgotten about the secret room himself – or wanted to. It must be a reminder of how and why his father had died, even while he was becoming Deriu's hero.

'The theatre fell into disrepair after the war,' he said. 'It was more or less abandoned until the Rinaldis organised a restoration in the 1960s. I do not imagine they found it.' His expression seemed to suggest that they wouldn't have had the wit.

'So Alessandro doesn't know about it either?' she asked.

'*Non.*'

Faye noticed his frown when Alessandro's name was mentioned. 'Why do you dislike him so much, Pasquale?' she asked.

'Is it just because he's Bruno Rinaldi's son? And what about Marisa? They are your Sofia's children, remember.'

'How could I forget?' He clenched his fists and a shudder seemed to travel the length of his body.

'But, Marisa—'

'I tried to help Marisa,' he said. 'I never disliked her. I felt sorry for her.'

'Why?'

He shook his head sadly. 'Her parents – they did not understand her. They wanted to change her. They did not see the truth.'

'And what was the truth?' Faye was intrigued. She realised that although she had spent a fair bit of time with Marisa Rinaldi, she still didn't know her very well. She knew that she spent some weekends in Rome with her boyfriend, she knew that she was eager to leave Deriu, and she knew that Alessandro had been protecting her from something. She also knew that once upon a time she had wanted to be on the stage just like her mother – was that what Pasquale was referring to?

'That she was like Sofia,' Pasquale whispered. 'So much like my Sofia.'

Faye was conscious of a flicker of unease. Pasquale still hadn't got over the love of his life, that much was clear. 'In what way?' she asked. 'How was she like Sofia? To look at, do you mean?'

'Yes, she was, but that is not what I meant.' Pasquale looked up at the ceiling and made a sudden movement, beating his chest with a fist. It was a comical sight, but also rather a tragic one. 'She was born to be an actress,' he declared.

'Ah.' Faye remembered that day in the theatre when Marisa had spoken of her dream. It had been the day they waited for

Alessandro, the day he had stormed off. As if someone had got to him, Faye thought now.

'But her mother hadn't wanted that life for her,' she reminded Pasquale gently.

He let out a snort of derision though Faye doubted it was directed at Sofia. Did he think Bruno was behind it?

'It was all Marisa Rinaldi wanted,' Pasquale said. His voice had taken on a dreamy quality now, as if he were reliving the memory of that time.

Or as if he were acting, Faye found herself thinking.

'And I could have helped her.' He turned once again to Faye. 'Me,' he said. 'Old Pasquale who was no longer required to play lead in any production. Yes! I could have helped her.'

'But she didn't want your help?' Faye didn't understand what he was getting at. She could see that he would encourage Marisa in her career choice – in memory of the time he had spent acting with Sofia if nothing else – but surely Bruno and Sofia wouldn't have welcomed his interference.

'It was not like that,' said Pasquale. He took a step inside the room at last. 'She came to me.' He smiled. 'To me.'

Faye could imagine how that would have massaged his ego. He might be unwanted by Sofia, he might have been looked over by Bruno and the directors here at the little theatre, but Marisa at least had still thought he was someone who might have influence. 'What did she want?' she asked.

He puffed out his chest. 'To use my contacts, of course. Do not think I did not have any.'

'Oh, I'm very sure you did.' Faye smiled to herself. Pasquale might no longer have been taking the leading roles, but he would still know the right people. In the eyes of a young girl who wanted to be an actress, a young girl whose parents opposed her decision, he might well be viewed as the next best option. 'And did you speak to someone about Marisa?'

'I was prepared to,' he said. Again his voice grew dreamy. 'There was one famous director in particular. If he could just see her, I thought – she did look so like Sofia – and I told her: *If he saw you, if I could simply take some photographs to show him . . .*'

'And did Marisa agree to that?' she asked. Once again she felt that flicker of unease.

'Of course.' He spread his hands. 'Who would not? Any girl would be glad of the opportunity.'

'So you took some photographs of her to show your director friend?' Faye kept her voice level. There was some connection, some significance that she was missing, but for the moment, it was eluding her.

'Ah, she was so lovely.' Pasquale had gone back off into his little world of memories. 'So perfectly lovely.'

Faye remained silent. She was uncomfortable about the way this was going. Marisa had been a girl of, what – fifteen at the most? And at the time, Pasquale a man of . . . fifty-something? Had anyone else been there at this photographic session? 'What happened, Pasquale?' she said at last.

His eyes were frightened as he looked back at her, almost as if he'd forgotten she was in the room. 'I had not intended—' He broke off. 'I did not mean—'

'What happened?' Faye said again.

He spread his hands in supplication. 'She was beautiful,' he said. 'And so like Sofia. When I looked into her eyes it almost seemed as if she was Sofia. For a moment I even thought . . .'

'Oh, Pasquale.' Faye had sensed this story wouldn't have a happy ending. 'What did you do?'

'Nothing.' He put up his hands, took a step away from her.

'Nothing. Of course. I did not touch her, if that is what you are suggesting.' He looked at Faye. 'Ask her if you do not believe me.'

'But you took photographs.' Faye's voice was soft. All she could see in her mind's eye was that brown paper package that Alessandro had tossed on to the bureau in Marisa's apartment. All she could see was the way Alessandro had comforted his sister. 'What kind of photographs did you take, Pasquale?'

He reared back as if she had struck him. 'Tasteful photographs,' he said. He licked his dry lips. 'What do you take me for?'

'But you thought she was Sofia?' pressed Faye. 'Didn't you say that, Pasquale?'

He nodded. 'She was not ashamed of anything back then,' he muttered. 'She had a lovely body. She—'

'You were the adult,' Faye snapped. 'What were you thinking, taking photographs of her without her parents' consent?' Faye shuddered. 'For God's sake, Pasquale. She wasn't much more than a child.'

He hung his head. 'You are right,' he said. 'You are right – of course. I had not meant . . . Things got out of hand . . .'

Faye thought once again of the mysterious package Alessandro had brought to Marisa's apartment that night. 'You didn't want the theatre to change,' she whispered. But she could hardly believe what she was thinking. Had he been so desperate for it not to change that he would . . .? Was it possible? Pasquale seemed so mild, so deferential. Yes, he was arrogant, but not in a threatening kind of way.

She took a deep breath. 'Did you try to blackmail Alessandro?' No wonder Alessandro and Marisa disliked him. No wonder Alessandro didn't want him to know about their plans for the little theatre. No wonder Marisa wanted to leave Deriu. She had stayed for her father's sake, but now that he was gone . . . How could Faye have missed so much?

'No.'

'No?' Faye was sure she was right.

'I would not call it blackmail.'

Faye stared at him in disbelief. 'What would you call it then, Pasquale?' And she had trusted him.

'I showed Rinaldi the photographs, yes. I thought he might want to reconsider his plans for the theatre. I admit it. But—'

'That's blackmail, Pasquale.' But Alessandro had challenged him. He couldn't tell the authorities – his sister's happiness and reputation was at stake. Apart from anything else, she was a teacher in the local school. But after Faye's visit to the boatyard, Alessandro had stood up to him and refused to give in to his demands.

'He threatened me, that Rinaldi bastard.'

Now Pasquale was playing the part of the wronged man, she realised. And very convincingly.

'He hit me.'

Faye remembered the state of Alessandro when he'd turned up at Marisa's apartment. It had been obvious he'd been in a fight. And now Faye knew why. As he'd told her, he had been protecting his sister from this man.

'They're all the same.' Pasquale looked bitter now, his mouth a thin line on his weather-beaten face.

'They?' Faye had had enough. She had thought Pasquale de Montis a pleasant and well-meaning man and now this. Not only had he taken advantage of a young girl in a way that could only be called abuse, but he had also tried to blackmail her family. And on top of all that, he didn't even seem aware that what he had done was wrong. There was no remorse. All he could think of was Sofia and his obsession with the Rinaldi family and *il Piccolo Teatro*.

'You know who,' he snarled. 'The Rinaldis. They think they own this town. They think they can have anyone they want.' He looked her up and down. 'Even you,' he said.

'That's enough.' She turned to go.

'Faye – please try to understand.' Pasquale grabbed her arm and Faye tried to shake him off. She moved backwards, slightly off balance, and almost tripped on the corner of the rug. Suddenly she was frightened. She just wanted to get out of here.

But Pasquale's grip on her arm was a strong one. 'Women,' he growled. 'They lead a man on, but they always want something different – someone different.' He glanced down at the floor.

Instinctively, Faye followed the direction of his gaze. There were some marks on the floorboards that had been covered by the rug, as if someone had taken the boards up and then tried to hide the fact.

'They want you to help them,' said Pasquale, half to himself. 'But when you try . . .'

Faye's mind went into overdrive. 'Them,' Pasquale had said. Who else had he tried to help? Was he talking about Sofia? Or was there someone else who had rejected his offer of help, his advances?

At that moment she heard a loud thud followed by voices and footsteps. She looked at Pasquale and he looked back at her. There was something hard in those piercing dark eyes . . . Belatedly, Faye realised that she should have been more afraid of this man. 'We can sort this out,' she said to him. 'We can—'

'Faye!' She heard someone shouting. Alessandro?

She opened her mouth to call back, but in a flash, Pasquale

had twisted her arm painfully behind her back and clamped his hand over her mouth. 'Be quiet or I will break it,' he muttered.

Faye struggled, but he was wiry and stronger than he looked. The next moment he was brandishing a small knife, its blade bright and steely. He held it to her throat. She went still. Oh my God, she thought. How had it come to this – and so fast? How could she have been so stupid?

She could hear Alessandro stomping around the back of the theatre. *Come into the costume room,* she thought. *Come into the costume room.*

Pasquale reached out with his foot and kicked the door. It clicked shut. Faye's shoulders slumped. That was it, then. Alessandro would never discover her now. He would look for her, think that she had gone home and leave. She was at the mercy of Pasquale de Montis and the blade at her throat. What could she say? How could she calm him down? How would she get out of here?

She tried to think, forced herself to stay quiet, to remain composed. 'It's only blackmail at the moment, Pasquale,' she whispered. She could smell the scent of him, the stale sweat and faintly rancid breath and had to suppress a shudder of revulsion. Was this how Sofia had felt? And Marisa? Had they been repulsed by this man with his needy ways, his blind arrogance? 'Let me go and that is all it is.' But she couldn't help looking down at the floorboards and she knew that he had seen her do it. What had been hidden under there?

'If she had only loved me,' Pasquale was muttering. 'If she had only remained my friend . . .'

Sofia again. Faye heard Alessandro in the room next door. She heard him swear and walk away. He had given up. Her eyes filled with tears. How could she let him know where she was? And what would happen to her now?

'Did you use this knife on Marisa, Pasquale?' Faye forced herself to ask. She wanted to know everything.

He was so close to her that she could feel him shake his head. 'I did nothing to Marisa Rinaldi, I told you that. I did not touch her. They were only photographs. She looked so like her mother . . .'

Faye bit her lip. 'On someone else then?' She carefully twisted her head, aware of the blade at her throat, so that at least she could see him.

His eyes glazed over. 'She laughed at me,' he whispered. 'She said I was an old man who knew nothing and who had nothing. She said that I had less talent in my whole body than Bruno Rinaldi had in his little finger.'

'Who did, Pasquale? Who said that?' But Faye thought she knew.

'It wasn't long since Sofia had died. I tell you – I went a little crazy . . .'

There was a loud grinding sound as the door swung open. In the split second that Pasquale was distracted, Faye grabbed his wrist, yanked it to her mouth and bit hard. He screeched like a wounded animal, dropped the knife and ran. Then she was in Alessandro's arms.

'I thought you'd gone,' she sobbed.

'I am here,' he whispered. 'I am not going anywhere.'

But Pasquale had run. He had run like a whippet through the other side of the doorway. Alessandro didn't even try and follow him. He just held her and Faye didn't think she had ever felt so safe in her life before.

CHAPTER 42

'Shouldn't we go after him?' Faye asked Alessandro. She didn't want to, she was still in shock. 'We can't let him get away.' Her face was still half-buried in the warmth of his chest.

'Hush.' His hand cradled her head. 'Do not worry. He is going nowhere. There are too many people who will stop him.'

Too many people? But Faye decided not to worry about it — not now.

'How did you know I was in here?' she asked at last, when she felt able to draw away from the warmth of Alessandro's hold, the strength of his arms. 'How did you know about the room?' They were still standing in the long narrow space that had saved an entire family from death.

'I did not know for sure.' He looked around him and she knew that he was thinking of the Bertelli family too. 'But there were some clues,' he added modestly. He stroked her hair. He was looking at her almost as if he'd never seen her before. And Faye liked that. For the moment she tried to put any negative thoughts out of her mind.

'I feel such an idiot,' she said. 'I always thought Pasquale was a nice man.' How wrong she was. 'A bit eccentric perhaps . . .' But not a bad person. 'I even felt sorry for him.' She thought of all those stories of the little theatre that Pasquale had told her, of the pride in his eyes, of what he had said about missing the stage, the limelight. He was an attention seeker – and worse. She should have guessed. She'd known right from the start that he didn't want the theatre to be restored; he'd made that plain enough. The man had always worn a mask and she hadn't been perceptive enough to see behind it.

'I blame myself.' Alessandro raked his fingers through his dark curly hair. 'I should have told you what he was.'

What he was . . . Faye wrapped her arms around herself. And she had been alone with him in this room. She had trusted him.

'But Mama always felt so sorry for him – she forgave him almost anything.'

It was strange, thought Faye, how different the same facts could be when viewed from the other end of the telescope, or spoken by a different voice. From what she'd heard before, she hadn't liked the sound of Sofia. But now she saw things differently. She had a picture in her head of Pasquale trailing after Sofia like a lovesick puppy. Sofia must have looked up to him in the beginning because of his experience in the theatre business, even flattered by his attentions. But as time went by her feelings would have changed. She hadn't been cruel to him at all; she had tolerated him and felt sorry for him. Sometimes though, that was worse.

'I think she felt guilty,' Alessandro said. 'He had been in love with her all those years and she'd never reciprocated the feeling. Then she met my father, and . . .'

'They fell in love,' said Faye. She thought of what her mother had told her about guilt being a powerful thing. 'But did she ever know what had happened to Marisa? About the photographs Pasquale had taken?'

'So you know about the photographs?' He sighed. 'I wanted to tell you, Faye. But it was not—'

'Not your secret to tell. I know.' Now, she understood. It had never been a case of Alessandro not trusting her enough; it had been a case of him keeping Marisa's secret safe.

'But, no, Mama never knew about the photographs. And neither did I until he approached me recently and tried to blackmail me, the scrawny little bastard.' He shook his dark head. 'Even Mama would not have forgiven him that.'

'He was very determined to stop the restoration of the theatre,' murmured Faye. She looked around the room. But why?

'He certainly was.' Alessandro's expression was grim. 'No doubt he instigated some of Enrico Volti's passion to dispute the ownership of the little theatre, hoping that might stop us. When it did not, when our project seemed likely to become a reality, he must have decided to use a different tactic.'

'Yes,' said Faye. It was a chilling thought. Had he kept those photos all this time for just such a reason? Or had he kept them because they reminded him of Sofia? It didn't much matter now. 'But you got them back,' she whispered.

'I got them back.' He shifted his weight, drawing further away from Faye as he did so. 'But when he returned the photographs to me – when I forced him to return the photographs to me –' He grimaced. 'He wept, he begged me to give him another chance. I promised the little weasel that I would not tell the world what he had done, what kind of person he was, for Marisa's sake.'

Faye nodded.

'If it had been up to me alone I would have contacted the police immediately.' His voice rose and he straightened his shoulders. 'But Marisa felt differently. She did not want any of it to come out into the open, to be public knowledge. I could not blame her. She had long put it behind her. She did not need any reminders.'

'I can understand that.' Marisa wanted to start a new life away from here, not be reminded of what had happened in the little theatre all those years ago. Faye looked once again around the secret room. She could hardly believe what had happened here. She'd known there was some disparity in her measurements, but she never would have guessed about this room and the secrets it held. She supposed that Pasquale had taken the photographs of Marisa in the costume room – it was the obvious choice; there was good light and plenty of fabulous costumes to choose from. But did those reasons include its proximity to the secret room? Faye shuddered. She didn't want to think about that.

'But how did you know I was in here – and with Pasquale?' she asked Alessandro. 'What made you come back to the theatre tonight?'

Alessandro led the way over to the small table and they sat on the very same chairs on which that poor family must have sat, night after night until Pasquale's father had arranged for them to be taken up into the mountains. And what, thought Faye, would Luigi de Montis have thought about his son's actions so many years later? She remembered what Dorotea de Montis had said about Pasquale being half the man. Faye supposed that she was right. And that had been Pasquale's burden to bear.

'It was the crucifix,' said Alessandro. 'The one you gave to Marisa.'

'The crucifix?' Faye frowned. She'd found it close to the doorway to this room, of course, under the floorboards by the mirror.

'Marisa and I bumped into Enrico and Carmela Volti earlier,' he said.

Faye sat up straighter. 'I saw them. I saw you all.'

'Arguing?'

'Yes.' *The crucifix* . . . She remembered what had happened when she found it. And now, Faye was beginning to see.

Alessandro put his elbows on the table and leaned forwards. 'We were passing by their house. Enrico came out. He spoke to us and then –'

Faye understood.

'He saw the crucifix around Marisa's neck.' Alessandro sat back. 'He went crazy. He said—'

'That the crucifix had belonged to Giorgia?'

Alessandro stared at her. 'You knew?'

'Only just.' It was all coming together now. 'It was something Pasquale said. I realised that it wasn't only Marisa he'd taken photographs of and made promises to. He kept referring to more than one person who had come to him, asking him for help. I remembered Carmela Volti telling me that Giorgia too had longed to be an actress. And so . . .'

'You started to speculate if Pasquale had also had something to do with Giorgia's disappearance.' Alessandro's voice was flat.

Faye hadn't wanted to, but, 'Yes.' She had thought a lot of things when she'd been trapped in this room, Pasquale's knife at her throat, her arm twisted painfully behind her back. She wriggled her shoulders to release the tension.

Once again, Alessandro sat forward in the tiny chair. He took hold of her hands. He looked exhausted. 'It is over now, Faye,' he said.

'I know.' She nodded, looked down at her hands in his. He was probably just being comforting. She was grateful.

'That was why I came back to the theatre,' he said. 'As soon as we realised that it was Giorgia's crucifix and Marisa said that it was you who found it but Pasquale who had said it belonged to Mama . . . We knew he must have lied for a reason.'

Faye remembered. 'It was the expression on his face when he saw it,' she said. 'He went white. As if he'd seen a ghost.' They exchanged a look. Faye glanced towards the floorboards where she had seen the marks and wondered what could have been hidden there. Surely not . . .?

Alessandro nodded. 'So he covered it up by pretending to be so affected because it had been Mama's crucifix,' he said. 'And you believed him, because . . .'

'He was obsessed by your mother.' Exactly.

Alessandro let go of her hands and got to his feet. He paced over to the other side of the narrow room. 'I did not come straight here, of course,' he said. 'I ran round to his house to challenge him – with Enrico and Carmela and Marisa close behind – but he was out. There was only one other place he would be.'

'So you came here.' Thank God, she thought.

He nodded. 'There was a light on in the auditorium. The Voltis and Marisa waited outside while I came in to find him. I saw immediately that you were here. Your laptop was in the doorway of the dressing room and I know you always take it home.'

Not tonight, thought Faye ruefully.

'And . . .' He paused. He seemed hesitant to go on. He was back at the table now.

'And?'

'Your perfume,' he said. 'It is distinctive.' He held her gaze for what seemed like a full minute before Faye at last looked down.

'So you shouted for me,' she said.

He nodded. 'But you did not answer. Which seemed odd.'

But he had known she was here. Faye was very glad now that Alessandro was a stubborn man, the kind who did not give up.

'When I came in here, I saw that the mirror had been taken off the wall – again, rather odd, but it might have been the builder – then I saw your handbag on the chair by the sewing machine.' He pointed to where it still sat.

'So you knew I was close by.'

'Precisely.' He shook his head. 'It seemed very strange – it was as if you had vanished into thin air.' He paused. 'And then I spotted the track marks in the dust coming out from the wall.'

'From the pivoting door.' Faye got up to take a look. She'd seen them herself; she'd created them, of course, when she first turned the candlestick and opened the door. She must have been right in her initial assumption – Pasquale hadn't entered this room for years. Too many bad memories, no doubt. Thank goodness, she thought. Otherwise there would have been no dust to move.

'I had a hunch. So I pretended to leave and then I waited and I listened and I heard your voices coming from the other side of the wall.'

In the secret room. They were both silent for a moment. Faye thought about what it must have been like for Pasquale, enduring at such a young age the death of the man he'd followed everywhere as a young boy, the man he looked up to and revered. She thought of how Dorotea de Montis must have taken him then and moulded him into the role she expected him to fulfil now that her husband was gone. But she never let him forget, did she, that his father had been a hero and that he was half the man. Acting had lifted Pasquale out of his real life, given him something else to live for, and a woman he adored – who didn't want him, who left him just as his father had done. She shook her head. It was no excuse. But life had not been easy for Pasquale de Montis.

'Which must have been a bit of a surprise,' Faye said.

'Yes and no. I was not entirely surprised,' Alessandro admitted. 'My father had spoken once of a secret room. I thought it was just an old family story. But I put together the track marks and the voices and I spotted the candlesticks and . . .'

'You came charging in. My hero,' she joked. Only, he was.

Alessandro grinned as if he liked this role. 'It was the least I could do,' he said.

'But what about Pasquale?'

His expression grew stern. 'Enrico was waiting at the theatre entrance. He will stop him from going anywhere.' They exchanged another look. 'Volti is made out of the same stones as the *nuraghi*,' Alessandro added.

Faye was beginning to understand what he meant. 'I hope Enrico won't do anything stupid.' Not that she would blame him, but the law wouldn't be so lenient. She realised that she'd made a mistake about Enrico. Another one, she thought ruefully. She had believed in the friendly, personable Pasquale de Montis. But he was an actor – a master of pretence. Enrico Volti was another matter. Like Alessandro, he was prickly on the outside, but the man was grieving for a loss that still remained unresolved.

'Marisa and Carmela are there too and probably half the village by now,' Alessandro said grimly. 'In fact, we should go and see what has happened. They will be wondering where we are. And Pasquale de Montis still has a lot of explaining to do.'

Yes, they should, although Faye was strangely reluctant to go anywhere. She looked around the room. How sad it was that this space had been created for such a worthwhile purpose and then . . . And then had gone on to fulfil such a bad one. She remembered something. 'The floorboards,' she whispered.

'The floorboards?' Alessandro looked down. 'What about them?'

'It seems as if someone has had them up. See? Just here.' She pointed to the marks on the wood.

Alessandro went over to take a look. He tried to prise the floorboard free and then he stopped. He turned to Faye, his expression serious. 'We will contact the police about it,' he said.

'But shouldn't we find out what's under there?' Faye realised that he was being protective once again, and this time of her. He knew what she'd been through. He didn't want her to see whatever might be there. Which made her guess what he thought it was. 'Oh, my God,' she said. 'Alessandro – do you really think it could be—?' She couldn't say it, couldn't think it.

'It might be some of the possessions of the Bertelli family,' he cut in. 'Or some of Deriu's valuables when they were hidden from the Fascists. Come, Faye.' He put an arm around her shoulders. 'For tonight, we have seen enough.'

They walked together out of the room and towards the auditorium of the little theatre, picking up Faye's bag and laptop on the way. Faye was still dazed and when she saw the shadow of a figure on the stage, she thought it was a mirage. She gasped. Grabbed on to Alessandro's arm.

Pasquale de Montis wouldn't be doing any more explaining and now they had seen more than enough. His body was hanging lifelessly from a rope tied to a beam above the stage, as scrawny and inelegant in death as he had often appeared in life – apart, that was, from when a character's personality had allowed him temporarily to forget his own . . .

CHAPTER 43

12 Months Later

Faye was in the window seat, stretching for her first glimpse of the island she had come to love so much last summer. In the seats beside her were her parents; the three of them were heading to the grand opening of the little theatre in its new role as Deriu Community Arts Centre. Marisa Rinaldi had sent the invitation: *You have to come,* she had written. *You were a big part of it. I am sorry that some bad things took place while you were here. But you made it happen, Faye, and we thank you for it.*

Faye wasn't sure that she had made it happen. She had been there at the beginning, of course, and there for most of the drama as it occurred, but after the death of Pasquale de Montis and the discovery of the remains of Giorgia Volti under the floorboards, it had not been long before Faye left the island. Marisa was right. So many bad things had happened. Too many, she thought. Despite everything, it had been a relief to leave Sardinia and return to the relative normality of life in London, where Faye had started working freelance for a design company and where she'd also completed a one-year part-time course in theatre and events design to add to her portfolio. She had finished the course in May. The freelance contract had come to an end less than a week ago.

A year ago, back in the Little Theatre of Deriu, after she and

Alessandro had found Pasquale, the police had been called and his body cut down from its macabre position front stage. As if, she thought, there was a part of him that still longed for the limelight, that was determined not to stay in the wings. Faye had been unable to stop shaking. It was so horrible. Pasquale's mother was distraught. She had hobbled into the theatre, wept, screamed and beat her fists on the wooden stage that had taken her son from her so many times. '*Non, non! Per l'amor di Dio, non!*' she'd cried in her brackish voice. 'I always tried to protect him. But even I could not protect him from that.'

Faye had been compelled to turn away from the old woman's grief; she couldn't bear to witness it. And she hadn't been at all surprised when she learned from Marisa three months later that Dorotea de Montis had died. She was very old, and when Pasquale killed himself, his mother must have finally lost the will to continue without the men in her life. Dorotea knew how brave her husband had been and how weak her son. And she had loved them both.

At last, Faye could make out the northern part of the island, see the blue-green shades of the translucent water in what she knew to be the picturesque coves and bays of Costa Smeralda. She leaned back so that her mother could see. Squeezed her arm. 'You'll love it, Mum,' she said. Faye was certain of that. And despite her own trepidation at coming back here, she also couldn't wait to see how the little theatre had progressed and to show her parents what she had designed. She was also looking forward to seeing Charlotte and the other friends she had made here. Not to mention Alessandro Rinaldi. Although a year had gone by, her emotions still became tangled when she thought of him.

'So this is Sardinia. It looks wonderful, darling.' And her mother glanced from one to the other of them and smiled.

Faye hadn't been present when they dug up the floorboards and found Giorgia Volti's body. There had been speculation – even before Faye left the island – of what must have happened the day Giorgia disappeared, but it seemed likely that the young girl had asked for Pasquale's help with her acting career just as Marisa Rinaldi had done before her, and that he had offered to take photographs of her, too (although these were never found, so perhaps in this case he had destroyed the evidence). It was also likely, Faye supposed – though she didn't want to think about this – that he had made some unwanted advance towards Giorgia which had made her laugh at him. Faye remembered Pasquale's disturbed ramblings about being mocked. By all accounts, Giorgia was a girl with an outgoing personality. She would not have taken kindly to Pasquale trying to take advantage of his position. And he would not have taken kindly to being laughed at.

Faye had visited Carmela and Enrico Volti before she left Deriu, to pay her respects and offer her condolences. Enrico had managed only a grudging nod of acknowledgement but Carmela had thanked her effusively and shown her a picture of her dark-eyed, laughing daughter. 'We were always scared for her,' she admitted. 'She was not a bad girl . . .'

'Of course not.' Faye hastened to reassure her.

'But she was daring and she was cheeky – her father was always battling with her about showing respect to her elders.' She gave Faye a sad but knowing look. 'Our Giorgia was never afraid to speak out and she would never be frightened of the consequences.'

Faye understood. Pasquale's ego, and the fact that Giorgia

didn't show him the respect he felt he deserved, had sealed her fate. She didn't look like Sofia, of course, in the way that Marisa did, but Faye guessed that after Sofia's death and by the time he came to lure another young girl into the costume room, Pasquale's mental health – probably never good – had deteriorated still further. Faye remembered what Pasquale had told her when they were alone in the secret room that night about his meeting with Giorgia – 'It wasn't long since Sofia had died'. Pasquale had gone, as he had said himself, a little crazy. Who knew what his original intentions had been? She wanted to think that Pasquale de Montis had not intended to hurt Giorgia Volti. Faye couldn't quite get out of her head his nostalgia and sadness about his life, about Sofia. She hoped that he was sorry. Though now of course she knew the real reasons behind his desperation not to have the theatre restored. He must have been terrified that his darkest secret would be revealed.

The plane had begun its descent and the flight attendants were checking seat belts and making sure bags were correctly stowed under seats. Faye could feel a churning in her stomach. She wasn't afraid of flying – on the contrary, the feeling of being high in the sky, of being hurtled to a new destination always gave her a thrill. But today, she was revisiting a place that had meant so much to her only a year ago. A place and a man that she had effectively run away from back then. And she wasn't at all sure how she felt about coming back.

When Charlotte and Fabio had returned to Deriu, Charlotte had scooped her up and insisted on looking after her at the house. When Faye went out, she went out with her. She felt terrible, she said, that Faye had been subjected to so much tragedy and distress. And it was all her fault. She had brought Faye over here in the first place, she had introduced her to

Marisa and Alessandro, and then she had gone away and not even been there to pick up the pieces.

'I'm not in pieces,' Faye had protested, half-laughing, half-enjoying the fuss her friend was making of her. 'I'm perfectly fine.'

And she had indeed been well enough to tie up a few loose ends and make sure the rest of the team knew what they were doing before she took a flight back to the UK. She wanted to see her parents too; they were worried about her, she knew, and Faye wanted to see for herself what was really happening between them. She had completed the drawings and handed over the project at that stage to a site manager, Rafiele Calia. But the truth was that she had been well and truly shaken up by her experience. Deriu – a place of sunshine and warmth – had become a place of deep shadows. And as for Alessandro . . .

Alessandro Rinaldi had kept his distance after they found Pasquale. She kept expecting him to contact her, but there was nothing – no phone call, no text, no email. As if nothing had ever happened between them, as if he had never held her and kissed her. Alessandro had rescued her from Pasquale de Montis, but he would have done the same for any woman in such a dangerous situation. He was attractive and he was a nice guy. He just wasn't her nice guy. Neither had he tried to influence her decision to leave. And why should he? He might have saved Faye's life, she realised, but he wasn't free to be anything other than Faye's client, and with the way she felt about him, Faye knew that he could never be a friend. Perhaps Alessandro too had finally realised that.

The plane landed with the usual rush of engine noise and before long everyone was taking off their safety belts, getting out of their seats, and searching for baggage in the overhead lockers. Faye stayed in her seat for a moment looking out of the window. They had landed in Olbia. Her father was hiring a car as he had done the last time he'd visited the island and they would be driving straight to Deriu. They were booked into Fabio's hotel, Hotel Azzurro, the one owned by Bruno Rinaldi before he sold it after Sofia's death. It seemed, thought Faye, that everything surrounding the little town of Deriu had something to do with the Rinaldi family.

She had been careful, after her departure, not to leave Marisa and Alessandro in the lurch. She communicated closely with Marisa, continued to source materials, and kept in touch with Rafiele who was very capable and who liaised directly with the builders and restoration experts. Alessandro had managed to get a good amount of funding for their project and they had upped their budget considerably to allow for all the improvements. Marisa and Charlotte had both tried to get Faye over to Deriu during the past months, but she had always found a reason not to go. She was too busy, too tired, she couldn't get time off work. It was unprofessional, she knew, but her part in the project was as good as over. And she didn't want to see Alessandro. It was already too hard to forget him.

CHAPTER 44

They settled in at the hotel and began to walk towards the old town of Deriu. Ade glanced across at his daughter and smiled. *Courage*, he wanted to tell her. Everything will be fine.

'So what happened, Dad?' Faye had asked Ade, back when she was still recovering from her own drama in the little theatre of Deriu. 'What happened with Mum when you went to see her?'

Ade was touched that she had still been worrying about them when she'd been holed up in that ghastly room with a madman holding a knife to her throat. Just the thought made him shudder and clench both fists. His little girl . . . He couldn't think about it without feeling the anger, red-hot and sweeping through him towards the man who had dared to touch Faye, dared threaten to hurt her.

When he and Molly had received that first tearful phone call from their daughter to tell them what had happened, they'd both had to hold back from insisting she took the next flight home. To his surprise it had been Molly who had been the braver. 'Let her stay, Ade,' she'd said after they'd heard Faye's story. 'She's safe now. She'll be back soon.'

'But . . .'

'It's better this way.'

Ade had blinked at her. He had been taken by surprise more than

423

once by the new, decisive Molly who seemed to know what she wanted. He liked this new Molly. And most importantly, he knew that she was vulnerable too. As for Faye, what had happened to her was out of his control, Ade knew that. His daughter was all grown up. But none of this logic mattered – he just wanted her where he could see her.

'She's got some things she has to sort out first,' Molly had said. 'We'll see her when she's done that. Okay?'

He had nodded. 'Okay.' Work things, he supposed. Or things to do with Alessandro Rinaldi – and Ade had to admit that the man had come good for Faye when it mattered the most. Molly was wiser about these things, he was coming to realise. One of the many things about her he was learning, come to think of it.

'We talked,' he told Faye in answer to her question. 'We're going to go away together for a while.'

'Together!' He heard the surprised delight in her voice. He'd been just as astonished himself when Molly had agreed.

'So we'll see how it goes,' Ade told Faye. He didn't want her to get all excited if it was going to come to nothing. But somehow, even then, he'd known it wasn't going to come to nothing. Had he been trapped all those years ago when he first married Molly? Or simply lucky enough to be accepted by a girl who could give him everything he'd ever want or need?

They had taken an early morning flight to Olbia because the opening celebrations were due to begin in the afternoon. As they'd driven through the town, Ade had already seen the colourful bunting, the musicians, the crowds of people filling the streets. Was this all for the little theatre? Faye had told them there would be an art exhibition and reception in the main auditorium, followed by a performance of singing and dancing by a local school's drama group, a dinner in the theatre for select guests catered for by a nearby restaurant, and finally a firework display at the marina, which could be viewed from the steps of *Piazza del Teatro*. The Rinaldis, as Faye had pointed out rather dryly, didn't do things by halves.

Ade exchanged a smile with Molly. When she saw the finished result of her very first design project, what would Faye's reaction be? He wasn't sure, but he was glad they were both here to offer moral support. It had been a difficult time for her; she shouldn't have to face this particular homecoming alone.

In the past six months, he and Molly had taken a trip to Australia and Singapore. It had been mind-blowing. This year they planned to focus on Europe. For Ade, it had been a revelation. Travelling, exploring another culture, meeting new people, seeing different landscapes was everything he had always hoped for and more. And another funny thing – travelling wasn't running away if the right person was sitting in the passenger seat beside you. Initially he wouldn't have expected Molly to enjoy it, but she had seemed to love every moment, as if now, for perhaps the first time in her life, she felt free. Was she still that girl with dreams he'd met in the Electric Palace all those years ago? He suspected that she was. And if Molly still had dreams, then Ade wanted to earn the right to be told what they were. You never know, he thought, he might be able to help a few of those dreams come true.

Faye was grinning. 'It's a *festa*,' she said. 'In Sardinia they have one whenever they get the chance. Religious anniversaries, bringing in the different seasons . . .' She gestured. 'Whenever they have something to celebrate.'

'Sounds an excellent idea to me.' Ade looked around as they approached the *centro storico*. It was a flamboyant display that must be deeply rooted in Sardinian culture. Masked dancers and women in traditional costume – full-length, fur-lined, embroidered dresses with wide red sashes and lace headdresses – were crowded into the main square. Street musicians were playing fast Sardinian folk music. Heels clicked on cobbles and women spun and twirled, their long skirts flying. It was a mass of frenzied and colourful activity.

A man in a scarlet bandana and yellow waistcoat bowed to them and offered Molly a sprig of myrtle. She accepted with a big smile and turned to Ade, her eyes shining.

'Let me.' He tucked it into the clasp of the silver brooch she was wearing.

'Thanks, Ade.'

His hands lingered on her shoulders, just for a moment. And now? He was living back in Dorset but nothing was the same. It wasn't all hearts and roses, but it was real life. They had never grieved together for their lost child; he could finally see that. But strangely, it wasn't too late. He hadn't been there for Molly – not then and not later. But he would be now for as long as she'd have him. Molly didn't have to be scared anymore. Had he learned the heart of her at last? Ade hoped so. But if not, he was going to keep trying.

The same Sardinian man turned his attention to Faye. She too accepted the sprig of myrtle with a smile, but Ade thought he could see some sadness too.

'*Grazie, Signor*,' she said.

Ade and Molly both took an arm and they walked with their daughter towards the *Piazza del Teatro*.

CHAPTER 45

As they walked through the piazza lined with food stalls selling local delicacies, they lingered to taste, and a hooded, masked dancer grabbed hold of Faye's hand and pulled her unceremoniously into the centre of the square. She tried to protest, but he was having none of it. He twirled her around to the musician's fiddle playing, with his feet stomping, hands clapping, cow-bells ringing, until Faye laughed and joined in. When the music came to an end, he gave a deep bow. '*Grazie, Signorina,*' he said. 'I can never thank you enough.'

And then he was gone, whisking through the streets with the rest of his merry band; one playing an unusual-looking woodwind instrument with three pipes, another a small drum hanging around his neck, another an old-fashioned accordion. Who was the dancer? The dark-brown painted mask – quite hideous really – had given nothing away. But from his stature and his voice, Faye thought she knew his identity. Enrico Volti had just thanked her for her part in finding out what had happened to his beloved daughter.

Deriu hadn't changed, she thought as they walked on, the music still echoing through the streets; every archway wound with palm leaves, every corner revealing another display, complete with garlands of flowers, religious effigies and metres of white netting. *Ballo sardo*, thought Faye. It was such a vibrant

427

spectacle. But take away the *festa* and the flag-waving, and the cerulean-blue river still snaked from the mountains to the sea, the boats still rocked gently on their moorings in the summer sunshine, and the old buildings still leaned precariously over narrow cobbled streets – though maybe their painted facades had peeled an inch or two more, their wrought-iron balconies were slightly more bent and worn, their stone steps just a bit more sunken. Women still gossiped outside their houses, children still played in the street. The *centro storico* still reeked of that wonderful Sardinian combination of blossoming jasmine, tomato with oregano and basil, aged stone and crumbling plaster. It was a unique scent. Faye took her time; breathed it in.

But somehow it felt different this time. Faye was still an outsider, but she didn't feel like one. Women who had sent sidelong glances her way now beamed at her and sang out a greeting, men smiled and nodded as they said, *Bon giorno*. There was no hostility in the looks and greetings sent their way. Everything about the place and the people was familiar. And Faye felt an unmistakeable sense of homecoming.

When they reached *Piazza del Teatro*, she gasped. The theatre stood at the top of the steps looking down on them with pride. It was still the little theatre in character and style and yet she saw immediately that its revamp had made it a different creature from the one she'd got to know so well. The little theatre had recovered its dignity.

'So this is the place.' Her mother tucked her hand in the crook of Faye's arm. 'It's splendid, Faye.'

And it was. The exterior of the little theatre had been restored in keeping with its original features. The old oak door remained – cleaned, polished, repaired and rehung – though the stonework around it had been rebuilt and the masonry re-crafted to combat many years of erosion from the salt air, exposure to all weathers and the passage of time. It had also been repainted, the exact shade chosen by studying the layers of paint already on the facade. The windows shone, especially the central rose window. And the little theatre was little no longer – there was a stylish, stone-built extension to the side and to the back, with wide windows and a glass roof that melded old and new in exactly the way Faye had hoped.

She noted the disabled access via a ramp to the right of the old steps. For the celebrations today there was a bit of extra flair: the door had been flung open and multi-coloured bunting had been draped around the building, flying victoriously from open windows. The music coming from inside the building was less Sardinian folk and more triumphal march. Faye grinned. It was perfect.

Faye's father took her other arm. 'What are we waiting for?' he said. 'Let's go in.'

What were they waiting for indeed? Faye took a deep breath and began to climb the stone steps.

Inside, the foyer was much lighter and more airy and had been reworked to create more of a sense of space. Sunlight shafted through the rose window and on the walls a colourful collage had been arranged, comprising the history of the theatre just as Faye had discussed with Alessandro and Marisa over a year ago. On display were faded photographs of local performances from times gone by, old programmes and posters of the theatre's stars – with the glamorous Sofia Rinaldi as the centrepiece. Faye paused. 'Alessandro's mother,' she murmured to her mother.

'Ah.' To Faye's surprise, her mother's eyes filled. 'It was so sad,' she said. 'So very sad.'

Next to this was another photograph, this time of Bruno and Sofia. The golden couple, thought Faye.

'And Bruno . . .' Her mother reached out towards the photo, a faint smile on her lips.

Faye glanced around but her father had hung back and was preoccupied in looking at some other photographs and reading the potted history of the building, displayed in Italian, German and English. 'I always wondered about you and Bruno, Mum,' Faye said. It probably didn't matter now, but she'd still like to know.

'He was a good man.' She didn't answer the question, but from the expression in her eyes, he had meant more to her than that.

'When I mentioned his name to you, you seemed . . .' Faye hesitated. How could she put it? 'Affected.'

'I was.' Her mother nodded. 'And you're right. Something could have happened between us.' She paused. 'But what Bruno Rinaldi gave me was much more important.'

'More important?' Her mother and Bruno Rinaldi . . . Faye and Alessandro . . . It was an interesting parallel. It seemed to Faye that while she had been getting closer to Alessandro, her parents had been moving apart. And when she had left Deriu and Alessandro, her parents had pulled together once more. There they all were – painted ponies on a carousel.

'He listened to me, Faye.' Her mother smiled. 'He heard what I told him and he tried to make me feel better – less guilty, if you like. We all have reasons for feeling guilt, you know. He came into my life – this unexpected stranger – and he gave me something special.'

Faye put her arm around her mother's shoulders and gave her a little squeeze. Though she couldn't imagine what her mother could have had to feel guilty about. 'We all need someone like that from time to time,' Faye said. And hadn't Alessandro done much the same for her?

'But there was only ever one man for me.' Her mother glanced across to where Faye's father was standing, wearing his reading glasses, peering at the photographs.

Faye smiled. That was nice. This new closeness between her parents made Faye feel warm inside. 'And for Bruno?' She thought of all the stories she'd heard in Deriu about Bruno Rinaldi. Like his son, he was a charming man – but like many charming men, he appeared to enjoy using that charm on the female population.

'There was only ever one woman for him too,' her mother said. 'That's why . . .' But her voice trailed.

'Why what?' Faye frowned, but her mother shook her head as if she had already said too much.

'We can't tell other people's secrets,' she said.

Faye remembered Alessandro saying the same thing. And he'd been right, of course.

'Whoever told you that Bruno was a womaniser,' her mother continued, 'may have had their own agenda for doing so, my darling. You know as well as I do that you can't believe everything people tell you.'

Faye considered this. It was true, of course. Much of what she'd heard had come from Pasquale de Montis – who was a noticeable omission from the hall of fame here in the theatre foyer and who had certainly had his own reasons for telling tales about Bruno Rinaldi. Enrico and Carmela had told her the same story – but who knew where they had got their information? Pasquale maybe? It would be a simple thing to start a rumour against somebody in a town like Deriu.

'So how do you know who's telling the truth?' Faye

murmured, half to herself. She gazed out through the rose window, which now gave an uninterrupted view of the sun glinting on to the blue sea beyond. It was dazzling.

Faye's mother squeezed her arm. 'You'll find the truth, darling,' she said. 'Just follow your heart.'

At the far end of the foyer the picture gallery had moved on in time to the current restoration and reinvention of the theatre. Faye looked at the pictures of 'before' and 'after'. Some of the photographs she remembered being taken – usually by Marisa. There was one she lingered over – it caught Faye and Alessandro debating one of her drawings, heads together over the table, one fair, one dark. Faye's breath caught. She hadn't even been aware that Marisa had taken it.

'So that is your Alessandro,' said her mother.

'He's not my—' Faye turned and he was there.

'Alessandro.' She cleared her throat. Damn it.

'*Buon giorno*, Faye.' He leaned forwards and kissed her on each cheek. He was so close. Faye could smell the scent of him and it brought it all back – warm sun and sandy beaches, swimming in turquoise water, arguing over the fate of the little theatre, and that awful evening in the secret part of the costume room, when he had held her and gently stroked her hair until she had finally stopped shaking.

His dark blue eyes grazed over her. 'You are looking well.'

'So are you.' He was wearing a dapper Italian suit in a shade of indigo so dense it was almost black. His curly hair was shorter than before, not quite reaching the collar of his dove-grey shirt, which, being Alessandro, was undone at the collar. 'I am pleased to see you,' he said. He seemed about to say more but then he became aware of Faye's mother, standing patiently waiting to be introduced.

'This is my mother, Molly Forrester,' she said. 'My father's here too.' She gestured towards him. 'Though you two have already met, of course.'

'Of course.' He smiled politely. 'I am very happy to meet you, *Signora*.'

'It's good to meet you too, Alessandro,' Faye's mother said smoothly. 'I met your father when he came over to Dorset for Charlotte and Fabio's wedding. He stayed with Ade and me, in fact.'

'Ah, yes.' Alessandro smiled. 'He spoke of you.'

'Good things, I hope,' Faye's mother said lightly. Faye could tell how delighted she was to finally meet Bruno Rinaldi's son.

'Good things, yes.' But Alessandro's expression was thoughtful.

Faye's father came over to join them. He shook Alessandro's hand energetically. 'The place looks magnificent,' he said. 'All worthwhile in the end, eh? Congratulations.'

'Yes, indeed.' Alessandro smiled his appreciation but once again he was looking at Faye. 'And it was thanks to your daughter,' he added. 'We could not have done it without her.' He took a step closer to Faye. 'Would you like—?'

But they never found out what he was going to say because Charlotte and Marisa came out of the auditorium at that moment, both shrieking with delight when they saw Faye. She found herself enveloped in a group hug and then propelled towards the auditorium. She didn't even have the chance to look back at Alessandro.

'I'm so glad you are here,' whispered Marisa. 'I need to talk to you later. But for now – come and look!'

Faye looked. The auditorium had been transformed. All the old musty and threadbare seating and carpeting had been removed and the ancient marble floor had been cleaned and restored so that its surface gleamed. There was still seating in a large area, but Faye had sourced the mobile variety in order to make the space more flexible. It worked. The auditorium seemed far bigger than it ever had before – which was a good thing, because it was filling up now with people from the village and beyond.

She had read an article recently in an online magazine where a Swiss architect was quoted as saying that a building's success should be judged on whether it was filled with people or not. If so, then theirs was doing well so far. It seemed that Faye, Alessandro and Marisa had every chance of fulfilling their original aim for the little theatre. It had never been just about the restoration and renovation of a historic building. It had also been about the townspeople – giving them what they wanted, what they would use, what would make their community richer.

Faye looked towards the stage. The proscenium arch had been one of their biggest challenges but it had now been painstakingly repaired and repainted, the plasterwork restored to its former splendour. The dusty lilac curtain had gone too. In its place was a curtain of fresh red brocade, which Faye had discovered was much closer to the original. There were new lighting fixtures and the orchestra pit had been enlarged and its wooden rail replaced. She gazed up at the ceiling, at the decorative stucco work. It had all been immaculately restored. The walls had been repainted too – a clean white that was perfect as a backdrop for the art exhibition but also accentuated the vibrant colours of the stucco, the stage curtain and the tiered seats above. The original features of the theatre had been enhanced just as Faye had hoped they would be.

'They did a great job,' she murmured to Marisa and Charlotte. She had been right in her first impressions. Everything was perfect.

'We've managed to improve the sound quality quite a bit,' Marisa told her. 'Taking away that old carpeting certainly helped. And the acoustic consultant you referred to us had some really good ideas about using a black absorptive material on the back of the stage. Reverberation, fluttering . . . sound quality is quite a science these days, it seems.'

Faye laughed. So she had discovered when she did her initial research. And it was something she knew even more about since she'd done her last course. Theatre design was a complex subject and perhaps it was a good thing she hadn't known more – she might have been too intimidated to ever take this project on.

'And you will see that we have reconstructed the stage along the lines we discussed.'

The stage . . . It was hidden for the moment, but Faye still couldn't get out of her head the grisly sight of Pasquale's body dangling from the rope. 'And is the backstage area working out?' she asked in a faint voice.

'Oh, yes.' Marisa was so full of enthusiasm – it was lovely to see. 'We have made the technical improvements. It is so much bigger and better organised – we can store more sets and be so much more flexible with the productions we put on.'

Faye nodded. Marisa sounded far more involved than Faye had expected her to be. It was all as Faye had planned, and yet seeing the reality was so very different from seeing drawings and plans. This was her first job – and once again the magnitude of it was hitting home. Now that she had gained more experience in architectural design she had no idea how she had ever considered herself qualified to take on a project like this one. And yet . . . it had come together. It was the hybrid of the traditional and the contemporary she had envisaged. And it had been lovingly restored. 'It's amazing,' she told Marisa and Charlotte. And it was.

During the champagne reception, Faye and her parents looked around the exhibition, which was celebrating the work of local artists. It was good to see that the community spirit was present from the start, thought Faye. And this impression was reinforced by the production – an all-singing, all-dancing affair performed by the local young people who would now have a venue for their drama group as well as a place in which to perform. As Faye waited for the curtain to rise, she felt it, just as she had felt it when she was a child sitting in the Theatre Royal: that excitement as the lights darkened; the tension and anticipation as the curtain was raised.

'We will have a good selection of professional performances too,' Marisa – who was sitting next to Faye – assured her. 'Later, I will show you our programme.'

Faye was surprised. Marisa sounded very involved with the future of the theatre too. 'Are you staying? What about Rome?' she said. 'What about Leo?' Last time she'd seen her, Marisa couldn't wait to get away from Deriu.

Marisa beamed at someone just behind Faye. 'This is Leo,' she said.

Faye found her hand clasped by the hand belonging to a big bear of a man with twinkly eyes and a wide smile. 'I am so very pleased to meet you, *Signorina*,' he said.

'And you.' Faye looked from one to the other of them. 'So . . .?'

'Leo has moved here to Sardinia,' Marisa said. 'He works in a bank and it was simple to get a transfer.'

'Well, that's great news.'

Marisa leaned closer to her. 'I escaped the past in a different way,' she said. 'You see I have always loved the little theatre and

I have always loved Deriu. He took that away from me and now I have taken it back.'

Faye nodded. She thought she understood. It had been different for Marisa when Pasquale de Montis was still alive. His death had freed her to remain in the place she loved the best. 'Will you be working with the theatre?' It sounded as if Marisa had taken charge of everything. 'I'm surprised you have time for it all.'

'I am my father's daughter as well as my mother's,' Marisa replied. 'I have formed a local amateur dramatic group and we may put on the occasional performance.'

'That's wonderful.' Faye smiled, remembering the time Marisa had climbed on to the stage and performed a little dance with Faye as her only audience. She was glad that Marisa had been able to put her ordeal to one side and was going to fulfil her ambitions at last. 'But how does that make you your father's daughter?'

'I will run the theatre too,' Marisa said. 'I have appointed a manager and there will be other staff, of course, but like my father, I want to be involved with the operations. And he ran his hotel at the same time. He was good,' she added, 'at juggling.'

'And your teaching?'

'I started working part-time several months ago,' Marisa admitted. 'I love it too much to give it up completely. But even I cannot do everything.'

Faye laughed. 'And do you think the town of Deriu has finally forgiven you and Alessandro for taking charge of the theatre?' she asked. 'They're pleased with the final result, aren't they?'

'They should be,' Marisa said happily. 'Because we have given the theatre back to them.'

'Yes. They're going to love using it,' Faye agreed.

'And owning it,' Marisa said. 'It is official. We run it, the townspeople possess it.'

'Really?' Faye clapped her hands in delight. 'Oh, Marisa. How lovely of you both. That was an incredibly generous thing to do.'

'Alessandro and I discussed it. The theatre was a community project. I think it always belonged to Deriu.'

Faye remembered what Alessandro had told her about the history of the theatre the evening they had first met. It had been built by a consortium of local families to celebrate the arts and identity of the town. And that was the role it was still playing. So there would be no more ownership disputes in Deriu, thought Faye. At least as far as the little theatre was concerned. Once again, the theatre belonged to the people who loved it.

'What about Alessandro?' she asked at last. The question had been on her lips all afternoon. She had not spoken to him since their meeting in the foyer but she had been aware of him the entire time; she always knew to whom he was speaking and where he was standing. She had seen Jana too, wearing a white dress with an abundance of gold jewellery, once by his side, once on the other side of the auditorium talking to a smooth-looking man in a dark grey suit and red tie.

Marisa shot her a curious look. 'It is different for my brother,' she said. 'He wanted to reopen this place as a tribute to Mama, but since everything that has happened . . .' Her voice lowered. 'Despite what we have achieved here – I think he has lost heart.'

Faye glanced towards the other side of the auditorium where Alessandro was sitting with Fabio and Charlotte. You too, she thought. You too.

It almost seemed a conspiracy. Faye had not wanted to be in close proximity to Alessandro Rinaldi and now it seemed as if her wishes had come true. Every time she thought that he would come closer, every time she saw him glancing across at her, someone else appeared whom Marisa or Charlotte insisted on introducing her to.

And now, Marisa had grabbed her arm. 'There is something else I must show you,' she said.

She led Faye up the steps and on to the stage. Faye hesitated, but Marisa held tightly to her arm. 'It is over, Faye,' she said. 'It is history.'

Faye knew she was right even though she still faltered. She wanted to see backstage of course, she wanted to look at the new bathroom facilities with their disabled access and the new dressing rooms, she wanted to see everything that had been done. She held back when they reached the costume room.

'You must see,' Marisa said sternly.

And of course Marisa was right. She had suffered far more than Faye. If Marisa could face up to it, then so could she.

There it was. The door to the secret room was wide open; and everything looked as it had on that night when she had first discovered the place. Faye looked down automatically to where the floorboards had clearly been sawn and prised up, but a rug covered the spot – the same rug, she realised, that had been there before. 'Oh, Marisa,' she said.

'See here.' Marisa drew her attention to an information plaque on the wall. Faye read it. It was a commemoration of the actions of Luigi de Montis from the town of Deriu. It told of how he had saved the lives of the Bertelli family by hiding them here and then helping them escape to the mountains. He lost his own life when he was later captured by the Fascists, but even under torture, he did not reveal the family's whereabouts nor where they had been hidden.

Faye nodded. 'That's a lovely tribute.'

'It is good to have the commemoration,' Marisa said. 'Because we need to remember.'

'Do we?' Faye asked her. She admired Marisa's bravery and she could acknowledge this room had certainly been used for good, but what about the other way in which the room had been used – for evil?

'Yes,' Marisa said. 'The good outweighs the bad, Faye. The room was conceived and used as a hiding place to help the village; it was for anyone who should need it. But when Pasquale de Montis disposed of Giorgia Volti's body under those floorboards . . .' She pointed and Faye winced. 'He had already done the bad deed. He could have hidden her anywhere.' She gestured. 'The room, you see, is not to blame.'

Faye conceded the point. Nevertheless . . . 'Did you ever wonder?' she asked Marisa. 'About Giorgia and Pasquale?' Giorgia had disappeared less than a year after Marisa's nightmare. Mightn't she have put two and two together?

'No.' Marisa shook her dark head. 'With me there was no question of violence or force.' She looked down. 'It was my fault too. I played my part. I used to go on and on at him to help me. I was young and stupid.' She sighed.

'He was an adult,' Faye said firmly. 'He took advantage of you.'

'Yes, that is what Alessandro says.' She looked up. 'And I know that it is true. But I never wanted him dead. Though now that he is, now that I know about Giorgia . . . I cannot be sorry.'

Faye put an arm around her shoulders and gave her a hug. 'Come.' She was glad to step away from the costume room and head back to the auditorium.

Marisa straightened her back and took a deep breath. 'I have someone else I would like you to meet, Faye,' she said. 'He will be sitting next to you at the dinner.'

Faye was curious. 'Why do you want me to meet him?' she asked. 'Who is he?'

'He is the chairperson of a committee in a town in the interior,' she said. 'A rich and powerful man in Sardinia. Very influential.'

'What sort of committee?'

'A restoration committee.'

Faye stared at her. 'Restoration of what?'

'Why, a theatre, of course.' Marisa laughed. 'People have come to see what we have done here,' she said. 'What *you* have done, Faye. Prepare yourself.'

For what, Faye wondered.

'You will be in demand.'

CHAPTER 46

The dinner was pleasant. Faye found Jagu Timpone an interesting companion, and Fabio had been placed on her other side so she had him to turn to for light relief. On Jagu's left sat Jana, with red-tie man sitting opposite her and another younger man on her left; it seemed she was receiving plenty of attention. Further up the table Faye saw that her mother was sitting beside Alessandro and on his other side was Charlotte. There was something different about Charlotte this summer. She seemed quieter and somehow more content. Faye watched her friend thoughtfully. Was Charlotte and Fabio's life about to change? Could she be . . .?

At that moment, Charlotte looked across and caught her eye. Her smile was slow and warm. She put a finger to her lips. Faye smiled. She knew it. Someone else was on their way to Deriu.

She brought her attention back to the man beside her. 'What's your theatre like? How old is it?' she asked Jagu. She hadn't known much about Sardinian theatres when she first came here, but she'd had to learn – and quickly. They had just finished eating their first course of *calamari ripiene* – spicy stuffed squid served with fresh basil. Faye realised how much she had missed Sardinian food; the squid was piquant and delicious.

'It has some similarities to this theatre,' he said. 'There is still beauty but there has been fire damage. It is much bigger. Older too.' He pulled his mobile from his pocket and showed her some images.

Faye leaned closer to see. The theatre must have been very grand in its day; there was a lot of ornate stucco work in the interior, though clearly it had been damaged by fire and was blackened and crumbling in places. The stage had been all but destroyed too, but the outside of the building seemed intact.

'There is some heritage protection for our theatre,' Jagu continued. 'But if we can create an arts centre as you have done here, we may apply for a grant.' He looked around the stage and auditorium, which was glowing now with the soft lamps and low lighting system Faye had designed. She was conscious of a flush of pride. 'If we can achieve even a fraction of what you have achieved,' he said, 'we shall be happy.'

They broke off their conversation as the waitress brought the next course – a creamy lemon risotto with seared prawns. Faye tucked in.

'It's very kind of you to say so,' she said, after she'd swallowed the first delicious mouthful. 'But you're giving me too much credit. We had an excellent team of builders and restorers here. Everyone made their own contribution.'

He raised an eyebrow. 'So Marisa Rinaldi told me.'

'We could certainly give you some names . . .'

He turned to her thoughtfully. 'It must be very rewarding to see people using the space you have created.'

'Oh, it is.' Faye thought of how hard she had worked at interpreting the purpose of the building, in trying to make it something that pleased both Alessandro and Marisa as well as benefitted the community of Deriu. It wasn't only the form of the building that was important – it was also the way in which people could use it, now and in the future too.

Jagu leaned closer and took her hand. 'And Marisa told me how dedicated and imaginative you are, my dear. How special.'

'Really?' Faye didn't know what to say.

'She also said that you have undertaken some further theatre studies.'

'Well, yes, I have.'

'And so the name I am most interested in – is yours, *Signora*.'

'Oh.' Faye glanced up the table and saw Alessandro looking her way. Noting the apparent intensity of the conversation she was having, no doubt. Seeing Jagu Timpone take her hand. She looked away. But it was hardly her fault. She hadn't devised the seating plan.

At last, with a dish of *amarettus* – almond macaroons with lemon peel – and fresh coffee Sardinian style, the dinner was over and they moved outside for the fireworks. Faye had a lot to think about. She saw her mother drift back to her father's side, watched the way they smiled at one another in the moonlight. She let out a small sigh of satisfaction.

'*Una bella copia*, I think.' The voice at her shoulder made her jump. It was Alessandro. *A fine couple.*

'Yes,' she said, still looking at her parents. 'They are.'

'So it worked out.' He nodded. 'I am glad.'

'Thank you.' Faye wasn't sure what to say to him, not now. 'And how is Jana?' she asked. 'Well, I hope?'

'Jana?' He arched a dark eyebrow.

'I saw her at the dinner, of course,' Faye said. 'But I didn't get the chance to—'

She was surprised when he gripped her arm. 'You know about Jana?' he asked.

'Yes.' She looked down at her arm until he released it. 'Of course I do.'

He nodded slowly. 'We have organised a firework display,' he said.

Faye remembered how he had always spoken in riddles. 'So I hear.'

He took her arm and drew her away from the rest of the crowd. 'Although there is a much better view from the castle, I believe.'

'But—'

'What do you think you know?' he asked her. 'About Jana?'

She didn't look at him. 'That you've been together forever. That you'll get married eventually, I suppose.'

'Faye, I kissed you,' he said. 'I held you in my arms and I kissed you.'

Did he think she didn't remember? 'I'm aware of that,' she said.

He took her arm, more gently this time. 'Faye, when I kissed you I was no longer involved with Jana. I ended the relationship before you even came to Deriu. She was far too emotional, too vulnerable for me. I no longer felt the same way about her. We were so young when we first were together; we had grown apart. It happens. But how could I extricate myself from the relationship? It seemed impossible. She became angry, possessive . . .'

Why was he bothering, Faye wondered. She had seen them with her own eyes. 'It doesn't matter,' she said. 'Not now.'

But he was still talking. 'She saw us together at the marina that day,' he said. 'She came to my house – she was furious, she was crying, she even threatened . . .' He sighed. 'To do herself harm.'

'What did you do?' Faye's voice was low.

'I tried to calm her, I tried to make her see that although we had been together for so long, that it was no longer working, that she could find someone who would give her more, who would be much better for her than me.'

'And did she believe you?'

'Not then. It was just a matter of time. And of course I cared for her welfare and safety, although I could no longer care for her in the way she wanted me to.'

At last Faye risked a glance at him. He had asked her to trust him and she never had before. But now . . . he seemed genuine. And what he was saying was making her think. What had she really seen that day at the boatyard? Jana had flung her arms around him, yes, but had he responded as a man in love? Or had he actually been comforting her, trying to calm her?

'I tried to stay away from you,' he said. 'I did not want to hurt her more.'

'And now?' Faye whispered. Was there a Jana and Alessandro now?

He shook his dark head. 'Jana has moved on,' he said. 'And I could not be happier for her.'

Red-tie man. Jana seemed brave on the outside, but she was vulnerable and she delighted in male attention, and she had clearly found someone who was happy to give it to her. Faye was jostled by the crowd on the steps, which seemed to have expanded since they left the theatre. There were too many people around. Everyone wanted to watch the fireworks. Faye smiled. 'You can always see more clearly from higher up,' she said.

'Then shall we?' He offered his arm.

Faye took it. It was a beautiful night. The clear sky was charcoal soft and the moon was fat and full. The stars were clear and bright and there was no breeze to ruffle the tranquillity of the night-time air. So why did Faye feel so stirred up inside? She guessed it was a mixture of things – coming back to Deriu, the conversation at dinner, and this man by her side.

'We have hardly spoken together all evening,' Alessandro said. He let his hand rest on hers, just for a moment.

Faye had noticed. They climbed slowly through the winding, cobbled streets of the *centro storico*; the evening views were very different from the daytime ones Faye had become used to last summer. The atmosphere had changed, too; she could still hear the voices from the steps of *Piazza del Teatro* down below, and music coming from the main town square. Were the masked men and women still dancing? she wondered. Despite the night of *festa* and the celebrations going on, there was a growing hush in the serene air that made her almost not want to break it. 'What a fantastic crowd,' she said. 'It's marvellous really – for the theatre. And for Deriu.'

'And for you?' he asked.

They had reached the wide steps that led up to the castle, set in the grove amongst the prickly pears and gnarled, ancient olive trees. 'And for me,' she said. 'I haven't seen you all for such a long time.'

He gave her a lingering look. They continued to climb. All was deserted; everything was still. Even the sound of voices back in *Piazza del Teatro* and the musical celebrations in the square seemed to have faded. 'And there are other people too who want to claim your attention,' he said. He glanced across at her. 'You have made a name for yourself in Sardinia, I think.'

'You mean Jagu Timpone?' Could he possibly be jealous?

'The very same.'

Faye nodded. 'He was trying to pick my brains for his own theatre project.' She had been flattered, but she had hardly made a name for herself.

447

'But now . . .' They had reached the summit of the hill and the castle walls. He drew her into the canopy of a myrtle tree. 'I have got you to myself at last.'

Faye trembled. She laughed uncertainly, but Alessandro looked very serious. He cupped the back of her head in his hand, moved his fingers down to her neck, and from there to her shoulders. He stared at her, with that navy gaze that looked almost black in the moonlight. '*Mi mancas*,' he murmured. 'I miss you, Faye.'

'I miss you too,' she whispered. So talk to me, she thought. Tell me how you feel.

'I tried to resist you,' he said. 'I felt the attraction from the moment we met. But I told myself that you were not one of us, that you were a stranger, that you had no place here in Deriu.'

Faye bowed her head.

'And then there was Jana.'

She looked up again. Reached out to touch his cheek. Tonight, he was clean-shaven, but she could already feel the roughness under her fingertips.

'And then I watched you becoming part of our town, just as my father must have watched my mother.'

It was true, she thought. She had. Deriu had taken her by surprise. Very slowly, it had wrapped its arms around her, enveloped her in its warmth, but also in its shadows.

'I wanted you, Faye,' he said. 'I was wary of moving too fast after what had happened with Jana. But I wanted you.'

She looked up, found herself staring at his mouth, his lips. 'I wanted you too, Alessandro,' she said.

He was silent for a moment. She thought he would kiss her but he held back. Clearly he had more to say. She tensed.

'And then when you would not trust me . . .'

'And you would not trust me.'

Their gazes locked. Impasse, thought Faye. They were too alike. Maybe that was what had kept them apart.

'But sometimes,' she added softly, 'it's hard to know who to trust.' She thought of Pasquale. She had trusted him without questioning his motives. But Alessandro had been an enigma. There had been many times when he could have approached her, when he could have made things right. Even at the end, after he'd rescued her. But he had always kept his distance, never come to her, never made that move. And she had thought she knew the reason why.

He acknowledged this with a nod. 'I believed in my father,' he said. 'All my life I trusted him. And then just before he died, he told me—' His voice broke off. Faye remembered that Alessandro had said this once before, on the day he'd taken her to the beach. She remembered that her mother too had spoken of Bruno Rinaldi having a secret.

'What did he say to you?' she asked.

'He told me that on the night of the accident, the night my mother died . . .' He clenched his fist. His mouth was set and grim. All of a sudden he seemed a long way away.

'What, Alessandro?' She touched his arm.

'They'd had a terrible row,' he said. 'It was about him – Pasquale. My father wanted him out of the theatre, my mother would not hear of it. Papa – he admitted to me that he had been angry, that he was trying to scare her that night on the *via della morte*. He was driving too fast, way too fast. He lost control of the car. There was no other car – that was a story he told so that no one would blame him for what he had done. But it was his fault alone. He killed her.'

Faye was shocked. 'The poor man,' she said, almost without

449

thinking. No wonder he had been so grief-stricken. He must have been tortured by guilt for the rest of his life. But she realised that Alessandro was glaring at her. 'And my mother?' he asked. 'What about my darling mother?'

'Oh, Alessandro.' Faye reached out for him again. 'It was tragic – for them both. But don't you think your father suffered enough as he went on living without her?'

She saw him thinking about this. And she knew that he had thought about it before.

'We all make mistakes,' she said. 'And your father's mistake was the worst kind. But you know, he was very brave to tell you the truth before he died.'

'You are right.' He half-turned away from her, staring out over the town in the darkness. Lit windows twinkled from houses, and bars and restaurants were still open; the street lamps emitted a soft orange glow.

Faye thought she could hear firecrackers being let off in the streets down below. This town was not yet settling down; people were continuing to spill around the streets, still celebrating.

'I know that you are right. Marisa says the same. She also says that I need a strong woman who will stand up to me and tell me what she thinks.' He gave her another long look. 'But it is hard to forgive him, Faye.'

'You must.' She spoke gently. She thought of how Alessandro had helped her come to terms with the fact that her parents were separating. It hadn't happened after all, but if it had, she knew that she would have accepted it. Their happiness was what mattered, whether they were together or alone. 'Would your mother have forgiven him?' she asked.

'Of course.' He sounded surprised. 'He was everything to her.'

'And she to him.'

He turned back to face her. 'And she to him,' he agreed. 'You know, Faye, my father was a successful businessman. But he could have done more to help Deriu. It is no wonder that there were voices raised against us Rinaldis.'

'We're all human, Alessandro,' she said.

'Yes, we are all human.' And she saw his frown fade. Forgiveness wouldn't come in one moment, she knew that. But she had the feeling that it would come in time.

'It is quite a responsibility,' she said, 'when you are expected to look after a whole town.' She touched his arm. 'But you and Marisa have done what your father was unable to do.' She thought of Sofia. If not for Sofia . . . 'You have given the theatre back to the people.' He and Marisa had healed the rift in the split community and that could only be a good thing.

He acknowledged this with an ironic bow of the head. 'And it is also a responsibility,' he said, his voice more serious now, 'when you fall in love.'

'That too.' She had to concede.

'For my father, falling in love put everything else out of his head. And for me . . .'

'You?' She could hardly speak.

'You seemed so distant,' he said. 'Every time I tried to get close to you, it was as if you had decided to stay away from me.'

Faye stared at him. Was that how it had appeared? 'I never knew that you were free,' she said.

'No? *Veramente, non?* You thought that I would be with a woman and run after another woman, is that it?'

'No – well, yes. I suppose that I did. People said things . . .'

He stiffened. 'People? De Montis, you mean?'

She nodded.

'And then when I found you – with him, in that hidden room . . .'

Faye shuddered. She didn't want to think about that time.

'I was so worried about you. I could not bear the thought of anything happening to you. I knew then the strength of my feelings. And I began to hope that we could start again, free from de Montis, free from whatever it was that had kept us apart.' He looked out into the night. 'But you were already planning to leave Deriu.'

'Yes.' It hadn't been the right time for so many reasons. If Faye had decided to stay in Deriu, if just once Alessandro had come to see her and told her how he felt, if she had known that his ties to Jana had already been broken . . . then it might have been different. But she saw now that he had been as uncertain of her as she had been of him. Jana hadn't been the only thing keeping them apart. Perhaps they had both known there was so much at stake. After what their parents had gone through, it was likely they had both been anxious about the sort of commitment they might be making. 'I thought that I should leave.' She looked up at him. Now was the time for truth, for communication. 'I didn't know how you felt and I couldn't stay here. It all seemed too difficult, too painful, too unsure.'

'So you left,' he said. 'You barely even said *A si biri*, goodbye.'

'I'm sorry,' she whispered.

Faye found then that she was crying; tears traced her cheeks. What was she mourning? Her life in Deriu? A relationship that hadn't worked out? Or the people in this town who had suffered – the Voltis, Marisa and Alessandro, Bruno and Sofia, and Pasquale de Montis?

When Alessandro kissed her this time it was the softest,

warmest sensation. The brush of his lips sent currents of pure longing running right through her body to her fingertips and toes. She reached up, put her arms around him and kissed him back. There were fireworks. A Roman candle fizzed slowly in her belly and rose up into something light, bright and wonderful; a dizzy Catherine wheel spun her senses out of control, a rocket shooting up to the skies.

They drew apart. 'Mmm,' she said. Wow.

He laughed. 'Look.'

The fireworks were for real. Faye laughed too as she watched them light up the night sky.

'Come on.' They ran up the steps on to the castle walls. Alessandro's arm was tight around her shoulders. They watched the cascading fountains of light, the bursts of colour; they heard the crack of the explosives, the rush of the speeding rockets. Faye didn't think she had ever been happier.

He pulled her round to face him. 'How can I persuade you to stay in Deriu?' he asked. 'What do I have to offer you?'

It seemed to Faye that the whole of Deriu and the countryside around it – the mountains, the river, the sea – were laid out in front of her, lit up by a myriad of shooting star-rockets that spun through the air and exploded into thousands of teardrops of light.

'All this is pretty good,' said Faye. And then there was this man . . .

'But what about your work? I know how important it is for you.'

'I'm still freelance,' Faye said. 'So in theory I could work anywhere.' She liked the look in his eyes. She'd like to kiss him again too.

'You could work here in Sardinia?' He was gripping her

shoulders very hard, as if he meant it. 'Would you work here in Sardinia? Would you come here – to be with me?'

To be with him . . . 'As a matter of fact, I've been offered a job here already,' she said. She had told Jagu that she would think about it, but she'd just made up her mind. No more running away. No more games. No more hiding what she really thought. She'd take the sunlight and the shadows. When she had left this place she had left a piece of herself behind. So she would come back here to Deriu. Faye reached for Alessandro. She would come back here to be with this man. She would follow her heart.

ACKNOWLEDGEMENTS AND THANKS

Thank you, thank you, everyone who takes the time to read this book. I hope you like it! I so appreciate your lovely comments and your continued support. Readers are the best . . .

I so enjoyed writing this book. I have always loved theatres – the atmosphere and feel of them as well as the theatre experience itself – and so it was fun to find out more about theatre design and especially old theatres in Italy and Sardinia. Books that were particularly helpful to me on *Little Theatre*'s journey include *Theatre and Architecture* by Juliet Rufford (Macmillan Education: Palgrave); *Sardinia Baby* by Malachi Bogdanov (Rogue University Press) and *Aurora, Me and Sardinia* by Terence Dillon (Austin Macauley Publishers Ltd). Malachi and Terry were both very helpful. Thanks to Terry for helping me with some research into listed buildings. Malachi has also kindly allowed me to mention one of his productions in Sardinia and the 'break a leg' ritual mentioned in *Sardinia Baby* in this book. I also read *Sea and Sardinia* by D.H. Lawrence, an author whose writing has influenced me hugely over the years. (It was fab.) These books helped me to understand Sardinia and theatres a little more – each in their own way. Sardinia is a stunning island and I loved spending time there doing research for *Little Theatre*. I just hope that I have done the place justice.

The hugest of thanks must go to my wonderful editor, Stef

Bierwerth, who is both clever and lovely and who always has time for me. And to the rest of the fabulous team at Quercus Books, who do such a great job. Equally massive thanks to my amazing agent Laura Longrigg at MBA who has such a perceptive editing eye and is always upbeat, encouraging and supportive. And thanks to Sophie Ransom, Eve Wersocki and Alice Geary at Midas PR – for their unflagging energy and enthusiasm. I am very fortunate to have such a great team of people behind me.

Special big thanks go to my talented and beautiful daughter Alexa Page for discussions on architecture and design and for reading bits of the book to check I haven't made any awful mistakes (any mistakes I have made are definitely my own). Thanks to Terry Milward for career advice. And to all my friends for their continued encouragement, for reading my books and for telling other people about them! (Special thanks to Wendy Tomlins and June Tate who are both generous and amazing.) My family are wonderful too . . . Big love to Luke and Agata and Little T (Tristan); to my lovely Ana, to my mum who never stops believing in me and to my husband and travelling companion Grey who is always there for me at every stage of every book helping me with technical advice, listening, making suggestions and of course driving the motor-home around Sardinia! I appreciate what you do so much. This is for you all. You know who you are. Thank you, my lovelies . . .